STEALING
GHOSTS

THE DEWITT AGENCY FILES #2

a novel by
LANCE CHARNES

WOMBAT GROUP MEDIA — ORANGE, CALIFORNIA

Wombat Group Media
Post Office Box 4908
Orange, CA 92863
https://www.wombatgroup.com/

First Printing November 2017
Second Printing October 2019
Third Printing December 2020
Fourth Printing September 2021
Fifth Printing September 2025

ISBN 978-0-9886903-8-7

This is a work of fiction. Names, characters, businesses, places, events and incidents are either the products of the author's imagination or used in a fictitious manner. Any resemblance to actual persons, living or dead, or actual events is purely coincidental.

No animals were harmed in the writing of this novel.

Printed in the United States of America

For Betty

Who's getting to believe this may be a thing

For bonus chapters from **Stealing Ghosts**, reading group questions, an interview with the author, and an art gallery, check out https://www.wombatgroup.com/dewitt-agency-files/stealing-ghosts/stealing-ghosts-bonus-material/

Chapter 1

The first thing you notice is her eyes.

Big, dark, luminous. She's no blushing ingénue; those eyes grab you and pin you to the wall. *Think you got what it takes?* they say. *Come find out.*

If you don't fall in, you see the face around those eyes. High cheekbones, a razor-sharp jaw, a long semi-Roman nose, full lips parted just a bit. Maybe you surprised her. The dark chestnut hair's cut at jaw level and shingled so it hugs the curve of her skull. Her graceful neck's arched just so, circled by a doubled strand of lapis and gold.

If you make it down that far—and you should, you really should—you'll see the moss-green silk yoke draped across the points of her shoulders, then plunging below her shoulder blades. That creamy bare back and her sleek, bare arms are a shade darker than your typical society woman's skin; she's from somewhere warm, where the cypress and olive trees outnumber the firs. An ibis outlined with silver embroidery and gold seed beading spreads its wings across her back. Beaded lotus flowers and papyrus stalks tangle on the yoke and skirt. The dress is fashionably shapeless, but it can't hide her curves.

The weathered Ionic column just to her right holds up a portico that casts a warm, brown shadow behind her. She glows against that darkness.

She's royalty. She's a young empress and you're the servant. You don't mind being the servant because you get to look at her. And sometimes—like right now—she looks back.

Her name's Dorotea. She's ninety-one years old. One look stole my heart.

Now I'm stealing her.

Chapter 2

EARLIER THAT DAY

Someone's pounding on my hotel room's door. I know what time the clock says, but my body says the clock's full of shit. Eleven hours on an airplane does that.

That pounding sounds familiar... doesn't it?

I'd crawled out of this humungous king-size bed at what my brain said was the middle of the night (even though it was light outside) to catch breakfast downstairs. When I got back, I closed my eyes for just a minute, I swear. Two hours vanished.

Where am I?

I let myself off the bed easy—the platform's high enough that if I jump, I'll break something—detour past the desk (Sofitel London Heathrow, that's where I am) and shuffle to the door peephole. *Knew it.* I yank open the door and catch her in mid-slam. "What?"

Carson folds her arms and glares at me. "Pack your shit. Allyson's waiting."

Allyson's... *what?* She's *here?* "Since when?"

"Since she emailed. It's almost nine. Haven't read your email yet?"

I try to grind the grit out of my eyes. "You know what time it is? It's twelve fifty-five a.m. Matt Daylight Time." I pull the door open. "You get to watch."

She swings a black laptop carry case into my chest as she stalks by. It doesn't knock me over, though it's a near thing. She scans the room, then flops in the butter-tan, wingback swivel armchair near the little round-topped cocktail table by the window. She doesn't say anything.

So I do. "Good to see you, Matt." Yes, I sound grumpy, even to me. "How're you doing? I'm fine, Carson, thanks for asking. What've you been up to?"

"Yeah. That."

"What's with you? I thought we'd moved past the I-hate-you stage in Milan."

"Supposed to get time off," she grumbles. "Allyson called me back."

"Sorry," I say, and I am. She shrugs.

Carson's in her mid-thirties (like me), about five-nine, and on the okay side of plain. Her ice-blue, long-sleeved tee is snug across her broad shoulders, biceps, and chest, and she fills her black jeans well. She'll never make the cover of *Vogue* (though you should see her in a tight dress), but she's smart and tough and good to have around when things go south.

"Anything in your backgrounder?" Carson asks. She's swiveling her chair back and forth, watching as I stumble around collecting my things.

"Who are you working for this time?"

"Allyson."

"Only?" Last time, I found out she had a second boss. Nobody was happy.

"Yeah. Your backgrounder?"

"I didn't *get* a backgrounder." In my two other agency projects, I got a little blue thumb drive with all the details Allyson decided to share about what I'd be doing. Not this time. "The only reason I knew to pack for cool weather was the itinerary had me terminating at Heathrow. What's in yours?"

"Fuck-all. Three to six weeks in northern Europe."

I concentrate on re-stuffing my bashed-up black roller bag so Carson doesn't see my reaction. Six weeks is a problem. I'm still on supervised release for two more years and I'm not supposed to leave the U.S. That's why I'm traveling on a fake passport. I can scam Len, my federal probation officer, for a couple weeks, but longer is gonna get complicated. "Still got your Brooklyn number?"

"Yeah." She snorts. "We still a thing?"

"As far as Len knows." On my first project with the agency and with Carson, I told my PO I was in New York City when I was really in Milan. To explain why I didn't come home on time, Carson pretended to be my new Brooklyn-Russian girlfriend. Hey, it worked.

I zip my luggage, stow my work phone (a big quad-band Samsung), and pile the duffel and laptop case on my roller for towing. "What's it like outside?"

"It's great. Let's go."

A sturdy South Asian in a black suit and peaked cap holds up a sign saying "Mr. Simon" (me for this trip) near the rectilinear marble water feature in the main lobby. I follow him out to the curb; Carson detours to the front desk. It's a clear and chilly morning, with a sharp breeze spiking down the road. I remind myself to never ask a Canadian (like Carson) about the weather.

The suit sets my bags in the trunk of an idling midnight-blue BMW 440i Gran Coupe and guides me to the left-front passenger's seat.

Allyson's behind the wheel.

I've never seen Allyson drive. I didn't know she could.

"Mr. Friedrich." She doesn't look at me. It's chillier inside the car than outside.

"Ms. DeWitt." The agency's formal name is DeWitt Associates. Yes, she's the boss.

I sit down and try not to stare. Her black wool pique pencil skirt is hiked halfway up her very shapely thighs. One night around five years ago—long before she hired me—I found out exactly what's under the several thousand dollars' worth of clothes she's wearing. If I close my eyes, I'll still be able to feel her skin under my fingertips. I keep my eyes open and locked on the Range Rover ahead of us. Getting fired isn't on my agenda.

"Acceptable work in Mexico," she says in that smooth, toe-curling alto of hers. It's the frostiest compliment I've ever gotten.

"Thanks. Everything went fine." As far as she needs to know.

Carson climbs into the back seat. "Why are you driving?"

Allyson flicks a glance in the rear-view mirror. "Please fasten your seat belt." Then we glide away from the curb like we're in a vintage Rolls and not an autobahn burner.

I risk a glance at Allyson while she negotiates the parking lot. She's somewhere in her mid-forties and not conventionally pretty, but her presence makes you look when she comes into the room. Unfortunately, she's everything I like in a woman—deep brown eyes, thick black hair that splashes off her shoulders when it isn't up in a bun like it is now, olive skin, great cheekbones. And the legs. And, for that matter, everything else.

Gar Heibrück, my ex-boss at my ex-gallery, schooled me in

high-end fashion so I could tell how much money our clients had. Allyson's wearing a flame-red St. John knit jacket with a shawl collar, one-button closure and belled three-quarter sleeves. It's a perfect color for her. She's one of those women who wears clothes and wears nothing equally well.

The little brain still wants a rematch with her. The big brain knows I'd have to sleep with one eye open and my back against a wall.

Allyson says, "I want to brief you both before you go on your way. I'm sure you noticed I provided no background information. I believe you know what that means, Ms. Carson."

"No documentation. Something illegal."

"Exactly."

I say, "You gave us background for Milan. We were doing illegal stuff there." Especially Carson. As illegal as it gets. "Why is this different?"

"That client wasn't likely to tell the world about it. This one is."

We circle a wide left-hand curve onto a two-lane frontage road that parallels a small river. The massive pewter brick of Terminal 5 slides by my window.

Allyson pulls a five-by-seven card from her door's side pocket and holds it out to me between two fingers. "What can you tell me about this?"

I can't control the gasp that slips out when I see the picture. "Wow. Sargent. *Dorotea DeVillardi*. The last portrait in oil he finished before he died." It's a gorgeous work, like John Singer Sargent knew this was the end and he wanted to go out with a bang.

Carson's leaning forward to peek over my shoulder. I hold up the postcard so she can see. She peers at it, grunts "Huh," then thumps back into her seat.

Allyson says, "Go on."

"It disappeared in World War Two. Everybody called it lost—the Ormond survey still has a black-and-white photo of it from the '30s. Then it resurfaced in the late '90s." I know this because Sargent is one of my favorite artists, and because I have this freak memory where if I read something a few times, I remember it basically forever. "It got a lot of play in the art press. Some Russian dude owns it. It's on loan to the Moscow Museum of Modern Art."

"It's in the Mainwaring Gallery in Portsmouth for the next nine weeks," Allyson says. We're poking along behind a box truck like we're part of a parade. Either she's stalling or she usually drives like a granny. "You left out the bit that's most important to this project: the original owners want it back."

"We're being followed," Carson announces. She's twisted around to look out the back.

"The black Audi? That's mine. Thank you for your attention."

While we've been talking, I've managed to get a data connection on my work phone. Good thing the agency pays the roaming charges. "Here it is. Ron Bowen. He says the Nazis took the portrait from his family and the Soviets took it from the Nazis. He sued the Russian dude—Arkady Tovorovsky—in federal court and lost twice. The Russians turned down his claim." I look up at Allyson. "Bowen's the client, isn't he."

She hesitates a moment. "Yes."

Carson lurches forward. "Stop. You're breaking the rules. You don't tell us who—"

"You'll find out almost immediately. I may as well tell you now."

When she hired me, Allyson said I'd never know who the client is. Carson went to a lot of trouble to keep it from me on my first project—just as well, as I found out. "You know, what I told you is all public information. Why didn't you send that?"

"'Cause we're stealing the picture," Carson says. "Right?"

"The client very much wants his property and doesn't care how we accomplish that." Allyson's voice is unusually guarded. "I'm reliably informed that he isn't a graceful winner. When he gets his painting, he'll tell everyone who'll listen. That may draw more attention to us than I'm interested in deflecting. It's why I'd appreciate you leaving as few fingerprints on this project as you can manage." She pauses for a lane change we don't need. "Which leads me to the next two points.

"This is our first project for Mr. Bowen. He's very wealthy in his own right, and his company is extremely successful. He can be an important client if he's pleased with your performance. I expect you to please him.

"Because it's important that we please the client, we all have to make certain… adjustments to the way we do things. Our client is not a trusting man. His representative will monitor you as—"

"A babysitter?" Carson's screech rattles the windows.

Another long pause. "Yeeesss." Allyson packs a lot into that word: *I'm sorry. I don't like it either. Just go with it, okay?* "Her name is Julie Arnlund. She's the client's cousin. I expect she'll report to him everything she sees and hears. Please—"

I ask, "How do we work with a spy?"

"Very carefully, I should—"

Carson lunges between the front seats. "Carefully? Really? How much do we tell her? What if she wants to 'help'? I'm—"

"Enough." The spring steel in Allyson's voice shuts up Carson like pulling a plug. "She'll supply any background information you need. Show her every courtesy. Protect her. Keep—"

"Does she need protecting?" I ask. This is sounding worse with every step.

"She may. The client referred to her as the 'family historian.' I doubt she has Ms. Carson's skill set."

Carson makes a rude noise.

"Keep her out of trouble. I understand what an imposition this is, but I have every confidence you'll meet the challenge."

I catch Carson rolling her eyes. Then I turn back to Allyson. "Carson's got a point. What if the cousin wants to do more than watch?"

"Dissuade her politely. If that doesn't work, find something… innocuous for her to do. Whatever you do, don't allow her to be arrested. That would be a disaster for us all."

We lost the box truck some way back and passed all the unloveliness of a major airport's infrastructure—warehouses, baggage-cart depots, anonymous, square windowless structures, above-ground pipelines. Allyson's dangerously close to matching the speed limit (40, though I don't know if it's MPH or KPH). We thread through a hairpin turn and into a traffic circle.

Carson asks, "Where are we going?"

"In this case, it's the journey that's important, not the destination." Allyson nudges us out of the traffic circle and suddenly we're off the airport grounds, driving a divided four-lane road lined with scrubby trees and pastures. "This is your car, by the way. Keep in mind that we don't have vehicle service arranged where you're going, so it's a minimum two-hour turnaround for a new one. Please try to not change cars every few hours the way you did in Milan. That was excessive."

I can hear Carson fuming behind me, but she doesn't say anything. I guess she's bitched out the boss enough today.

"One more thing." Allyson pulls off the highway onto a two-lane road, then stops. "There are two countries I absolutely detest working in. This is one of them. There are cameras everywhere. We know that GCHQ is monitoring the telephone system in a way your NSA could only dream about. The Tories have proposed a law that would let the security services keep records of every person's internet use for a year. That they're asking for permission tells me they're already doing it. Be very, very careful. I don't know how well I can protect you here."

I swap a glance with Carson. She blows out a long breath and shakes her head. The black Audi slips up behind us. "What's the other country?" I ask.

"Yours, of course." She pulls what looks like a black leather Lanvin Sugar shoulder bag from under her legs. Two months of my pay for pushing coffee, right there. "I suggest the A3 for Portsmouth. It's dual carriageway all the way, it's marginally more scenic than the M3, and there are slightly fewer traffic cameras. The M25 is infested with cameras from here to the A3, so behave yourselves. Olivia has your hotel arrangements."

"Olivia knows about all this?"

"Olivia knows everything, as usual." She pushes open her door, steps out, then leans into the opening. "Ms. Arnlund will join you tomorrow. I suggest you get as much done as you can today. Good luck."

Chapter 3

The BMW's loping along half-asleep, heading southwest on the A3 through a whole lot of Technicolor green trees and pastures. Carson apparently took Allyson seriously and isn't practicing for the Indy 500 as usual.

Carson almost always drives. When we first met, she said she's a "bad passenger"—a huge understatement—so I'm happy to let her have her way and avoid the explosions. It's one of the few things I know about her.

"You're quiet," she says.

"You should talk."

"I'm always quiet."

True enough. "Ripping off a museum's like scamming a granny. It's not all that hard, but it's a pretty scummy thing to do. And it's seriously illegal."

"So?"

"'So?' You're sure you were a cop?" That gets me The Look. "I haven't had to do anything seriously illegal so far."

"Fraud? Transporting stolen goods?"

"You know what I mean. Nothing really bad. Not like *some of us.*" I go for the laser stare, but her shields are up. "I mean, sure, I've cut some corners, blurred some lines. But in Milan and Mexico? I just let crooked people do what they wanted to anyway and took advantage of it. Nothing like this."

"Get over it. You know you gotta do it." Carson tears herself away from the road for a moment to scowl at me. "Same reason I do."

Yeah. For the money.

I owe $530,000 in mostly non-dischargeable debt. Some is student loans, more's medical bills, and a lot is restitution. Being a convicted felon limits my (legal) career options. That's how a graduate architecture degree qualifies me for a not-full-time job with the Green Coffee Empire. My pay's going up to ten bucks an hour in January—thank you, California minimum wage—which makes it even easier to figure out how long it'll take to get out of hock.

As a junior associate, Allyson pays me a thousand euros a day on this job plus "reasonable" expenses, including really nice hotel rooms and all the food I can shove in my mouth. Put another way: each *day* spent stealing one already-stolen painting pays more than a whole *month* feeding West L.A.'s caffeine addictions.

But there's a downside: what if Inspector Morse busts me? (Yes, I know, he's dead. Lewis, then. Pick a copper, anyone but Luther.)

It won't be pretty. I'll be at Her Majesty's pleasure for however long she wants me. When the Brits finally give me back to the feds, they'll throw me into the hole again for busting my probation in all kinds of ways. It won't be a nice, safe pen like PEN (Federal Prison Camp Pensacola), where I did time with naughty Wall Street types who had bad lawyers. This time, it'll be a real prison with real prisoners. Animals. Predators.

As much as I hated the confinement and dehumanization at PEN, I didn't have to worry about getting knifed in a race riot.

But being half a million in the hole to the government and the banks truly sucks.

I turn to watch the greenery slide by and start to obsess about something else: why am I even *here?*

I'm not a burglar—that's Carson's thing. It's not like this project is going to take much art knowledge to pull off. Does Allyson think I know more about museums than I do? I grew up in museums, true. Mom would take me every time she had a chance. But we never got past the "Authorized Staff Only" signs.

So, what's she up to? She's got an angle. She's *always* got an angle.

Maybe it's because of Ida Rothenberg. Maybe Allyson thinks I have something to make right, some long-term guilt to bury. Maybe she thinks that's more of an incentive than the money.

Maybe she's right.

Chapter 4

The Mainwaring Gallery is on Commercial Road in downtown Portsmouth. An online PDF of a quaint 1955 pamphlet says it's in what used to be the city's main Lloyd's Bank building: a pale gray, four-story, Art Deco-style limestone block built in 1950. Two banners hang from the second-floor cornice to the thin granite band course ringing the top of the ground floor. The garnet one on the left reads "Mainwaring," and the other's for the special exhibit.

The pedestrianized street's lined with places like this, built after the war to replace what the Blitz wiped out. The ground-floor facades have been updated, but a surprising amount of the upper-story work is more-or-less intact. It's not bad for a commercial strip.

I'm sitting on the edge of the Jubilee Fountain in the busy plaza where Commercial Road and Arundel Street meet. It's a quirky two-tier concrete basin circled by bronze royal beasts—unicorns, griffins, lions, even what I think is a kangaroo—holding coats of arms. It's just a few steps from the museum's front door.

Carson plops down next to me. Halfway here, she'd started crabbing about the client. We both adjusted our attitudes at lunch in the mall next to the museum.

"Feeling better?" I ask.

She shrugs. "Bitching at you won't fix it. You?"

"It's amazing what a good sandwich can do." I lurch off the ledge. "Time to go to work."

The museum's ground floor is rose-and-gray checkerboard granite floors and printed vinyl overlays on the walls featuring art's greatest hits (most of them not here). A big gift shop is on our left, the café's straight ahead, and there's a seating area to our right with teak benches that look like they belong on the *Titanic*. We buy our £10 special exhibit tickets from a chirpy young blonde at the rosewood information desk. Like the other customer-facing staff, she wears a garnet long-sleeved button-down with a gold "MWG" logo on the left breast. She hands us a gallery map, and off we go.

In the elevator, Carson wraps her hands around my arm and leans into me. We don't want to look like we're casing the place—though that's exactly what we're doing—so we agreed we'd play it like a couple here for an afternoon of culture. This'll be the third time we've played house like this (twice in Milan), and we've gotten better at it with practice. It's pretty okay to pretend; the women who interest me aren't interested in an ex-con. Carson's so far outside my usual type, though, that it's hard to see an "us" working for real.

The elevator rumbles open at the special exhibit's entry lobby. White copperplate script dominates the textured scarlet wall in front of us: "Stealing Beauty: Portraits of Women, 1750-1950."

"Getting one of those," Carson whispers at me. She nods toward the cart renting the audio guides.

Not what I expected from her. "Why?"

"Excuse to stand around."

I read the thesis statement under the exhibit title—*art reflects the changing roles of women* yadda yadda—and check out the corporate sponsor logos while Carson gets her guide. Then she takes my arm and lets me lead her into the gallery.

The exhibit's laid out thematically in a serpentine plan. Each theme's partitions have a key color. The first one, "Class," is imperial purple; appropriate, I guess, but awfully damn dark. The ambient lighting's restrained, which is a nice way of saying "dim." It doesn't take long to feel like we're walking through a maze. The labels could stand to be bigger, though I can't remember ever being in a museum that didn't need bigger labels.

You're not writing a review. You're ripping this place off. Concentrate.

We drift past the artwork, sometimes together but often a few feet apart, like we've been a couple for a long time and don't need to constantly hang on each other. From time to time I'll catch Carson standing in front of a canvas holding her audio guide (an overgrown TV remote on a red lanyard) to her ear, but instead of studying the portrait, her eyes are roving all over. I should be looking for stuff, too, but there's a problem.

I have no idea what to look for.

I did some sketchy things at Heibrück Pacific, my now-dead gallery in L.A., but someone else always stole the hot pieces we sold. So I notice the cameras, but that's about it. Besides, it's so easy to get lost in all the beautiful things here. The first inevitable Gainsborough, for one: *Ann Ford*, an apple-cheeked young woman wearing a billowing brocaded-silver gown and holding a lute.

My mom was an artist and an art teacher. Some of my earliest memories are of her leading me and my sister through one museum or another, talking about color and light. She helped me fall in love with art—hers first, then everyone else's. When I close my eyes, I hear her asking, *What do you see?*

Carson slips up behind me, props a fist on my shoulder, and rests her chin on the fist. "Where's the guards?" she whispers.

"They're the docents." I get a blank look. "Red shirts with the logo? iPads? That's them."

She purses her lips. "They're guards?"

"It's a new thing. Some museums have merged their docent and security staffs. They say it's to make the place less intimidating, but it's also about saving money. The Broad back home does it."

"Whatever." Carson chews over this for a moment. "What about after hours?"

"No clue."

Over three-quarters of the works are on loan, either from private collections or other museums. The logistics of putting this show together must've been brutal.

Stop. Think like a thief.

The displays use what looks like a standard wire hanging system—two-millimeter aircraft-grade stainless cables mounted on a track under the crown molding, then hooked to whatever mounting hardware's on the backs of the works. We used Griplock at Heibrück, but the major systems are mostly variations on the same theme. I'd like to look behind a canvas to see if they're using open or gated hooks or some kind of theft-proof hangers, but even the docents would notice that.

At the beginning of "Motherhood" (shell pink, of course), I find Carson stalled in front of a Millais piece lent by the Tate: *Mrs. James Wyatt Jr. and Her Daughter Sarah.* I clear my throat gently so I don't startle her—which could be deadly—and wrap an arm around her waist. Every time I do this, I'm surprised by how solid she is. I make like I'm nuzzling her ear and whisper, "What've you got?"

She fiddles with her audio guide and holds it between our ears, like we're both listening. "Two wireless cameras per room. Opposite corners. Hundred-percent coverage. No motion detectors. Can't tell about thermals or sound. Probably not. You?"

I tell her about the hanging hardware. Her eyes glaze after my first sentence. She says "So?" when I'm done.

"We have to get the piece off the wall. The hardware makes a difference."

"Ask a docent-person." Carson nods at the Millais. "What's wrong with this thing? Looks weird."

"What do you see?" I'll teach her how to look at art if it kills me. Which it might.

She frowns at the double-portrait for a few moments. "Mom and the kid aren't looking at each other. All those"—she waves the audio guide behind us—"happy moms, happy babies. This one..." more frowning "...reminds me of home."

Wow. Personal insight. There must be a blue moon out.

We finally find the first exit partway through "Work," which is mustard yellow and the exhibit's halfway point. Carson grabs my hand in both of hers and nods toward the passageway. "I need to..."

Check out the stairwell, I finish for her. "Okay. I'll wait here."

She waves me away. "You go on. I'll catch up." A nice little playlet for the half-dozen people milling around in this room.

So I go on. Carson's right—I have to get farther out on a limb if I'm going to learn what I need to. But if I do, I make myself memorable. Memorable's great if I'm after a woman; not so much if I'm about to knock over the place.

I'm looking over a Jean-François Millet scene of a woman shoveling raw bread into an open-flame oven—she has Carson's arms—when I realize I'm alone for the first time since I walked in here. Crazy me says, *look behind the canvas.*

Are you nuts?

Do it now.

I pull my phone and switch it to camera mode before I can think about all the good reasons I shouldn't. I edge to my left, reach for the frame's corner... and freeze. Security cameras. I'll be on tape.

I jump at a flash of red in the corner of my right eye. A docent. Shit.

A young black woman comes steaming toward me. She has colored threads woven into her cornrows, and she's wearing a red museum shirt and a name badge—Kwana—decorated like an illuminated manuscript with what looks like colored Sharpies. "Can I tell you anything about that, sir?"

Did she see me go for the frame? Did the cameras? "Um, no, thanks. I'm fine."

Kwana looks up with big, eager eyes, like she's glad to finally have someone to talk to. "That's why I'm here, yeah? Like to know more about the artist? I can look him up." Her English accent isn't one you hear on PBS very often, though God knows what it is.

"Actually, I'm familiar with Millet. Thanks, though."

Her eyebrows arch. "Are you, now?"

I had to say that, didn't I?

"How's this—I give you a quiz. If you answer the questions, you get a prize. Have a go?"

Aw, hell. Is she being helpful, or stalling until the real guards can get here? She hasn't wrestled me to the floor yet. Maybe that's because I haven't moved. What if I walk away?

No. If I brush her off, she'll remember me as the jerk who told her to get lost. She might start wondering what I was doing right before she showed up. Why I was so startled. I can hear the interview a couple weeks from now when the detective asks Kwana if she remembers anything unusual. *Yeah, there was this bloke...*

She's got me. Maybe I can get something out of it. "Where's your blue blazer?"

"My...?" After a moment, the light dawns. "Oh! Like museum guards, yeah? We don't do that here. Just me, red shirt."

"Do they make you sleep here to keep the place safe after they close?"

"Oh, no, there's proper guards for that."

Just what I wanted to find out.

She leans in, perfectly straight-faced. "You're not gonna nick something, are you?"

Oh hell...

Then I notice her sly smile and drag my heart out of my throat. "Sure I am. I want one of everything."

She giggles. At least someone thinks it's funny. "Well, don't, or I gotta bop you about a bit with this." She holds up her iPad. "It's a deadly weapon, you know."

I paste on a smile. "I'll be good."

I play along with her quiz. Three Millet canvases passed through

Heibrück while I was there, so I'd read up on him. I answer four out of five questions—I forgot he had nine kids—but Kwana gives me a red Mainwaring pen anyway. "No souvenirs off the walls, now, yeah?" she says as she walks away.

Blend in echoes in my ears as I finish the "Work" theme. Carson's not back yet. She's been gone almost twenty minutes. I text her but she doesn't answer. Is she okay? Did she get caught? Did she leave?

Then I enter "Fashion" and its powder-blue partitions. I instantly forget Carson and Kwana and everything else.

There she is, at the opposite end of the room. All alone in a pool of light.

I finally meet Dorotea DeVillardi.

Carson slides onto the Nelson bench and drapes a hand over my thigh. It's the hand that brings me back into the gallery.

"You're still alive." I try not to show how relieved I am.

"Uh-huh." I can feel her breath on my ear. "Stairs and toilets all the way down. No cameras, no alarms, one-way latches on all three levels."

I nod. I'm still distracted—it's not often you get to see a lost masterpiece in person, especially one like this.

Carson figures this out and spends a few moments checking out the portrait. "Just your type. Dark eyes, dark hair." She flicks a snide glance my way. "Big tits."

That describes Carson, too, but I know better than to point that out. "You know, I like a nice rack as much as the next guy, but if I have to choose, I go for legs."

"Did I ask?" She squeezes my thigh hard enough to hurt, then braces her hands behind her and leans back. "Bigger'n I thought."

"Her boobs?"

This look is less playful and more slicing-open-arteries. "The picture."

"Fifty by thirty-six and a half. That's not unusual for Sargent's three-quarter-length portraits. His second portrait of Sybil Sassoon is over five feet tall."

"So who is this guy?"

"John Singer Sargent?"

Carson shrugs. "Never heard of him."

How sad. "An American who did most of his work in Europe. He was the top portrait artist of the late nineteenth and early twentieth centuries. He also did landscapes, watercolors, murals. But this is what we know him for." I wave toward Dorotea. "See how alive she is? It's like she could just climb out of that frame. That's why people wanted to sit to him."

Carson pushes off the bench and fiddles with her audio guide while she strolls to the canvas. She stands right in front of it, blocking my view. Deliberately? Probably. I follow and stand close enough to hear a voice buzzing from the guide. For once she's actually listening to the thing. When the voice stops, she lets the guide dangle from the lanyard around her neck. "What's with the bird?" she finally asks.

"It's an ibis. Ever hear of Howard Carter?" She shakes her head. "He opened up King Tut's tomb in 1923. Everybody went nuts for Egypt. You see it a lot in early Art Deco, and in period jewelry and clothes. This dress would've been very *au courant* in 1924."

She scowls at me. "*Au courant*? Really?"

"It comes with the master's." That would be the M.Arch I didn't get to use for very long, but I'm still paying off. "This Tovorovsky dude's going to be pissed when he loses this."

"Know what that means, right?"

"One of Putin's buddies? I've got an idea." Not a very happy idea, either. "We've gotta do this smart, but we've gotta do it. He went public with the portrait almost twenty years ago and this is the first time he's let it out of Russia. Best reason I can think of for that is, he's pumping it up for a sale. If he sells it, it may disappear again for another fifty years."

Chapter 5

Carson asks me, "Got a plan yet?"

"No. Do you?"

We left the museum just before it closed at six. Now we're in Nando's in Gunwharf Quays, the splashy shopping center on the edge of the channel leading to Portsmouth Harbor. From the mezzanine, we can look down on the semicircular booths with bright geometric upholstery, full of Saturday-night party groups. There's lots of warm wood and tile and Afro-Portuguese music throbbing in the background.

Carson wipes her mouth and leans her elbows on the wooden two-top. Her half-chicken looks like it lost a fight with a train. "Don't know enough yet. Be a bitch to take it at the museum. Have to pack it past ten cameras, at least." We don't have to worry about being overheard; all the noise comes up here, and I can barely hear her two feet away. She bobs to the rhythm a bit. "How do they move these things?"

"Honestly? I don't know. I never did museums. I used to haul around six figures worth of canvas in the trunk of Gar's Mercedes. I doubt they do that."

She snorts. "Yeah. Too easy. I'll look at it. Truck's gotta be easier to boost than that gallery."

I set down what's left of my huge chicken sandwich. The nuclear-level peri-peri sauce will keep my sinuses clear for a week. "You know, I've been thinking about this whole stealing-the-portrait thing. It's not that simple."

"No shit."

"Let me finish. Let's go back to why we're doing this. The client wants his painting back. If we just steal it, it's, well, stolen. He gets two choices: he either sticks it in his basement until the statute runs out—whatever that is in Britain—or he tells the world he's got it, which is like saying 'come arrest me.' There's blowback either way, and it's gonna go straight through Allyson back to us. The client's not spending all this money to get a dust-catcher."

Carson's getting that sucking-a-lemon look. "So?"

This is another of those half-assed ideas I really should keep to myself until it turns into something, but it's too late to stop now. "We have to steal it so nobody notices."

She screws her eyes shut. "How the *fuck* do we do that?"

That question's why I should've kept this to myself. "Look, we've got three problems to solve. First, we gotta get it out of the museum. Second, we have to get it out of the country. Third, we have to launder it so the client can show it to his buddies sometime in his lifetime. Each problem depends on us solving the previous one."

"So how do we do it?"

"I'm thinking… we swap in a copy." I get the are-you-shitting-me look I expect. "It'll have to be a damn good copy so the museum and Tovorovsky don't realize the original's gone, at least, until it's time for them to know. If the museum doesn't know anything happened, we can get the original out of the country easy. Then we can figure out how to doctor its provenance so Bowen can claim it."

Now Carson's rubbing both temples. "How'd Tovorovsky get a fake?"

"For real, or in the story?"

"The story."

"There were forgers around back then." Now I really am saying the words as I think of them, like I'm re-learning how to talk after a stroke. "Han van Meegeren was the most famous. He cooked up Vermeers—new ones, not copies—sold them to the Nazis. Goering got at least one. Maybe… some guy was working that angle in Austria. Copying paintings stolen from the Jews, selling them under the table. The Russians rolled through in '45, grabbed everything they could carry, took the copy back home. It knocked around there until Tovorovsky got it. He didn't have any reason to think it was fake." I hold up my hands. "Or something."

"Fucking lame."

"Give me a break. I just thought of it thirty seconds ago."

Carson sighs and picks at her chicken. "What really happened?"

"Nobody knows. At least, not that I've seen written down. We can ask the cousin when we meet her. Maybe she knows something. But… it's the only way I can see of solving all three problems. You got a better idea?"

She doesn't answer. I've learned that means *no*. She fiddles with her fork with her eyes focused miles away. "Where we get the copy from?"

"I'll find a guy who can do the job."

"Just happen to know art forgers?"

"Allyson's paying me for something." Before I can pursue that idea, reality sticks a shiv in my ribs. "Shit. The copy."

"Now what?" Her voice is getting crabbier.

Now I'm rubbing my forehead. It'd seemed like such a good idea. At least, it'd seemed like an idea. "If we're going to fool the museum and the Russian dude, we have to copy *both sides*."

"What? Why? Nobody looks at the back."

"You do when you take it off the wall." I pound the rest of my second Sagres beer. "The back of a painting… it's like the piece's life history. You see the aging, how the canvas was prepared, the stretcher design. Maker's stamps if it's the right period. Gallery stickers, pencil markings, inscriptions, damage. You flip over a hundred-year-old work and it's all shiny new on the back? You know it's a fake—anyone can tell."

"Wait. That thing about someone forging the picture back before the Russians got it? Wouldn't they have the same problem with the back then?"

"Not necessarily, not if the forger was working from the original. Also, remember that the portrait would've been only fourteen or fifteen years old then, with only one owner. The back would've been pretty clean."

Carson spears the chicken carcass with her fork. That takes some effort. "We gotta break into the museum, take the thing down, so we can look at the back? Really?" She shakes her head. "Fuck it. Let's just take the damn thing."

For a moment, that sounds really good. Simple. Even a caveman can do it. "What's the statute of limitations for grand theft in England?"

She hauls out her phone and stabs at it for a while. Her face gets darker as she goes along. "None for criminal, just civil. Huh." She shakes her head. "Something new for Allyson to hold over us."

"She'd do that?"

"She'll do anything that gets her ahead."

Great. My boss is keeping a permanent file on me. At least I have practice being thrown to the wolves.

It looks like we have to pass on the hard thing to do and try the damn-near-impossible thing to do.

We finally check into our hotel after eight. When Olivia mentioned the Florence Suite on our call during the drive from Heathrow, I pictured a multi-story glass box surrounded by parking lots. But the Florence Suite is one of a series of newish multi-gabled brick townhouses that blend in with the older buildings along a street in a neighborhood called Southsea. The front office is in the next building. We're both up a winding staircase to the fourth floor, me in Room 6, Carson across the hall in Room 5.

The desk clerk hands me a note-sized envelope when I check in. "Mr. Simon" is handwritten on the front. After I get done unpacking, I slump in a Danish Modern armchair and rip open the envelope. Smooth, practiced script on a folded sheet:

```
Mr. Simon,

I hope you had a good trip. I'd love
to meet you for breakfast tomorrow
at the hotel restaurant. Can you
come at 8:00? I'll have a Hartford
newspaper.

Julie
```

A newspaper. Someone's been reading too many spy novels.

Chapter 6

"Play nice," I tell Carson when we enter The Kitchen. It's the common restaurant for the flock of pint-sized hotels on this block. "Don't piss her off."

"You do the talking, then," she grumps. Her hair's still damp from the shower and she's wearing her usual jeans and long-sleeved tee (forest green today).

The Kitchen is hardwood floors, slate-blue walls, white wainscoting, and shuttered bay windows. It's early-Sunday quiet and there's only a scattering of other hotel inmates waiting for breakfast at the wood-topped tables.

We poke our heads into a room with three four-tops, two of them still empty. A lone woman's sitting at the one closest to the broad bay window. She looks up from what she's reading, then lifts it off the table: the Hartford *Courant*. By the time we reach her, she's stood and thrust her hand in my direction. "Mr. Simon! I'm Julie Arnlund. I'm so glad to meet you!"

A good, firm grip. Middle-aged—forties, maybe?—with an open, oval face and soft eyes the color of strong coffee. Handsome rather than pretty. Her straight chestnut hair is cut at her collar and curled under. The drapey, blush-pink, long-sleeved polo and double-pleated khakis don't do her any favors.

"Nice to meet you. Call me Matt."

She smiles. Straight white teeth. "Julie." Her hand lingers a moment before she takes it back and turns to Carson. "And you're…?"

"Carson." She says it like she's trying to push it through the blinds.

Julie's mouth pops open for a moment. Then she coughs out the start of a laugh. "Like on *Downton Abbey?*"

Carson's lips mash flat. She shakes Julie's hand—Julie winces—then steps back so she won't catch anything.

We sit in the artfully mismatched wooden chairs and

immediately get one of those awkward pauses where everyone knows they should say something but nobody knows what to say. I cover by picking up the menu. It's short, but we all spend a lot of time going over it. A waitress eventually comes to take our orders, then leaves us with the awkward pause again.

"Well," Julie finally announces. She's perched on the front edge of her chair with her hands folded in her lap. I can't tell yet if she's normally uptight or if today's special. "I guess I should start. I'm… really excited to have you here, to *be* here. I've been hoping for this for years, and I'm really, really looking forward to working with both of you to finally get our painting home. So, thank you."

The nervous smile is kind of cute, but it makes me wonder if she's making this up as she goes along, like I am. I exchange a glance with Carson. She's biting both her lips, maybe so she won't say *God help us*, which her eyes are doing. She hikes her eyebrows at me. I guess she's serious about me being the mouthpiece.

I turn back to Julie, who's been watching us. "We'll do our best." That didn't relax her a bit. "I tried Googling you last night–"

"I'm the high-school teacher, not the porn star. Disappointed?"

"Devastated." Actually, not. Juliet Arnlund—a.k.a. Jewels Starr—is a skinny twenty-something blonde with too much body art. I wasn't even tempted to watch the videos.

"Maybe if you keep looking…" Julie says this with such a straight face that for a moment I wonder if I really missed something. Then another smile creeps out of hiding. She touches my forearm. "Just kidding."

At least she's got a sense of humor. "What I was going to say was, I was looking to see how public you've been about the painting."

Julie purses her lips. "I'm sorry, I don't understand."

"Do you blog about the portrait? Have you talked to the media about it? Testified in court? Are you named in any legal papers? Had your picture on the news with Bowen?"

Her eyes get big. "No. No. Nothing like that. Ron doesn't share the spotlight." She holds up both hands palms out. "Which is fine with me. I don't want to be a celebrity."

"Okay. All I found for you was stuff on the school and district websites. You're not on social media at all?"

"No, I'm not." Julie finally settles back into her chair. "It's hard to share anything publicly when you're a teacher. Students might see it. Worse, *parents* might see it. Say one 'wrong' word or share one 'wrong' post and you get a complaint, or…well, you know how kids are. It's not worth it."

That confirms what I saw, but it never hurts to ask. At least we don't have to worry about her live-tweeting everything we do.

"Why aren't you teaching?" Carson's hunched over what's left of her coffee. "School's open, right?"

If Julie catches the borderline-accusing tone in Carson's voice, she doesn't show it. "I'm on sabbatical this term. I needed some time off. Of course, what am I doing?" She turns up her palms. "I'm writing a book about our family, about how we're trying to get back the things the Nazis stole from us."

"That's getting to be a pretty crowded bookshelf," I say.

"I know. It's not really to make any money. It's so we don't lose the information. It's for my son so he'll know who he is."

The waitress trundles in with our orders: waffles for me, porridge and sliced bananas for Julie, and the "farmer's breakfast" (a.k.a., the "full English") for Carson. It occurs to me that this is the first time I've seen Carson eat breakfast. She can't scarf all that down all the time, can she?

We take a break from talking while we feed. Carson demolishes her pile of food. Julie's careful, doesn't spill a drop. She sits up straight and keeps one hand in her lap. Someone got a dose of old-fashioned table manners.

After a few minutes of peeking at Carson, Julie shakes her head. "Ms. Carson, I'm *so* jealous you can eat all that and still keep your figure. I'm gaining weight just watching you."

The look she gets back is a tiger interrupted while eating a yak.

I need to head off the food fight. "How long have you been working on this?"

"Oh… seven, almost eight years. That's nothing compared to some people I've met. Some of them have been chipping away at this for decades. I can see why—it's incredibly complicated, and it seems like everyone wants to get in our way."

"That's a lot of work. Who's Dorotea to you?"

Julie cocks her head. "She's my *oma*. Sorry, my grandmother. Ron's too. You didn't know?"

Now I feel dumb. I don't like that. Why didn't Allyson tell us more? "No, sorry. All we know is, the portrait belongs to your family.

We don't know how. Who was she?"

"Oh, wow." Her face absolutely lights up. "The short version… Errico and Francesca DeVillardi were our great-grandparents. They were rich Venetian Jews. Dorotea was their only daughter. She was born in 1906. They raised her basically as a princess—the palazzo on a canal, servants, foreign tutors, the whole thing."

Now that she's not strangling inside, her voice is warm and clear and lively. Her face is very mobile. Her eyes look vaguely familiar, but I can't place why.

"She was very smart. By the end she spoke three and a half languages, and—"

I ask, "A half?"

"She was teaching herself English. You know, reading the *Times of London*, listening to the BBC on the radio. She learned about business from Errico and about art from Francesca. Her mom was a big patron of the arts. That's how the family knew John Singer Sargent—you know who he is, right? Sorry, of course you do. He visited Venice a lot. He was the first person outside the family to visit after Oma was born…"

Julie's eyes are sparkling, she's smiling, she's using her hands more. But I start to notice other things, too: the crinkles at the corners of her eyes, the smile lines around her mouth, the softening at her jaw and under her eyes and chin. She's closer to fifty than forty. Unlike a lot of Westside women I see, she hasn't had work done. Good for her.

"…how they finally got him to paint Oma's portrait."

"Great. Thanks." Now she's finally relaxed, I hate to bring up the next subject. We've got to talk about it, though, sooner rather than later, and I'd better do it before Carson does. "You mentioned 'working together' earlier. What does that mean to you?"

Julie gives me a slow blink. "Well… I need to be involved in your planning. Ron wants regular updates. I want to help as much as I can."

Carson's eyes slam shut.

I check the room; we're still alone. Here we go. "Do you know what 'accessory' means? I don't mean belts and scarves."

What's left of Julie's smile melts like ice in a microwave. "Ron hired you"—she glances from me to Carson and back—"to get Oma back. He told me he didn't say how. That means he doesn't care how, or he'd be very specific with you. I think he expects you to steal her. Frankly, so do I."

Carson asks, "That bother you?"

"Usually it would, but not this time." She's perched again. "She's already stolen—we're just taking her back. That's how I look at it. And I intend to help. So, to answer your question, yes, I know what 'accessory' means."

Oh, hell. This is just what Carson was afraid of. "You know, 'helping' is a big step past 'accessory.' 'Helping' means you're doing the crime. If we're caught—and we could be—you're going to jail. That's no fun."

Julie's jaw is getting tighter. "Ron told your boss that you're supposed to cooperate with me."

"Our boss also told us to protect you."

"I'm not a child."

"I've noticed." So much for staying on her good side. "Seriously. How much are you willing to risk for Cousin Ron? He's not the one who'll get the cuffs. If you go inside, you'll come out someone else. You won't be able to teach anymore. Your life'll be very, very different, and not in a good way. Just saying."

Julie sits there staring past me for a few moments. She sets down her spoon very carefully. "Mr. Simon. Ms. Carson. I understand you're professionals at this, and I respect that. But you're here because you're getting paid to be. This is personal for me. That's my grandmother on that painting. Did you ever get to meet your grandmother, Mr. Simon?"

"On my mom's side. Dad's mom died young."

She nods. "So did mine. I'm sixteen years older than she ever got to be. That painting's the closest I'll ever get to meeting her. She's been stolen from us twice. I *won't*"—she slaps the table's edge with her fingers—"sit around and watch *that man* take her back to Russia. Please don't shut me out. I'm helping." Julie leans forward and folds her hands on the table. "Do you have a plan yet?"

I have to think of what to say that'll satisfy her and not have Carson kick the shit out of me afterwards. That's a hard square to circle. "We've been here less than a day. We haven't had time to build a plan. We're still doing research."

"I have everything you'll need about Oma or the portrait."

"Not that kind of research," Carson says. There's more of an edge on her voice than I like.

I put up my hands: *slow down.* "We're still figuring out how the museum works. Getting the lay of the land. You can't help us with that. We don't know enough yet to know what we don't know." Did that make sense? Whatever. I try to come up with something that'll make her feel valuable without giving her an inflated idea of how involved she's going to be. "It's great that you have all the background on the portrait. We'll totally need that really soon, but we're working on basics right now. So relax. Catch up on the jet lag."

Julie's jawline gets a little tighter. "I can't tell Ron that. How long have you been here?"

"None of your business." Carson's eyes are stripping the skin off Julie's face. "Not like buying a Coffee Crisp at Mac's. Gotta scope it out first. That takes time."

I cut off Julie before she can jump on Carson. "Tell him we're doing our due diligence. He'll understand that. We'll let you know as soon as we have a plan."

Carson kicks my shin. I try not to react, but *damn,* that hurt.

Julie carefully folds her napkin on the table. She looks appeased but not happy. "This isn't a vacation for me. I have to work on my book. And today I'm finally going to see Oma's portrait." She aims a flat, direct look at me; not quite a challenge but close. "That's not going to be a problem, right?"

I start counting the ways it could be but stop. "Um, well, not necessarily…"

"Stay away from the staff." Carson's leaning in with her forearms on the table edge. "Don't look at it more than the other pictures. Don't drool on it. You'll be on camera."

"Don't take it off the wall, either. Let us do that. We're professionals." I say it like it's a joke, but it might not be for her.

Julie aims a not-quite-irritated look at Carson for a few uncomfortable moments. Then she puts on a stiff smile. "Thank you, Ms. Carson. I have experience at being… invisible." She pushes away from the table, stands, and gives me a softer-but-not-soft look. "Please let me know when you're getting ready to do something. Have a nice day."

Then she marches out.

Chapter 7

Carson and I check out the museum's conservation lab. *The Mainwaring at Thirty,* a slick coffee-table book I bought at the museum shop on our way out yesterday, calls it the Dundas Lane Support Facility. It's in a light-industrial area northeast of central Portsmouth that looks like light-industrial areas everywhere else.

The DLSF is two adjoining structures. The first is a narrow two-story brick office block that parallels the road, with garnet trim and a flat roof. Behind it, a warehouse sided in concrete panels stretches back what looks like a hundred feet or so. Only the discreet museum logo on the office building's front door gives away what's inside.

Carson scans the complex through her mini-binoculars. She insists on having the car window open even though it's just over fifty outside. "Keypad on the front door," she says. "Another keypad on the double doors into the warehouse. Lights and cameras over both entries. Floodlights around the perimeter." She lowers her binoculars and frowns.

I'm on the lookout for the owners of the parking lot we're squatting in. "Can you get us in?"

She shrugs. "Probably. But what's in there? Alarms, locks, motion sensors, guards? Wanna walk into that?"

No. Just another complication.

How do we get into that lab?

I'm on my surprisingly comfortable queen-sized bed staring up at the ceiling light fixture, which looks like a large, white, upside-down artichoke. The radiator's on and I'm finally warm again. My brain's back online, but it's got no ideas.

We need detailed pictures of the portrait so we can get a good copy made. The conservation lab has the best camera setup available. But getting the portrait sent to the lab doesn't do us any good if we can't get in there afterwards. We need to check out the security inside the building before we knock over the first domino. How?

I think about bringing flowers for Ms. Vivian Whitehaven, the senior conservator in the Mainwaring's YouTube promo videos. Sixtyish, grayish, roundish, but even grandmas deserve flowers, right? Chances are, I'd never get past the front door or the security guard. The old repairman/janitor/city inspector trick falls apart because it's too easy for the museum to poke holes in it. Can Olivia scrape up someone legit? It seems like she can do anything, so maybe. Would they be able to get the info we need? Unless we buy somebody from the alarm company, probably not.

What we need is access and time. Access to the whole facility and the equipment in it so we can see what's there. Time enough for thorough fact-finding so nothing bites us in the ass when we come back.

That sounds like a tour, not reconnaissance. And it sounds like the longest long shot.

Carson asks, "Why do we need someone else?"

This is my first time in Carson's room this trip. It's shallower but a little wider than mine, with the same cream walls and gold carpet. I'm in an armchair next to the radiator, in a little patch of early-afternoon sun. Warm is good. "To be a potential donor. Buy our way into the lab."

She scrubs her hands over her face and slumps lower in the black wooden armchair in front of her Shaker-style desk by the window. "You do it. Be Hoskins again."

I was Richard Hoskins for my first project. He was a zillionaire property developer and a shady art collector. He'd be just the kind of guy who'd lay a multi-zero check on someone and demand whatever he wanted in return.

I shake my head. "They wouldn't buy it. There's no reason in the world he'd want anything from a regional art museum in England."

"Be someone like him, then."

"I don't think that'll work this time. A rich guy my age is all ego. He'd drop money on the museum, but he'd want his name on a gallery or an exhibition catalog or the whole building. We need either an old dude or a woman."

"Don't look at me. What's he gonna do?"

"Actually, I think we're better off with a woman. She needs to pass as a museum patron. Offer to grant ten or twenty grand for support services, like the lab or storage."

"And she wants a tour before she cuts the check?"

I nod. In poker, this is called *betting on the come*.

She grimaces. "This' nutser than that 'copy the back' thing."

"Just hear me out. The local council's cut its arts grants to almost nothing. The museum's subsidies are drying up. I doubt they'll turn down free money."

"Will Bowen cough it up?"

"I don't know. I'll have to ask the cousin."

"Yeah, you do that. Do they even let people into the lab?"

I'd spent some time on the website's "Support MWG" page looking for this answer. "Yeah. Every year you give them £5000 to be in their Collector's Circle, you get a tour of Dundas Lane with a curator."

"When's that?"

"June." Nine months away.

"Wonderful." Carson shoves her butt against the chair back and drapes her forearms over her knees. She looks tired and disgusted. "All we need is a hole, and you're building a fucking subway."

She's got a point. We haven't even started and this is getting convoluted. Allyson's notion of keeping it small and contained is already falling apart. And the more I get into it, the more I realize I only sort-of know what I'm doing.

She asks, "No other way to do this? Nothing?" It's almost a plea.

"Not that solves all three of our problems. There's ways we can do one or two, but..."

Carson sits staring at the carpet, breathing like it's hard. "Calling it. Ain't gonna work."

"Any other ideas that get us where we need to go?"

"No. That's what 'calling it' means." She waves in my direction. "All this shit, and the Princess breathing down our necks? Miss I'm-helping-whether-you-want-it-or-not?" She grunts out of her chair and starts pacing. "I'm out. You should be too."

Wait... *out?* Like, *quitting?* "Can we do that?"

"It costs. We get on Allyson's shit list. Some other darts'll get tagged with it. Better them than me. Cops don't do so good in prison. And *you*…"

I know what she means. "What's being on Allyson's shit list like?"

Carson shrugs. "We don't get projects. She forgets we're alive. How's it end? Depends. Replacements get busted? She'll see we were right. They pull it off? She fires us. You. Me she keeps for Rodievsky and shit work." Rodievsky is Carson's boss in the Russian mob. She owes them money for something—a *lot* of money. I've seen how she works it off.

None of this sounds good to me. Neither does getting busted. "How's this work? Is there a form or something?"

Carson snorts. "Not that easy. I call Olivia. She tells Allyson. Then our world gets fucked up. But we get to sleep in our own beds. You in?"

I don't want to lose this job; it's the only way I'll get out of debt in my lifetime. But I can't pay off those debts in prison, either.

No matter which way it goes, it'll suck. But I'd rather have it suck with me outside the fence. "Make the call."

Chapter 8

I spend the rest of the afternoon... not exactly *hiding* in my room but keeping on the down-low. The last thing I need is to run into Julie and have her start grilling me about our plans, especially since those plans are all about dropping her like a hot rock and running the other way.

I keep researching the museum while I wait for Carson to reappear. Partly it's a way to pass time, and partly it's to see if maybe I missed the easy, risk-free way to boost the portrait and make everybody happy. It doesn't look like I did.

Even though I'm trying to duck Julie, a little something in the back of my head is thinking about her. As potentially scary as she is to have around, I get where she's coming from. She's like Ida was— she wants her stuff back, and "no" isn't the right answer.

Is she worth having my probation yanked?

Would it have been worth having Gar fire me to keep Ida from living in my head for the past five years?

Around six, I wander to the window, stretch out my back, and watch the day start to turn into dusk. I haven't been able to decide whether I should feel guilty for dropping this project, anxious about losing the job and being in debt for the rest of my life, or relieved that I won't be setting myself up to spend a lot of poor-quality time with people not evil enough to be politicians or bank executives. So I've done all three in a loop, over and over, which is exhausting.

When Carson pounds on my door, I don't know what I want her to tell me. Her face and neck are scalding red, though, so whatever it is, it's not good.

She stalks to the window and braces her palms on the sill. I don't think I'm imagining the low grinding sound coming from her direction; it may be her teeth. She doesn't say anything for what seems like a long time.

Eventually I say, "Allyson's pissed?"

"Oh, yeah."

"How pissed? Like we're-fired-instantly pissed, or she's-sending-a-hit-man pissed?"

"Worse."

That vaguely queasy feeling I've been working on turns into full-blown nausea. "When do we leave?"

"We don't." She spins around, folds her arms, and leans her butt against the windowsill. Her face still looks like it belongs on a lobster. "Can't quit. Can't ditch the Princess. She said, 'The only way out is forward.'"

I thump down on the bed and let my stomach finish balling up in a knot. Not only are we stuck, but she blew us off with a line from a motivational poster. "You explained it to her?"

"Tried. This went through Olivia. Never get read out by Olivia. Can't fight back."

"Why not?"

I get The Look. "Think. She sends you to some shithole, then your return ticket disappears."

I guess there are teeth behind Olivia's gorgeous voice. "So now what do we do?"

Carson shakes her head slowly. "You think of a better plan?"

"No."

"Then we go with the old one. Allyson'll send someone to be rich. We gotta get the Princess sorted, too."

"What's that mean?"

She spends a lot of time peering at me, like she can't decide if I'm real. "You tell your wife everything you did at your gallery?"

"No." Knowing Janine, though, she'd want to help if she was in the right mood.

"Your boss tell you everything?"

"Enough. But no, not everything."

Carson points through the floor. "Think Princess is gonna let us get away with that?"

"She won't know what we're not telling her."

"Really? She's a pain, but she ain't stupid." She sighs, then tumbles into one of my armchairs. "Gotta watch Every. Single. Word we say around her. Gotta hide our movements. When we get the picture, gotta hide that, too. And guess what—she's still got enough to burn us if she gets scared or pissed or we get caught."

"I bet not telling her anything will piss her off, too."

"No shit?" Carson plants her elbows on her knees. "Gotta get her dirty. She wants to help? Fine. Get it on video. That way, she flips on us? We got plenty to throw back on her."

I let that filter through my skull. According to Carson, we have to turn Julie into a criminal. I get where Carson's coming from—we have no idea what Julie will do if this project goes sideways—but it feels almost as scummy as ripping off a museum. Well, I've done scummier things before when the stakes were lower. "How do we do this?"

Carson rocks out of the chair. "Give her a choice."

Julie looks at Carson, then me. Her eyes are blown. She works her mouth a few times before any sound comes out. "Let me see if I understand. I can either hide in my room and let you ignore me, or I can steal something. Is that what you're saying?"

Carson's arms are folded hard. It always makes her look bigger, like she really needs that. "You got it. You wanna be our partner? You gotta have skin in the game."

"I have plenty of 'skin in the game,'" Julie snaps. "More than either of you. I—"

"Wrong kind." Carson steps closer so she can loom over Julie. "Don't know you. You don't work for the agency. Maybe you're a cop. Wanna get in our panties? Drop yours first."

So many reactions are crawling across Julie's face—shock, anger, embarrassment, disbelief—that it looks like it's trying to jump off. The look she's giving Carson is straight out of a horror movie. She finally remembers to close her mouth.

Carson says, "Figure it out. We got work to do." Then she grabs my arm and drags me out of Julie's room.

I don't dare look back.

Chapter 9

Portsmouth has only a handful of buildings taller than half-a-dozen stories, including the Spinnaker, the city's answer to Seattle's Space Needle. Most everything is low-rise red brick. As we chug through endless streets of two-story townhouses, it's hard to remember that Portsmouth is the most densely populated city in the U.K. and that downtown is only a few minutes behind us. At night, on empty roads with mist halos around the spotty lighting, it seems like we're passing through an endless village on our way to stake out the lab.

"Why aren't we going the same way we did last time?" I ask after the umpty-eleventh turn down another side street. For once, I'm driving. Carson's navigating. Bad passenger or not, she's behaved herself so far.

"Avoiding cameras."

"How do you know where the cameras are?"

"Found a map online." So that's why she's squinting at her phone. "Turn left up there."

I turn more carefully than I need to. Everything's backwards, so I can't drive on autopilot like I'm back home. "Did you find out anything else today?"

"Left again at the end. Yeah. City's got this thing online. You can look up planning docs for permitted projects. Museum reno'd the warehouse in '07. Lab's where you called it."

"Office building, ground floor, south end?"

"Yeah. No electrical plan, though. Figures."

"Good work." Carson finds the damnedest things online.

"Better slow down," Carson says. "Might get there tonight."

"Gimme a break." I leave out the *fuck you* I'm thinking. "I'm driving a too-big car on the wrong side of a too-small road, at night."

"Wimp." She snickers a little. "What do you think the Princess'll do?"

"Hard telling. She's got a good reason to go all-in."

Carson sits up straight and drops her hands into her lap. "I'm *so* glad to meet you. I'm *so* excited you're here. What can I do to get in your way?" The voice isn't quite Julie's, but she nails the cadence, her posture and gestures.

"Cute. Just saying. She might surprise us."

"Doubt she's got the stones. Right at the roundabout."

I'm still not used to these. "I have to go left to go right, right?"

We survive the traffic circle, several more turns, an overpass, and roads the size of goat paths. Then I see tilt-ups and light industrial development. We're not out in the country.

Carson tosses her gray hoodie into the back seat. She's wearing a black turtleneck to go with her black jeans and black gym shoes. I'll bet she's got one of her black hoods in that black backpack under her legs. I avoid making a ninja joke.

She screws a Bluetooth into her ear. "Right at the end, then a quick left."

Tilt-ups aren't any prettier here than they are back home; they just have more trees and grass around them. After I make that quick left, I start to recognize where we are from Google StreetView— we're at the north end of Dundas Lane.

The next time I look toward Carson, she's got her black hood on. All I can see is a couple shiny spots where her eyes are. "Slow way down when you get to the blue fence." She throws off her seat belt and hauls her backpack into her lap.

"Then what?"

"Keep driving. Right at the intersection, park someplace close."

A royal-blue fence appears in the headlights at the end of a long brick wall to my right. There's a blue warehouse just ahead; the museum building's on the other side, surrounded by a pool of light. I slow to walking speed. "Tell me when to stop—"

The passenger door clunks open, then shut. Carson disappears into the dark.

"Okay then." I cruise past the museum complex, turn right on Quatremaine and park in front of the white cube of a Greggs bakery. My phone rings before I shut off the engine. "Yeah?"

"Keep the line open." Carson, whispering.

"Are you okay?"

"Fine." There's rustling on her end. "Good view of the warehouse."

"Okay." I have no idea where she's hiding—there's a twelve-foot-fence across the road from the museum property—and she won't tell me if I ask. "How long are we staying?"

"Long as it takes."

Before I turned off the car, the screen in the middle of the dash said it's 5° C outside. That's 42° F, cold even for Carson. "You need some coffee? Something warm? I can go—"

"No. Got a Thermos." She pauses. "Thanks for asking." There's a funny something in her voice, like she's surprised I'd think about it.

For the next half-hour, we sit there with the line open between us, not saying much. Every car that passes on Quatremaine makes me jump. I hear leaves rattling on her end, the wind blowing, the odd engine going by. Now she's sipping coffee. It's weirdly intimate, like we're sitting in the car in the dark, only she's not here.

"Guard's on his rounds," she whispers. "Her rounds. A woman."

I check my phone: 1:04 a.m. "Hourly?"

"We'll see at two."

Another hour of this? Gack. Then I remind myself that I'm in a nice, warm car, and Carson's out there under a bush in the cold. She's got the experience and skills to be out there and I don't, but I shouldn't complain. At least the jet lag's working for me for once.

After a stretch of silence, I pull my personal phone and bring up a website I've been following for a few weeks. A new video dropped in the blog yesterday that I haven't had a chance to watch. I mute my work phone and punch the "play" icon on the embedded viewer.

"*Buon giorno*—good morning—I am Gianna Comici, and today I show to you the building of my gallery…"

She's practically bouncing past the stud walls and bundles of electrical cable dripping from the ceiling. Her sleeveless, fire engine-red '60s-style minidress matches her lipstick. Bright white stripes cut down her sides and around her hips. She's a swirl of color when she spins around a corner.

Gianna was the assistant at a Milanese gallery I was nosing around to find a cache of stolen artworks. She's beautiful and smart and ambitious and if I could've figured out how to tell her I wasn't a millionaire, I'd have brought her home with me. But I couldn't. Now all I can do is watch her weekly videos and think about what could've happened if I hadn't grown a conscience. And hope the world changes.

Carson startles me out of the swamp I'm diving down. "Cop."

What? I un-mute. "After you?"

"Shh." I hear engine noise and tires pass by on asphalt. After a moment, Carson says, "Patrol."

I note the time: 1:16. It's now I realize that my parking spot next to Gregg's doesn't let me see very far down the road. I slide down in the seat until I can just see out the windshield and stow my phone in the center console so there's no light. A couple minutes later, a white Ford five-door hatchback rolls by, taking its time. It has blue-and-yellow color blocks along the side and a blue light bar on top. I don't dare move until it disappears from my rear-view mirror. "It's gone."

"For now."

More silence. Thirty minutes crawl by. My heart settles down.

"Matt?"

"Yeah?"

"Talk to me."

"About what?"

"Anything. Just talk." Her voice is getting shaky.

"Are you okay?"

"Tired. Wet. Dead out here. Need something to focus on."

"Okay." The mist has turned to fog. It must be bad out there for her to admit it's bad. "What were you going to do on your time off?"

"Home. Toronto."

"Not a beach somewhere?"

"Can't afford a holiday."

She's paid twice what I am and she works a lot. But she owes four times as much as I do to someone who's worse than any bank. "What do you do at home?"

"Sleep. Wash clothes. Work out, play some hockey. Watch movies."

"Visit friends?" No answer. "Got anybody?"

"None of"—She stops. I can hear her think. "How? I'm gone all the time. You?"

"I've got a roommate. She's also my best friend. Nobody else special."

"You live with a woman?"

"It's not what you think—she likes girls. We don't sleep together."

That kills that subject. After a couple minutes, she says, "Keep talking."

"About what?"

She sighs. "Princess tell you anything?"

"She gave me a draft of her book."

"Email?" That comes out pretty sharp.

"No, thumb drive. Don't worry, the NSA didn't get a shot at it. Anyway, I looked over what she wrote about what happened to the canvas during the war."

"And?"

"You want to hear it?"

"Talk."

"Okay. What do you know about Germany before the war?"

"Headline stuff. Nazis, Kristallnacht, Munich."

"Okay. Germany swallowed Austria in March '38. First thing the Nazis did was throw all the Jewish community leaders in Dachau. People started just taking stuff from the Jews. It was a feeding frenzy. Ever hear of Adolf Eichmann?"

"Israelis got him, right?"

"Yeah, twenty years later. He was a father of the Holocaust. He was a young SS captain in '38. They sent him to Vienna and he got the bright idea to let the Jews leave, but tax them for the privilege. 'Tax' meant, take everything they owned. He set up an agency with one of those twenty-syllable German names? Julie can pronounce it; I can't. VVSt, the Property Registration Office. Jews had to register all their stuff, and the VVSt took what it wanted and sold it to 'good Germans.'"

"They took Bowen's picture."

"They took twelve canvases from the Meckelsohn family—Julie's grandparents—in July, all Moderns. The Nazis called Modern art 'degenerate,' so the VVSt consigned them to one of its pet art dealers, Otto—"

"Wait. Nazis had art dealers?"

"Yeah. Just because you sell art doesn't mean you have a conscience. Look at me."

She makes a choking sound. "You got too much conscience for your own good."

She may be right. "Thanks. Where was I?"

"Otto something."

"Right. Otto Scheunebrunner. Nine of the Meckelsohn pieces show up in his inventory in November '38, including the Sargent. The thing is, Scheunebrunner never sells it. It's still in the last inventory Julie has, May '43. She thinks the rest of his papers burned. The Red Army got him in April '45 and he disappears after that. Nobody knows what happened to him."

"Knowing the Soviets, probably went in the Danube. No loss."

If I'd been alive in Vienna back then, I might've ended up like Scheunebrunner. "You know, he could've just burned the portrait. He didn't have to hold onto it."

"Fucking leech. Maybe he sold it before then."

"Maybe. There's no—"

"Shh!" I hear a *crunch*. "Security."

"Police again?"

"Private. Silver minivan."

That wakes me up. "Are they—"

"Shh."

I strain to hear any background sounds. There's a wimpy *beep*, a distant low hum, rattling metal. An engine revs. It's 1:57. Is this routine, or did the security guard spot Carson?

"Going inside," Carson whispers. "Gate opens by remote."

"Why are they there? Does it look like an alarm?" Why am I whispering?

"Can't tell." After a few moments: "They stopped. Guy getting out. Armed, pistol holstered. Carrying a bag. Doesn't look like a response." Pause. "Guard from inside opened the door." Another pause. "Fuck."

"What? What happened?" I start the car in case I have to rescue Carson.

"They're kissing. They got practice."

"Seriously?"

"Both going in."

Just our luck. Even if this is a booty call, now there's two guards to deal with—one of them armed.

The security guy leaves at 2:43. His girlfriend does another circuit of the property starting at 3:02. The cop car doesn't come back. At 3:20, Carson says, "Come get me. Dundas at Quatremaine."

A flashlight blinks twice at me from behind a hedge at the intersection of the two streets. I stop only long enough for Carson to tumble in. I've already got the heater blasting. "Thanks," she says. "Hang a U, go up Quatremaine."

"Get what you need?"

She loses the hood, pulls off her black gloves with her teeth, then holds her hands in front of the heater vents. "Close enough. Should watch all night, but we can't." She lets out a heavy sigh. "Someone else was watching."

Chapter 10

Opposition.

That's Carson's word for the dude with the nicotine habit (an e-cigarette's blue glow tipped her to him) in a plain-wrap black sedan in the parking lot next door to the DLSF. When Olivia runs the plate, it comes up in the Avis fleet at Southampton's airport.

The good news: it's probably not the cops.

The bad news: it could be almost anybody else.

"Don't you fucking tell the Princess," Carson growls at me. "Not 'til we figure it out."

"You think it's Bowen?"

"Could be. Could be Tovorovsky—doesn't trust the museum. Could be a third party looking to score something." She aims a loaded finger at me. "Keep your mouth shut 'til we know more."

"Even with Allyson?"

Carson's face gets darker. "*Especially* Allyson."

I don't see Julie at breakfast this morning—Monday—and don't hear a peep out of her after that. A couple times I wonder if I should check if she's still here. Or maybe she told Ron, and I should be worried about the Wrath of Allyson coming down on us.

At 11:40-ish, I hear a tapping on my door. It's Julie, completely stone-faced and radiating resentment. "Where is she?"

Do you have a gun? "Did you try her door?"

Her lips lose more color. "Yes."

"Let me check. Come in."

I sit in my desk chair, Julie in the far armchair. While I text Carson, I ask, "You saw the portrait yesterday?"

"I did. Oma looks beautiful." Her voice is calm but tight.

"She does. I'm glad you got to see her."

A cold front settles between us. A tense few minutes later,

Carson bursts through the cracked-open door, then stops when she sees Julie. "Looking for me?"

"Yes." Julie rummages through her purse, stands, then holds out something shiny in Carson's direction. It's too small to be a weapon. "Here. Satisfied?"

When I get up, I see that it's a woman's watch with a stainless-steel case and band and a rose-gold bezel. At least she's got some taste. I reach out my hand. "Let me see that."

"Don't touch it." Carson closes in, bends to examine the watch. "Where'd you get it?"

"At the mall."

Carson's eyebrow arches. She pulls her phone, pokes at it, then holds it in front of Julie's face. "Details."

She starts and stops a few times—I think having Carson's phone in her face recording everything freaks her out—but Julie finally gets through it. She went to Gunwharf Quays and entered the Ernest & Jones jewelry store behind a gaggle of Chinese tourists. The tourists got the salesgirl all wrapped around the axle, and in the confusion, Julie picked up the watch and walked out. She spent an hour on three buses to make sure mall security wasn't on her.

"How do I know this isn't yours?" Carson asks. Her tone's hard, but I get the idea she's enjoying this.

"On a teacher's salary?" Julie's voice is almost as hard as Carson's. "This is a $4000 watch. Besides, there's still a tag."

Carson finishes recording the confession and has Julie drop the watch into a Kleenex from the bathroom. "I'll keep this." She looks Julie up and down, then snorts. "Welcome to the team."

Chapter 11

Malvern Road is the one-lane-wide, two-lane street running past the hotel. Carson says there's no cameras here, which is convenient. As quiet and low-slung as it is, it could be in some remote exurb of Portsmouth. It's not. Stop signs are the only reason it takes maybe fifteen minutes to get to the city center from here.

Julie and I are pacing along the east side of the street in whatever post-lunch sun sneaks through the clouds.

"I know you're pissed about what happened," I tell her. "It sucks, but you've gotta look at it from our—"

"Why? You work for me."

This probably isn't what Carson had in mind by *get Princess on board*. "She's your headache now," Carson told me. "Keep her away from me. Keep her happy." I'm pretty sure all three things in this to-do list don't go together.

"Actually, we work for our boss. She accepted a project from your cousin. You're a spectator. It may seem like splitting hairs, but it's an important hair."

Julie doesn't say anything out loud, but her disappearing lips are doing all the talking.

It's nice enough out, but the nagging wind makes me glad I've got my windbreaker on. Julie's still in her pink polo with her sleeves pushed up to her elbows. I don't have to work hard to see the goosebumps on her forearms. "Cold?"

"No. This is just like home." She looks over my windbreaker. "Are you cold?"

"Not with this on."

She scowls. "Where are you from?"

"Los Angeles, born and bred."

"Oh, no wonder."

"It's supposed to be ninety today back home. We'll know it's fall when the hills start burning." That usually gets a reaction from non-Angelenos, but Julie just marches along silently. I need to get her past the resentment so we can deal with each other in some nontoxic way. "That was pretty slick, with the watch. Good job."

"Congratulations on stealing well?" She shakes her head.

"Not everybody has the knack." That doesn't get me the reaction I was looking for. "You said you have all your research material with you. Can I get a copy?"

Julie's walking with her hands folded in front of her hips. I'm not sure she even knows she's doing it. Somehow, it brings out the schoolmarm in her. "Of course. Give me your email address and I'll send it all to you. There's a lot."

I'm about to say "sure" when I think back to Saturday's paranoia party with Allyson—GCHQ looking over our shoulders, Big Brother reading our email. "Um… we probably shouldn't send emails back and forth. We need to protect each other. How much is 'a lot'?"

She shrugs. "A lot. Thousands of pages."

Paper's more secure than bits until you start talking reams of the stuff, then it's a liability. "Let's use the flash drive again."

"Okay. I hope it helps."

I have extensive experience with pissed-off women—enough to recognize it in her. One cure for that is to get her talking about herself. There's no good segue into that, though. "Look, I can tell you're seriously invested in this. What you did this morning proves it. I get that it's your grandma's portrait, and you want it back. Most people in your position are willing to spend a lot of money and time to get their art, but they aren't ready to wreck their lives to do it." Except Ida Rothenberg. She gave everything she had—*everything*—to get her painting back. "Why are you?"

We walk a few paces before she answers. "Is there anything you'd risk everything for?"

I glance at her to gauge where she's coming from. There's no heat in her face; it's not a challenge. Yet. "That's an awfully personal question."

"It's the same one you just asked me."

True enough. I have to think hard to come up with an answer. "There was, but not anymore." Then I decide this should be what they call a *teachable moment*. "I lost it when I went to prison, and I went there because I risked everything."

Julie stops, which makes me stop and turn toward her. She

frowns up at me with her head tilted a bit to one side, like she can't figure out what I am. "You were in jail?"

"Federal prison. One of the nicer ones, but still." I probably shouldn't tell her this, but I need her to understand that I'm serious and I know what I'm talking about for once.

Her eyes don't break lock with mine. "Now I know why you're afraid of getting caught. Was Ms. Carson in prison too?"

"Carson's got her own issues. It wouldn't go any better for her, though."

She nods slowly. "You don't look like a criminal. I mean, it makes sense that you are, but you don't look it."

Like I've never heard that before. "The best criminals don't. You know Don Henley? He said, 'A man with a briefcase can steal more money than a man with a gun.' It's true."

"You were the man with the briefcase?"

"Metaphorically."

Julie nods solemnly. "This thing you lost… was it someone you loved?"

The last thing I want to do is drag Janine into this. But I opened this door, and if I don't let her in, she may clam up on me. That'll bite us in the butt later. "Yeah."

She watches my face for a while, maybe waiting for me to show her I'm making all this up. I'm not, so I don't. "Thank you for being honest with me." Her tone is more gentle than I expected. "You already knew the answer to that question before you asked me, didn't you?"

"I know the general answer, not the specific one. You have a son. You have a good job you're apparently good at, if those awards mean anything. Why's an old portrait worth risking all that? Why does it mean so much to you?"

Her lips purse. Then she glances past my shoulder. "Let's go over to that park."

It's a wedge-shaped plot sandwiched between two intersecting streets, overlooked by a sprawling brick preschool and some unlovely recent brick-and-glass townhouses. But it has leafy green trees and green grass, all very exotic after the palms and brown lawns back home.

"You said your grandmother died young," Julie says. "How did she die?"

"She had a stroke. I never met her, so it's all pretty abstract to me. Dad's dad remarried by the time I showed up."

"But you still had your grandfather, and their house, and their world, right?"

"Sure."

"I don't." She glances at me for the first time since we entered the park, maybe looking for a reaction. I'm waiting for the punchline so I can figure out how to react. "Oma was murdered. So was my *opa*, Herschel Meckelsohn. The Nazis did everything they could to wipe out their world. As far as I can tell, her portrait and some letters are all that proves she ever existed. If *that man* takes her back to Russia, she disappears, maybe forever, and so does her world." She stops to face me. "And a part of me. If she disappears—if she's forgotten—the Nazis win. I won't let that happen."

I will not let the Nazis win. Ida Rothenberg said that right before she showed us all what she was willing to do. By then, it was too late to do anything about it.

It's a quiet, thinky walk to the Florence Arms, the local pub, around a couple corners and down half a block from the park. The pub's clean and freshly painted in whites and sage greens and buff-brown wainscoting and a busy, figured brown carpet. The bar advertises wine. It's nothing like the old-school pubs on *Masterpiece Mystery*.

I duck into the nook behind the snooker table and push Julie's glass of Chenin Blanc across the butcher-block tabletop. Then I give my ale a try: it starts out tasting like malt and honey, then a little lemon and orange sneak in. Not bad.

Julie gives her wine a closed-lip smile. "We should've started here. Wine makes everything better."

"Next time, we'll know."

She sips. "Mmm. You can stop asking why I want to do this, right?"

"I can." That doesn't mean I won't worry about it.

She lays her fingertips lightly on my forearm. "At least you asked. Ron just said, 'You. Go. Keep track of these people.' He didn't ask if I wanted to. I did, but it would've been nice."

"I don't get that 'nice' is part of his program."

The corners of her mouth turn up a little. After some more wine, the shadow-smile fades. "What did you do to get sent to jail? Specifically, not metaphorically."

I guess I asked for that. I stall with my beer for a few moments while I figure out how to tell her without giving her so much information that she can figure out my real identity. She's watching every move I make, maybe trying to catch me winding up to a lie.

"The micro answer is, interstate transportation of stolen property." Her eyebrows do a little dance. "That's a federal beef, which is why I went to federal prison. The macro answer is, I worked for an art gallery that had a very... *flexible* code of ethics. We did all kinds of things the government didn't approve of. Our clients asked us to do a lot of it or they went along with it. We didn't cheat anyone who couldn't afford it."

"Does that make it better?" There's no judgment in Julie's voice or eyes... yet.

I hope I can keep it that way. So far she doesn't look at me like vermin, and I hope she doesn't start. I get enough of that back home. "I think it does. It's not like we were taking people's life's savings or destroying families. Most of our clients had more money than sense—we just found interesting ways to help spread some of that money around."

"It's still illegal."

"Yeah. Unethical and immoral and fattening, too. So's what Wels Fargo and JP Morgan did before the crash. I spent more time in a cell than Jamie Dimon did, and I didn't drive the world economy off a cliff." I stop when I realize I'm *this* close to ranting. "Sorry. That's probably more than you wanted to know."

"I asked the question, remember?" She stares into her mostly empty glass, swirling the dregs around. "You don't have to justify yourself to me. Ron hired you to steal Oma's painting—I don't expect you to be an angel. But I'm glad you didn't hurt any normal people. I'd have to hate you if you did, and I don't want to." She drains what's left in her glass, then gives me the most open look since yesterday's breakfast. "I really mean that. I understand that you have to be careful, and now I know why. But you need to understand that Ron sent me here to do something."

"Tell him what we're doing."

Julie nods. "If I don't do that, he'll take me back home and send someone else. Someone you… well, they won't be as easy to work with. They'll tell you what to do, they won't ask."

God help us.

She folds her hands on the edge of the table and leans in. "We both want to get Oma's portrait back. I'll help you as long as you help me. If there's something you don't want me to tell Ron, explain why and I'll work around it. I showed you this morning what this means to me. Can we work together, please?"

This is where I hoped we'd end up. "Let's give it a try." We shake hands. Carson would kill me for saying that, but she also said "keep her happy," right?

It takes another wine and another ale to get the conversation going again. "What are you telling Cousin Ron?"

She leans back against the banquette and arches her eyebrows. "I haven't told him anything yet. You haven't told me anything yet."

"What *will* you tell him?"

"What I think will keep him happy and make him feel like he knows what's happening." She smiles for the first time since we turned her into a felon. "Even if he doesn't."

I almost choke on my beer. For some reason, I've got the impression that Julie isn't a great poker player. Maybe it's because I can read everything that rolls across her face. Then again, maybe she's a fantastic poker player and I'm reading what she wants me to. I know I'm going to chase that idea down a rabbit hole later on today.

"You're handling him," I say.

"If that's what it's called. I've had almost eight years to learn how." She peeks at the lack of people outside the booth, then leans toward me. "What's our plan?"

I hear Carson saying, *don't tell her shit.* Right now, that's easy— there's nothing much to tell her. It's going to get harder later. "We still don't have a plan. We need to do this right. It'll take some time to figure out what 'right' is."

"Hm. I can tell Ron we're 'exploring possibilities.'" She uses finger quotes.

That's even true. "Why doesn't Cousin Ron just buy the piece from Tovorovsky? Why go to all this trouble?"

Her eyes go wide. "Are you kidding? Ron? Let someone beat him? I asked him once and he just hit the roof." She drops her voice an octave and starts shaking her fists. "I won't let that Russian so-and-so sell me my own property! It's like paying ransom! I'll be damned if I give him a penny!" She holds her hands palms-up. "That's how he is."

I've met guys like him before. The upside—if there is one—is that no matter how much we spend to get the portrait away from Tovorovsky, Cousin Ron will pay it. No wonder Allyson wants his business.

The downside: guys like those are usually assholes.

Chapter 12

I spend the rest of Monday in my room, piling up background information for whoever Allyson sends to be our pretend rich person—museum administration, British arts and culture grants, the fine arts scene around the Solent (the body of water next to Portsmouth and Southampton), and the Mainwaring. In between, I wonder who Carson saw in that car last night, and what they want.

It's all stalling. I have to—but don't want to—figure out how to get Dorotea sent to the lab. Which means I have to decide how to vandalize her portrait.

The Mainwaring at Thirty talks about an incident in 1986 when some dude who was wound up about Margaret Thatcher (which apparently describes about half of Britain then) threw red paint on an 1838 Robert Ladbrooke landscape in the permanent collection. The lead curator took the canvas down the moment the museum closed, cleaned it overnight, and had it back on the wall when the museum opened the next morning.

That's what I want for Dorotea.

What I *don't* want is to permanently damage her. That's one of those open-a-vein things. It's beautiful, it's Sargent's last oil, and we have to get it to the client.

I also don't want to get caught doing it. Remember the cameras? Carson said, "One hundred percent coverage." That means when they discover the damage, they'll run through the security video until they find me dumping paint or whatever on her. Then everybody gets out pitchforks to chase down the barbarian who attacked Dorotea.

A grand a day isn't enough to put up with that.

I need something that starts out transparent and doesn't turn opaque until I'm long gone.

Google hands me 148,000 hits for "photoreactive dye." Leafing through the first three pages is how I learn these dyes are used for (among other things) medicine, clinical research, and CD-Rs. On page four, I find Inkodye. "Print your logo on anything," they say.

It apparently reacts to the ultraviolet rays in sunshine or artificial lighting. That may be a problem; most gallery and museum lights use low-UV lamps to protect what they're lighting. But then I think: *no problem. Lots of time to get away.*

I'd made the mistake of propping Dorotea's postcard against the base of my chrome articulated desk lamp. She's giving me the evil eye. "It's for your own good," I tell her.

The more I read the FAQs, the more I like this stuff. It doesn't adhere to non-fibrous materials. Oil paint pretty much seals the canvas it's on; after ninety years, it's like plastic. The dye's non-toxic and water-based, so it won't react with the paint or varnish. It washes off skin with soap and warm water—no stains on my hands for the people with pitchforks to find.

A few minutes later, I find a competing product—SolarFast, by Jacquard—and decide to run a test. I could order samples online, but I'd have to give them a shipping name and address. That doesn't sound too smart. Each brand has a local outlet—SolarFast north of here, Inkodye east of here, both roughly the same distance away. The deciding factor: the Inkodye outlet, T.N. Lawrence & Son, is just outside Brighton. I can get the dye and go see the Brighton Pavilion, the most wonderfully silly architecture to come out of Regency England.

It's dinner time; too late to do anything about this today. Road trip tomorrow.

Chapter 13

I run into Julie coming up the stairs. She's added a white zip-up fleece cardigan to her outfit. She asks, "Have you had dinner yet?"

"Just going. Have you?"

"Not yet. Is Ms. Carson here?"

This is the second time today she's come looking for Carson. Maybe she's packing this time. "Why do you ask?"

She hesitates a moment, like I asked something complicated. "Well… I want to invite both of you to dinner. My treat—well, Ron's, but you get the idea. I thought we could try to put our relationship back on track."

Even if Carson was here, I wouldn't tell Julie. I'm about 99% sure Carson would rather pull her own molars than socialize with *the Princess*. "I'm game, but Carson's out."

"Doing something fun, I hope." She says it light, but I know she wants an update.

"I doubt it."

Julie shrugs. "Okay. Just you and me, then." She doesn't sound disappointed. "I picked a place and everything—all you have to do is say 'yes.'" Her smile's innocent.

I doubt she is, though. "Yes."

We end up at Las Iguanas, a loud, busy, mid-range pseudo-Latin American restaurant at Gunwharf Quays. The décor's a weird mix of tropical and Mid-Century Modern—globe light fixtures, color panels, mosaic tile, bamboo, hot colors. We get a booth upholstered in a green Op Art floral pattern set against a wall-length photomural of Rio.

The menu's all over the place, but nothing's all that spendy. "You're not used to an expense account yet, are you?"

She glances up from her menu and over her reading glasses. "I wanted to go someplace fun, not fancy. For fancy, we'd have to dress up and behave ourselves."

"You're planning to misbehave?"

She smiles. "We'll see."

Once the waitress takes our orders and brings back our drinks—a Long Island Iced Tea for Julie, Brahma on draft for me—I ask, "How do you think Cousin Ron would react if you asked him to lay a ten- or twenty-grand donation on the museum?"

"If he thinks it'll get Oma's portrait back, he won't even blink. He makes that much in a few hours." She considers me over the tip of her straw. "Why would he do that?"

Now I get to discover where the line is between too much information and not enough to keep Julie happy. "To gain us access."

"Can't you just buy a ticket?"

"Different access. Inside access." I plot out how to say this. "Make the museum think a rich person wants to drizzle money on it."

"And what does that do for us?"

"Like I said, the kind of access we can potentially exploit. It's not a real plan yet"—that she needs to know about—"but more like…"

"Exploring possibilities?"

"That sounds familiar."

"I'll ask." We drink to possibilities.

It's time to give her a few strokes. "I've been reading your book. You're a good writer."

"Oh. Thank you." She ducks her head and blushes a little. "How far did you get?"

"Dorotea and Herschel are about to get married. All the Meckelsohns are catting about the Italian girl he's dragging back to Vienna with him."

She makes an exasperated sound. "They were *awful*. I had no idea Jews would be that way to each other. It was like, 'what, Austrian girls aren't good enough?'" She shakes her head. "It's amazing they got together."

We chat until the food arrives on heavy, colorful crockery, along with a bottle of Argentinian Pinot grigio. The servings are big and they smell great, especially since I had potato chips and Coke for lunch. I make a big dent in my *xinxim* (Brazilian chicken and crayfish in a peanut-and-lime sauce) before I come up for air.

It's also an opportunity to keep Julie feeling important. "Before we go into a food coma, I want to ask… can you look through your notes and see if there's anything your grandparents did that can help us build a new story for the portrait?"

I caught her in mid-chew on her salad. She holds up an index finger until she swallows. "Sorry. What are you looking for?"

I explain about needing to come up with a new narrative for the canvas' history so it's not officially stolen goods forever. She concentrates hard until I'm done. Then she rolls a sip of wine around her mouth for a moment. "There's absolutely nothing legal about any of that, is there?"

That doesn't seem to bother her. "No. But we've gotta do it unless Cousin Ron wants to keep the piece in storage for the rest of his life."

She shakes her head. "He wouldn't like that. You know, I think there is, but let me check and I'll let you know tomorrow..." she raises her eyebrows "...at lunch?"

I'm about to say *yes* when I remember the road trip to Brighton. "Um... I'm going to be out until probably mid-afternoon. Let's see when I get back. Definitely no later than lunch Wednesday. Okay?"

Her smile dims a few watts. Oh, hell. "Going someplace interesting?"

"Chores. I'll let you know if it turns into something." I need to buy back some goodwill. "Thanks for looking into this. It's really helpful."

We get back to our food. Julie flicks a glance at me now and then, watching. It's not because I have sauce running down my chin (I check); I think she's sizing me up. For what, I can't tell. She seems happiest when she's talking, so I give her a topic. "How'd you get involved in all this?"

No answer for a few moments. Then she sighs. "I divorced my husband."

I wait for her to go on, which she doesn't. "And?"

She carefully refills her wine goblet. "It wasn't very much fun."

"Divorces suck, even when you want them."

"All I know is, once was enough. Anyway, there I was, forty-two years old, a son about to go off to college, I'm alone for the first time in almost twenty years, and I realize I don't know who I am. I don't mean some New Agey thing—I had no clue about Mom's side of the family. She never talked about it."

That's weird. I've known a couple grandchildren of Holocaust survivors, and they said they heard about it from the time they could walk. "You were a history teacher with no history?"

"I know, right? Mom was sick by then, so I knew if I was going to get anything out of her, I'd better do it fast. One day I sat her down and said, 'Okay, Mom, it's time to talk. Who are you?' And she laid back in her couch like she's watching TV and she nodded and nodded. Then she said, 'Well, honey, we're Jewish.'"

"Surprise!"

She laughs. "Right? So I got up off the floor and got her talking again and... it was *amazing*. This whole world I never knew about. I started writing it down right away so I wouldn't forget anything. Then I researched it and filled in some of the blanks."

"How'd Cousin Ron get involved? Or did he already know?"

"No, that's the thing. Uncle Leo didn't tell him anything, either. When Mom told me what happened to Oma and Opa, I wanted to try to fix it. I went to Ron." She tosses up her hands. "Eight years later, here I am."

Her eyes are bright and lively and her face is alive, like she's reliving that moment of discovery. I don't know anything about my family before my grandparents—there must be a horse thief back there somewhere to account for me—and I can't imagine having all this dropped on me in midlife. "I'm glad we get to help you," I finally say.

Julie turns her big, soft brown eyes on me. She presses her fingertips against my forearm. "Me, too." A few long seconds later, she takes her hand away and returns to her salad.

We talk for almost an hour about movies and books, this and that, nothing more about work. She has a nice smile and a good laugh.

The only other date-like evening I've had this year—with Gianna in Milan—was totally different: lots more electricity, but lots more stress. I had to be some other guy with her, play a role, try to fight my own feelings so I could react the way my character should.

It's not as hard with Julie. She knows what I am, if not who I am. While I can't exactly relax around her—there's all that what-part-of-the-plan-am-I-hiding-today? stuff—I can be more-or-less myself, and she's good with it. How long has it been since I could say that?

By the time the taxi drops us at the hotel, we're getting along okay.

Now I need to get us a forger.

Chapter 14

Why would a respectable art gallery need a forger?

Well, for one thing, Heibrück Pacific wasn't respectable. We weren't as dirty as some of our competition, but we were pretty untidy. Second, Simpson Boutelle's a total wizard at retouching, which is perfectly legitimate when you restore a canvas. And third... some pieces just *need* a signature. The artist may not have remembered or bothered to put one on. And if the name Boutelle puts on the canvas just happens to be a bit more marketable than the one that should go on... well, who can say for certain the name artist *didn't* have something to do with it?

That's why I have the number for the best art forger in the western U.S. on my personal phone.

The problem is, his line's disconnected, and the recording says there's no new number. This could mean one of two things: either Boutelle's in a cell somewhere, or he forgot to pay his phone bill. They're equally likely.

A couple web searches don't pull up anything useful, just some references on the Studio Direct website that sells his unsigned "fine art reproductions" (legal counterfeits). So I go to the best resource I know for contacting people on the shady side of the art world—Getz.

"You got balls, calling me again," he growls. As usual, there's music blasting in the background, even though it's just past noon L.A. time. "You fucked me with Burim."

An Albanian gangster I needed in Milan. "He fucked himself. He got cute with somebody who didn't appreciate it." The *somebody* was Carson, but... details.

Getz is a runner: an art dealer with no fixed business address. I met him through my roommate Chloe and used him for some side deals I worked outside Heibrück. He always played straight with me, which is why I didn't sell him to the feds in my plea deal. Getz still owes me for that.

"Whaddaya want?"

"Is Boutelle still working? The number I've got is stale."

"Think he wants to talk to you?"

"He should. For the same reason you do."

I hear Getz simmering on the other end of the line. "Fuck me on this, we're done. Got it?"

"No problem."

He gives me a 424 area code, which is the less-fashionable overlay on the 310 part of West L.A. "Too early to call him, you know."

"I know. Thanks, Getz."

"Fuck you very much."

Some people just don't do gratitude.

Three hours later, I've looked up the local news and weather in New York City and watched a webcam feed from a craft brewery a few blocks from where I'm supposedly staying. I make my three-times-a-week call to my probation officer in L.A. After a little back-and-forth, I convince him that everything's fine on my business trip to Brooklyn and that my imaginary girlfriend's keeping tabs on me. I've been on the straight-and-narrow (as far as he knows) and he's way too busy to follow up. It's a win-win for us both.

Now it's time to try the number Getz gave me.

He picks up after six rings. "Simpson Boutelle, at your service." He booms, he doesn't speak.

"Hey, Sim. It's Matt."

There's a beat. "Matt Friedrich? Is that you? What a surprise, m'lad! Are you at liberty again?"

The dictionary entry for "Falstaffian" inspired somebody to create Boutelle. He's from somewhere in the middle of England, barrel-shaped, and about as tall as he is hairy, which means he's a good hand taller than me. Like Sir John, his favorite sports are drinking and wenching. I have no idea what women see in him.

"Yeah, I've been out for over a year now. What are you up to?"

We spend a few minutes catching up. He's somehow avoided arrest, cirrhosis, and STDs since we talked last.

After a socially correct amount of chat, I say, "Hey, this is sort of a business call. Can you recommend a copyist in England?" *Forger* is apparently an impolite word.

"That depends, that depends." Suddenly he's cagey. "Who d'you want copied?"

"Sargent. A portrait."

A long inhale. "Oh, m'lad, m'lad, your taste is impeccable. Any piece in particular?"

"Yeah, but I'll talk about that with the copyist."

"And you need it to be *accurate*, I expect." That was his code for a complete forgery, front and back.

"Yeah."

"Hmpf. Well, of course, of course, I *know* people in England. I *may* be able to find someone." Here's the windup… "But I couldn't *vouch*. Really, m'lad, why go to a stranger?" …and there's the pitch. "I know your discretion, you know my work. Sargent, Boldini, Tarbell, Zorn, Chase—I do them all, don't you know."

Yes, I know he has an affection for pre-Modern portraitists—he does a mean Van Dyck and a very credible Gainsborough, too. But his hobbies make him more than a little unreliable, and I hadn't been looking forward to trying to ship such a big canvas from the U.S., either. "I don't know, Sim —"

"You're not copying from the original, are you?"

"Um, no. Photos."

"Well, then. I'm your man. Won't take 'no' for an answer. Gratitude and old times' sake, and all that. When d'you need it?"

"Can you just give me a couple names—"

"Lay some coppers on an old man. Can you do it, m'lad? Can you? If I do another *Pinkie*, I'll die, I swear it! I need a challenge."

Oh, for chrissake. I've forgotten how needy and wheedling he is. I weigh the pros and cons. Pro: he's very good, especially in this genre; I already know him; he won't try to screw me. Con: he's never seen a drug he can't drink, swallow, or smoke; he takes an unhealthy number of women to his studio, meaning lots of witnesses; and his concept of time is hugely elastic. On the other hand, it's hard telling what vices come along with any forger he sends me.

Go with the devil I know?

"It's fifty by thirty-six," I say. "How much? How long?"

"For you? A special price, a *very* special price. Couldn't do it for any less. I'm practically *losing* money, don't—"

"How much?" With Sim, you have to speak firmly, like with a large dog.

"Um, well. For you… twenty."

"Thousand? U.S.? Seriously?" That's double what I expected.

"You want it *accurate,* no? You did say that? Come now—"

Since it's not my money, do I care enough to bargain? No, but I have to try. "Do you have the right canvas? You have to source it, and it comes out of your fee."

"Which is the 'right' one, can you say? He used two then, you know. Winsor & Newton, and Newman's."

It's a semi-good point, except there's no evidence Sargent used Newman's canvas for anything but studies after *Mannikin in the Snow* in 1892. If I bring that up, we'll spend the next half-hour arguing about art materials. "We'll find out soon enough. How long?"

His laugh would rattle the windows if he was here. He thinks he's won. "Well, of course, this is a priority, my *top* priority. But it's Sargent, it must be right. Late or early?"

He means, *which period of Sargent's work?* "As late as it gets."

I hear a few *hmms.* "Four weeks *may* be possible," he says like he's discovering the words for the first time. "Five is better. Eight would be ideal—"

Sixteen would be more ideal, never would be perfect… "Make it four. We've got a schedule. I know you can do it."

"One more thing, m'lad, and I must insist. I need to see the original—"

"Oh, *hell* no."

"—touch it, smell it. You said you want this *accurate,* I remember that clearly. There's no better way. Snaps alone won't—"

"Don't push it, Sim."

He's quiet for a few moments. "I need to go home." His voice is so low, I can barely hear it through the ringing in my ears. "I've not been for years. I can't afford to go."

I've heard this story before. "If you stop blowing money on women with hard-luck stories—"

"I know, I know. But you're not paying for this, I know you're not. What does it matter to you? Just a few bob to see me home again, to smell the country air—"

Shit. He'll sing *God Save the Queen* next. "If you go, you get one shot at it. You'll have to be there on time and sober. You follow my rules. Otherwise, you're out. Understand?"

"Of course, of course, bless you—"

"Airfare and hotel comes out of your fee. Expenses, too." Because he's sure to ask for first class next.

"That's hardly fair—"

"That's how it works. Take it or leave it."

There's a lot of quiet on the other end. After a while, he sighs. "Well, if that's how it is, then of course. When d'you need me?"

I check my Outlook calendar and make some wild-assed guesses about how long it'll take to pull this together. "We'll try for two weeks from now. I'll know better in the next few days."

"Thank you, m'lad. I'll not let you down."

Oh, God. He just jinxed it.

Chapter 15

Carson pushes back some when I go to get the car keys from her Tuesday morning. She gives them up when I threaten to have the dye sent to her.

I return by early afternoon with a couple bags of stuff and my brain full of the Pavilion. It's garish and over the top and it started falling apart as soon as it was built, but you can't look at it without smiling.

I put the "Do Not Disturb" flag in the door's card slot, throw a fluffy white towel over the desk, and empty the bags. There's a dreadful little marine oil-on-canvas, a sort of Victorian motel art; an eight-ounce bottle of Inkodye magenta (a compliment to the green of Dorotea's dress); a small can of turpentine; a box of a hundred art swabs; blue nitrile gloves; and an LED lightbulb.

Before I go anywhere near Dorotea, I want to make sure the dye will come off her. I also want to see if the dye will develop in a low-UV environment. Even if I completely ruin this miserable £45 excuse for a painting, it'll be an improvement.

I lay the canvas on its back on the desk, open the Inkodye bottle, and carefully pour a quarter-sized dot right in the middle of the distorted sailing ship wallowing in really badly drafted waves. I tilt the piece to let the dye run down almost to the frame. It's totally clear and flows like thick water. Then I swap the new LED bulb into the reading light at the head of my bed. The sales guy said it emits "almost no" UV rays, so I figure it's as good a match for the museum's lighting as I'll get. The painting goes on the walnut drum table next to my bed, then I fiddle with the lamp's wall-mounted articulated arm to center the light on the canvas.

It's 2:18.

At 4:35, the dye's still completely clear. I go back to studying the "Stealing Beauty" exhibition catalog and thinking about Plan B. There isn't one.

◧

Carson's pounding on my door breaks my concentration. It's 6:20, the dye's still clear, and I realize I'm hungry. I find Carson standing outside with her arms folded. "Yeah?"

She tosses her head toward the stairs. "C'mon."

"Where?"

"Pub."

"Why?"

She rolls her eyes. "Just fucking *come.*"

The Florence Arms is buzzing with after-work business. There's a snooker game happening, and the nook I shared with Julie on Sunday is now stuffed with working guys. Carson orders drinks at the bar, then leads me back into a larger, open function room set with ranks of wooden four-tops. We head for a table in the far corner. It's held down by an older woman who's watching us like we're a bad floorshow.

She squints up at Carson. "Aye, hen, Ah ken nae be rid'v ye."

Oh, hell. She's Scottish. Subtitles *on.*

Carson stops on the other side of the table, puts her fists on her hips and shakes her head. "They still let you out with that face?"

For the record, it's not a bad face, but it has miles on it. A roundish head, smallish mouth, apple cheeks, steel-gray hair cropped almost as short as Carson's. It's her eyes that catch me: bright blue, but hard, like thick ice in sunshine.

"It only scares the bairns." It doesn't sound that way; I'm translating. She stands and circles the table, then opens her arms wide. "C'mon, hen." Now she sounds like a mom. "Give us a hug."

Carson hugs?

Miranda's a head shorter than Carson and sturdy, like you could drop her off the Spinnaker and she wouldn't break. Her heathery tweed suit's respectable enough for the Rotary or whatever it's called over here. Look at her on the street and you'd see someone's granny.

Carson and I sit opposite the woman. She gives Carson a once-over and chuckles. "Yer still too feckin' tall." She thumbs in my direction. "What's this, then?"

"The art guy. Matt? Miranda."

I expect to arm-wrestle, but her handshake's dry and gentle. "You work for Allyson?"

"Aye, for years. Number Forty-Six." The agency gives us all numbers; I'm 179. She turns to Carson. "Herself says you need a posh lass. What's the job?"

Carson nudges me. I give Miranda an outline of what we need. She listens carefully, pecking at her red wine now and then. I pause when the barmaid sets down our order (Carson remembered I drink vodka). Miranda says "Ta, lass" in a grandmotherly way that fits her look.

When I'm done, Miranda sits there staring at me with her mouth collapsed on itself. Finally she says, "Right. When do we start?"

"Tomorrow," Carson says. "We need—"

"Wait." I hold up my hand. "Do you have any questions? Problems?"

Her mouth twists like it's fighting to keep a laugh in. "Laddie, I was doing this when you were a wean. Questions? There's time. Problems? The whole thing's daft, you ask me." She shrugs. "I've done daft things me whole life, so it's no bother."

Fine, except nobody south of Hadrian's Wall can understand her. I'm not sure there's a graceful way to bring that up, though. "Well, we'll have to figure out why you're down here—"

"Instead of Glesca where I belong?" She laughs. It's not a pretty laugh. "What's a wee Scots hen doing in the South splashing money about? That's your question?"

"Um… yeah."

"Dinna fash yirsel. I can be a right booley mooth when I please." Huh? Her features even out and she holds her head like she's sitting for a portrait. "Is this more what you've in mind?" The accent comes from closer to the Thames than the Clyde. "I can be as posh as you need." She smiles for the portrait.

I turn to Carson. "You could've told me."

She smirks. "More fun watching you find out."

I negotiate with Miranda over when and where we'll meet tomorrow morning so I can fill her in on the plan and turn over the background material. She changes her accent every answer, wearing a cat-digesting-the-bird smile the whole time. It sounds like she can place herself in any part of the English-speaking world. "What do you do for Allyson?" I finally ask her.

"Why, sugar, I do this." This time, it's a dead-on Deep South drawl. "I pretend I'm someone else. Ain't nobody cottons on, on account I look like Great-Aunt Lulie."

This is going to be interesting.

I order takeout lamb *rogan josh* from the bar. By the time I get back to my room, it's 7:26.

There's a hazy magenta splotch on the painting. Yes!

By eight, the blob is clearly visible even on the dark paint. The dye's dry to the touch, which doesn't necessarily mean "dry." I'll let it sit some more.

At 10:31, the magenta has stopped getting brighter and the blob feels flat and dry. I move the painting to the desk. I pour some turpentine into a bathroom glass, snap on a pair of gloves, and start to clean the canvas.

At the gallery, we'd send pieces that needed lots of work to a restorer, but we'd do our own light cleaning—removing dust and dirt, foxing and other mildew, and the occasional dried-on food, cigarette smoke, or other gunk we didn't try to identify. It was slow then and it's slow now. I grab a swab (like a Q-tip with a six-inch handle), dip it in the turpentine, squeeze it out against the glass, then dab at a small stained area until the cotton's too gunky to use anymore. Reload, repeat. The dye's stubborn, but each swab comes away tinted red.

By midnight, I have a mound of used swabs—they'll go down the toilet—and a bad painting that's cleaner than it's been since World War One.

It works.

Chapter 16

Carson pounds my door at about five to nine, just before Miranda's scheduled arrival. I let her in and get back to copying background stuff on a thumb drive.

"Be good to Miranda," she warns me. The *or else* doesn't need to be mentioned.

"How do you know her?"

"What I did for you in Milan? Broke you in, taught you the ropes? She did for me when I came on. More'n just knocking the cop out of me. I was an angry fucker after TPS flushed me. She straightened me out, taught me things. Still talk to her."

There's more affection in Carson's voice than I've heard her use on any other creature. I watch her face for a moment, though I'm not sure what I'm looking for. "What's her work like?"

"Nothing better. Been on the grift her whole life. Learn everything you can from her." She shakes a finger at me. "Give her respect. Got it?"

She's so serious, I don't even consider saying anything other than "Got it." Then a thought kicks me. "If we're gonna ferry a rich woman around, we need to upgrade our ride."

"Not getting a Rolls."

"Don't need one. A nice Jag or Mercedes will do."

Carson nods. "I'll swing it." She checks the time on her phone. "Outta here. Still working the alarm angle."

"Smoking Man still around?" I haven't forgotten our shadow at the lab.

"Yeah. Later." Carson lets herself out. Judging from the greeting sounds I hear through the door, she must've run into Miranda in the hall. When I open the door, I do a double-take.

Miranda's holding both of Carson's hands, giving her a grandmotherly smile. That's not what confuses me. It's the chic silver-white bob with the bangs swept over her left eye—I've seen Helen Mirren with that do—the tasteful, understated makeup, and the Chanel suit (black wool skirt below the knee, scarlet bouclé cardigan-jacket with black trim and brass buttons) that make me wonder who this person is and what she did with the woman I met last night.

She squeezes, then drops Carson's hands, turns and gives me a cool smile, perfect for greeting someone from a lower caste. "Good morning, Mr. Simon."

Other than the softest overlay of a southern Thames accent, she could be a newscaster on TV back home.

Carson disappears with a warning glare for me. I usher Miranda in and lead her to the armchair I've pulled up next to the desk. "You look great," I say.

She stops and poses with a hand on her hip. "This is what you had in mind?"

"Totally. I don't get your accent, though. Who are you?"

"I'm someone who explains you and the hen." She sets her quilted black Chanel shoulder bag on the desk, unbuttons her jacket, then turns to let me slip it off her shoulders. She's wearing a simple bone-white, boat-necked silk shell underneath. She's mostly cylindrical, but that's not unusual for a woman in her sixties. "I was a young Surrey lass when I married a handsome Yank airman. I've lived with you lot ever since." She sits more daintily than I would've expected. With her ankles crossed and her hands folded primly in her lap, she looks every bit like a society matron who managed to hold onto her original husband on his road to CEO.

Just what I'd hoped for. It all seems a little too easy.

Chapter 17

After Miranda packs off with the mound of background material, Julie drags me to lunch. We drop just shy of a hundred pounds at Samphire, which Tripadvisor says has the best seafood in Portsmouth. I guess she's learning the joys of expense accounts.

After we order, she says, "Ron will give us money for the donation to the museum. He's setting up an account for me with one of his shell companies."

That was fast. "One of them?"

"I guess you get bored with only one."

Being rich gives you ADHD? "Okay. What's our limit?"

She gives me a crafty smile. "He said, 'whatever it takes.' Now I'm wondering where he was when I was in grad school."

We chat while we eat. She keeps poking at me to tell her what's going on, which I manage to do without giving her much detail. After the plates are cleared, Julie tells me where to look in her notes for info on how her grandparents handled their assets but won't say anything more about it. "Every time we're together, you're trying to dig information out of me," she says. "That's not really fair, is it? I mean, considering how little you're giving me."

I don't tell her that it's not about fair. She'll learn that eventually. Besides, there are worse ways to spend lunch than with her.

I catch Carson in her room later that afternoon. She lets me let myself in as she ambles back to her desk chair.

I drop into one of the plusher armchairs on the other side of the bed. Carson's duffel sags on the twin end tables next to me, but I won't snoop… while she's looking. "Find out anything?"

"Service panels for the museum's power."

I sit up straighter. "Seriously? How'd you do that? The city website?"

She shoves her chair around to face me and puts her gym shoes up on the bed. "No electricals there. Tried to pull plans at the Council, but they don't play that way. Went to the museum and looked."

"Whoa, wait a minute." I restart my heart. "If they saw you, you can't go back."

"Won't recognize me."

Sometimes I think Carson doesn't know what an impression she makes. "Some Amazon goes wandering around backstage and nobody's going to notice?"

"Didn't say that." She smirks. "Said they won't recognize me."

I must be wearing my *yeah, sure* look, because she swings out of her chair, strolls to her duffel, drags out a white plastic trash bag, then disappears into her bathroom.

This is the first time I've been in Carson's room unsupervised, so of course I poke around. She apparently doesn't unpack—the only things hanging in her armoire are her simple navy pantsuit (Tahari—probably from Canada's version of Macy's) and a conservative Ann Taylor LBD. Everything else is in her duffel. I guess that's how she can pack and leave so fast.

I pretend to look out the window when I hear her doorknob rattle. I turn when she clears her throat. "What the hell?"

Carson's short, dark-chocolate hair has turned thick, wavy, and dirty-blond. It hangs in a mop down to where her collar would be if she had one. The bangs almost reach her big, round, black-rimmed glasses. The geometry of her face has completely changed. I don't recognize her.

"Told you." Carson's voice.

"Did you have that in Milan?"

"Yeah. Didn't need it." She pulls off the glasses. With her eyes out in the open, I can tell it's her. "Mash my tits flat, nobody notices me."

"But you're not invisible. How'd you get in?"

"Service door, in back." Carson grabs the wig's front edge and drags it back over her head, then spreads it out on the duffel. She finger-fluffs her hair. "Museum's got a contract florist. Bought a couple dozen flowers from them, grabbed their card, went to the museum."

"Not in the Beemer...?" She's smarter than that, right?

"Rented a Transit van. I was the Polish flower girl. They—"

"Polish?"

"Yeah. They're everywhere. Locals don't expect much out of them." She slams on the glasses and hunches her shoulders. "The boss, he send me, with flowers?" Her voice is about an octave higher and thick with a semi-Slavic accent I assume is Polish. "Miss Grant, yes? Up?" Then she loses the glasses and switches back to her normal voice. "Jenna Grant's the Development Office secretary. Took the elevator back to the basement and started looking."

I have to shake my head. "You really were a detective, weren't you."

"Finally believe me?" She snorts. "Two panels: one for domestic power, one for security. Honeywell security system, can't tell which model. Get this—no cameras in the support areas except the back door."

That's huge. If we can get into the staff area, we're clear to the second floor. "Get any ideas out of this?"

"A few." She settles in her desk chair and puts her feet up again. She looks pretty pleased with herself. She deserves to.

I perch on the edge of Carson's bed, then get self-conscious and stand up again. "Does Miranda have a name yet?"

"Yeah. Olivia told me. Gillian Hardwick."

I roll that around my tongue. "Good name. Time to set up her meeting with the museum?"

We eye-wrestle for a few moments. I bump up my eyebrows. She sighs. "I'm the assistant again?" I nod. "You're, what, the art guy?" I nod. She growls. "Why can't I be the art guy and you're the gofer?"

"Well, first, you don't know anything about art. Second, it still looks weird for a woman to have a male assistant. People get ideas."

Carson makes a face. "With Miranda?"

"You'd be surprised."

She peers at me, frowning. I nod. She shivers a little, then reaches for her phone.

Most of us have some idea what happened in Germany between the wars, even if it's only from watching *Cabaret*. (By the way,

"Tomorrow Belongs to Me" is probably the best three-minute explanation I've ever seen for how the Nazis came to power.) Teacher Julie's homework assignment shows me that interwar Austrian politics were a train wreck, too.

The twenty years after the end of World War One were all about thug-on-thug violence and political infighting in Austria. The chancellor started ruling by decree when the government finally collapsed in February '33. In September, he announced Austria was going to be a one-party, Catholic, ethnic-German state "based on new principles and ideals which in reality are very old ones for a Christian and German people."

You can imagine what Vienna's Jews thought about all this.

In February '34, the government tried to break up the Social Democrats' militia and started a week-long civil war in some major cities, including Vienna.

According to Julie's research—including letters from Viktor (Julie's great-grandfather) to his brother Hermann in New York—this was when the Meckelsohns decided to bury their money in Switzerland. Viktor hired a Swiss lawyer to set up a front company (yes, they did this even back then) and started shuttling cash and bonds from Vienna to Zurich. Herschel and his two brothers also smuggled money; it wasn't exactly illegal yet, but it would've been unpleasant if they were caught. Even Dorotea pitched in. Between '34 and '38, they moved almost 200,000 schillings in cash (roughly $660,000 in today's dollars) and maybe another $230,000 worth of bonds and securities.

Good thinking, but it screwed them when the Nazis took over. When the Meckelsohns tried to ransom Viktor out of Dachau, they didn't have enough cash to buy off the Germans—and by then, they couldn't get to what they had in Zurich.

I could sense Viktor's desperation spike in his letters as Austria slid downhill. I can't understand why he didn't buy a little lakeside apartment in Zurich and stash the family there when it became obvious what was happening. True, the Swiss were being asshats about letting in refugee Jews, but money could get past the hurdles (then as now). With six figures in a local bank, they wouldn't exactly be refugees, would they? Then again, people aren't great at believing the worst-case scenario can actually happen. That's how people like me make money.

Anyway, the Swiss accounts show the Meckelsohns' financial assets, but nothing else. Why didn't they move their other valuables, like the silver or jewelry… or the art?

Who says they didn't?

I watch the sky get dark outside my window while I think about this. Julie clearly has Viktor's original letters. How hard would it be to discover another one—one from, say, late 1937, when things were turning to absolute shit in Austria? One that tells Hermann about how Herschel had the bright idea to get the paintings copied and move the originals to storage in Zurich? What a clever boy, that son of his!

Hmm. I'd like to ask Julie, but if I do, she'll hand me the forged letter three days later. I need to think this through, look at all the angles, all the potential problems. But it feels doable.

Everything feels doable until you have to do it.

It's almost seven-thirty by the time I realize that Julie hasn't come to take me to dinner, like she said she would when we got back from lunch. I could go eat now without her, but how would she react to me running out on her plan? I finally knock on her door to see if she's still around. It's part of keeping her happy, and I'm enjoying the company when I eat.

I hear, "Coming!" then the door opens. She's barefoot, wearing charcoal yoga pants and a powder-blue fleece pullover.

"You almost match the drapes," I say.

"I know." She laughs a little. "It's not on purpose, I promise. Are you here about dinner?"

"Yeah."

She pats her stomach. "Sorry. I'm still getting over lunch. But…" She holds up a white Chinese takeout box with a plastic fork sticking out. "I got way too much. Want to help me finish it?"

It doesn't occur to me until after she lets me in that, except for Carson and Chloe, I haven't been alone with a woman in her bedroom for over four years. Julie's desk is busy but tidy, and she's built a neat little nest of pillows and blankets on her bed. This feels more intimate than I'd planned.

"Did you see this?" She holds up a Blu-ray case of *Woman in*

Gold.

"No, I missed it." I wanted to (I'll see Helen Mirren in anything), but I can't afford to go to movies in West L.A. Julie doesn't need to know that detail.

She gives me a big smile. "With what we're doing? You *have* to watch it. Come on."

That's how we end up curled up in adjoining armchairs, eating bad Chinese takeout and watching Julie's laptop play a movie about Nazi-looted art on the room's TV. Helen's appropriately flinty, and Tatiana Maslany plays only one character, which is like a vacation for her. The good guys win (not a spoiler).

I hope that's the way our story ends... if we're the good guys.

Chapter 18

Thursday's visit to the museum has a whole different vibe than the one five days ago. The museum hasn't changed; we have. Miranda's polishing up her rich-widow persona, and Carson and I have pulled on our cover roles along with dress slacks and open-necked suit shirts.

Are there more docents today? Are they more alert? It's hard to kick the feeling that they know we're rehearsing, not just visiting. Will someone recognize us from last time? Does the museum keep track? Every time we turn a corner of the serpentine, I expect Kwana—or the "proper guards" she mentioned—to be waiting for us.

Miranda asks, "This is the one?" when we reach Dorotea. Her semi-American accent's pretty solid by now.

"How'd you know?"

"The postcard on your desk. Mind you don't leave it out for the cleaners."

I don't, but I hadn't thought to hide it from her. Clearly I'm not paranoid enough yet.

Miranda studies the portrait for a moment. She's in a cream suit with black trim that looks a lot like the famous Chanel from the early '70s. A knockoff? I can't tell, and I sure won't ask.

It's nice to see Dorotea full-size again. I risk a long look. She gives me an impatient stare: *aren't you done screwing around yet?* "Sorry," I whisper. "Not too long now. Hang on." By the time I think to find Miranda again, she's moved on.

Miranda insists on lunching at the Marks & Spencer Café in the mall next door. "Don't ask why," she warns us both. It's small, busy, full of laminate and sandwiches in plastic bags, and totally empty of any character. If K-mart had cafes, they'd be like this. Miranda's suit is probably the first and last Chanel to ever cross the threshold.

"I've been thinking about this scheme of yours," she says between bites of her chicken, leek, and mustard pie. It's ugly, but probably not the worst thing she could've ordered. "What will you do if you can nae get into the laboratory?"

Her lapse into Scottish sounds doubly weird since she's still using her cover accent. "'Can't,' not 'can nae.' Also, we say 'lab-ra-tory,' not 'la-bora-tree.'"

She bobs her head. "Of course. Ta, lad. The question stands, though."

"There's too much security?" Carson asks. "Plan B."

We have a Plan B?

"And what's that, then?"

I exchange looks with Carson. She wins the staring match. I feel foolish for not having thought this out better. "We're still working on that."

Miranda sighs. "I thought as much. Never leave yourself only one escape. Always have a backup plan. It may be a daft plan, but it's a plan." She downs some mashed potatoes. "Your Plan A—that's what this is?—it's daft, too, but I've worked with worse."

Great. This is the second time she's called my plan "daft," and it's after I've made most of the changes she suggested. But she's the pro. There's nothing like having my nose rubbed in my own inadequacy.

"I wanna just take the damn thing," Carson says. She's been bulldozing a baked potato covered with what M&S claims is chili, though it doesn't look like any chili I've seen lately.

"No, hen. The lad's instinct is good. If you leave a blank bit on the wall, the plods'll be on you in a shot. You have to give yourself a good chance to get away with the touch."

That was nice of her. "How would you do it?"

She finishes off over half her pie before she answers. "Nobody questions the police or the security services anymore. It's nae healthy." I'm not going to correct her in the middle of this. "Give two or three lads in naff suits and not enough hair the right warrant cards and papers with enough crests, and they'll get their way." She switches to an Oxbridge accent. "Have you any artworks from Russia or the Mideast? You do? Smashing. We'll need to photograph them front and back and place a small chip on the stretcher. Sorry, can't explain, national security, you know. Needs must. Of course your staff can handle them, we shouldn't want to risk it ourselves. No, no, no damage at all. Just a precaution, you know. Shall we?'"

I pick at my chicken sandwich. It's a good plan, and a whole lot less complicated than mine. We'd have to get the actors. Allyson's guy would have to forge the IDs and warrants. But if he's really ex-MI-6, at least he'd know what they're supposed to look like. Could it work?

Can mine?

After lunch, I spend another five hours with Miranda. It's not constant attention; she reads and asks questions while I look up more background and burp up my sandwich's cranberry spread (it's no better the second time around). We keep working on her semi-American accent and vocabulary. At one point, she asks me to read from part of a Reacher paperback she'd scored from somewhere, just so she can hear my voice and how I pronounce things. I don't have the heart to tell her that Lee Child is English.

Carson joins us for a while to hang around Miranda. She's so much like the good daughter that it's kinda cute to watch. She fetches water, gets a pillow for Miranda's back, turns on the lights when Miranda mentions it's getting dark. When they talk, it's shorthand, or maybe code. Is Carson this way with her real mom? Or did biology and history screw up that relationship—like it did with Dad and me—and Miranda's the substitute? However it goes, as Carson leaves to "check on something," she gets a mom-hug from Miranda.

Miranda's nice to me in a kind of maiden-aunt way. Maybe she thinks she bruised my feelings at lunch (she did, sort of, but that's nothing new). Whatever the reason, by the time we pack it up, we're getting along okay and she's stopped calling my plan daft. "This should work fine," she tells me on her way out the door. "There's a good lad."

Tomorrow—Friday—she's going to stay in Southampton to get a feel for the place in case someone asks her about it. She'll be in London over the weekend, cramming in all the art museums she can stand. Monday, I'll give her an online tour of L.A.'s art and museum scene. I have no doubt that when we meet the Mainwaring's administration on Wednesday morning, she'll be more convincing than I am. Once again, I feel like a fraud.

■

Carson abuses my door around six-thirty. She doesn't look happy. "Let's go."

"Where?"

"Eat. Fucking starving. Potato wore off two hours ago."

Mine, too. Plus, I think she wants to talk—she usually doesn't ask me to dinner just for my company. Julie left me a note saying she wanted to have dinner, but it's time we had a break from each other. "Indian?"

Carson makes a face. "Pub."

I give in on the pub but insist on going somewhere other than the Florence Arms. The Brewhouse & Kitchen is a half-timbered, multi-gabled pile on Guildhall Walk next to the university. It's jumbled and funky inside and full of the after-class and after-work crowd. We grab a high table and two stools from a departing herd of college dudes and get a view of the copper kettles where the beer's brewed.

"Been staking out the lab." Carson's downed half her stout in about three draws. I let her discover her own foam moustache.

"Why didn't you tell me? I could've driven you."

"Didn't need that. That fence across the street? Golf course. Go through the front gate, never get close to the lab. Anyway, there's a pattern. PD goes by one-fifteen, boyfriend shows at two, leaves around two forty-five. Guard patrols at one and three."

"What happens when she's off?"

"Don't know yet."

I think about all the hours she's spent out in the cold and wet getting this information, and I feel guilty for sleeping in a bed. "Is Smoking Man still around?"

"Came back Monday and Tuesday." Carson scans around us, then lowers her voice, though nobody can hear us with all the noise. "Not last night. Maybe he knows I made him."

"Think he's a coincidence?"

She concentrates on a mouthful of stout, then leans in close enough for me to smell the hops. "Someone random casing the same place we are? Doesn't feel right. But if he's tracking us, he'd know where we're staying. Someone'd be on us. Haven't seen anyone."

"Doesn't mean they're not there."

"You're learning. You tell the Princess about the lab?"

I know exactly where she's going with this. "Not yet. I told her about the fake museum donor. She needed to know so she could ask for the money. By the way, she's got it already."

"At least that's going right." Carson backs off a little. "Say Bowen's having her followed, or us followed. Say the Princess knows. Would she tell you?"

I try to untangle Julie the person from Julie the client's rep. It's hard, and not just because I'm starting to like her. If she really is in on having Carson followed, then Julie's up to something. If she's not, and the shadow belongs to Cousin Ron, then he doesn't trust her, meaning we have the worst of both worlds here.

There's an old poker saying: "If you can't spot the sucker, you're it." Gar and the FBI beat that lesson into my head, but guys like me have a hard time believing we can be suckers. Right now, there's not enough info to make me believe that Smoking Man's connected to Julie.

"I think if she knew, she'd be more careful about being seen with me in public."

Carson snorts. "Unless she wants Bowen to think she's cozy with you. What do we know about Tovorovsky?"

"Bowen with a Russian accent. He's got a different racket, but it's still a racket." If I have to believe something, I'd believe the Russian's up to no good before I decide that Julie is.

Carson nods. "Look at him some more. I'll call Olivia about Bowen." She shakes a finger at me. "In case the Princess is part of this? Watch your ass around her. *And* your other parts."

"Wait, what? What're you—"

"You got like this around the Italian girl. I got it with her—she was cute if you're into that kinda thing. The Princess? She's the *client*. And she's just… old."

"She's not old."

"Older'n us."

"You're older than blondie over there behind the bar. Does that make you old?"

Carson growls. "She's still the client. Just think with this"—she stabs my forehead with an index finger—"and not that." The same finger aims through the table.

Goddamnit! Before I can process anything, I grab the finger. "When's the last time I told you what part to use when you think?"

She glares at her trapped finger. "Don't have this problem."

"Yeah? This' the second time in a row you've harshed on a woman I've paid attention to on a job." That fires up a red flush on Carson's neck. "You told me to keep her happy, remember? So whatever part *you're* thinking with, use it on this: I think Bowen's a means to an end for her. I also think she thinks we're the people who can get her what she wants, whatever that is. So maybe, if we can keep her on our side? She can do us some good." I throw back the finger.

Carson glooms at me. She reaches for her glass, realizes it's empty, then flags down a waitress. "Whatever. She blows up, it's all on you."

She doesn't throw me out. We have dinner and do those little things that mean "sorry" without saying it out loud. I hate fighting with Carson, but I've found she plays nicer when I draw lines.

Her pounding on the door blows me out of a sound sleep at four in the morning. While I pull on some shorts, I wonder what the hell's gotten into her now.

She's in her ninja outfit. Her eyes are huge and hot. "Miranda's been hurt."

Chapter 19

After I put on some clothes, I go to Carson's room to find her charging around in a circle by the window. Her arms are crossed as tight as her jaw.

I ask, "What happened?"

"Olivia called. Car wreck outside Southampton. Thick fog. Six cars piled up."

Shit. I fall into an armchair and knuckle the crud out of my eyes. Of course this happens—things were going too well. "How is she?"

"Don't know." Her voice is thinner than usual, with a little waver. She's worried, not just surprised.

"How are you?"

She shoots me a sharp look. "Stop headshrinking—" She paces a full lap before she stops to suck in a deep breath. "She's old. Hospital's no place for an old woman. After Olivia calls, I'm heading up."

It's nice to learn that Carson can care about another person. I'll have to redo the mental picture of her I've built. But I don't think she should be alone right now, and she sure shouldn't be driving. "I'll go with you."

The look she gives me is surprise mixed with a little gratitude. "Thanks. No. Stay here, keep track of the Princess. I'll—" Her phone rings (2Pac rapping "Dear Mama"). "Yeah...? Okay... How is she...? Fuck... Okay... Yeah, leaving now... No, he's staying... I'm fine, okay?" The way she says it screams *I'm not fine*. "Right, bye." She hits the disconnect button so hard, I expect her thumb to go through the glass. She stands there staring at the phone for a few moments before she glances up at me. "Out of surgery, in ICU."

At least Miranda's still alive. I bolt out of the chair and stride to Carson before she can avoid me. I take the phone and wrap my hand around hers. "Let me drive you there. You're too freaked to drive at night in the fog. I can't have both of you laid up."

She squeezes my hand hard enough to make me fear for my

fingers. After a moment, she swallows. "Thanks. Really. I'm okay. Hold things together down here. Don't know how long I'll be gone. She's all alone; no family left. Won't just leave her there."

Jesus, she's stubborn. "You haven't slept."

"Think I will now?"

We stand staring at each other for a few long moments. Her face is fighting with itself. I can't think of anything to say that'll help her, so I pull her into a hug that she doesn't fight. She's usually solid as a sack of cement, but right now she's trembling—not a lot, enough to feel. So I stroke her back and whisper "It's okay" and let her hold on as long as she wants. I got lots of practice at this with Janine; never thought I'd have to use it on Carson. I'm glad I can, though.

She eventually pulls back, whispers "thanks," then scrubs her face with her palms. She grabs her computer bag. "Okay, I'm going."

"You should probably change out of your burglar outfit."

She strips off her turtleneck on the way to her duffel. Under any other circumstances, I'd be impressed by the way she fills out her black longline sports bra, but my brain's not in that place right now. She wrestles on a slate-blue, long-sleeved tee, then finger-combs her hair. "*Now* I'm going."

"Call me when you get there. If you don't call in an hour, I'm coming after you."

Of course, I can't get back to sleep, not that I try hard. I go from being worried about Carson (until she calls around 4:55 to say she's at University Hospital Southampton), to worrying about Miranda, to worrying about the plan, then back around. When I figure out that there's a limit to how much trouble Carson can get into in a hospital and that Miranda's too sturdy to break in any serious way, I concentrate on the plan. Which is in pieces on the floor.

It's Friday. Gillian Hardwick's supposed to meet with the Mainwaring's development director Wednesday morning at ten. What happens if we don't have a Gillian?

The exhibit closes in eight weeks and two days. Even if everything goes right, Dorotea won't be in the lab for another two weeks. Assuming Boutelle gets the copy done in four weeks (not a bet I'd like to take) and we can get it shipped here without any customs problems, we'll have maybe a week to make the swap. A week can go by like *that.*

So unless Miranda is out of the hospital by Tuesday—or her replacement shows up today—Dorotea goes back to Russia. We're screwed.

I take my phone on my morning run. Of course, it doesn't ring until I'm in the shower. I manage to grab it just before it rolls to voicemail. "Yeah?"

"Please hold." Olivia's voice. There's dead air and a couple clicks. I wrap a towel around me so I don't leave puddles. Then she's back. "One-Seven-Nine?"

"That's me."

"I know." That sounds like *duh.* "One-Two-Six is with us."

Carson says, "Hey."

Olivia says, "I need to pass on something important from Allyson. First, though, have you any news about Forty-Six?"

Olivia's voice is mezzo, smooth as clotted cream, and carries an Oxbridge accent that makes me want to melt. Carson says nobody's ever met Olivia or knows what she looks like. I think of Jane Seymour in *Dr. Quinn* and I'm good.

"Yeah. She's awake. Talked to her a few minutes." Carson's voice echoes. "Still in ICU. Busted arm, busted nose, cracked ribs, concussion."

Ouch. "What'd she hit?"

"A Mini. Delivery truck hit her." Carson sighs. "Won't be out of ICU 'til maybe tomorrow."

I ask, "When'll she get out of the hospital?" Like that makes any difference now, with those injuries.

"Doctors won't say. Waiting for the MRI to come back."

Shit. I mean, yes, this sucks for Miranda, and I'm sorry she's been hurt. But it majorly sucks for us. Our Gillian's going to be laid up for weeks. I mute the phone and kick the bed a few times before I trust myself to say anything. "Olivia…can we get a replacement?"

"I've already investigated that avenue." Of course she has. "We have two associates who would be appropriate for what you propose. Both are assigned to projects that won't end for several weeks. Sorry."

"You're gonna take care of her, right?" Carson, sounding anxious. "Forty-Six?"

"Of course. We always do. You know that." Olivia sounds like she's calming a pit bull.

"Can we hire someone?" I ask. "An actor or something?"

Olivia clears her throat. "I asked about that. Please pay attention, both of you. Allyson says you can't hire outside talent unless it's truly vital. Do remember that she wants as few people as possible involved in this affair."

I try to kick the bed again but connect with my ankle and not my foot. God*damn*, that hurts. "It's vital. Our plan—"

"I explained the situation to her. She doesn't consider this vital enough."

Carson mutters "fuck." I agree.

"I understand this is difficult for you, but—"

"You think?" Carson, done muttering.

"Please. I'm merely the messenger."

My brain's spinning out from Gillian to the rest of the plan. "We can still hire a forger, right?"

"Of course. We haven't those resources in-house, sadly enough."

"How about the Swiss collector?" A possible way to launder the portrait.

"I'm not hopeful that we'll find a cooperative one, but if we do, we can hire him."

Not everything's broken... yet. I shuffle around my room to vent some of the steam in my head. "It seemed like you could buy off anybody in Milan. What changed?"

"That was Italy. It's much easier there." She tsks. "Allyson's in a state about this project's size. Especially—this is important, so please listen, both of you—she's adamant that we not use people known to be associated with us who aren't under our direct control. The car service, for instance, is an independent group we've not used before and won't again."

Carson blurts, "But why—"

"I can't tell you more beyond that, so please don't ask."

Did Allyson finally stumble over the line from paranoia to full-up tinfoil hatness? The fog that used to be outside is clogging my brain. I can't decide whether I should get mad or curl up on the floor and cover my head with a pillow. I settle for pacing in a circle until I can put together a coherent thought. "So the three of us have to do everything."

"I fear so."

"Wait. Three?" Carson.

I let that go by. "Can we get new identities?"

"Of course."

"What do you mean 'three'?" Carson's getting louder.

"New wardrobes?"

"If you must. Do be mature about it."

I look out at the baby-blue sky and wonder if the clothes have to be mature, or our requests. "You know, this pretty much forces us to use Ju—um, the client's rep. Allyson was hard-over against—"

Carson says, "Are you fucking *crazy?*" I think the stray dogs outside hear her.

I probably *am* crazy, but as usual my mouth's running faster than my brain. That means I should shut up, except there's no time to be rational. "We need a replacement for Forty-Six. You wanna do it?"

"Fuck, no. But *her?*"

"What other choice do we have? Besides, you're the one who wanted to get her dirty. This is as dirty as it gets. Olivia, has Allyson changed her mind?"

Olivia's quiet for a moment. "To a degree, perhaps. You're still to protect her from unnecessary danger."

"How about *necessary* danger?"

"Understand my words in any way it helps you. Also…" she hesitates a moment "…please know that I argued on your behalf. However, it *is* Allyson's name on the doorplate. Even my powers have limits."

"Since when?" Carson barks.

I never expected to hear this from Olivia. "That's like saying Santa Claus doesn't exist."

"Oh, buck up, both of you." Olivia sounds like an exasperated mom. "Father Christmas exists. I know him personally. And when all is cold and dark, he *will* deliver. Or perhaps I will in his stead."

Carson calls me before my phone can cool off. By now I'm dry, and my hair's sticking up all over.

The first thing she says is "This is bullshit," skipping "hello."

"What part of it?"

"The 'no outside people' part. Never bugged her before."

"There's lots of that going around this time."

"No shit. Something's chapping her ass. Gotta make some calls."

"To Olivia?"

"She's said all she's going to. Other ops. See if Allyson's cut them off, too. Meet any agency people in Mexico?"

"Um… there was this dude at the airport. He got me set up in—"

"Get his number?"

"No."

She makes a disgusted noise. "*Always* get numbers. It's your network. Allyson gets pissed when we go around her, but we do it. Saved my ass more'n once."

That makes sense, I guess. Not the Allyson-getting-mad part, but the personal network. When I was in the art business, I got digits for every gallery owner, assistant, and vendor I could. I had something like five hundred contacts on my phone when the music stopped.

"Don't get the Princess into this," Carson growls. "Doesn't need to know."

I don't even try to stop the sigh. "She's Plan B. What's Plan C?"

Dead air. Then, "Take it from the museum."

"And how far past the parking lot will we get?"

"Not hard to get past the cops if we—"

"It's not about the cops. Did you know Tovorovsky's got his own army?" I started researching Tovorovsky when I couldn't get back to sleep. "Sorry, security contractors. Russian Blackwater. Those dudes in eastern Ukraine? Some of them are his guys."

"Wonderful," Carson grumbles. "Anything else I should know?"

"He's got a lot of money stranded in Russia and Putin doesn't invite him to parties anymore. With the sanctions and capital controls, some of the financial press thinks Tovorovsky and some of his buddies may be having a cash crunch."

"Huh." More dead air. "Can the Princess even *do* this?"

I've been asking myself that. I don't like any of the answers I'm getting. "That's what I'm gonna find out."

Chapter 20

Julie lets me into her room. It's tidier than it was Wednesday night. We sit in the tufted beige armchairs by the window.

This was my idea. She's Plan B. But I don't know whether it'll work, or whether I even *want* it to work. For once, I can't figure out how to start. So I stall. "What've you been up to?"

"Writing. I'm about halfway through the second draft." Her laptop's open on the little white spindle-leg desk. As usual, she's stock upright with her hands in her lap. "I've been wondering what to do for lunch. Do you have plans?"

"Not yet." I watch her perch for a few beats, thinking on what I'm about to get us both into. "Ever done any acting? Dance, maybe?" Movement is movement.

Her eyebrows go up. "I took ballet and jazz dance until I was in high school, just like every other little girl back then. I was in a couple of plays—musicals—in college. Why?"

"Anything recently?"

"Not really unless you count my job. Teaching teenagers is all about acting." She folds her arms. Her face gets serious. "Why do you ask?"

Tell her? I'd rather see if she can take direction first. It doesn't look like our time together has built enough trust to get away with that. "I need to see if you can be rich."

Julie sits there blinking. Her eyes slowly widen. "Ohhh. This is for the museum donation, isn't it?"

"Yeah."

"It's a real plan now?"

"Yeah." As close to one as we have, at least.

Her jaw gets just a little stiff. "Is this another way to make me guilty of something? I thought I already proved myself to you."

"You did." I think about the least damaging way to say what I need to. "We had someone tagged to do it, but she's not available anymore. You're already part of the team, and you're motivated."

There's a lot going on behind her eyes now. Her lips purse. She focuses on something across the street. When she looks back to me, her face is set and determined. "If you want me to do this, you have to tell me why. What your plan is. I'm not doing anything until I know that."

I screwed up by telling her we're in a bind. She knows she has leverage now.

I tell her as little as I can and still get the point across. Since Cousin Ron's paying the bills, he'll find out one way or another anyway. The funny thing is, she doesn't tell me I'm crazy like Carson did. She asks questions—good questions—but otherwise she listens carefully and nods and looks at me like... well, like she'd been looking for something and just found it.

"That sounds like something out of a movie," Julie finally says.

"Is that good or bad?"

She laughs. "*I* think it's good. It's imaginative. You know *The Sting?* Paul Newman and Robert Redford? It's one of my favorite movies. This plan sounds like that." Pause. "Will it work?"

"No clue. I'm hoping for a better idea." Deep breath. "Are you in?"

She goes back to the distant stare. I hope she remembers that five days ago she was fighting to help. If she says *are you crazy?* we're stuck with Carson's Plan C, and it sucks.

"I guess I'm already an accessory, or whatever it's called."

"This goes way past that. We're talking fraud, now."

"I said I wanted this, didn't I?" More thinking. "Okay. What do you want me to do?"

I swallow my sigh of relief. "First, wardrobe. Can I see what you brought with you?"

She shoots a loaded eyebrow at me, but she opens the white armoire next to the desk.

I already know she doesn't have any clothes we can use for Gillian; she's a schoolteacher. This is more a gauge of her self-image. I see the mom jeans and Dockers and pastel knits I expected, nothing a parent or school honcho could get worked up about. It's also nothing a rich woman would wear to paint her house if she ever decided to try manual labor.

I want Julie to wear something dressier than jeans to help her get in the mood. I hand her a conservative navy-blue Ann Taylor suit and a white button-down blouse with three-quarter sleeves. "Try these. You can leave the jacket off."

She opens her mouth to ask why—it's like there's neon on her forehead—but then she scoops up a pair of black pumps and retreats to the bathroom.

I poke around some while she changes. She shops at mid-market malls and she's neater than anyone else I know. I spin away from the armoire when I hear the bathroom door open again.

Julie's shirt is tucked into her pencil skirt, which cuts across the exact center of her kneecaps. She's got an hourglass figure—not quite Joan on *Mad Men,* but in that neighborhood—and the skirt emphasizes the swell of her hips below her nipped-in waist. She has sturdy but decent calves. I hadn't expected much; I'd figured there was a reason for all the loose clothes. She sure doesn't need to hide anything.

She holds her hands away from her hips, palms forward. "Is this okay?"

"More than okay. I bet if you wore that to school, the boys would pay a lot more attention."

"The wrong kind. The last thing I need to do is show off the girls to a bunch of hormonal teenagers." But she has this little half-smile that tells me she's at least sort-of flattered.

"I'll bet. Now I need you to do something really hard. I need you to walk from the door to the window and back."

Her frown comes back. "Walk how?"

I settle into the left armchair. "The way you normally would. It's a baseline."

Hers is a calm, leisurely stride, almost polite in the way it doesn't take up too much space. She still keeps her hands folded at lap level. There's nothing bad about it except that it's totally wrong for Gillian. She turns when she reaches the door again and raises her eyebrows. "Do I pass?"

Pass for what? Gillian's all about the conservation lab. I'm sure the Mainwaring's development people will have their own agenda— to get Gillian to throw a check at whatever their highest priority is, which probably doesn't involve the lab. She's going to have to stick to her plan like Gorilla Glue if we want to accomplish anything more than spending a lot of Cousin Ron's money.

I know Julie can push back; she did it the day we met. But that was about something that mattered to her. She was mostly nice and polite about it, too, which sharks (meaning salespeople) read as weakness. Her nice, polite walk will read that way, too, and so will her nervous smile. Predators love weakness. I loved to see clients like Julie walk into the gallery. I hated dealing with other, bigger sharks because they usually got what they wanted and they'd take chunks out of my fins.

We need Julie to become a great white. Look like one, sound like one. Move like one.

So we work on walking.

It's the first thing anyone sees. I can look at somebody's walk and tell what basic personality type they are after a few strides. It's really useful in sales. A lot of alpha predators—male and female— visited my gallery, and I could pick them out even before they passed through our door. Their walk's strong and full of confidence, head up, shoulders back, not afraid to take up space. If Julie can't get the walk right, there's no point going on.

So that's what I teach her. But how do you change something so automatic, after so many years, in just a few hours?

We spend some time watching YouTube videos of Olivia Pope from *Scandal* and a couple female CEOs. I have her do confidence builders like roaring (hey, it works). I tell her to push me out of the way without stopping.

The first couple times, she can't. "I don't want to hurt you."

"I'm not that fragile. Push."

She moves me maybe one step. "I just don't shove people."

"Gillian does. Learn." I pull it in; snapping won't help. "Think about work. Is there someone you hate?"

Julie thinks on her way to her starting point. "There's a woman in Instructional Services who I'd like to throw out a window."

"Pretend I'm her. Go."

Three tries later, Julie almost puts me through the wall.

She fights with getting way out of her comfort zone. We both get frustrated. There's a lot of long pauses while we try to not say something that'll blow this up. I grow a headache. Julie storms out of the room a few times... but she always comes back.

Three hours-plus later, she turns around (she's been facing the door while she prepares) and walks. *Struts.* Head up, chest out, arms strong. Squashing the peons under her heels. She ends with her hands on her hips. It's that Eliza Doolittle "The Rain in Spain" moment.

"How's that feel to you?" I ask.

She gives me her best shark smile. "Like I can kill and eat a buffalo."

While I coach Julie after our lunch at the Florence Arms (I bought her a steak, rare, to get her in the right mindset), Carson starts peppering me with emails about Bowen. She must be researching him while she's sitting in the hospital.

They start off fairly neutral—links to profiles in *Forbes* and the *New York Times* and so on—but get hotter as she gets wound up by what she's reading. I can't just ignore my phone's buzzing, either; the message I blow off will be the one saying Carson's been arrested or that there's a hit team looking for us. Every time I pull my phone, Julie gives me the side-eye. "Progress reports," I tell her, hoping she won't see email subjects like "Bastard" and "Only in America."

"Ms. Carson's making a lot of progress?" Julie doesn't sound convinced.

"She's very talented."

When Julie ducks into the bathroom, I skim a few of Carson's links. They're all about Bowen's general douchery at Alivian Healthways, the big pharma company he runs. The latest one—the subject's "Asshole"—is about how he fired all 217 employees of Prosilix, a pharma company Alivian devoured a few months ago. Not laid off; *fired*, for cause, so he could skip the mandatory 60-day notice and avoid paying severance. His reason? "If they'd been doing their jobs, I couldn't have bought the company so cheap."

I click off my phone when Julie walks out of the bathroom. How can someone like her be related to someone like him?

Carson texts me around 3:20 to say she's coming back to pick up some clothes and her bathroom stuff. I keep drilling Julie until 4:15, then park her just inside the door to my room upstairs.

Carson answers on my second knock. "Give up on her already?"

"Not quite." I slip inside when she opens the door, but I don't close it all the way when she paces back to her desk. Her backpack's on the bed alongside a couple folded shirts and a pair of jeans. Next to that is a small mountain of paper I recognize—it's books and the stuff I printed for Miranda. "How is she?"

"Doped up." She flops into the black chair by her desk. She looks absolutely whipped. "Looks so old in that bed. Fragile. I know she's not, but…" Her neck vertebrae pop when she rolls her head through a circle.

I point to the pile of paper. "You cleaned out her hotel room?"

"Yeah. Nothing left to tie her to us." She rubs her eyes. "Gotta get back. Whaddaya want?"

"I'd like to introduce you to someone." I lean out the door and wave in Julie.

She enters using the power strut we worked on, with just enough hip swing to notice but not enough to make her Jessica Rabbit. Her "Good afternoon" is the cool-calm-confident tone of someone who's damn well made sure it *is* a good afternoon. She stops a couple paces from the desk and extends her hand. Carson will have to get up to shake it. *Make them come to you,* I'd told her. "Gillian Hardwick," Julie announces.

Carson's eyes rack up miles scanning Julie from hair to heels and back again. She slowly gets out of her chair to take Julie's hand. What she doesn't know is that I taught Julie to equal the force the other person puts into the handshake. Julie shakes twice, then pushes Carson's hand back to her.

Julie sweeps her free hand toward the two armchairs in the corner. "Let's sit." She glides onto the far seat, throws one leg over the other, smooths down her skirt, then lounges against the chair's arm with her chin lightly touching her extended index finger. It took over an hour to get her to lounge in a chair in a natural way. Her smile is the expectant kind that says *entertain me.*

Carson gives me a *WTF?* look.

"We started at nine," I say. "Think she'll do?"

She stands there staring at Julie for what turns into an uncomfortably long time. Props to Julie—she doesn't fold up or break character. She just stares back.

Carson finally says, "Fuck. Me."

Chapter 21

We check out of the Florence Suite an hour later.

Carson tells me, "Can't risk having Princess here. Should've moved when Miranda signed up. At least she stayed in London."

I get her point. From now on, Julie's going to be switching between being herself and being Gillian. If some Mainwaring person—even a docent—sees her down here as Julie while Gillian's in play, we could be in trouble. So Julie has to officially leave town.

We end up about twenty-five miles northwest of Portsmouth on the east edge of Southampton, in the Hilton at The Ageas Bowl, a brand-new business hotel grafted onto the side of a cricket stadium. There's easy access to the M27 freeway, which dumps us off on the northern edge of Portsmouth. The hotel's big and anonymous and busy. Perfect for letting us fade into the woodwork.

Now we have to build us a Gillian.

That mound of stuff I dug up for Miranda? I drop it on Julie after we get settled in.

Her eyes get real big. "All that?"

"Yeah. By Tuesday night."

She sorts through the pile with an *I'm doomed* look on her face. "This is like grad school all over," she mumbles. Then she pastes on a smile and starts sorting the different subjects into stacks on her king bed's white duvet. "Is there a final?"

"Wednesday morning. Closed-book."

I sit in one of the squarish gray armchairs while Julie sits crosslegged on the bed, reading and looking at videos online and asking about a million questions. She uses both yellow and pink highlighters on the papers (not the books, or I'd have to kill her) and burns out a pen taking notes. In a way, it's like a study session for me, too, because I have to remember the material and figure out how it goes together so I can explain it to Julie.

Like in my room, the glass wall behind me looks out on the cricket ground. The sky gets darker and the sun gets lower until only the safety lights show up in the stands. We work through a dinner that's everything I expect from room service (bland and overpriced).

When Julie overloads, I put her through more charm school. She can become Gillian, but only for a minute or so at a time. Still, it's a little distressing to see her switch from a cheerful, generally pleasant schoolteacher into a cool, proud, brisk ex-trophy wife.

I hope I'm not creating a monster.

We make it to just past eleven before Julie drops the exhibit catalog and falls back on the bed. "I can't do this anymore tonight. My head hurts. Can we start again in the morning?"

I've been trying to figure out what to tell her when she got to this point and still don't like my options. "No. We're going to be busy tomorrow."

"What are we doing?"

Here's the hard part. "There's something we haven't talked about, but we need to."

She sits up. "That sounds serious. What?"

"We need to buy you some clothes."

She looks puzzled. "Why? What's wrong with what I have?"

"It's fine for you. It's wrong for Gillian. You need clothes a millionaire would have." This is *really* going to blow the mood. "The same with your hair."

"What's wrong with my hair?" Her voice threatens to crack.

"It's not Gillian's. When you walk in there Wednesday, we need them to take one look at you and believe you're who you say you are. You've gotta look the part. The sooner that happens, the better it is for all of us."

Her smile's turned into a frown that's getting darker. "What does 'look the part' mean, exactly?"

"I have some ideas. I'd like to find some things online for you to look at before we go buying. What are your sizes?"

Julie's jaw clenches. "That's an awfully personal question."

I kick myself for not bringing this up earlier or breaking it more gently. "I know. I'm sorry. It's just that Gillian would shop in London, so that's where we'll need to go. I want us to be smart about our time there, pre-shop online. But—"

"We're going shopping?" A light shines through the darkness.

"Yeah. We have to."

"In London?"

"Yeah."

"With Ron's money?"

"Ultimately, yeah."

The light takes over her whole face. "I wear a dress size ten or twelve, depending on the cut, a medium to large shirt, a seven and a half shoe, and usually a 38C bra. Does that help?"

"That's… great." *Shopping in London* is a magic phrase. I'll have to remember that.

"I have conditions."

"Um… conditions?"

She nods. "Nothing above the knee, nothing sleeveless, and no cutouts. Gillian wouldn't wear them, and I won't either."

I grind this over in the back of my brain. It's good she's starting to channel Gillian, but she just disqualified about three-quarters of the dresses out there. "Can I ask why?"

Julie pats her thighs. "Our husbands were surrounded by girls in short dresses and low necklines, showing lots of skin. We can't pull that off anymore without looking ridiculous. What we *can* do is remind our men what grown-up women can do for them. Things girls can't."

The way she's looking at me—the way *Gillian's* looking at me— I see her point. "If you don't mind my saying, you look great."

She gives me a subdued smile. "That's very kind. I'm good at camouflage." She holds her arms out at her sides. "I'd prefer that you see less of my figure and think more of it." The arms drop, and so does the smile. "Don't make me look desperate. That's all I ask." She slides to the edge of the bed and extends her hand to shake. "Promise me."

I take her hand. "Julie, you're gonna look like a million bucks."

Chapter 22

I love London. I've been here a couple times on gallery business. If it was up to me, I'd spend all day just wandering around looking at stuff. But London's also a shopping playground for the 1%, and we're here for a reason—turn the duckling Julie into the swan Gillian.

We start at the Daniel Galvin salon in Marylebone. For roughly the monthly lease payment on the BMW back in Portsmouth, Julie comes out with her hair off her neck and swept back over her ears, with a little lift on top to soften the look. It suits Gillian, but it's great for Julie too. A MAC Cosmetics consult in Covent Garden gives her subtle but sophisticated makeup that adds a couple zeroes to her net worth.

Now it's time to work on the rest.

I spent a lot of time at the gallery watching well-kept women wear a huge variety of clothes. I know the look I'm going for: quiet, flattering, jewel tones. That's what I showed Julie on the computer on our way here.

We shop our way through the brick-and-granite-lined heart of Knightsbridge. I shepherd her through her initial money freakout ("I can't wear this! Look at the price!") and creeping sensory overload. She tries things on. She gives them back to me. All we accomplish is sending a bunch of head-and-shoulders shots to Olivia for Gillian's fake ID.

Half a dozen boutiques and a dozen tried-and-discarded finds pass by. She looks great in at least two-thirds of the outfits she passes up. Each time, it's the same story: I ask, "What is it that you don't like?"

She sighs. "I don't know. It just doesn't... *do* anything for me. I'm sorry."

Everything crashes in Armani's three-story, ultra-minimalist flagship on Sloane Street. Julie stalls out in front of a full-length mirror, wearing an Armani Collezioni long-sleeved, color-block sheath that looks dynamite on her. Her face gets more glum the longer she stares at herself.

I watch her swivel left and right, trying to work up some enthusiasm it's clear she can't find. "Are you okay?"

Her shoulders slowly droop. "I'm sorry, Matt. All these things you've shown me, they're beautiful and they look wonderful on me, but..."

"Too tight? Too blue?" The Armani's center panel is ultramarine.

"Too... boring."

That I didn't expect. Land's End and Ann Taylor, her go-to faves, aren't exactly the cutting edge of fashion. I've kept the clothes simple and elegant so they don't scare her. But, *boring?* "Can you explain that some more?"

She turns a 180 so she can check out her butt in the mirror. For the record, it looks just fine. "I've been thinking a lot about Gillian."

Early this morning, while Julie was checking out of the Hilton, I got an email from Olivia with an update to Gillian's backstory. It's like the one for Miranda, except this time Gillian divorced her husband and got a $30 million settlement. I gave it to Julie to study on the train.

By the way... Gillian's ex? Richard Hoskins, my cover identity from the Milan project. I bet this is Allyson's idea of a joke.

Julie starts pacing barefoot on the parchment-colored limestone, touching racks and tables like she's counting them. "What's happened with her, where she is in her life. She gave up three hundred million dollars when she left Hoskins—when she was almost *fifty*. I think it's because she couldn't stand looking foolish anymore. She couldn't take people talking behind her back. 'Doesn't she see what he's doing? Why does she put up with that?'" She shakes her head. "She's had to look perfect all those years. That's what you said, right? That was her job?"

"Right." I don't know where this came from or where she's going with it, but I've learned the hard way that when a woman wants to talk, you listen. You might learn something important.

"But that means *his* idea of 'perfect,' doesn't it? I mean"—she pats her own shoulders—"is this what he likes?"

"I guess."

"See?" She throws up her hands. "All those years she's been

dressing for someone else. Now she's free and she's got her own money. Is she going to wear the same clothes? No! She's done with pleasing other people. She's ready to please herself."

How much of this is about Gillian, and how much is about Julie? Does it matter?

Her eyes skewer me. "Gillian likes art, right? Colors? Shapes? Why doesn't she have that in what she wears? She wants something fun. Something that says"—she spreads her arms—"'Look at me! I'm still here!'" Her arms drop. "Does that make sense?"

At the gallery, ex-wives tended to disappear. I can't remember ever seeing that post-split transformation. It sounds right. But how did she burrow so far into Gillian's head? What else has she figured out about Gillian that I haven't?

We give the dress back to Giorgio and head north on Sloane toward the Millennium Hotel, where we can pick up a cab. I ask, "What does Gillian think is fun?"

"I don't know." Julie's using her Gillian walk. After she's practiced almost non-stop all day, I wonder if she even realizes it. "I'll know it if I see it, but I haven't yet. It wasn't back there."

"Nobody ever called Armani 'fun.'" I'm trying to work out Plan B, because her epiphany shredded what was left of Plan A. Then I notice she's staring toward Hermès across the street. Purses already?

"That's it." She points. "That's what I mean."

An ice blonde with Slavic cheekbones is rearranging her shopping bags just outside Hermès. She's wearing a mango crew-neck sweater over a mid-calf plum skirt with a thick freeform fuchsia squggle running diagonally across the front. It's bold and graphic and I'd never figure Julie for wanting it. But there she is, trotting across the street, waving at the blonde. The hand gestures say what I can't hear: *Who are you wearing? Where did you get it?*

Julie scurries back to my side of the street. "The designer's name is Roksanda. I don't know how to spell it. She says she got it at a place called Browns. Do you know where that is?"

"I can find it." I pull my phone. What Gillian wants, she gets.

It's pitch dark by the time we're on the train heading southwest to Southampton. Once we pass London's M25 beltway, the suburban lights look like low-flying rectangular stars.

I watch Julie fight off sleep for a while. We'd started early and we were on the go all day, doing way more than our fair share to support the British economy. Our shopping bags fill the two seats ahead of us. I'm still wondering what she and Gillian are talking about together.

After the fifth or sixth time she jerks semi-awake, I ask, "What's Cousin Ron like for real?"

She yawns. "Do you mean, is he as big a jerk as he is in public?"

"Um… yeah, I suppose. He comes off like a real piece of work."

"He can be. He's nice to me, but I don't threaten him." She stretches out her legs and rotates her feet. Her ankles crackle. "Sometimes he does things that make me want to kick him. Like when he bought that company—four years ago, maybe?—that made some kind of cancer drug and put the price up ten thousand percent or something ridiculous like that. Mom had cancer, but not the kind the drug worked on. I asked him, 'What if my mom needed that drug? How would you feel?' and he said, 'I'd just give it to her.'" She motions like she's slapping somebody upside the head. "'That's not the point.' I didn't talk to him for weeks."

"That's his whole business model. Buy a company, cut its R&D, jack up the prices on its catalog, sell as much as he can until there's no market anymore."

"Don't forget laying off the people he got with the other company." She sighs. "I think he's got his own personal chair at that Senate committee he keeps talking to. You know, with a little nameplate on the back?"

"How'd he like *Time* calling him 'the Darth Vader of big pharma'?"

"He *loved* that. He's got a framed copy of that cover in his office."

"What does he want with Dorotea? He collects photography." I read that he has some heavy hitters on his walls—Stieglitz, Lange, Arbus, Sherman. That sounds like collecting names rather than things he loves.

Julie shrugs. "I'm not sure he knows. He's never talked about it. You know what I think?" She sits up and leans on my armrest. "I think it's all about winning. He just wants to beat that Russian person who has her now"—she waves a finger toward the window, like Tovorovsky's sitting out there—"it doesn't matter what happens after. I'm not sure he even *likes* Oma's portrait."

I lean back and roll that over in my head while the train gently sways under us. This always bugged me at the gallery: the people who buy things not because they love them, but because they want to keep other people from having them. Gar had a couple clients he could always manipulate into buying canvases he couldn't move otherwise; all he had to do was tell them someone else was interested.

"Can you talk him into putting her in a museum?" I ask. "That's where she belongs."

"I know, right? That's what I'd want for her. Let people see her, learn about her, know what happened to her. That way, she'll never be forgotten again. Will Ron do that?" She turns up her hands. "It's not his style."

"Guys like him need tax breaks. I know people who can give him a really inflated valuation on the portrait. Nice write-off."

"Do you honestly think he pays taxes?"

Silly me. "Maybe you can work on the wife, get her invested in it."

"Maria?" Julie snickers. "Don't get me wrong—Maria's a sweet girl, but this kind of thing bores her. I've tried talking to her about it and her eyes go a million miles away."

When I saw she'd been a model, I looked up Maria Duprovic (Mrs. Bowen Number Three). Just to be thorough, you know. She was in the 2008 and 2009 *Sports Illustrated* swimsuit editions. She wears body paint well.

"Ever consider slipping him poison?" I ask.

Julie gives me a sad little smile. "I don't think like him."

Chapter 23

Sunday. Three prep days left.

Carson ushers me into her room after my run and breakfast. She's got huge bags under her eyes and her hair's squashed flat, but she seems to be in an okay mood.

"Out of ICU," she says when I ask about Miranda. "They're keeping her another couple days. Swelling in her brain's going down." She collapses into an armchair. "Princess?"

"She's good." I rattle around her room as I give her the highlights.

Carson never takes her eyes off me, even though none of the rest of her moves. "She gonna be ready in time? What's left to do?"

She had to ask. "I've gotta work on her physical presentation. Drill her on Art 101 so she can talk the talk. Run her through the L.A. art scene. Build out her life with Hoskins…" The list grows as I tell her about it.

When I'm done, Carson shakes her head. "Whatever. Be careful. Too much prep's as bad as not enough. Don't break her."

Another thing to worry about. I notice a yellow squirt gun on the bed next to her backpack. I pick it up and aim it at her. "Allyson's finally arming you?"

Carson rolls her eyes. "Working out how you deliver that dye."

She means the Inkodye I need to shoot Dorotea with. "Does it work?"

"Too thick. Thin it out enough to shoot, can't see it when it dries."

Figures. It would've been a great way to get the stuff on the canvas. "Any other ideas?"

"One." She drags her backpack across the bed, pulls out a plastic bag and tosses something to me. It looks like a mini slingshot without the frame: stiff tan elastic looped at each end with a soft plastic pad in the middle. She rocks out of the chair. "C'mon."

I've never seen so little stuff in a woman's bathroom before. She grabs the slingshot from me, then pushes the loops over her right thumb and forefinger. Her hand's now a slingshot frame. She takes a small, round red ball from the bag, grips it in the plastic pad, pulls back, and *splat*—there's a red splotch on the white subway tiles in the walk-in shower.

I ask, "Make the dye into a paintball?"

"Yeah. Found some guys in Southampton who make custom paintballs." She holds the slingshot out to me. "Try it."

The elastic's so stiff, it feels like it's going to tear my fingers off when I pull on it. The upside is that I only have to extend it four or five inches to launch a paintball more than six feet, and I can keep my elbow clamped to my side. I can consistently hit a foot-square area of the shower's back wall after three or four tries. Nobody behind me can see what I'm doing. In front? Well, it'll be pretty obvious.

Carson rinses off the paint with the handheld showerhead. "I'll go in with you, screen you from the second camera."

"How long to get them?"

"Two Mondays from now. Works for you? I'll order them."

"Yeah, go ahead. Good job." Now all I have to worry about is putting a paintball through the canvas. "We can do this the Wednesday after if we can figure out the lab's security by then."

Carson plucks the slingshot off my hand. "If your girlfriend doesn't fuck it up."

When Gillian checked into the Hilton last night, she got a King Junior Suite. I'm not sure what's "junior" about it; the place is bigger than the pool house I live in. The living room, where we settle, is separated from the sleeping area by a wall holding a flat-screen TV. I'd expect a suite to have more interesting décor, but it's done in the same tints and shades of gray that we plebes get in our normal rooms.

If Friday was about museums, today's about art. She's going to have to talk about art like she knows something about it, with people who really *do* know something about it. So it's Art History 101 all day, broken up with virtual tours of various L.A. museums. I did this with Carson in Milan. She was a lot crankier about it, but Julie's having to absorb a lot more, so the tension level's about the same.

She's a trouper, though; she never complains.

We work our way through a room-service lunch and another sunset over the stadium. It's hard to straddle that line between being tough on her and being an asshole, but Julie grinds away at it with the help of aspirin and a bottle of French Sauvignon Blanc. By dinner, we're both cooked.

Julie's stretched out on the slab-sided loveseat with her head and feet propped on opposite arms. She's wrapped an icepack in a hand towel and draped it across her eyes. "Do you ever lose track?"

I'm at the window, trying to stretch out the kink in my back. "Of what?"

"Of why we're doing this? I mean, we've got this big... *thing* we're doing, and I think about it and I can hardly remember why. Does that happen to you?"

All the time. I can't say that to her, though, not with that lost-tired sound in her voice. "I just think about the end result and it all straightens out."

Julie nods. I can't tell if she's convinced. Probably not. I didn't convince myself.

Chapter 24

Monday. Two days left.

Today is Julie's first day on the town as Gillian in full costume. She does okay—she's got the walk down as long as she doesn't have to think about anything else. Our visit to the Southampton City Art Gallery is pleasant but not very useful; much of the place is taken up by a traveling road show of contemporary art that's not part of Gillian's world.

I've barely turned the lights on in my room after dinner when it sounds like someone's trying to bash in the windows. It's Carson, of course. We've started using the hotel-length balcony overlooking the field to go between rooms to avoid the cameras in the hallways.

Carson pushes her way through the moment I crack open the sliding glass door. She sidesteps to the chairs by the window. "Why don't you come in?" I ask her back.

Once I've settled in the other chair, she leans forward with her elbows on her knees. "Think I know what set off Allyson." Her voice is a hair above a murmur.

I have to lean in just to hear her. "Cops? Spooks?"

She shakes her head. "Client."

"Bowen? Why—"

"No, not him." She pauses, glances at the door. "Tovorovsky."

As usual, my mouth works faster than my brain. "He's not the cli—" The brain catches up. A bunch of synapses line up all at once. "He's a *client?*"

Carson nods. Her lips have almost disappeared.

I wilt into the chair. It doesn't take a lot of agency experience to know that screwing one client to benefit another one isn't a good long-term strategy. Allyson's not dumb—she couldn't have gotten this far if she was. "That's nuts. Are you sure?"

"About 95%. Talked to some other ops, Russian-speakers. Three did jobs for him."

My stomach curdles at all the implications. "Why would she do that?"

Carson shakes her head. "Fucking stupid, right? Hasn't ordered a project for two years. Word is, he didn't pay for the last one."

Even oligarchs can be deadbeats. "No surprise—a lot of his money's stuck in Russia." My sinking feeling is still sinking. "What do we do?"

"Do? Can't *do* shit, except be careful." She points through the wall. "Princess on board?"

"Yeah."

"You sure?"

"Yes. She's seriously invested. She let me change her hair."

"Whatever." Carson sits back and chews her lip for a moment. "Tell her to say nothing to nobody. What—"

"She reports to Bowen, remember? She has to tell him something. She says she's telling him what'll keep him happy, but still."

Carson rubs her eyes with her fingertips. "Tell her, no names. No descriptions. If Tovorovsky wants to torch the agency, maybe he won't know who we are." She stands and frowns down on me. "Keep her on a leash, or we all get to die."

Chapter 25

Tuesday morning. We go to the museum tomorrow. I hope.

Julie looks exhausted at breakfast, with big, dark circles under her bloodshot eyes. "Did you sleep last night?" I ask. She shakes her head.

We take her out to the seriously charmless Old Town Southampton. Julie can get some practice being Gillian in a low-threat environment. I figure some history will help ground her in something she's comfortable with. Carson tags along to let her get used to having an assistant. The salt air and the tang of fresh rain clear out the cobwebs and funk between my ears.

Julie at least *looks* the part—black Prada straight-leg capris, Tods black suede pumps, and a white micropleated Issey Miyake long-sleeved tee splashed with what looks like black lines drawn with a fountain pen the size of a tree. Her makeup mostly covers her raccoon circles. Today's her first try with the final part of her costume—hazel non-correcting contact lenses. Her idea. It's surprising how big a change it is.

"Let's start out easy," I tell her on our way down the High Street. "Posture and stride. Just stand up and walk."

"No," she snaps back. "I need to be Gillian. Don't baby me."

I can't tell if this is Julie in character or Julie about to lose it. I'm not sure which option I like less. I glance at Carson for some help and get her sucking-lemons look. "Suit yourself," I tell Julie.

Julie's biggest Gillian problem is still walking and talking at the same time, so that's what we drill her on. I take it easy on her, lobbing her softballs. Carson's throwing rockets. By now Julie's got the basics down—her bio, her life in L.A. with Hoskins, what she's been up to for the past year—but only when she's standing still. She still gets lost when she's moving.

Then Carson asks just the wrong question just the wrong way, and Julie has both a meltdown and a hot flash—or, as she puts it, a "personal power surge"—at the same time. She storms into a Burger

King restroom.

"Good work," I tell Carson.

She grumbles something I probably don't need to hear. "I'll check on her."

"Think she wants to see you?"

"I broke it, I fix it." She jogs after Julie.

I pace in a circle in front of the medieval Bargate—one of Southampton's civic symbols—with my brain in a downward spiral. Carson warned me that Julie might snap if I push her too hard. Is that what just happened? Did Carson's question set her off? The lack of sleep? Or was it her "personal power surge"? WebMD says that stress and caffeine can trigger hot flashes. She's had a bucketload of both these past few days.

Carson finally strolls out and stops in front of me. Her hands are shoved into the back pockets of her black jeans. "Out in a couple."

"Is she okay?"

She shrugs. "Cooling off. Told her to go in a stall and take her clothes off."

I'm not sure I should let myself form that picture. "Does that help?"

"Dunno. I don't get hot flashes. Can't hurt. She won't sweat on the clothes." She looks away. "Sorry. I was trying to get under her skin. It worked."

"No shit. What part of that sounded like a good idea to you?"

Carson scorches me with a look. "Questions you don't see coming kill you. She needs to learn that."

Now? I pause for a deep breath that isn't as cleansing as I'd like. "What do we do?"

"Ease off. Let her be her."

"She needs practice being Gillian. Tomorrow's the big show."

"She's gotta settle down." Carson thumbs toward the door. "No good to us like this."

Julie retreats to her room as soon as we get back to the hotel in midafternoon. I start to follow her, but Carson grabs my arm. "Leave her alone. Done all you can. Up to her now."

We spend an hour trying to work out what we'll do if Julie

implodes or freezes tomorrow. We don't have a lot of options. The museum's expecting Ms. Hardwick, and all of her ID has Julie's picture on it. Substituting Carson for her won't work past the first time somebody asks to see her driver's license.

"We do what we can do," Carson says. She's sprawled in her desk chair with her feet on her bed. "Doesn't have to be perfect, just good enough."

"Easy for you to say." I'm leaning against the glass wall, watching the late-afternoon rain. The gray outside is about the same shade as the gray inside me.

The worst-case scenario loops through my head: Julie loses it in the museum. Best outcome: we slink away like whipped dogs and don't get to preview the lab until we try to break in. Going in cold ups the odds that we'll fail and get to hang out with cops. Worst outcome: the museum people smell a rat. The police show up. We have to either hide out or talk to cops. I don't know what comes up when a cop runs Carson's prints, but with mine they get my probation officer's name and I get a return trip to prison.

Carson swings out of her chair, disappears into her bathroom to rustle around, then reappears. "Here, give her this."

It's a big, chalky white lozenge. "What is it?"

"Knock her out for eight-ten hours. She needs sleep."

She's got a point. "You just happen to have this around?"

"Got all kinds of shit." She smirks. "Need anything?"

I'm sitting at my desk, having a staring match with Dorotea while I wonder what I've forgotten to do. There's a light tap on my sliding glass door. It's not Carson; when she knocks, the whole room shakes.

It's Julie, makeup-free, swaddled in her powder-blue fleece. "Oh, good. I didn't wake you."

"It's not that late. Come in, I've got something for you." She drifts in while I duck into the bathroom to grab Carson's sleeping pill. By the time I come out, she's standing at my desk, looking at the postcard like it's a picture of her new baby. "Here. This'll help you sleep tonight."

She unfolds the hotel notepaper I wrapped around the pill, nods, then refolds and pushes it into her jeans pocket. "Thank you. I had dinner in my room, in case you wondered."

"That's what I thought. I figured you needed some alone time." Watching her stand there in a self-hug, looking everywhere but at me, tells me she didn't come up here just to say that. I'll wait.

A stretch of uncomfortable silence follows. "I'm sorry about this morning. I know Ms. Carson was trying to teach me something. It's just... well, I know this is important. I don't want to let us down. Let Oma down."

"You'll do fine." I squeeze her shoulder. "Take tonight off. Watch bad TV. I'd say 'paint your nails,' but the salon already did that." She fumbles a bleak smile. "How are your eyes?"

"Okay. It's strange, wearing contacts again. What's really strange is looking in the mirror and not recognizing myself."

"That's a good thing. If you can't recognize yourself, nobody else will, either." I brush a stray bundle of hair off her forehead. "Go relax. I'll see you at breakfast."

But she doesn't go. She stands there peering up at me with her head cocked a little to one side. After a couple moments, she takes a deep breath, like she's about to jump in a shark pool. "Remember Stefan, my Austrian lawyer? I talked to him Sunday. He says he's found something important. I thought... well, since I'm so close, I should go meet him for real finally, so he's more than an email or a voice on the phone. I'm thinking I'll fly to Vienna on Friday... unless you have something planned for then?"

"When will you come back?"

"I want to spend the weekend. I'd like to see where my grandparents lived. See what's left of their world. If anything is."

I crunch on this for a few moments. As long as the museum doesn't want Gillian to stage an instant encore, we'll be in a holding pattern until next Wednesday anyway. "That should be fine. It'll be a good adventure for you." I'm envious as hell.

Something clicks in her eyes, and I see some of Gillian flow into her face. "You should come."

Wait, what?

"I think you and Stefan have a lot to talk about. You may be able to ask him questions I can't. Maybe he can help you make Oma legal again."

She may have a point. Maybe the lawyer can help scrape up more information about where Dorotea's been all this time. Maybe he can help with the provenance problem.

One problem: my spidey sense is telling me that spending an entire weekend alone with Julie, on her agenda in a place like Vienna, wouldn't be the smartest thing I've ever done.

It's not because I expect her to make a move on me (not that that would be a bad thing); I learned a long time ago that I'm not exactly irresistible. No, it's because she'll have two uninterrupted days to try to pry information out of me. There's only so much pestering I can take before I'll spill something I shouldn't about the project, the agency, or myself. I've come close a couple times already.

That hint of Gillian in her face is gone. Julie's eyes and half-smile are soft and warm again. She's inviting a friend to come on an adventure with her, not leading a mark into a trap.

Maybe I *should* go. A free trip to one of the great cities of Europe, somewhere I've wanted to go for ages. Talk to the lawyer. Make Julie happy, like Carson said. Keep an eye on her. Keep her out of trouble.

"I'd love to," I hear myself say. "I'll take care of the arrangements." Or, Olivia will. Carson's gonna kill me.

A big grin washes across Julie's face. "Thank you! I'm so glad you're coming. It'll be fun." She sets her hands on my shoulders, pops up on tiptoes, and kisses my cheek. Just a soft, warm brush I'll be thinking about later. She steps back, beaming. "I'll be ready tomorrow. I promise."

Chapter 26

She may be ready, but she's not ready to go.

It's nine Wednesday morning. We have to be at the museum by ten. Our preferred route—the one with the fewest cameras—takes forty-ish minutes. Carson and I are standing outside Julie's door in our sincere blue suits. Carson looks very corporate and respectable: low-heeled black pumps, a button-down white blouse, and a simple string of pearls.

I knock on the door again. "Gillian, it's time. We gotta go."

"Coming! I'm coming!"

I exchange a glance with Carson. She bobs her head at the door. "Break it down?"

"Not yet. The hotel will notice."

Finally, the latch rattles and the door swings open.

Wow.

Julie's wearing a knee-length Roksanda sheath that highlights all her curves. It's covered with bold Cubist shapes in scarlet, fuchsia, coral, turquoise, and a white-streaked, color-flecked medium gray. The dress is sleeveless, but she's got a thin half-sleeve sweater under it that almost exactly matches the red. Lanvin Pearl pumps and a black woven-leather Bottega Veneta shoulder bag finish the look. Even Carson is surprised—her eyebrows have climbed halfway up her forehead. Julie really does look like thirty million bucks.

"Sorry." Her voice is thinner than I like. "I couldn't decide what to wear."

I give her my best calming smile. "You look great."

We bomb down the A334 through trees and brick suburbs, trying to stay ahead of the clock. Our burgundy Jaguar XJ—the Beemer's replacement—glides like a living room on wheels. Still, it's not fast going. I keep an eye on a grimly quiet Julie in the back while Carson navigates through the local traffic. Once we're on the M275, which injects us right into downtown Portsmouth, I notice the shake in Julie's hands and her deer-in-the-crosshairs eyes.

I reach over the seat back toward her. "Hold my hand." She does, like a flood's about to drag her away. "Good. Focus on that." I ask Carson, "How close are we?"

"Ten, maybe twelve."

Too far? Too close? "Okay, Julie. Close your eyes. Breathe slow and deep." I got a lot of experience doing this with Janine when she started coming unglued. Sometimes it even worked.

Julie mashes her eyes shut and sucks in shuddery breaths.

If I don't play this right, we could have a full-up panic attack on our hands. "Listen to me, Julie. I'll give you a four-count. Breathe in on the count, then out through your nose. Concentrate on that. Don't think about anything else."

"Sorry," she whispers.

"Suck it up," Carson growls. "You're on in twenty."

I snap "Shut up!" at Carson, then turn back to Julie in time to see her look like she's going to hurl. "It's okay. Just breathe." I start a series of slow four-counts. She breathes, more or less. We're in a stretch of the freeway where you can barely see there's a city. My arm's starting to go numb, but I don't dare move. Every exit reminds me we're getting closer to showtime.

Then suddenly the city appears, and so does the city traffic. We wait across from All Saint's Church at one of the few stoplights along the way. Carson whispers in my ear, "Will she make it?"

I shrug. Julie's hand is shaking even through her death grip.

Carson pulls a few semi-illegal driving tricks and gets us to the Stanhope Road lot—where the museum people told us to park—faster than we should have. She launches herself out of the car, rounds its nose, then yanks open my door. "Take a walk."

"What?"

"Get out."

Julie's eyes jerk wide open. "Don't…" she whispers.

Ignoring Carson hasn't ever gone well. I get out. She dives into the back seat and slams the door behind her.

I walk a circle around the string of parking spaces we're in, trying to ignore whatever Carson's doing to Julie. What if we can't get her out of the car… or worse, if we can and she loses it in the museum? Maybe I should've tried to turn Carson into the rich chick. Yeah, that'd work great. *Not.* The clock on the brick-and-stone Victorian train station across the street says it's less than ten minutes to late for the meeting and way, *way* late to be thinking about this.

On my third lap, I glance in our Jag's back window and see something I never expected: Carson holding Julie's face between her hands with their foreheads touching. A headlock wouldn't surprise me, but this? *The moment will melt if you watch. Keep moving.*

A few minutes later, Carson waves me back to the car. She's standing behind the trunk when I reach her, arms folded. "She's better. Get her moving."

Julie *is* better. At least, she's breathing unassisted, though she looks very serious. We power-walk down a block of Commercial Street still open to traffic—buses and delivery vans lining both sides—while Carson talks on her phone behind us in her corporate-smooth voice ("we'll just be a minute—we ran into some traffic…").

We reach the museum's front door at 10:08. I'm about to walk in when Julie grabs my arm. I turn to face her. It's weird, looking into her eyes and seeing green. "How are you doing?"

"Terrified." She slowly inflates, then sets her head and neck. She's Gillian, at least for now. "Let's do this."

Chapter 27

Miss Grant, the Development Office secretary—a thirtyish honey-blonde in a pale-yellow twin set, not a good color on her—meets us in the elevator lobby for the Mainwaring's fourth-floor administrative offices. She doesn't recognize Carson as the Polish flower girl. We follow her past blandly modern glass-walled offices along the street frontages and cool gray modular furniture along the courtyard exposure. Julie's got the Gillian power strut on; so far, so good.

Three suits are waiting for us inside a small conference room overlooking the Jubilee Fountain.

"So pleased to meet you." Gordon Fallbrook, the museum director, beams at Julie as he wraps her hand in both of his. He's wearing a navy English-cut three-piece suit, French cuffs, and a quiet maroon tie. He looks a bit like the Earl of Grantham in *Downton Abbey*. "I understand you found some of our traffic."

"It was annoying, but we finally made it." Good; Julie didn't apologize. Rich people don't apologize except to a judge or Congress.

Introductions all around. We settle into the swiveling brown-leather desk chairs ringing the stained-oak conference table. Julie's at one end with the museum wheels; I'm at the other end with Carson and Miss Grant, who flips open a pewter netbook and starts tapping in notes.

Fallbrook folds his hands on the tabletop. "Well then, Ms. Hardwick, I understand you're interested in helping the Mainwaring in its mission." I expect an *old chap* to pop out of his hail-fellow enthusiasm. He must be the cheerleader for the bunch. "And we're *delighted* to have you here, of course. Perhaps you could tell us something about yourself? Your interests?"

Before Julie can answer, Carolyn de Maziere, the Director of Development, drawls, "If I may—pardon me, Gordon—I must ask... are you American?"

Julie's lounging in her chair, her legs crossed, one wrist draped over a chair arm, an index finger resting on her jaw. She swivels slowly toward de Maziere. Her eyes narrow a tick. "Would that be a problem?" A slight edge to her voice. Good; she's got the attitude down. I hope she can carry it for the next few hours.

"No, no, not at all." De Maziere puts up her hands: *don't shoot me*. She's probably Julie's age, lacquered hair, thin, in a khaki Balmain double-breasted tuxedo jacket over a black knee-length flare skirt. "It's that… it's unusual, you see. We're not the British Museum or the V&A or the Tate. We're a regional museum, and nearly all our members and patrons live near the Solent. I believe—correct me if I'm wrong, Gordon—you'd be our first American patron."

Julie lets the question lie on the ground for a few seconds. Then she swivels back to Fallbrook. "Yes, I'm American. But I'm also English. I was born here. Not *here* here"—she pushes down with one hand, like she's patting the carpet—"in Southampton. My parents took me to America when I was three…"

I've heard this story before, multiple times, so I check how it's going down with the museum wheels. Fallbrook's smiling; Anson Berkeley, the third museum wheel, leans forward with his hands folded on the table; de Maziere has an index finger propped on the end of her pointy chin. Julie's owning this. If I didn't know her, I'd buy her story.

"… I needed to start over. I've always loved it here, so I thought, why not just go home?"

"Why not, indeed?" Fallbrook says.

Now the polite first-date getting-to-know-you chatter starts. Berkeley (pronounced "Barkley"), the forty-something Director of Administration in an off-the-rack black suit, mostly sits and watches, and mostly watches Julie. I hope he's crushing on her and not seeing some hole in her story the rest of us missed.

Fallbrook leaves us "in Carolyn's capable hands" after half an hour. When Julie sits again, I notice something I didn't need to see: the hand she's keeping under the table is trembling.

Oh, shit.

De Maziere settles into the chair at the head of the table, the one Fallbrook just abandoned. "Ms. Hardwick. I believe your assistant told Miss Grant that you're interested in our support services." She sounds like it's exhausting to push the words out. "That's rather unusual. I must ask: why? What attracts you to that?"

Julie reaches for the tea service. I get there first; I can just see her spewing tea all over the table. As I hand her the cup and saucer, I realize the last thing I should be doing is feeding her more caffeine. Can a hot flash be far behind? One disaster at a time, please.

"That's right," Julie says after a long sip. Her voice is tight but steady. "There's no shortage of people who want to help sponsor the public programs or the collection. The Arts Council's certainly active in that area. But..." another sip—she's covering "...I've learned that the public face gets what it wants, but the support areas don't always get the funding they deserve. They're important. If you can't *run* your museum, you can't keep the public programs going."

De Maziere and Berkeley swap a significant glance. I can't tell whether it means *we got a live one* or *who is she kidding?* Then she swivels toward Julie. "I've asked Anson to give you an overview of our support services and our plans for them. Anson?"

It's PowerPoint. It had to be. For the next almost thirty minutes, Berkeley drags us through all the parts of his empire—facilities, collection management, conservation, HR, finance, security—and some pieces of the Operations kingdom, like staff development and retail operations, along with a review of the strategic plan for each one.

Don't get me wrong: I love museums. But I want to stab myself with my pen after fifteen minutes. Carson's eyes are like glazed donuts. Worse yet: I can tell that even with this dose of verbal Prozac, Julie's way too wired to calm down.

Berkeley doesn't finish; he just finally stops. He and de Maziere zoom in on Julie. She stares at the final slide on the flat screen mounted on the wall behind Miss Grant.

Julie swivels to face de Maziere. "You have a lot of work ahead of you. It's all very worthwhile, but I'm afraid I have to pick and choose. The projects I'm most interested in are the lab equipment upgrades and the new inventory database." Then she stops. I expect her to ask me to talk with her outside or say something about the slideshow, but she doesn't. I expect her to ask for a tour, but she doesn't.

I lean in a smidge and see a shiny bead of sweat roll from behind her ear down into her neckline. A couple others pop up on her temple. *No, not now, not yet…* I wheel on Berkeley. "Do you have cost estimates and timelines for those projects?"

His head swivels from me to Julie to de Maziere and back. "Yes… yes, we do. I can get them for you—"

"Please do." At least Julie's talking again, though it comes out harsher than I like. She dabs at her mouth with her white linen napkin, then at her nose and temples. "Ms. De Maziere—may I call you Carolyn?"

"Well… of course."

"Thank you. I'd like to see Dundas Lane." I can hear the strain in Julie's voice, but that may be because I've been with her almost non-stop for six days. She's holding the chair arm so tight, her knuckles glow. Another rogue sweat trail crawls down the back of her neck.

I tap Carson's shin and roll my eyes toward Julie. Carson nods once; she's noticed already.

More glances between de Maziere and Berkeley. "Well, of course we can arrange that." De Maziere's smile is brittle. "Perhaps next week? It takes some preparation, you understand. Visits can be so disruptive."

Oh, *hell* no. A week sitting around, waiting? I don't mind the extra money, but we're on a schedule and it gives them a chance to check out Gillian's story some more. I have no idea how sturdy it is. I don't want to find out the hard way.

Julie sits still, aimed at de Maziere. I can't see her face, but I can see the point of her jaw going pale. The red sweater's now darker under her arms. It must be torture for her to sit there and not do anything to cool off. How can she concentrate?

Carson's leaning forward, ready to sweep her out of here.

Julie's neck arches. "Perhaps I didn't make myself clear." She leans toward de Maziere. "Depending on the cost and schedule, I'm prepared to fund one of these projects *today*. I don't need a big show with a lot of people standing around, but I do need to see where my money's going." She sounds just irritated enough to sell it. "Now, I have a busy schedule next week and I'm going to London and Paris after that to visit friends. I want to settle this *today*."

Good job. Keep it up. You're doing—

There's a double rap at the door, followed by Fallbrook's head poking in. He beams. "Oh, excellent! You're all still here." He ushers in another man. "Ms. Hardwick, I thought you'd enjoy meeting one of our…" His words melt into *blah-blah-blah*.

The other guy's in his fifties. Five-six or -seven, maybe. Gelled dark hair brushed back to show off his widow's peak. Sturdy; not fat. A sharp camel-hair blazer over an open-necked olive dress shirt and black slacks.

No way. No. Fucking. Way.

"…introduce you to Arkady Tovorovsky."

Chapter 28

Julie stands carefully. The back of her dress is soaked, but she maneuvers around the chair so her back's always to me and Carson.

I can't see her face. I can't tell what she's thinking. I need to catch her before she goes for Tovorovsky's throat. Carson's already a step ahead of me.

Julie extends her right hand. "So pleased to meet you." Cool, correct. That's better than screaming. For now.

I reach her in two strides and arrange myself so I can see her face but stay out of the way. Carson's behind and to her right. Between us, we should be able to pull her off him before she chokes him to death.

Tovorovsky takes her hand and nods his roundish head over it. "The pleasure is mine." An accent, but not Boris Badenov. He holds her hand a few seconds longer than necessary while he gives her a good scan. His eyes narrow when they finally get to her face. Is that *hey there, hot mama* or *where do I know you from?*

Julie's expression is carefully neutral, but her eyes are tight. She pulls her shoulders back and stands as straight as she can. In her heels, she's an inch taller than Tovorovsky. By the way she holds her head, I can tell she wants him to notice. "May I ask which piece is yours?"

He smiles and tries to grow that extra inch. "Of course. The Sargent. *Dorotea DeVillardi.* You have seen it?"

"I did. It's lovely. Thank you for sharing her with us." Still reserved, but not cold. A sweat droplet the size of a BB creeps down the back of her neck.

I flick a glance at Carson. Her face is as blank as I've ever seen it. Her right hand's buried in her boxy purse, the one that's like a mobile storage cube. I hope she's holding a Taser and not a hand grenade.

"Of course." Tovorovsky nods once. "It is an obligation. Owners of significant art should share it with the world." His English is better than the last Russian dude I met on the job, though that's a pretty low bar.

Julie's lips flatten for a moment, then she pushes out the coolest smile I've ever seen on her. "I believe that too. You're a long way from home. What brings you here today, if I may ask?"

Fallbrook steps forward and lays his fingertips on Tovorovsky's upper sleeve. "Arkady's been a regular visitor since the show opened. He's been very generous. We're always glad to have him."

If he wasn't Russian, I'd say Tovorovsky gives Julie an aw-shucks look. "I have a home in Knightsbridge, in London. Not so far. I come to see my investment is safe. It gives me peace." He nods at Fallbrook. "I do not distrust you, Gordon, of course."

"Of course not." Fallbrook's smile looks nervous, like he's figuring out this intro may not have been his best idea.

"I don't blame you," Julie says. "I'd want to make sure she's safe if she were mine."

Tovorovsky's eyebrows bunch. "She? The portrait is alive to you?"

"Of course she is." Julie slides half a step closer to him. I follow. I'm sweating almost as much as she is. "All great art is alive, isn't it? It wants to live. It wants to be loved. Cared for. If it gets lost, it wants to go home."

Oh, no. She didn't.

Carson slides to her side in a second to whisper in her ear. Julie tilts her head down to listen, but her eyes don't break lock on Tovorovsky's. The museum wheels are like smiling mannequins.

Tovorovsky has that look yellow labs get when you hide the ball. "The portrait will not be lost again, Miss Hardwick. It goes to my home."

Julie nods to Carson, then laughs a little. "That'll be a happy ending for you then, won't it?" She thrusts out her hand. "My assistant says I need to return a call. So very nice to meet you. I hope your painting stays safe."

Tovorovsky takes her hand in both of his. He seems to have found the ball again. "I thank you for your concern. I hope we meet again... perhaps when we have more time to talk?"

Seriously? Is he asking her out?

"Who knows?" Julie flashes him an almost-genuine smile. "Fate is a funny thing."

Chapter 29

The lab's smaller than it looks on video, maybe fifty feet deep by at most twenty wide. The walls are stark white with art posters tacked up where windows used to be. Three large laminate-topped worktables take up a lot of floor space: two to the left, one close to the door on the right with a chunky white microscope hooked to a big flatscreen. The place is filled with crap, like every other workshop I've seen.

Berkeley stops us just inside the door. Julie's up front with de Maziere glued to her side; I'm in back with Carson. Berkeley clasps his hands at chin height. "Right. Well. This is our conservation laboratory." He focuses on Julie. "Mum, do you—of course you do?—know what happens here?"

"I'm aware of what a conservator does, yes." Ooh, frosty.

A pained smile cracks his face. "Of course, mum. Um, well, we do that for our own collection and for works on loan, like at the 'Stealing Beauty' exhibition." His hand movements don't always look voluntary. His puppeteer's having seizures? "We do all our own cleaning, repair, some restoration work, relining, restretching, some frame repairs. The conservators in their spare time"—a nervous laugh—"they consider that a joke, um, they shoot archival snaps of our own collection…"

Julie crosses her arms. "I'm aware of all this."

Carson splits off from the herd and starts poking around this end of the lab. I'm jealous.

"Of course, mum." Berkeley's face wrinkles, like he has to concentrate to find his next line. "Um, the conservation proposal brings in a new camera for multispectral analysis. You have that proposal, mum?"

"I do." Since meeting Tovorovsky, Julie's doubled down on Gillian's attitude. The green contacts seem to have turned into ice; there's a sharper edge to her voice. She took charge during the twenty-plus minutes we spent in the warehouse, pushing Berkeley through his spiel when he threatened to get lost in his own words. She's skating up to that line between take-charge and pushy—I hope she doesn't cross it.

After more of Berkeley's rambling, Julie clears her throat. "I'd like to see the camera now."

We shuffle to the camera stand that fills the hole where the fourth worktable should be. If I hadn't been reading up on reprographic systems, I'd never recognize the camera; it looks like some weird kind of power tool mounted on an eight-foot-tall, square column of black anodized aluminum. The five-by-four-foot repro table hits me about mid-thigh. They can shoot large-format works here—like Dorotea's portrait.

I stand next to a rolling metal cart with a Dell minitower and a big flatscreen monitor. Thin cables tie it to the camera. When Berkeley stumbles into his pitch, I press the computer's power button and hope it doesn't beep too loud. It does, but nobody seems to notice or care.

Windows 7 comes up. No login, no password. Yes!

Everybody's busy looking somewhere else. I pull my phone and start pounding in notes. Capture One CH 9 controls the Digital Transitions rCam camera with an IQ180 back. The stand is a DT RG3040. The two Kaiser Lightbox floods are hooked to the repro stand somehow. How much of this means anything to me? None. A week from now, I need to be able to run this thing.

Good luck to me.

I've just put my phone away when I hear Berkeley's voice behind me. "You're interested in these systems, Mr. Simon?"

I almost jump but manage not to. Instead, I turn around and smile. "Just admiring the hardware. Nice setup you've got here. This all moves to collections management when the new camera comes in?" Not that I care. We'll be long gone by then. Still, I have to play the part.

"Oh, yes, yes it will. Wonderful increase in their capability. If you would…?" He waves toward the worktable with the microscope. Then he turns to Julie and de Maziere. "Carolyn, mum, please, over here? I have samples from the new system?"

Julie fiddles with her earring. That's the circle-the-wagons signal. I nod once. She aims a cool almost-smile at Berkeley. "Mr. Berkeley, I need a moment with Mr. Simon and Ms. Carson."

"Of course, of course, yes. I'll be right, um, here. Yes."

Carson and I converge on Julie in the middle of the room. De Maziere's at her side and hasn't budged. After a moment, Julie sighs and turns on her. "Privately."

De Maziere's brittle smile slinks out. "Of course. I misunderstood. Sorry." She bows out.

We form a tight knot as far from the two museum weenies as we can be and not be on top of Aurora Tunstall, the conservator who's been totally ignoring us at the far worktable. Julie opens the lab proposal so it looks like we're talking business. She whispers, "How much longer do we need to be here?"

"I've got what I need off the camera." Something finally occurs to me. "Can you read that without your glasses?"

"Only if I squint and concentrate really hard. I've got a headache now."

"Talk to Carson. She's got the pharmacy."

Carson's way ahead of me. She pulls a small, translucent white box from her purse and flips it open. Its six compartments hold different sizes, shapes, or colors of pills. She drops one into Julie's outstretched hand.

Julie eyes the tiny orange pill. "Will this put me to sleep?"

"If you're a lightweight." Carson stashes the box, produces a bottle of water and hands it to Julie. Someday I'll find out everything that's in that purse, and it'll scare me.

Julie gulps down some water, then gives back the bottle. "Thank you. Do you need anything else here, Ms. Carson?"

"Fob's a problem."

Berkeley let us into the lab using a gray plastic doover at the end of a scarlet Mainwaring lanyard—a key fob. "That fob's a big problem," I say. "Can you break the system?"

Carson shrugs. "It's passive. That pad out there interrogates it. Have to get a fob, grab the frequency and code, then burn a new RFID. It's doable, but good fucking luck."

Why isn't it ever easy?

Julie's hand goes to pinch the bridge of her nose. She must remember that her entire face is covered with foundation and powder and fixer; her hand detours to her throat. It's about the only place on her head that she can touch safely. "Do we need to be here to work that out?"

"Still looking for an alarm panel, motion detectors, cameras." Carson nods toward the far end of the room. "Need to look down there if someone keeps the girlie busy." She aims a your-turn look at me.

"All right. Julie, keep those two out of our way." I angle my head toward the museum weenies. "Talk to them about money and timing. How long before the project's up and running? Are operations costs budgeted? That kind of thing."

"Okay." She squeezes her eyes closed. "This is really, really hard. I had no idea."

"It is. I know." I touch the back of her wrist so nobody else can see. "You can do it."

"You're doing great," Carson says. "Keep at it. They're scared of you."

Huh? Carson said that?

Julie blinks open her eyes and smiles at Carson. "Thanks. Really." She swallows a deep breath and arranges her head and shoulders. "Here I go."

We watch her parade across the room. I say, "Never figured you'd be in her corner."

Carson shrugs. "I'm not. Wish she'd go away. She won't, so we need her to win."

True enough.

I work my way down the edge of the room, checking out what's tacked or taped to the wall—art postcards, drawings, pictures cut from magazines, a selfie of two youngish women in front of the London Eye. The pictures turn into a dense collage on the wall closest to Aurora's table, including elements from graphic novels, book covers, and high-concept business cards.

I watch her work for a while. She's maybe in her late twenties, nice-looking but nothing spectacular, with thin strawberry-blond eyebrows. Her white lab coat and white nylon bonnet bleach out her pale skin. I've never liked nose studs, but at least hers matches the electric blue lock of hair that's escaped her bonnet.

She's cleaning an unframed canvas on a metal easel. Art swabs, a glass bowl of what smells like acetone. When she reaches out to dab at the surface, I catch the swirl of a tattoo on the inside of her wrist between her coat cuff and blue nitrile glove. I hate tattoos.

The canvas is Impressionist: a small steamboat churning down a mirror-like river, trees on either side, fluffy clouds ahead. The uncleaned part looks like someone chain-smoked next to it for a century. I can just make out a signature in the lower-right corner.

"Maximilien Luce?"

Aurora glances up at me, then plucks an earbud out of her left ear. "Sorry?"

I point at the canvas. "Maximilien Luce?"

"Uh-huh." She drops a used swab into the plastic bag next to her, then reloads.

"What happened to it? It shouldn't be this dirty. It's not old enough."

"Attic."

All right. This one's a chatterbox. I notice Carson drifting down the opposite wall. "You've been at this, what, four-five days?"

"Three."

Works fast, too. "Is it a donation?"

"Uh-huh."

"It must be hard, being the only conservator here now." Berkeley said Ms. Whitehaven retired four months ago.

"Hm."

"I've cleaned my share of canvases. It's hard, boring work." I lean closer to the Luce. "You're doing great. Really thorough."

"Ta."

"I'm Matt, by the way. You're…?"

Aurora glances up at me. Her eyes are almost turquoise. "Busy." She plugs in her earbud.

Okay, then. Either I'm way off my game, or I've reached the age where I'm invisible to millennial women. Either way, there's some ego repair in my near future.

Carson's reached the corner nearest Aurora's workstation. She took off her suit coat somewhere along the way and has it slung over her shoulder. Then I notice that Aurora's noticed. She tilts her head to see around the canvas… and check out Carson's butt.

Seriously?

I don't feel so old and washed-up now.

Carson strolls along the wall toward me. She's not scanning the ceiling, so she must've seen what she needed to. When she draws even with the canvas, she glances at it, then at Aurora.

Both of Aurora's earbuds come out. "Hullo."

"Hi."

"Who're *you?*" It sounds like, *where have you been all my life?*

"Ms. Hardwick's assistant." And Carson's oblivious.

"Oh. You're with this lot." She waves at me, then holds her hand out to Carson. "I'm Aurora. What's your name?"

Carson flicks a glance at me. Is she getting a clue? "Carson." She hesitates, then shakes Aurora's hand.

My job is done here. By now I've drifted back a couple paces behind Aurora, not that she notices. Carson frowns at me. I tap my chest, then thumb over my shoulder at Julie and the museum weenies. When I start to turn, Carson takes a step after me. I hold up my hand for *stop,* point to Aurora, then make a quacking duck beak with my fingers.

Julie waves me over to the microscope worktable. While we go over the project details with Berkeley and de Maziere, I occasionally glance toward Carson. She still looks a little dubious, but Aurora's into it, leaning forward, lots of hand gestures. She pulls off her bonnet. The blue streak winds through the brassy blond hair piled on top of her head. I feel a little guilty, but not a whole lot. Carson's a grown-up. She can cope.

"So, £18,400?" Julie says. "We should round it up to twenty thousand just in case something's more expensive."

Berkeley and de Maziere exchange a we-just-hit-the-lotto look. De Maziere drawls, "That would be lovely if that's what you'd like. We should chat about naming rights, of course."

Julie sniffs. "Really, I'm not doing this for that. My name's on enough walls already. If you must, a little plate on the camera stand is fine." She smiles up at me. "What do you think?"

"Sounds great. You can get this project going, move this camera out to collections. They can start shooting the art right away even without the database. When that comes in, they're ahead of the curve." That may actually make sense. I hope.

De Maziere's smile starts taking over her face. "My thoughts exactly."

Does she ever disagree with a prospect? Naaaah.

Julie calls out, "Carson, dear," and waves her to us. It takes Carson a few moments to get away from Aurora. She works with Berkeley to twiddle around $30,000 from the Barbados account Cousin Ron set up for Julie to the museum's oh-so-boring HSBC account. De Maziere grins like a new dad.

While Julie swaps compliments with the museum people, Carson grabs my lapel. "You didn't tell me," she hisses.

"About Aurora? How long did it take you to figure it out?"

"Not the point." She pushes me away. "She asked me out."

"Yeah? What'd you tell her?"

Julie slides in between us. "You two look awfully serious."

"Miss Tunstall's got a thing for Carson."

"Really?" Julie giggles, then presses her fingertips to her lips. "Sorry. Did you find a door thingie?"

Carson looks disgusted. "No such luck."

"Is she our only way to get one?"

"Berkeley got his from the security office." Carson twitches her chin in that direction. "Hangs on the wall next to the door."

I ask, "Can we get to it?"

"Not with guards there."

Julie purses her lips. "If you use the girl's door thingie, will she get in trouble?"

Carson glances back over her shoulder at Aurora. "If they look, yeah."

"I won't allow that." Julie's voice is sharp. "We don't hurt innocent people. Do we need to stay here so you can work out what to do?"

Carson and I stare at each other for a moment. I think we're both hoping the other one has an answer. She finally says, "No."

"Okay. I'll tell them we're ready to go." Julie bustles off to corner de Maziere.

Carson blows out a long exhale. "We're fucked."

I turn my back on Julie and lean in to Carson. "Get Aurora's digits, just in case."

"She asked me out!"

"I got that part. Tell her you have to look at Gillian's schedule. You'll get back to her."

"You heard the Princess. Girl's off limits."

"I heard. I don't like it either. But we don't have a lot of choices, and we're running out of time. We've gotta get into this place one way or another."

Chapter 30

Julie's hyped by the time we leave the museum and get in the Jag. It's like that I-just-won-the-Super-Bowl-and-now-I'm-going-to-Disneyland! mood, where the sun is brighter and the air is cleaner and she just can't stop being all *wow* about the morning. Which is kinda cute, but tiring.

On the other hand, the set of Carson's jaw tells me she's worried about something. When she worries, so do I.

My adrenaline and Carson's is mostly gone by the time we trudge into our hotel. When we step into the elevator, Julie says, "I want to celebrate. Will you come with me?"

"Sure." I don't know what her definition of *celebrate* is, but it probably requires adult supervision.

"Ms. Carson? Will you come too?"

Carson frowns at the elevator door.

"Get changed," I tell Julie. "I'll be down in a few."

I catch up to Carson as she's opening her door and tailgate inside. She throws her coat on the bed and stalks to the window. Her face's almost as cloudy as the sky. "Goddamnit."

"Anything in particular?"

"Tovorovsky got a good look at her. And she had to shoot her mouth off."

"Yeah, that wasn't so great. I can't tell if he was checking her out or trying to figure out where he'd seen her before. She said she never testified in court and never went on TV, so—"

"Forgot a question. She ever go to the courthouse with Bowen after he sued? Lawyer's office? His house?"

I roll that around to see where Carson's coming from. Then it hits me. "You think Tovorovsky's been watching Bowen?"

"Since they served him, yeah. He's got the people."

"Aw, shit." I pace a couple circles, trying to figure out how worried I should be. "Different name, different hair, different eyes. She's out of context. There's no reason he should make that connection." But…

"Hope you're right. Saw us, too."

If I didn't already have heartburn, I'd get it now. "Did they follow us?"

She shakes her head. "I checked. Need to scan the car for a tracker."

"You can do that?"

She gives me The Look. Of course, she can do that.

The farther we get from this topic, the better I'll feel. "What about the lab? See anything there that's a problem?"

Carson grunts into the desk chair. "Camera at the front door, but we knew that. No alarms, no cameras in the hallway or the lab. No sensors I could see. When we're in, we're *in*."

"If we've got a fob."

"Yeah. Front door has a keypad and a sensor pad. Fob gets you through that and the lab."

"If we've got one."

She glares at me. "Heard you the first time." She's sounding a bit cranky.

I perch on the foot of her bed. She doesn't react, so I stay there this time. "Can we get the fob from the security office?"

She shrugs. "Thinking about it. Got a good look at the fob. Berkeley left it on the table. Easy for Olivia to order one."

"A swap?"

"Maybe. Gotta think about it more. It's risky."

Like I didn't already know that. "Just in case…did you get Aurora's number?"

"You trying to hook me up with her?" Full-up cranky. "'Cause I don't play on that team."

I put up my hands. "I know, I know. It's just in case. Did you?"

Carson lurches out of her chair, back to the window. Her neck and ears are turning red. "Yeah. Got it. Happy?"

"Overjoyed. Text her after lunch. Tell her Gillian wants you in Southampton today. You'll get in touch when you can see her. Pretend she's a dude. Okay?"

"Fine. You ever do this? Date a guy for your gallery or whatever?"

"Not really. We had a couple clients who were out. Gar threw me at them once or twice. All I had to do was be nice to them and laugh at their jokes." I step up to her so I can look into her eyes.

"Which is all you have to do."

She snorts. "Never been a honey trap before."

Chapter 31

Our white Mercedes taxi rolls past the five- and six-story monuments to Hapsburg excess that line Vienna's Ringstrasse. Neoclassical, neo-Renaissance, and neo-Baroque showpieces loom over the broad, tree-lined street.

Julie nudges me with her elbow. She's reading from her guidebook. "One of the reasons Franz Joseph wanted the Ring Road this wide was so revolutionaries couldn't build barricades the way they did in 1848."

She's been doing this since we left Heathrow—reading factoids from the guidebook, reviewing the list of places she wants to visit, making notes on her laptop. It's fun to see her so excited. Julie's finally going to see her grandparents' and great-grandparents' home.

It's catching, too. Sure, after spending Wednesday afternoon and all of Thursday learning about the lab's camera and its software, I'd be excited about dental work. But I'm stoked about seeing *Jugendstil* (Art Nouveau everywhere else), the Wiener Werkstätte, and the Secession (the roots of modern architecture). It's nice to be able to share it with another newbie.

My first clue that this may not be a normal trip comes when we finally arrive at 25hours, a modernist boutique hotel across Museumstrasse from the huge Second Empire Palace of Justice. Big orange letters over the hotel's main entrance say in English, "We are all mad here." The lobby is design chaos, an explosion of funky mismatched furniture, bright colors, funhouse mirrors, and oddball tabletop sculptures. My queen room has a full-wall mural of vaguely sinister circus performers. A throw pillow's embroidered with *Let's spend the night together*. A Marriott, this ain't.

We take a quick march through the history of Jewish Vienna that afternoon. It's easy to think the Nazis invented antisemitism, but Austrian Jews first had to wear yellow badges in the sixteenth century. Still, they survived somehow and became Vienna's cultured bourgeoisie. Julie reads me a bunch of statistics, but one sticks with me: in 1934 there were over 176,000 Jews in Vienna. In 1945, there were a thousand. The rest escaped or died.

We make a pilgrimage from the Stadttempel (a Biedermeier-era synagogue that looks like nothing outside and like a marble wedding cake inside) through the old Textile Quarter to the Jewish Museum and Holocaust Memorial.

Julie amazes me with her drive and energy. She's organized and focused and totally in charge. She marches into the bus and tram systems fearlessly. She doesn't speak a word of German, but a smile and a touch gets her anything she wants. It's actually pretty hot. I keep wondering, *who is this woman? Why isn't she like this in Portsmouth? Is this Gillian... or the real Julie?*

By the end of the afternoon, we're both ready to do something decadent.

That would be Café Central, a 130-year-old marble shrine to caffeine and sugar. Waiters in tuxedos, *lieder* playing on the grand piano, stenciled cream walls, vaulted ceilings, swagged curtains on the twenty-foot-tall arched windows. This is what Starbucks wants to be. It's beautiful. And it smells fantastic.

This is where we're supposed to meet Julie's Austrian lawyer. Our reservation lets us walk right past the growing line of people waiting for a table and slip into a booth against the east wall. The upholstery matches the brick-red marble tabletop.

"Let's go look at the sweets," Julie says. We race to the cases in the south end of the room and drool on the glass. The pastry selection should be a UNESCO World Heritage site. She asks, "Dessert before dinner?"

"How about dessert *instead* of dinner?"

She grins. She's got a great smile.

We get our order numbers from the grim-looking woman behind the counter and get back to our table in time for our drinks to arrive. The waiter also brings our pastries: chocolate and chocolate iced in chocolate for me; chocolate and raspberry iced in chocolate for her. This is what heaven's cafeteria serves.

"Here's a fun fact." Julie's still reading from her guidebook. "Hitler, Lenin, Trotsky, Freud, and Tito were all regulars here in

1913." She looks up with a smile. "I'd pay to see them all at the same table."

We're both about to lapse into sugar overdose when the seater brings a guy to our table. He's maybe forty, shaggy sandy-brown hair, and a short, wispy beard and moustache. His tweed jacket is about the same color as my cake. He peers at me, then Julie, then says, "Excuse me. You are Julie Arnlund?"

She breaks out her sunniest smile. "Stefan?"

There's some how-good-to-meet-you-finallys and hugging and so on that doesn't involve me but distracts me from trying to stop my heart with chocolate. It's too bad she's back in her Julie clothes (khakis and a moss-green sweater) instead of one of Gillian's outfits. That would've really given the lawyer something to coo over.

Julie finally turns him my way. "Stefan, this is my friend Matt Simon. He's helping me with Oma's portrait. Matt, Stefan Geisman."

We shake. There's no tie: an Austrian thing or an after-work thing? "*Grüss Gott*, Herr Simon. I am glad Julie has someone else to look after her." His English is fast and his accent ices it without smothering it.

The waiter materializes the moment Geisman sits opposite Julie. He orders, then drops his beat-up brown leather messenger bag in his lap and hauls out a medium-thick manila file folder. "You should find some exciting things in these." He passes it across the table to her.

She pounces on the papers. "What is it? What'd you find?"

Geisman holds up his hands. "Julie, if you will allow me, please. I need my drink. Three hours I was on the telephone before I come here." He turns to me. "What is your role in this affair?"

I've been practicing a non-answer for the past couple hours. "Mr. Bowen engaged my firm to come up with new ideas for securing the canvas."

"I see. Do you have any?"

"Nothing we can discuss right now."

He nods. "Of course. Well, if I can be of any assistance, please, contact me." He pulls a silver case from his inside coat pocket, peels off a business card and sets it carefully next to my coffee. There's a geometric black Wiener Werkstätte design on the case's cover. I want it.

"Well, there *is* something. We need more information about how and when the Sargent got from Vienna to Russia."

He nods again. "Then it is very good that you are here today. That is exactly what I want to tell Julie."

Now he's got my attention.

The waiter drops off a glass mug half-full of brown and half-full of whipped cream, topped with a cherry. Julie's eyes drink it all in one gulp. "What's that?"

"This is a *pharisäer*." He carves off some whipped cream with a spoon and downs it. "It is what you might call a double espresso with a bit of rum, and the cream you see. It is perfect for when you are on the telephone for three hours."

Now *that's* a drink we could sell at Starbucks.

We wait until Geisman digs out enough whipped cream to get to his coffee. Then Julie holds up a fistful of paper. "This is all in German. You know I can't read this."

Geisman holds up a hand while he wipes his mouth on a napkin. "Yes, I must apologize. I have had these for two weeks only. I have not yet had the time to translate. If you wish, I can—"

"No, that's okay, I'll have it done." She drops the papers on the stack and peers at him over the top of her readers. "What did you find? What's so exciting?"

"Yes, of course." Geisman leans his forearms against the table edge and presses his palms together. "One of my cases involves a Hungarian family. The grandparents were deported to Auschwitz and murdered when the Wehrmacht occupied Budapest in 1944. Their artworks somehow came to be in Salzburg. The Americans found them in 1945 and gave them to the Austrian government once the State Treaty came into force."

Déjà vu stabs me in the shin. This is too close to Ida Rothenberg's story: the looted painting ending up in the wrong hands in the wrong country. For her, that was a little museum in Prague. Then it got stolen. That damn thing ruined every life it ever touched—including mine.

"None of this is important except to say it requires research involving Salzburg." He pats the file with the spread fingertips of his right hand. "My researcher found these in the *Staatsarchiv*." He turns toward me. "Herr Simon, you know of Otto Scheunebrunner, yes?"

"Yeah. He's the dealer who got the Meckelsohn collection from the VVSt."

"Yes, very good." He turns back to Julie, flips over the stack's first few pages, then taps the new top page. "This is a report about Wolf Kinigader. He also was an art dealer tolerated by the National Socialists, and he also sold or traded artworks taken from Jewish families. We knew *of* him but knew very little *about* him until my researcher found this in the Archive misfiled." He flips some more pages until he reaches a list. "Look at the yellow, please."

Julie squints at the list through her readers. As faint as the printing is, it looks like a sixtieth-generation copy. She gasps. "'Italienischen Mädchen,' J. Sargent. Oma's portrait." Her eyes get big. "What *is* this?"

He drains the rest of his coffee. "That is a list of one hundred thirty-four paintings that Herr Scheunebrunner sold to Herr Kinigader on 21st January of 1945."

Day-om. I ask, "This Kinigader—did he work out of Vienna?"

"Yes, until the end of the war nearly."

"Wait, I recognize these." Julie holds up another page. "Aren't these more of their paintings?"

"Yes, they are so. We have to assume that Herr Scheunebrunner sold or traded the rest between May of 1943 and then."

I take the page from Julie. There's an Auchentaller (a Secession portrait and landscape artist), a Schiele (a German Expressionist Ralph Steadman filtered through Robert Mapplethorpe) and an artist (Bolesław Biegas) I have to look up (soft-core vampire porn?). "Dorotea had adventurous tastes. I'm surprised these didn't go straight into a bonfire."

Julie smiles. "I know, right? You should see some of the others."

The pianist starts playing something dramatic and Germanic. I don't know what it is—my memory's visual, not aural—but it's a good soundtrack for talking about dead people.

I give Julie her paper back and turn to Geisman. "I've been wondering. Scheunebrunner held onto these way longer than should've been good for him. When he figured out he couldn't sell them, why didn't he just ditch them?"

Geisman nods and flags down a waiter. "Julie, would you like to try a *pharisäer*? It may help you with the rest of the story."

Her eyebrows jump. "I'd love to."

"Herr Simon?"

"No, thanks. I'll take another *grosser brauner*." Unfiltered coffee steamed like espresso.

"Of course." He orders in German, then turns to me when the waiter disappears. "Herr Scheunebrunner was not the barbarian you may think. He did have affection for the new art. He thought he was saving it from the real barbarians. In a way, he was. When he traded it with the Swiss or Swedes for more… acceptable, should I say? Yes. More *acceptable* art that he could sell to the National Socialists or place in the *Führermuseum*. When he did this, the newer art went to a safer place. This is why he held these paintings for, as you say, longer than was good for him."

Which all sounds reasonable until you connect the artworks to the people they were stolen from. It's not so noble then. But, like I said, if I was alive back then, I might've done what Scheunebrunner and Kinigader did. I'm in no position to get all moral on them.

Julie says, "You said 'Salzburg.' Did Oma's portrait go there?"

"A very good question. His last written inventory is from February of 1945. It lists the Meckelsohn artworks." He turns more papers over. "Herr Kinigader applied to the Salzburg government for a petrol ration for two lorries on 2nd April of 1945. This is the day the Soviets began their attack on Vienna. He must have left Vienna in late March and drove on roads that would be full of the Reich's rubbish. It is remarkable he arrived in Salzburg alive and with his property."

I say, "The trucks were hauling his art inventory?"

"That is less certain. If so, how does the DeVillardi portrait go to the Soviet Union? Salzburg was in the American occupation zone. If not, then what is in the lorries? Yes, it could be that they are valuable in themselves. A clever man would find ways to profit from two large lorries and the petrol to drive them. Was Herr Kinigader clever enough?" Geisman shrugs.

The waiter returns with our drinks and clears our empties. Julie starts excavating her tower of whipped cream. While the waiter's fussing, I take a quick scan of the café. It's full, now, mostly with tired-looking tourists. The noise level hasn't gone up as much as I expected, considering it's all hard surfaces in here. Maybe you don't raise your voice in the coffee temple.

The waiter leaves. I say, "There's another option—Kinigader unloaded the portrait before he blew town. The Russians got it from the new owner."

Geisman nods as he stirs his coffee, which looks like mine. "That is of course possible. However, in those final few weeks, there must have been many people selling art and very few buying it. They would need money for their passage to someplace far away, or at least to the American or British sectors. But yes, that could be the answer. We have no evidence."

Julie takes her first sip and comes away wearing bliss all over her face. "Ooh, that's lovely. Stefan, what happened to Kinigader?"

He turns more pages. "He stayed. Here you see his registration with the occupation authority in June. This copy was sent to the Austrian police in November—that is the mark you see here. Salzburg was a very… *interesting* place after the war. The Allies bombed nearly half the buildings in the city. However, compared to German cities, it was not so ruined. German and Austrian refugees all came there. There were eight displaced persons camps in the city. It was also the seat of the American occupation authority in Austria. That drew many kinds of people, not all of them good people."

Geisman spends some quality time with his coffee. "All we know is that Herr Kinigader did not live in any of the displaced persons camps. He did not have official contact with what very little there was of the new Austrian government. We have requested already access to the U.S. Army's records in your National Archives to see if he had any dealings with the Americans. However." He flips to the file's last page and taps it. "Here is the city police report of one Wolf Kinigader, found dead by a knife wound on the Lagerhausstrasse on 19th January of 1946. No arrest was accomplished. It was an industrial area, heavily bombed by the Allies. We can only imagine why he was there."

So much for going to talk to a hundred-year-old dude about where he put the paintings.

Julie asks, "What happened to his trucks?"

"The request for a petrol ration is the first, last, and only reference we have to his lorries."

That would've been too easy, anyway. "There's salt mines around Salzburg, right?"

He smiles. "Yes, of course. The name means 'Salt City.'" He waves his mug my way. "You are thinking that he put his artworks in a salt mine, yes?"

"He wouldn't be the first one. Didn't Cornelius Gurlitt have some of his stash there?"

"In a house, not a mine. But yes, he did, in Bad Aussee. The police found it last year. You may be interested to know that it is the same place where your famous Monuments Men found six thousand artworks in May of 1945."

Julie taps the stack of papers. "Any of the ones on these lists?"

"No, sadly not."

Figures. I ask, "Let me ask my earlier question another way: how *could* the portrait end up in Russia?"

Geisman not-quite frowns. "You are asking me to speculate."

"I'm asking you to make an educated guess. Or maybe come up with a theory, based on your experience."

He studies the bottom of his empty cup. "There is so little information…" He pokes at the handle a few times. "Perhaps… the portrait was stolen in Vienna before Herr Kinigader left. Perhaps he sold it in Salzburg, and it went east with its new owner." He throws up his hands. "I really cannot say."

I'd already figured out those two stories. Thanks for not much.

Geisman rebuckles his messenger bag. "Julie, I believe by now you know that what we do is a series of small steps that seem to mean nothing until they mean everything. We will research this problem and find what we can." He drains the last of his coffee. "Now is not the time to stop. I hope for your sake that this nothing can also become something."

Chapter 32

The DO & CO restaurant is on the sixth floor of the hotel with the same name. It's white ceilings, black columns, wood-plank flooring, white furnishings, and an entire wall of glass overlooking Stephansplatz in the center of the *Innere Stadt*. No wonder Julie reminded me to dress up.

Julie walks ahead of me, following the seater. I was expecting one of Gillian's outfits, but instead she's chosen the little black dress I saw hanging in her armoire. The velvet sheath hugs every one of her curves from her collarbones to her knees. Mid-heeled black pumps give her hips a roll I don't mind following. She's wrapped a silk pashmina she bought in Southampton around her shoulders; it looks like a tropical lagoon. When she stepped out of her room, I said "wow," and meant every word.

When we pass the cylindrical glass sushi kitchen, Julie stops hard. "Oh, my God," she gasps. "It's like the world's biggest jewelry box."

"It" is the enormous St. Stephen's Cathedral—the *Stephansdom*—right across the plaza, floodlit against the early evening sky. With all its Gothic ornament and Romanesque massing, it does look like something carved on a bench by a master craftsman instead of built out of stone. The roof's spectacular: a mosaic of tens of thousands of glazed ceramic tiles, tracing blue, green, yellow, and white zigzags and diamond shapes from ridge to eaves.

The seater shows us to a rectangular four-top just inside of the window tables. Julie takes the cathedral view while I get a Second Empire office building on the plaza's other end. She slides off the pashmina, revealing her dress' cold-shoulder cutouts. Whatever beef she has with her biceps, there's nothing at all wrong with her shoulders. She leans toward me and whispers, "Do you see these couples?"

There's a lot of older man/expensive suit-young woman/barely-there dress combinations around us. I overheard almost as much Russian as German on the way to our table. Clichés have to come from somewhere.

We finally get to order. A wine steward brings out the €76 bottle of Riesling I asked for without knowing what we'd get. Luckily, it doesn't suck. Julie swirls the wine in her glass so it catches the candlelight. "You know, I'd never come to a place like this on my own."

"Why not?"

"Well, for one thing, I can't afford it. But these people, that menu… I feel like a little girl playing dress-up. This isn't part of my life; it never has been. I just don't belong here."

The imposter syndrome. I get that, too. "My mom was a teacher and my dad was a contractor. A big night out was Outback or Black Angus. You know what I've learned? It's all money and attitude. These people aren't any better than you. A lot of them aren't as good. We could dress you up as Gillian and march you in here with her attitude and as far as any of this crowd would know, you'd be one of them."

"You make it sound so easy." She sets an elbow on the gray tablecloth and props her chin on her fist. "Was anything Stefan told us helpful?"

"It could be. Kinigader's trucks are just the kind of thing I can use to cover a provenance change. We need to know more about him and what he did in Salzburg." I cross my arms on the table and lean in. "You know, I really don't want this to be about work. All I want is to have a good dinner with a nice woman and be myself for once. Just a nice evening together. Can we do that?"

Julie's eyebrows arch. "So this is a date?"

"If you'd like that."

She puts on a mischievous smile. "Thought you'd never ask."

We find other things to talk about through our shared appetizer and into our entrees. I can feel our guards slowly come down. I can't help but notice how the candles make her face glow and put little flickering spots of light in her eyes.

After we finish our entrees (lobster for her, dover sole *meunière* for me, beautifully presented on heavy white crockery), we collapse into our white wraparound armchairs and sigh in unison. She drapes her pashmina over her shoulders. I ask, "Dessert?"

Julie cocks an eyebrow. "We already had dessert."

"That was hours ago. The chocolate mousse is calling our names."

"Are you crazy? I'll pop right out of this dress."

"Promise?"

She gives me a smile I can't quite read. "Can we just walk around outside? Look at the lights?"

So we walk around outside and look at the lights, and the people, and the buildings. The temperature's down around fifty with a light breeze. Julie doesn't seem to notice—this is probably summer weather in the Great White North—but I'm glad I'm wearing my blue Canali single-breasted. Her hand is soft and radiating heat when she wraps it around mine. I've forgotten how nice it is to hold hands.

"I'd like to ask you something," Julie says. We're circling St. Peter's, a Catholic church that's basically all dome. "Please be honest with me."

Nothing good starts this way. "O-*kay*."

"Are you married?"

I hesitate. I don't really want to get into this, but... "Not anymore. Why?"

"I was thinking about London. You seemed awfully comfortable with hair salons and women's clothing." She waits for a horse-drawn carriage to clop past. "What was she like?"

Even if I tell the story straight, I'll sound like one of those guys who's pathological about his ex. I'm not; when I think about Janine, I get sad, not mad.

"I met her in college. She was the smartest person in class."

Julie shoots me a skeptical look. "Really? You were attracted to her brain?"

"Well... she was pretty, too. Had a nice pair of legs. Pretty *and* smart makes you pay attention. She was fun. Fearless. She'd say anything, do anything, because she could."

We walk a few yards. "What happened?"

What didn't? "She was severely bipolar. She'd controlled it with meds for years. I didn't find out until we were living together when we were seniors. By then, I was too far gone. We got married right after graduation. Then she decided she hated her meds and stopped taking them."

Julie's mouth turns down. "Oh, no."

"Oh, yeah. The next eleven years were like a bad roller-coaster ride. I'd get new scrips for her and she'd try them for a few weeks, then give up on them. She left with some dude the day after I got arrested. I haven't heard from her since." I have to stop a moment to let the catch out of my voice. "I don't even know if she's still alive."

Julie squeezes my arm. "I'm so sorry. That must've been awful for you."

"Yeah." We walk quietly down Kohlmarkt for a while. The storefronts are still lit, and the sidewalks reflect a gentle warm wash from the windows. "What about your ex?"

"Scott?" She sighs. "Fair's fair, I guess. I was a brand-new teacher in middle school. We were having Career Day. I was writing his name on the chalkboard—that should tell you how long ago this was—and I turned around and saw this beautiful man in a blue fireman's uniform. I think I actually said, 'Will you rescue me?'"

I have to chuckle. "Did he?"

"For a while, I guess." She looks out into the night. "We got married after a few months. Anthony came along a couple years later." She lets a few steps go by. "It took me almost twenty years to leave that man. I couldn't take smelling another woman on him anymore. I left a lot behind. But it was *so* worth it."

Like Gillian. "Got anyone back home?"

"Just a cat with a lot of opinions."

"So, Connecticut men are idiots?"

She sputters like she just choked on a drink. "I'm not sure about that. The single men my age are chasing girls half my age. The ones who aren't… well, it doesn't take long to figure out why."

I hear the edge of disappointment gone hard in her voice. It makes me realize that I don't want to be the next guy who lets her down. "Can we stop telling depressing stories now?"

"Yes, please." Julie hugs my arm. I could get used to that. "That 'Connecticut men are idiots' line? Thank you for that."

We pass into Michaelerplatz, the Hofburg Palace's back door. Floodlights silhouette the Corinthian columns marching across the Baroque façade's first floor, the statues on the cornice, and the ornate green-and-gilt dome.

Julie shakes her head. "The man who designed this—he works in Las Vegas now?"

"Not quite. Joseph Emanuel Fischer von Erlach designed it in the early eighteenth century, but it didn't get built until 1889."

"You just happen to know that?"

"You're not the only one who can read a guidebook."

She hip-checks me. "Showoff."

I catch the note of a fragrance on the breeze. "You're wearing Gillian's perfume."

"Uh-huh. It's really the only thing I like about her."

I'm glad to hear that. "That's okay. It makes it easier to turn her off when you don't need her. I'd be worried if you decided she's the new you."

"No worries there."

We stroll through the open gate, through the well-lit rotunda, and into a large but not-so-well-lit courtyard. We pick it up a bit, but not enough to need to let go of each other.

"One good thing about being by myself?" Julie looks up at me with a brave smile. "I can pack up and go on an adventure and not have to worry about what's happening at home."

"Is that what this is? An adventure?"

"Are you kidding? Of course it is. I've never done anything like this before."

"Like walking through an imperial palace with a strange man?"

"You're not strange." She stretches up to peck my cheek. "You're part of the adventure. I'm so glad you came."

"So am I." You know what? I really am. This is the most fun I've had in ages.

We stroll through another arched passage and enter the Heldenplatz. This huge plaza and parade ground was supposed to have been more palace if the rest of it had been built. The farther we walk, the more light we see off to our left. When we clear the corner, Julie stops and gasps.

The Neue Berg stretches out in front of us, a 400-foot-wide, semi-circular, neoclassical celebration of a dying monarchy. It glows gold in the floodlights. A two-story-tall colonnade cuts a bright white stripe across the façade's center. Each course of twenty paired columns meets at the central triumphal entry, topped by a gilded eagle holding the Austrian flag. *This* is how you do a power statement.

Julie drifts a few paces away from me, clutching her pashmina tight. She's locked onto the palace. When I step behind her, she murmurs, "I don't think I'm in Kansas anymore."

"They finished it in 1913. Think they knew there'd never be another one?"

She settles back against me and pulls my arms around her waist. I wasn't planning this, but it's nice. "Could you do this if you knew your world's ending?"

No. Buildings are an expression of hope. "Can you—"

"Shhhhhhh."

We stand pressed together for an enjoyably long time. Julie eventually swivels in my arms until she's facing me, then stretches up on tiptoes to kiss me. It's a long, full, lovely kiss I feel all the way down to my heels.

I shouldn't be surprised. I am a little. Yeah, we've been heading here since we left the hotel. But Julie's not really my type, and I'm pretty sure I'm not hers. Then again, that was a real nice kiss. She feels great in my arms. And what's a type, anyway?

"How far are we from the hotel?" she whispers.

Seriously? Is she thinking what I've started thinking? "A ten-minute walk, maybe."

"So close…"

On the way, when my big brain manages to think, I try to decide why this is okay now when it wasn't in Milan. Is it because Julie's older and wiser than Gianna? Or is it simpler than that? Gianna always thought I was someone else, someone I could never be. The real me would've scared her. Julie knows what I am and accepts it. God knows why.

We neck in the elevator to make sure we haven't lost the knack. When the door opens on our floor, she says, "Do you mind if we go to my room?"

It's been four years and some since a woman asked me that.

She snaps on the bedside lights and steps out of her heels. We pick up where we left off in the elevator, except now it's more urgent. We start peeling off each other's clothes.

I'm fascinated by her skin. Its visual texture is nothing like Janine's or the other women I've been with. The freckles splashed across her shoulders and collarbones. The sunspots, a mole. Different shades and tints. Nicks, scars, a couple small, shiny pink patches that might be healed burns. A road map of her life.

Road map or not, it's still skin. My senses overload when she presses it against me. She feels… so… good. And it's been so long. "I, um… I'm really rusty at this."

"So am I." She slides her way up until her lips are brushing my earlobe. "Let's see if we still remember how."

Chapter 33

The *Cottageviertel*—Cottage Quarter—in Döbling northwest of downtown Vienna started out in the 1870s as a stab at recreating the British "garden city" model for the middle class. But (surprise!) gentrification drove up land costs. By the 1880s, the "cottages" had turned into the bourgeois mansions and proto-McMansions now lining Felix-Mottl-Strasse.

It's a nice place for a walk.

Julie insisted we ride the streetcars up here so we could see the city. Now we're strolling past the suburban villas of the *haute bourgeois* under trees still painted with golds, russets, and persimmons. All the usual turn-of-the-century styles are here: Italianate, the revivals, *Jugendstil*, Deco, even a couple examples of International Style. Lots of stone and stucco, Dutch gables (or whatever they call them here), mansard and hip roofs, and bay windows.

It's cloudy, breezy, and in the mid-forties. Even with Julie cuddling up next to me, I'm glad I wore the hip-length Barbour Bedale jacket I bought at Harrods when Julie was busy ransacking women's shoes. The waxed cotton swishes when I walk, but it's warm. Julie's very cute in a pink knit cap and matching scarf (and cheeks and nose) over her black car coat. We keep each other's hands warm.

It felt strange waking up next to someone this morning. Good strange. I think the same went for her, too—after we got out of the shower, there was a lot of mutual awkwardness as we tried to remember how to be with a lover when we're vertical. We're getting back into the swing of it, though. She's very touchy-feely, and I've been starved for physical affection for a long time. There's been maybe two or three minutes in the past hour when we haven't been touching.

"That's it." She stops and points across the street. "Over there. Number forty-two."

I can see why she sounds disappointed. It's a zero-lot-line, four-story gray stucco box with balconies stacked above a pair of prominent ground-floor bay windows. It's completely out of scale and context with the neighbors.

"This is what's supposed to be there." Julie shows me a black-and-white photo on her phone. It's a light-colored, three-story Italianate villa with a projecting central bay and a dark mansard roof. A black 1920s town car sits at the curb. Handsome in its own stodgy kind of way.

She sighs and stuffs her phone into her coat pocket. Her shoulders slump.

I wrap my arms around her waist and kiss the back of her head through the cap. "I'm sorry this isn't what you wanted."

She sniffs and leans back against me. "I know it's just a house." The air's gone out of her voice. "I wanted…"

"Something to survive?" She nods. "Maybe, go knock on the door and say, 'My grandparents used to live here, can I look around?'"

"A girl can dream, can't she?"

I kiss her cap again. She twists around and I get lips to practice on. Lips taste better than wool.

After a few moments, she grabs my hand and tows me to the next corner. She stares toward the apartment building that should be her grandparents' house.

When she doesn't say anything for a while, I ask, "What is it?"

"The last time Mom saw Oma was right here. This corner. While they were taking Oma away."

"How old was she?"

"Eight." She glances at me. "Have you met Trudi in my book yet?"

"She just showed up." Trudi was Gertrude Berrisch, a blond, blue-eyed Jewish girl from Innsbruck who went to Vienna to make her fortune. The Meckelsohns hired her as a nanny for Lea and Lothar, Dorotea's twins. Lea was Julie's mother.

"Good. She took the kids to Türkenschanzpark—just over there—every day it wasn't raining or snowing. She grew up outdoors and she thought the exercise would make them stronger."

Julie drops my hand and drifts to the curb. Her eyes are still locked on the apartments, but I get the feeling she's not seeing them anymore. "Trudi was bringing them back home when the police took

Oma." She shivers, then hugs herself. "I keep wondering what would've happened if they'd come back ten minutes earlier. I wouldn't have been born. Just ten minutes."

I think about Geisman's story as we stroll through the heavily wooded park that had been a playground for Julie's mom and uncle. By the time we start heading back to the nearest streetcar stop to go downtown, I've spooled up a couple ideas that need airing out. "I had a thought. How are property records handled here?"

"The registry's in what they call the *Grundbuch*. Every city and district has one. Why?"

"I was thinking. Kinigader maybe took a load of paintings to Salzburg, but they're still missing. That sounds like he hid them somewhere. So either he bought some property himself, or he made a deal with someone whose family still owns the place. We need to go through this *Grundbuch* for Salzburg to see if there's any property in his name or that used to be, or anything that hasn't sold since the war."

Julie frowns. "Well, the first is easy, but the second? People here don't move around like they do back home."

"I know. Still, it's somewhere to start. He might've bought something."

"I guess." She peers up at me. "Why does it matter? Oma still ended up in Russia."

"Well... a *version* of Dorotea ended up in Russia. We have to think about it that way. Maybe a copy went there, and the original's in some attic. If everything goes right, we'll have the original in a few weeks. We still have to explain how we got it."

She thinks this over as we wander past the serious pre-war mansions on Sternwartestrasse. "Let me see if I get this right," she finally says. "You're hoping to find the paintings this Kinigader hid seventy years ago, that no one's found yet, so you can put Oma in there and 'discover' her. Is that your plan?"

"Well, when you put it that way..." It sounds lame, I know, but it's something.

"Wishful thinking much?" She pulls me to a stop and plays with the flaps on my coat pockets. She starts to sing: "You may say I'm a dreamer…"

"Let's hear your better idea. I'm all ears."

"You're the one who's supposed to know how to do all this." She tweaks my nose. "I think it's cute."

I call Olivia on our way down the Operngasse downtown toward lunch and the Secession Hall (Joseph Maria Olbrich's Art Nouveau masterpiece). Her reaction to my plan is about the same as Julie's, minus the singing, but she says she'll get someone after it. "Don't expect it quickly," she warns me.

We stop in Café Museum, a clean, airy coffee house with arched white ceilings. We luck into an empty two-top in the back corner, still warm from its last occupants. I chase another idea on my phone after we order. A foot knocking on my ankle makes me look up.

"Hey, you." Julie's got her elbow on the cream marble tabletop, her chin on her fist, and a sour look on her face. "If I wanted to watch my man play with his phone, I'd have found a twenty-year-old."

Every so often, she says something that reminds me how much older she is. It doesn't bother me—pretty obviously, I don't have a problem with older women—but does it bother her? "Sorry. I had another thought. What happened to Kinigader's body? Did somebody claim it?"

"You mean, did he have someone in Salzburg?" Her face gets slightly less sour.

"Yeah. I was looking at the website for the office that runs cemeteries in Salzburg. Burial plots have to be paid for every ten years. Who paid to plant him? Is someone still paying for it? That could give us a big hint."

She thinks about this for a few moments. "I'll ask Stefan to look into that."

"If you could. That would be great."

Julie pulls the phone out of my hand. "Now push my buttons for a while."

Sunday's all about museums. So much so that we make it onto

our flight back to England with maybe ten minutes to spare. Julie falls asleep on my shoulder not too long after the plane's wheels tuck up. This gives me time to dredge up two very unhelpful thoughts. One: I'm sleeping with the client. Two: if Carson finds out, she'll kill me. *Now* I think of it...

We get back to the Hilton at around eleven that night. Carson's not in her room and she doesn't answer my text. I haven't heard from her all weekend. What's she been up to?

As I unpack, I wonder how this (that is, me and Julie) works. Was it a what-happens-in-Vienna-stays-in-Vienna thing, or does it follow us back here? Do I wait for her to come up here and look passive, or do I go to her room and look pushy? I haven't done this for so long, I have no idea what the rules are now. Are they different for Boomers like Julie than they are for Xers like me?

"She's your granddaughter," I tell Dorotea's postcard. "What should I do?" She just looks smug.

I'm just about to turn in when I hear tapping on my glass door. It's Julie. "Hi."

My dilemma's solved. "Hi. Unpacked?"

"Uh-huh. Can I come in?" She's wearing her white fleece. It's unzipped far enough to make it reasonable to wonder whether she's wearing anything under it.

"I don't know... it's pretty tight in here. We might have to stand really close together."

She gives me a sly smile. "Let's see if that works."

Chapter 34

Something's seriously wrong with Carson on Monday morning. She's humming. She's *happy.*

"You're in a good mood," I say when she lets me into her room after breakfast.

"That a problem?" Normally, that would have sharp edges on it. Not today. It's weird, but I could get used to this.

"It's rare. What makes Carson happy?"

"Not your business." She didn't say *none of your* fucking *business,* so she really is flying.

I catch her up on Vienna except for the sleeping-with-Julie parts. She asks a couple questions, but I can tell she's not all here. "Are we ready for Wednesday?" I ask.

"Mostly. Paintballs are done today. When's the forger coming?"

"This afternoon. Two-forty."

"Have a nice drive."

"Thanks a lot. How are we getting into the lab?"

"Working on it."

It's good that I trust her—otherwise, the squinchy feeling I get in my gut would be a lot worse. "Don't think too long. Sure you're okay?"

A little of the normal Carson scowls at me. She points toward the door. "Out."

Boutelle's flight is late getting to Heathrow, of course. This gives me plenty of time to puzzle over Carson's bizarre behavior this morning.

Another wave of shell-shocked international travelers starts spilling out Terminal Five's arrivals doors. You can always tell the first-class passengers—they're the ones who look fit, rested, and well-fed. Coach always looks like refugees. Replace the off-white back wall with an Aegean beach and it'd be the evening news.

"Matthew, m'lad!"

The unmade bed shambling toward me turns into Boutelle. He's lost weight (maybe down to 225) but somehow gained hair since the last time I saw him. I'm *so* glad I didn't have to sit next to him for ten hours on an airplane. "Jesus, they'll let anybody into this country."

"It's a bloody scandal!" He pulls me into a bear hug. I leave the ground at least once. Then he thrusts me out to arm's length with a paw on each of my shoulders. "Let me look at you. Fitter than ever! They didn't break you in prison, I'm—"

"Can you say that a little louder?" I manage to squirm away. "The guards didn't hear you."

"Oh, they're harmless." He grabs his roller bag's handle. It's the size of a small steamer trunk and makes mine look pristine. "Come, m'lad. I need to feel the English sunshine."

"There's no sunshine here."

I get him shoveled into the Jag and drive off before Her Majesty's Border Force changes its mind. Boutelle futzes with the radio until he finds a sports-talk show with guys arguing over soccer. At least, I think that's what it is; everybody needs subtitles. "I do appreciate you coming for me, really," he booms. "Needn't have done, you know. I'm perfectly capable of taking the train."

"Yeah, and ending up in Scotland. The fewer people who see you around, the better. Besides, this is faster."

"And which Sargent will I have the pleasure of copying?"

I pass him the Dorotea postcard. He stares at it for a good, long time, almost like he's looking at an icon. "Never thought I'd see this with my own eyes. Well done, m'lad, well done. You have it now?"

"Wednesday night."

"Of course, of course." He sighs. "His last portrait. This *is* special. I'm honored you'd have me for this, m'lad, honored. You'll not be sorry you called on this old man."

I take the postcard from him before it disappears. We squirt down the onramp to the M25 southbound and avoid getting squished by semis. "Pull that bag out from under your seat."

He does. Out comes a phone in a plastic clamshell. "A mobile?"

"Your phone while you're here. You'll carry it on you and answer it at all times—I don't care when. It's UK-only service, so don't go trying to call home with it. Got it?"

"Well… of course, yes. Though I must say, it sounds more like a lead than a mobile."

"If by 'lead' you mean 'leash,' then yeah, you're right. This is work, not play. You stay sober between now and Thursday morning. 'Sober' means no booze or drugs—"

"That's hardly necessary—"

"—of any kind. You want an aspirin, you call me first. And no hookers—"

"This is outrageous! Am I to be in prison these three days? I mean—"

"Remember what I said before? My money, my rules. Understand?"

He sulks, but he eventually grumps, "I understand. Tyrant."

Chapter 35

Fifty-seven hours until we break into the lab. Yikes.

After I stash Boutelle, I check in with Carson. Predictably, this morning's good mood fizzled out. "Olivia says, no Swiss collector."

Aw, hell. I drop into one of her armchairs. "Did she say why?"

"Only one they trust said no." She's in her desk chair, feet on the bed.

I know: *trustworthy crooked collector* sounds fishy, especially when you add "Swiss" to the description. The "anonymous Swiss collector" is such a notorious ruse for faking up provenance that there's an art-crime blog with that name. Even crooks need to play it straight with their contacts, though; nobody ever got dumped in the river for filling their end of a bargain. If we're going to enlist some shady collector to say he's been sitting on Dorotea for years, we need to know he's going to say exactly that, on cue, even when the heat gets turned up.

I say, "Well, so much for that idea." I have no clue what our fallback is right now.

"Forger here?"

"Yeah. He's at the Holiday Inn Express up the road. Now all I have to do is keep him there until Wednesday night."

"I got cuffs."

No surprise there. "No, he'll just seduce the first housekeeper through the door and get out. I gave him a burner phone. With any luck, I can use Allyson's tracker app to keep tabs on him. Are we missing anything for Wednesday? Like, how we're getting in?"

"Like I said, working on it. Tied up everything else while you and Princess were gone." She scowls at me. "What's with her? Saw her after lunch. She was *singing*."

I try to not let my *oh, great* reaction out on my face. The last thing we need is for Carson to figure out what happened in Vienna. "What was she singing?"

"Dunno, some shit. Sounded like a Disney-princess kinda song."

"How do you know what those sound like?"

"Really? Those flicks were my babysitters." She sings "A dream is a wish your heart makes" like she's one of Cinderella's magic mice, then aims two fingers at her open mouth.

I need to have a talk with Julie. "Weird. Kind of like you humming this morning."

"Was not."

"Was. You were making a humming sound that followed a tune." I hold up my best Boy Scout salute. I was never a Boy Scout.

Carson's face crinkles a little. She knows I caught her.

Tuesday afternoon. The hours refuse to go away.

I run a second time. I read more of Julie's book. I call Boutelle every few hours. I go to the Walmart-sized Marks & Spencer across the freeway and buy a black wool turtleneck for skulking and black leather gloves with knitted cuffs to go with the turtleneck. Now I can do team dressing with Carson. Still, time seems stuck.

I call Boutelle again. This time, he doesn't answer.

Allyson's tracking app shows his phone's inside his hotel. He was there at five, before my second run. It's now a bit after nine. Time for a visit.

The sky's finally clear, though there's no moon and most of the stars lose out to the city's glow. Boutelle's hotel is a less-than-ten-minute walk from the Hilton's front door. The place looks like every other Holiday Inn Express I've ever seen.

I march through the lobby like I belong there and charge up the stairs to the second floor and Boutelle's room. I rap on the door. "Sim? Are you in there?"

No answer. If he dumped his phone, I'll...

This time, I use Carson's police knock. "Sim, open up. Now."

Still no answer. I use the key card. The room's dark. I hit the switches.

No Boutelle.

I should've checked on him more often. I should've used

Carson's handcuffs. *Goddamnit, Sim, where are you?*

The phone's on the wall-mounted laminate counter next to the bed. The room looks like the day after a riot, which lets me imagine for half a second that someone kidnapped him. Then I remember what his studio looks like.

I stand in the middle of the debris, feeling the first taste of panic in my mouth. Call Carson for help? I'll never hear the end of that. What do I do?

Where could he walk to? He's not in the bar or restaurant downstairs.

He's not in the warehouse-sized gym across the parking lot. Not that he'd be working out—I doubt he ever has—but he could be scoping out the women.

He's not in the bar or restaurant at the Hilton. The spa's closed.

I race-walk the three-quarters of a mile to big-box heaven across the freeway in Hedge End (I expect the place to be full of talking rabbits). KFC, Pizza Hut, McDonald's, Burger King... Boutelle's not in any of them.

We're surrounded by suburbia on all sides. Unless he picked up some yummy mummy (a Brit term, but I get it) at Marks & Spencer, where in hell would he go?

I end up standing in the streetlights at the main traffic circle into the "retail park," wondering how it got to be almost eleven at night. At least the Thinsulate in my new gloves keeps my hands from freezing. On the downside, the rest of me *is* frozen, and it feels like I've walked about ten miles.

I've been ignoring another possibility: he got a taxi. If he did, he could be anywhere. He could be halfway to Lincoln or wherever he's from. *Good going, idiot.* That's me I'm talking to.

It's time to admit I'm powerless over this situation and that I've come to believe a power greater than myself can restore me to sanity. I start my phone's encryption app, let my thumb hover over the contact labeled "Mom" for a couple last thoughts, then push it.

After two rings, Olivia's voice says, "Good evening."

"Hi. One-Seven-Nine." I hesitate, then jump. "I have a problem. I lost my copyist."

"I see. Did he abandon you, or did you mislay him?"

"I think the first."

"I see. Is One-Two-Six there with you?"

"Um… I don't want her to know I screwed up like this." Every confession shrinks me another foot. Soon I'll be G.I. Joe-sized.

"Ah. How can I help?"

"I checked all the places in walking distance. Can you see if he called a cab?" I tell her the hotel's address and give her Boutelle's general description, all while trying to figure out what to do if she can't find anything.

Olivia's keyboard clicks in the background. "Very good. There's a limited number of cab companies in Southampton. You should return to his hotel while I ring them. It may take some time."

I start trudging back to the hotel. "Any ideas on what I should do 'til then?"

"Let me see. Is your copyist fond of nightlife? Clubs and such?"

"Ducks like water, right?"

"Hm." There's a lot of typing going on at Olivia's end. "Bedford Place is the hub of the world for uni students on Tuesday nights. It mightn't be amiss to look there whilst I deal with the cab companies."

"Okay." The Holiday Inn seems miles away. Plenty of time to feel stupid.

"I understand you're afraid of disappointing One-Two-Six, but I suggest you ask for her help. She has much more experience with this sort of thing. She'll understand."

"Thanks. You're a lifesaver." Not what I wanted to hear, but she's right. I'll take my lumps from Carson if it gets Boutelle back in his cage.

Bedford Place skirts the west edge of a several-block warren of two- and three-story commercial buildings threaded with barely-two-way streets. Every other business seems to be a club, bar, pub, or sketchy-looking takeout or café. I pity the people living in the few apartment buildings around here.

Gangs of proto-adults cruise from bar to bar. Children's music (EDM, trance) throbs out to the street. Cars thread through the drunks on roads that are already too crowded. It's late enough that the smell of barf overwhelms the smell of spilled beer. I'd say it reminds me of my UCLA days, but Westwood had stopped being this grungy by the time I got there.

I thread through a couple groups of milling pub-crawlers and manage to get next to the doorman for the Buddha Lounge, a tan box of a place attached to a three-story brick 1960s office building. The doorman's about Boutelle's size, has no hair, and wears head-to-toe black. "Looking for someone," I yell.

He holds in a laugh, but only just. "Really, mate? Here?"

"He won't look like anybody else you've seen. Late fifties"—Boutelle's not that old, he just looks it—"six-four, a hundred kilos, scrubby red beard, light-socket hair. My girlfriend's dad. Gets confused easy. Seen him?" I hold up a folded twenty-pound note to goose his memory.

The doorman rubs his jaw with the back of his hand. He may actually be thinking; I smell burning. Then he shakes his head. "Naw, mate. Nothin' like. Sorry."

What I'd expected; not what I'd hoped for. "Thanks anyway."

Same answer I got at Tokyo Bar next door, and The Social, and Popworld, and Ninety Degrees, and the Tap Room, and Seymour's. Somewhere out there, Carson's going through the same routine, only Boutelle's her boyfriend's dad. We decided to risk looking like cradle-robbers so we won't look like cops.

My phone buzzes against my hip. It's Carson. I ask, "Any luck?"

"Nope. Outa places to check. Sainsbury's, Bedford Place."

I wind my way back to where we started. Carson's leaning against a ramp railing in front of Sainsbury's Local, a grocery store too big to be a 7-Eleven and too small to be a supermarket. The Revolution Bar rumbles away next door. Other than rolling her eyes, she didn't give me too much shit when I went to her for help, for which I'm hugely grateful.

"Fucking hate college crowds" is how she says "hello" when I catch up to her. "Almost got puked on twice. You?"

"Nobody said they'd seen him."

"Yeah, bullshit." She watches a gaggle of young male humans—I can't quite call them men—stagger down the sidewalk past us, singing loudly and accidentally-on-purpose bouncing off any stray female humans within reach. "Glad I skipped college," Carson growls. "Do we need him?"

"For tomorrow?" I check the time on my phone. "I mean, tonight? He wanted to see the painting in person. What worries me is that he'll get plastered and arrested and tell the cops why he's here. Or some college girl will give him a heart attack and we won't find out for weeks. We need him alive and back home in his studio by this weekend."

It's Carson's turn to sigh. "Got another forger?"

"I can probably dig one up. It'll take time. I doubt I can find another one as good—" My phone rings. It's Olivia, finally. "Yeah?"

"Answer with your number, please."

I plug my free ear so I can hear her. "Sorry. One-Seven-Nine. Did you find him?"

"Not... exactly. He didn't ring a cab. However, I was able to persuade the night man at his hotel—"

"Persuade? How?"

"If I explain , it won't seem magic. As I began to say, I persuaded him to check his security video of the exits. A man answering your copyist's description left via a side door in the company of two other rather large men at 20:19. They did not appear to be mates."

Oh, shit. I sag against the railing. My heart drops into my knees.

Carson snaps, "What? What's happened?"

It takes a couple tries to form words. "Someone stole Boutelle."

Chapter 36

It's clear and cold—like, almost freezing—when I go running with Carson too early on Wednesday morning. She wanted to talk to me without Julie around. It's really hard to crawl out of that nice, warm bed with that nice, warm woman in it just so Carson can run me into the ground.

"No stiffs turned up last night," she says as we chug through the brick houses and townhouses of West End. "Nothing at A&E, no reported murders. Any smart ideas?"

"You mean. More than. Last night?" I can talk or breathe, not both. "Could be anybody. Maybe Smoking Man?"

On our way back to the hotel last night, we'd tried to figure out who might want to snatch Boutelle. The possibilities were endless.

"Naw. If you didn't tell the Princess"—Carson shoots me a loaded look—"it's gotta be someone who knows him."

Someone who knows him *over here*. The problem is, I know nothing about Boutelle's life before he came to L.A. ten or so years ago.

"How do we. Find him?"

"We don't. You find another forger. We do the lab tonight. Woman guard's off tomorrow and Friday. We need her there with the boyfriend."

"We go in. When there's. Two guards. Not one."

"Yeah."

"Why?"

"Duh. They're busy."

"You sure?"

"Listened at the window last night. They're *busy*."

So I was right—it's not just lunch; it's a booty call. "That's why. You were awake. At midnight. Last night."

"Yeah." She slides her knit mittens into her gray hoodie's pouch pocket. This slows her down enough that I won't die in the next few minutes. "Should watch 'em take the picture out of the museum tonight. See how they move it. Might be a better way to grab it later."

"Okay. How're we. Getting in?"

"Got it wired. One more thing—bring the Princess."

What? "Why?"

"Get her in deeper."

I stop dead and try to grab enough air to stop panting. "She's already Gillian. The face of this whole scam. That's not deep enough?"

"You think it is?" Carson's glaring at me from a couple paces away. Her fists are on her hips. "You trust her?"

The last thing I want is to risk Julie in something like this. Yes, because we're sleeping together. But also because making her go through another hoop will piss her off, for no good reason. "At this point, yeah. She's in too deep to pull out. Besides, she'll be a distraction."

"For you, maybe." She makes a sound like spitting out a sunflower seed. "Your call. Hope you're right. Nine-thirty." Carson turns and runs off. A few beats later, she charges around a corner and disappears.

We enter the Mainwaring at around ten-thirty right before a bus unloads a slug of Chinese tourists. If we can time it just right, they can cover us as I mark Dorotea.

Yeah. "Mark" Dorotea. I already feel like world's biggest asshole, and I'm not even in the gallery yet.

The elevator lets us out in the same entry lobby as before. We skip the audio guide this time. We're not even us this time. Carson's wearing her Polish flower girl disguise and a ratty mustard-colored sweater long enough to cover the seat of her jeans. She's managed to lose a couple cup sizes, too. I've borrowed one of her hoodies (which could stand a wash) and I'm wearing some faded second-hand jeans I bought from a thrift shop a couple days ago.

When we step into the exhibit, my heart starts pounding like it did when I was running with Carson this morning.

We try to keep ahead of the Chinese tourists chattering a few steps behind us. Luckily, their tour guide's keeping them in a herd. But we also have to establish a "pattern of behavior," as Carson put it, without getting too far ahead or behind or tangling with the docents.

"Can't treat Bowen's picture any different," Carson said in the car on our way here. "Gotta stop, spend a minute in front of a few pictures. Then it'll look normal. Got it?"

Yeah, sure.

Each theme has a signature piece. Gainsborough's *Ann Ford* is the one for "Class" (she's on the exhibit's poster, after all); a pretty, later Cassatt for "Motherhood"; "Leisure" features Fragonard's *The Musical Contest*; and "Work" has Paxton's *The Housemaid*. Even though we spend a minute or two with each, I can't remember a thing about them other than the names. I'm too busy trying not to watch the other visitors shuffle past, trying not to plot every inch of the Chinese group's progress, and trying not to freak every time I see a docent... which seems like every thirty seconds.

A docent veers toward us as we pretend to study the Cassatt. I didn't think my heart could go any faster or get any louder, but it does. Every step closer he gets, the more sweat seeps down my back. The slingshot in the hoodie's pouch turns broiling hot against my stomach. Did the Eye in the Sky flag us?

I lean toward Carson's ear and whisper, "See him?"

The docent's about two paces away, unlimbering his tablet, when Carson starts murmuring to me. In Russian. If Russian twentysomething girls talk like American twentysomething girls, this is what they sound like—lots of lifts at the ends of sentences and a couple words (something like *krutoy* and *vyezzhaesh*) coming up over and over. Most of her hand gestures involve the Cassatt. Is she trying to explain it to me? Hope not.

Am I supposed to answer? Hope not.

The docent's close enough for me to read his name tag: Loren. I wonder for a second what happens if he speaks Russian. Nothing good. Getting caught with the stuff in my pockets means a one-way trip to the local lockup.

He stops. He frowns.

Carson gets her second wind. Her hand gestures get broader.

Loren gives us an apologetic smile and detours around us.

I can breathe again. Just.

I wait until we reach "Work" before I ask Carson, "What were you saying back there?"

She smirks. "Dirty story from a hooker in Riga."

It takes almost an hour, going at exactly the right speed, to get to "Fashion." Two turns and we'll be at Dorotea.

One turn.

Carson says, "Ready?"

No. "Sure."

We stop in front of a portrait of a sour-looking woman in an early-eighteenth-century black dress and white headdress (a Mrs. Margaret Wilson of Bantaskine, wherever that is). A few seconds later, we're swarmed by the Chinese. They rumble past in a cloud of whispers and phone noises. We ride their coattails around the corner.

They stop at Dorotea. We're on the fringes of the mob. I can see the top of her head, nothing more. My fingers fumble for the slingshot.

I'm sorry, I tell her. *Really. It's for the best. It's so you can go home.*

The tour guide gives us a nasty look but keeps on with her spiel, like we're freeloading on her commentary or something. You think we understand Mandarin, lady?

I keep wiping my left hand on the inside of the pouch. I don't want my fingers to be too wet when I handle the paintballs. The coating makes eggshells look bulletproof.

After about three hours of talking, the tour guide waves her herd along. We wait for some strays to get done with their selfies. Then it's just us and Dorotea.

Carson nudges me around the bench we sat on the first visit. We stop about four feet away from the portrait, off to the left a bit. This puts one camera directly behind me, blocking its view of Dorotea. Carson crowds me from the left to cut off the other camera. I know I'm as sheltered as I'll ever get, but it still feels like one of those naked-in-the-stadium nightmares.

"Ready," she whispers.

I get the slingshot looped over the fingers of my right hand. With my left, I seat a translucent white paintball in the slingshot's plastic pad. Now the hard part: pull back the slingshot without crushing the paintball.

I crush the paintball.

"Shit!" I yank a paper napkin out of the pouch and wipe up the mess on my hands. *At least it's clear,* I think, not that it helps. "Sorry."

Carson's jaw has turned to steel. "On your right."

A mom and her little girl pull up next to us in matching fall sweaters. I stuff the slingshot back in my pouch and try to look like I'm having a great time. Carson starts murmuring some more Russian at me. Another dirty story? Chekhov? Pussy Riot lyrics?

The family unit moves on after an agonizing few seconds. Carson says, "Go."

Out comes the slingshot. In goes the paintball. This time, I manage to pull back the elastic. I try to aim without looking at my hands, then let go.

The paintball *snicks* against the frame's left edge. A thimbleful of shiny trickles down the dark-stained wood. There's nothing left of the shell.

"Running out of time," Carson reminds me, like I don't already know.

Last chance. I pull out another paintball, get it seated, try to remember what I did last time. I turn twice as much as I did, mentally cross my fingers.

Thwap. Bullseye. On Dorotea's butt.

I'm sorry, Dorotea. Please forgive me. I'll make it right.

Carson drives me toward the exit. "Let's go."

We get two turns away before I hear, "Sir? Mum?" A woman, behind us. Don't look back.

Carson opens a gap between us, a couple feet that feel like a couple miles.

"Sir? Mum? Is this yours, please?"

Definitely don't look back. We can't run—that looks bad—and walking starts to feel like standing in place. What did we drop? Did the camera see us after all?

We turn another corner. The docent/guard behind us is close enough to hear her footsteps. When we're halfway down the corridor, another docent—a big Slavic-looking dude—swings around the next corner, stares past us, then holds his arms out to block the corridor. Shit!

We stop. They got us. The slingshot glows blue-hot in my pouch.

The woman docent trots around to face us. No wonder she couldn't catch up—she's tiny. She pants a couple times, then steps closer. "Sir, mum, is this yours?"

I expect a broken paintball shell, or the sign with the target on it that fell off my back.

"Sorry. It was by the Sargent painting? I saw you there just now."

Carson shifts away from me. The muscles in her neck are quivering.

The docent holds up a blue fanny pack.

Chapter 37

I spend the afternoon worrying about Boutelle and waiting for the cops to come get me.

I happen to have two other forgers in my contacts list. Neither of them works in Sargent's genre. I've put feelers out to both, asking if they have any ideas. I can go back to Getz (much as I hate to) if I don't get anything from the other two.

More than that, though, I'm worried about Boutelle. I hate that we can't do anything to find him. We sure can't go to the cops. Yeah, it was his idea to come over here, but I let him do it, so it's partly my fault that someone grabbed him. How'd they find him? What are they doing to him? Is this about old business, or about this project?

When my brain isn't busy burning holes in itself over Boutelle, it's remembering the splat of dye I left on Dorotea in the museum.

I've never deliberately defaced a work of art before (that nasty little thrift-shop painting I tested the dye on doesn't count). Now that I have, I feel lower than a junk-bond salesman. I apologize to Dorotea's postcard two or three times an hour. She just looks pissed.

Worse yet: I can't tell Julie about it. She might understand, but I doubt Cousin Ron will. When she comes up to visit after lunch, I tell her I'm nervous about breaking into the lab. She suggests a few ways she can help me calm down. I know I won't be able to concentrate enough to make sex enjoyable for either of us—that's how wound up I am—so I ask her to read her book to me instead. The sound of her voice settles me some, but not enough.

Carson collects me at 4:30 to go back to the museum. "Spending a lot of time with the Princess," she grumbles. "That healthy?"

Does she suspect something? "You told me to keep her happy."

"Didn't mean you get stapled to her."

"Well, it's nice to hang out with a completely normal person for a change."

"Here we go," she mutters. "Hot for her?"

Careful. "She's an attractive woman."

"She's fucking *old*."

"Like you'd turn down Harrison Ford if he showed up at your door."

"Not my type." We bash through a traffic circle. "I'd do Neeson. Hell, I'd do his voice."

We park at the mall and weave our way onto Fountain Street, which dead-ends into a courtyard behind the Mainwaring. The five-story brick building opposite the museum is being renoed; there's scaffolding, stacks of materials, and an industrial-sized dumpster out back. No workers. Carson picks the padlock on a plywood door faster than I could open it with a key. We trudge up to the fourth floor and settle into what looks like a gutted apartment (stud walls, no fixtures) that has a primo view of the museum's limestone butt.

It's 5:39. The museum closes at six.

"Enough with the mystery," I say. "How are we getting into the lab?"

"You'll find out when we're done here. Stop asking."

At 5:52, an unmarked white Transit van loops into the courtyard and backs up to the shallow canopy over the museum's rear entrance. Two guys in safety-yellow parkas hop out. They walk past the back of the van to the double doors.

"Dome on the cargo box?" Carson's examining the van through her mini-binoculars. "Satellite antenna. Bet there's a tracker." She peers some more. "Bullet-resistant glass in the cab. Box's probably armored."

At 5:57, a black Range Rover busts into the courtyard and screeches to a stop about two feet from the van. Two dudes in matching black mercenary outfits rocket out of the back seat and stalk toward the guys from the van. I ask, "What's this? Guards?"

Carson's got her binoculars glued to them. "One on the left's got a Russian prison tat on his neck. Gotta be Tovorovsky's dogs." She lowers the binoculars and lets out a lungful of air. "That idea I had? Grabbing the picture on the street? Officially fucked."

A real bad thought shoves itself into my brain. "What if these guys—"

"Shut up."

"—stick around at the lab?"

"Shut up!"

All the museum's back windows are glowing pale yellow against the twilight in the courtyard. Occasional dark people-shapes pass behind the obscure glass. A good thing to know; if we end up out there, nobody can see us from inside.

The back entrance opens at 6:13. A man wearing a dark suit and a guy in gray coveralls carry out a rectangular something, about four feet by three, wrapped in tan muslin. Unless somebody else vandalized another painting today, it's Dorotea on her way to the lab. A yellow-parka guy opens the van's cargo doors, cutting off my view. The twin mercenaries flank the cargo box, holding pistols. After a minute, the suit and coveralls reappear without the covered thing. The driver slams shut the van's doors, signs the clipboard that coveralls hands him, then marches to the van's cab. The mercenaries trot back to the Range Rover.

A minute later, they're gone.

Chapter 38

Carson drops me at the Florence Arms while she "takes care of something." I hold down a table in the back room while I nurse a beer. It's the first time since I met Miranda that I have nothing to do. It's not a good thing.

Allyson's voice echoes in my head. It's a question she asked at my interview for the agency: *Is there anything you regret about your time at the gallery?*

Yeah. The face I see when I close my eyes. The Steel Sparrow.

Five years or so ago, a canvas snuck through Heibrück Pacific's back door wrapped in a green-black trash bag, what every well-dressed stolen painting wears. *Italian Landscape*, 1876, by Oswald Achenbach. Thirty by forty-five. Tawny hills, cypress and plane trees, a ruined Roman temple in the background, tiny sheep and a miniature shepherd. The Romantic movement never did much for me—it's like the art version of high-fructose corn syrup—but this piece is in my head Every. Damn. Day. Art has ghosts, too.

I discovered the canvas hiding under a bedsheet on our workbench. "Want me to look up the provenance?"

"No. Research the market for Achenbach. Quickly, quickly." Gar had this non-specific *Mitteleuropa* accent that went with the umlaut in his name. After everything fell apart, I found out he was born in Indiana.

I heard a lot of *quickly, quickly* in the next couple days as I helped Gar fake up a provenance for the canvas. Gar had a stealth client in town: Feng, a Shanghai developer who had a serious jones for *Gründerzeit*-era (roughly, our Gilded Age) German and Austrian art. Our cash flow had hit a rough patch, and Gar wanted to unload the landscape on Feng before the man climbed into his Gulfstream and jumped the Pacific.

Feng liked *Italian Landscape*. He paid Gar a price that had more to do with Chinese commercial real estate values than it did with auction results. He left humming a tune that sounded like it would use all the black keys on a piano.

Three days later, the Steel Sparrow walked into the gallery.

That was Gar's name for Ida Rothenberg, a Ravensbrück survivor. She was five-foot-one, weighed about ten pounds, and was made of old nails. She brought a grandniece, her lawyer, and some dude with a video camera. She said, "You have something that belongs to me." Which wasn't true anymore.

Later—when I had plenty of time on my hands in PEN—I learned all about *Italian Landscape*. It'd been Ida's father's back in Dresden in the '30s. The Nazis loved pre-Modern art, so Israel Rothenberg's small collection of German Romantic landscapes became state property and he became a statistic. A wheel in the SS hung the Achenbach in his confiscated Bohemian castle. That's why the Americans gave the painting to Czechoslovakia in 1945.

I learned a lot about Ida, too. She'd recorded her testimony for Spielberg's Shoah Foundation. I endured all four hours of it twice, and cried my eyes out both times. She almost died at least six times at Ravensbrück. She told how she'd been trying to get her family's art back since the '80s, how she found *Italian Landscape* in a small state-owned Prague gallery, how it and six other pieces disappeared in 2001 while she was still wrestling with the Czechs. Newspapers and *60 Minutes* filled in the rest: nine years tracking the Achenbach from one set of thieves to another, from Europe to America, to a crooked little L.A. gallery that sent her dad's favorite painting to China just days before she could rescue it. That was the last straw for Ida.

I helped do that to her.

I used to like to think that I never cheated anybody who couldn't afford it or didn't deserve it. Ida keeps telling me that's not true. She guilted me into turning state's evidence. She won't let me forget what I am. I met her only once and didn't say much to her, but she's always in the back of my head, my own personal Fury. All she ever says—all she ever has to say—is, *you should have tried.*

I should have, but I didn't. Not trying destroyed the gallery, then a chunk of L.A.'s art scene, then my life.

I'm gonna try now, Ida. I'm gonna make it right. I hope.

Not that that's really possible.

Chapter 39

Half an hour later, I get Carson's text: outside.

It's twilight and getting colder by the minute. I don't see the Jag anywhere. I plod up the street a few yards until a little white Ford hatchback flashes its lights at me. I can't see who's inside. With Smoking Man and maybe Tovorovsky's goons around, I'm not sure I want to get close enough to find out.

The driver's door swings open. Carson stares at me over the roof. "Get in."

My next surprise happens when I slide into the passenger's seat. Carson's not alone.

"Miranda?"

She looks like absolute hell. Huge black eyes, nose taped, safety-glass nicks scattered around her puffy face. Her right arm's in a royal-blue sling. She's back in tweed and seems perfectly comfortable in the back seat, though. "Evenin', laddie."

A few seconds of being speechless lets my mental universal translator boot up. I finally squeak out, "What... what are you doing here? Should you even be out?"

She gives me a you-poor-thing look. "Once I chored a necklace—a wee bauble, worth a million quid near enough—from a bedroom on the third floor of a terrace house in Lennox Gardens, with a bullet in me arse."

All right, then. I turn back to Carson, who looks like she's trying to keep in World's Best Joke. "What's going on?"

"Gonna get the fob from the security office."

"Just like that?"

"Least I can do," Miranda says. "Considerin'."

I look from one to the other a couple times. They're both totally serious. "Okay. What do you want me to do?"

Carson shoves her phone into my hand. "Navigate."

We retrace the camera-free route we drove about five hundred years ago. It's not as late as before and there's more traffic, so I'm glad Carson's driving. Miranda's calmly watching the lights go by like she's out sightseeing. I guess this is what a pro looks like.

"Is there a plan?" I ask on a long straightaway.

Miranda doesn't even turn away from the window. "What's the most harmless thing in the world, lad?"

When Dan Ackroyd answered that question, he came up with the Sta-Puft Marshmallow Man. Look where it got him. "What?"

"A wee Scots granny in a stookie." She pats the plaster cast sticking out of the sling. "And doan you know? I'm in a smashup, then me hire car goes oof."

Carson finishes for her. "Lab's the only place with someone onsite 24/7."

I get it now. "So she asks to use the phone in the guard office and steals the fob off the wall by the door."

"Swaps, but yeah."

I practically know Dundas Lane by heart now. When we pass the lab, it's like coming home. As we pass the big blue warehouse next to the lab, Carson swerves to the curb and punches on the flashers.

She pulls a tiny tissue-wrapped bundle from her jeans pocket and carefully fits it into the gap between the cast and the base of Miranda's thumb. "There's the decoy. Sure you don't want me to come?"

Miranda squeezes Carson's hand. "If I got you, I doan need them. Help me out, hen."

Carson levers Miranda out of the back seat like she's a box of antique bone china. They have a brief conference I can't hear, then Miranda starts hobbling toward the lab. Even in the near-dark, I can tell she's trying not to move her upper body any more than she has to. That must be the broken ribs talking.

Carson raps on the driver's-side window, then stabs a thumb toward the back of the car. I follow her to the other side of the chain-link enclosure around the blue warehouse's buzzing transformer. There's a couple-foot gap between it and the warehouse's wall, and that's where we hide. At least it's sheltered from the wind. "Why aren't we in the nice, warm car?"

"Guard comes out, sees us in it? It's over for Miranda."

"Okay. Who cooked this up?" When I left the hotel, I didn't figure we'd be outside very long, so of course I didn't bring my gloves.

At least my coat's warm.

"Me and Miranda. She felt bad about jilting us."

"It wasn't her fault she—"

"Not how she thinks. Way she sees it, she made a commitment, didn't see it through. She's paying her debt."

"Isn't she still on pain meds?"

"Nope. Went off 'em to do this."

This is totally what a pro looks like. Will I ever be that dedicated to anything?

I have a long time to think about that. My legs start to scream after about ten minutes of squatting. Carson's next to me, playing with her phone, preoccupied. I try to start a conversation a couple times and get nothing back. The points of her jaw are glowing. She's worried.

She must feel me start to shiver, because she skins off her black watch cap and jams it on my head before I can even squawk. It's still warm.

"I don't want to take your—"

"Shut up. You'll freeze."

I shoulder deeper into my coat. What's taking Miranda so long? She's been in there over fifteen minutes. Did the guard bust her? Did she pass out from the pain? "When do we start worrying?"

"When she got out of the car."

"So you didn't talk her into this?"

Carson shoots me sharp-edged look. "Tried to talk her *out* of it. I was gonna do it."

After another five minutes or so, I have to get up or my legs will fall off. When I turn toward the road, a short, stout, dark silhouette's looking at me. "Miranda?"

I feel Carson bounce up behind me. "You okay? How'd it go?"

Shadow-Miranda lets out a deep sigh. "Sorry, hen. I could'na get tha thingme. It's gone."

Of course. I turn to Carson. "Still got Aurora's number?"

It's 12:18 when I get Carson's next text: coming in.

I'm sitting in a room in the Portsmouth Park Hotel less than a mile from Dundas Lane. The room, like the rest of the hotel, is tired.

I'm not; I'm wide awake, as in wired. Yesterday morning, Carson said we have to be at the lab by two to take advantage of the guards being "busy." It'll take at least twenty minutes to get there using a no-camera route. We're cutting it awfully thin.

Carson left at ten right after she got a text from Aurora. I was glad to see she still has the black leather skirt we bought for her in Milan, but I had to convince her to pop the top two buttons on the long-sleeved white dress shirt she'd paired it with. "It's supposed to be a date," I reminded her. "Look like you're trying." She just snarled at me.

Eleven minutes after her text, she starts stress-testing the room's door. She bursts in when I get it open a couple inches, knocking me back a few feet. Her face and neck are bright red, and her glare tells me it's not from embarrassment. She storms halfway to the windows, then swivels, stalks up to me, grabs my head with both hands and shoves her tongue down my throat.

Uh, okay. Not what I expected, but I can cope. She has a very energetic tongue. When I start to reciprocate, she shoves me against the wall.

I manage to gasp out, "What was *that?*"

She wipes her mouth on the back of her hand. "Had to kiss a guy. You're the closest thing I got."

Did she just diss me? "What happened?"

"None of your fucking business." She yanks something out of her purse and hurls it at me. "Here."

It's the fob. She got the fob. "When will Aurora miss this?"

"When she goes to the lab and the one she's got doesn't work." She's not swearing, but she sounds like she's swearing.

"Are you okay? What happened? You guys fight?"

She grabs her backpack off the bed and bulls past me toward the bathroom. "Nothing you need to know. Be ready in ten. Time to work."

Chapter 40

Dundas Lane is sound asleep when we pull into a parking lot next to a tilt-up with channeled gray siding. The mercury-vapor lamps mounted on the eaves paint the space with a warm orange glow it doesn't earn.

"Cameras?" I ask.

"Other end," she says. "Pointing back, not out. Come on."

We close our doors as quietly as we can. Carson and I match: black everything, neck to toes. All I need is a *katana* and I'll feel like a grown-up ninja.

It's almost time for the guard-on-wheels to show up. We jog a block down the sidewalk to the big blue warehouse next to the Mainwaring's property, then stash ourselves in the shadows behind a white Prius plastered with company logos. Carson pulls on her black hood, then scuttles across the asphalt to the Mainwaring's fence.

While I slip on my hood (it's weird how good I'm getting at that) and put on nitrile gloves under my leather ones, I wonder for the umpteenth time about Boutelle. He's still gone. As far as Carson can tell, he's not on a slab. Is he ever coming back? Is he still alive?

I can't think about that now. I hope I don't have to think about it later.

Less than fifteen minutes after we take cover, a silver minivan rolls up to the Mainwaring's gate and toots once. The gate rattles open. Carson waves me over to her as the van pulls up to the front door. She whispers, "We go inside when they do. Takes 'em a couple minutes to close the gate."

A few moments later, Carson says "Go."

We scramble around the corner and through the gate, bent double, trying to avoid making noise. The parking lot's like the inside of a stadium with all the lights on. Carson points to me, then to the ground: *stay here*. She dashes across the driveway, disappearing behind the van. I have a good idea where she went—she's going to listen at the security office's window until she hears the sounds of love, sweet love.

Carson reappears after a few minutes, sprints around the van to approach the front door from slightly behind the camera. She slams her back against the brick next to the alcove, pulls a dark spray bottle out of her pocket, pumps it three or four times at the camera lens, then flings some powder out of a baggie at the camera's nose. She waves me over.

My heart leaps from running-a-six-minute-mile to jumping-out-of-an-airplane speed in an instant. This is worse than in the gallery this morning. This shit's getting serious.

I hit the wall next to Carson. There's gunk on the camera lens, but you have to look really close to see it. I point up at the camera and whisper, "What was that?"

"Hairspray and dirt. Blurs out the picture."

We slip blue hospital booties over our shoes so we don't leave identifiable shoeprints. Carson holds her hand out toward me. "Fob." I fork it over. She palms it onto the black plastic pad next to the reinforced glass door. The light turns from red to green with a *peep.*

We're inside.

We pad toward the lab. I hear the two guards when we pass the security office door. They're not coming out anytime soon.

The lab door's electric bolt sounds like a hammer hitting a steel box when it throws. We stand frozen for a moment, surprised. The guards must've heard that... right?

Nobody comes out to look.

The lab's pitch dark inside. Once I ease the door closed, Carson shines her flashlight on the floor. I stuff rolled hotel towels against the threshold to block any light leaks. Only when Carson snaps on the lights for the far end of the room do I stop to take a full breath.

Dorotea's on the metal easel next to Aurora's worktable. Her frame lies flat on the table on a layer of white cotton towels. There's no trace of dye on either piece. Yes!

Carson says, "We can take it now. In and out, ten minutes."

"And do what with her?"

She glares at me. "Get to work. Clock's ticking."

Carson said Lover Boy usually stays about forty minutes. We have to be out in thirty.

My leather gloves go in my backpack. I mark the canvas' position on the easel rail with two dabs of blue painter's tape. I get everything turned on at the copy stand, take a couple quick measurements of the canvas, then haul Dorotea to the stage. I've never carried an artwork worth this much in my whole life, so I take very careful steps. Dropping her isn't part of the program.

The floodlights take their time to warm up. I notice Carson standing next to the door's latch edge with her metal baton in her hand. We don't want to bust heads—we don't want to leave any sign we've been here—but it's better to tap a guard on the bean than it is for us to get Tasered to the floor.

I was okay when I was busy, but my yips come back while I'm waiting. I try deep, cleansing breaths, like the therapist taught me while I was dealing with Janine. I try walking in a tight circle. My hands flutter as fast as my heart. *Come on, come on, we're on the clock…*

The floods stabilize after a long few minutes. I click "live view" on the CaptureOne camera menu so I can see what the lens sees.

Nothing happens.

Don't panic. It's something easy.

Then I notice the camera information is greyed out on the menu. I run back through the checklist and realize I skipped a step. I switch on the camera back. Nothing happens. Shit. I check the cables. The ones going into the camera are fine.

Carson says, "Twenty minutes."

The data cable going into the computer snagged on the copy stand's edge and pulled partway out when I raised the camera. I plug it back in, hoping I didn't break the damn thing.

The software recognizes the camera. I start breathing again.

Using live-view mode, I raise the camera until the whole canvas appears on the computer screen. Then I go through the checklist I put together based on the National Archives job aid, making sure all the software settings are correct, noting the couple I need to change. There's no gray card, so I drop a piece of notepaper on the portrait's center and set the white balance.

Autofocus, manual focus. Sweat's rolling down my back, into my waistband. Set up the session folder on the computer so I can find the pictures once they're shot.

Carson says, "Fifteen."

I shake out my hands, step back to the computer, switch off live view. "Turn off the overheads," I stage-whisper to Carson. The room lights click off so only the photo floods light the place. I click on "capture."

In an instant, a high-res picture fills the monitor. It's a huge version of the postcard back in my room. Eighty megapixels worth of detail in one frame. Try *that* with your iPhone.

I zoom in on a one-inch patch of the image to check the focus. The brush strokes look like a satellite photo. Zoom out, crop, de-skew, adjust the color and luminosity curves. The only reason I know how to do all this is by reading the manuals and watching YouTube videos; I hope I'm not screwing things up. There'd be 99% fewer selfies on the internet if everyone had to go through all this to take a picture.

I shoot an insurance image using these settings. "Halfway there."

I turn Dorotea on her face like I'm handling Roman glass. This is the first time I've seen the back of an actual Sargent in person, though I've seen a couple pictures. This one's got all the yellowing and wear-and-tear I'd expect for a ninety-year-old painting. The mid-gray priming reaches to the canvas' edges, typical for Sargent. There's six labels—three in German, three in Cyrillic—and a label-sized rough patch. Future homework.

The next two images go faster since I don't need to monkey with the settings.

Carson says, "Ten."

Shit! I get the software churning out TIFs of the four photos. Then I whip out my phone, sit next to the stage and start shooting the painting's edges. Boutelle needs pictures of the edges so he can reproduce the paint runs and wear. After each shot, I slide on my butt across the linoleum to line up the next one.

I have to turn the painting around to get the fourth edge, so while I'm up, I check the computer. Its disk light is still solid white. Windows Explorer shows me that the RAW files are eighty megabytes plus or minus, but the TIFs are at least *four hundred megabytes* each. What? That'll take forever to copy, and forever's something we ain't got. I plug in the thumb drive I brought, wait what seems like hours for the computer to recognize it, then start the copy.

It's not going to finish on time.

I trot over to Carson and tell her the good news. She snaps,

"Why's this a surprise?"

"Nothing I saw online said they'd get so big."

She winces, like this physically hurts. "How long?"

"Can't tell. It should speed up once the new files are done. I still have to put the canvas back and clean up. Ten minutes?"

"Pushing it. Better hope they don't check out the camera before he leaves." She sounds more resigned than irritated. "Get it done."

The file conversions are finally finished by the time I get back to the computer. I shoot the last edge, then carry Dorotea back to her easel. It doesn't take too long to clean up after myself, but I keep feeling like I'm forgetting something. Now I wish I'd taken a picture of the workstation so I could tell if I've moved anything. Too late now.

I finally get to start the second half of the copy. My nerves are back now that I literally can't do a thing. My hands feel clammy and thick in the nitrile gloves, my back is soaked, I can't stand still. *Tick tick tick tick tick…*

Carson flips on the lights at this end of the room. "Five."

I shut down the rest of the camera equipment and check the file copy progress: 64% and getting *slower*. A glance at the system tray shows me why—the computer's antivirus software started a disk scan a couple minutes ago. A reasonable thing to do at two in the morning, but now? Seriously?

"Voices!" Carson hisses at me. "Footsteps!"

I switch off the computer monitor, then dash to the end of Aurora's table farthest from the door. The room lights click off before I can get on the floor. Carson's hospital booties make a sandpaper noise ending in the *thump* of her back hitting the far worktable. My breathing's so fast I'm starting to see static.

The electric bolt clacks. The door swings open. The lights snap on, blinding me.

A woman's voice says, "See that?" She's in the room.

See what? *What?* I pry open one eye just enough to glance up at Dorotea. I didn't leave her upside-down, thank God, but the painter's tape is still on the easel rail. Will they notice?

A guy's voice says, "Another one of your pictures?"

"Hush, you. You know I love these things. C'mon."

Two pairs of footsteps clomp down the aisle. They're coming to see Dorotea.

The woman says, "Some wanker threw paint on it today."

"Why?"

"Christ knows. Charlie told me. It's pretty, innit?"

"Yeah, she's right fit." The guy's voice goes flirty. "Looks like you."

"She does *not*. Don't be daft." But she sounds a little pleased.

The easel is maybe four feet to my left, between Aurora's table and the wall. No matter which way they get here, I'm going to have to move twice. But which way?

The footsteps cross behind me. I get down on all fours and crawl very carefully around the corner of the table so I don't make a sound.

The guards are almost to the easel.

"How much is it worth?" the guy asks.

"An arse load, I reckon."

I squat against the table's aisle side just as the guards' shoes clump to a stop by the easel.

"She's a cracker," the guy says. "I'd put this on my wall."

"Yeah, your wall in Mayfair. You want me to compete with that?"

"No competition, luv. She's dead, yeah? You're not."

"Glad you noticed." She giggles. "Stop! Haven't had enough already?"

"I never get enough of you."

Get a room, for chrissake!

Their feet scrape. "C'mon, you," the woman says, "while I've still got me knickers."

It sounds like they're going back the way they came. I slink around the corner to the far end of Aurora's table. With any luck, the guards are too busy molesting each other to notice.

Footsteps leave. Lights out. Door closes.

All my bones have turned to Jell-O.

After a minute of silence, my skeleton solidifies and I can crawl my way upright. Everything's inside-a-whale black except the pulsing white disk light on the front of the computer. I fumble my Mini-Maglite out of my backpack, use it to work my way past Aurora's table, then creep to the computer as silently as I can.

When I turn it on, the monitor's glow turns the whole back half of the room blue. The "copying files" dialog box is gone—everything's on the thumb drive. I delete the files from the hard drive, pocket the thumb drive, then shut down the computer.

Carson grabs my arm. "Gotta go *now*."

I get Dorotea settled and pull the tape off the easel. "Towels?"

"Backpack."

Great—I can use them to dry off.

Carson listens at the door for a while, then waves me into the hallway. We creep along the west wall. The security office door is open.

"She goes around that side first." Carson thumbs toward the building's other side. "We got five minutes. Let's go."

Chapter 41

"Why are we still here?"

Carson takes her eyes off the internet long enough to give me a sharp look. "Gotta see if we fucked up."

It's past four in the morning. Carson's stretched out on the bed with her feet crossed on the rust-and-buff bed scarf. Her laptop's on her thighs. I'm at the faux-maple desk, hard awake, combing through the local news websites, hoping to not find any stories about break-ins on Dundas Lane.

"I mean, why aren't we headed for Heathrow by now?"

Carson sighs. "Bust out of here in a hurry, in the middle of the night? That's suspicious. People remember. Cops look for that. We leave after breakfast."

Which makes perfect sense, other than it's totally unnatural. I feel like a sitting duck. Every time a car goes by outside, I'm sure it's the cops. But Carson's the one who knows how this part works, so I force myself to trust her judgement and keep looking for news I don't want to see.

By eight, I'm prying my eyelids open with my fingers and Carson's grinding the heels of her hands into her eye sockets. None of the TV morning news shows even mention Portsmouth, and no local news websites say a thing about the Mainwaring.

We're safe. Maybe.

We leave Portsmouth before nine and clear out of the Hilton in Southampton just after ten. Carson drops me at the main train station before taking Miranda to Glasgow to recover. Julie's already on a train heading for London.

Boutelle's still MIA. I really hope he's having a great time with some young blonde. In case he's not, I ask Olivia to start making discreet calls to hospitals and the police. She'll arrange to get him out of the country… *if* she finds him. He doesn't get the thumb drive with the photos until he shows up at his studio, and he doesn't get his money until he's done with the copy. If he's still alive, he'll make sure he gets back home if he has to swim. If not…

Since I haven't slept for over a day, I go through a huge amount of fully-leaded black coffee, usually bad, to keep me awake during the two-hour train ride to London. I spend almost as much time in the toilet as I do in my seat. At least it keeps me awake.

I finally reach the Sofitel at Heathrow's Terminal 5 around one. Olivia got me on a flight tomorrow morning, so all I can do until then is chill. I leave a note at reception for Julie with my room number. Then just like when I got here three weeks ago, I stumble to my room and immediately go face-down on the bed.

The next morning, I'm on a British Airways flight home to Los Angeles.

Chapter 42

I've been home eight days. As usual, I was back at work the day after I got here, jet lag and all. Allyson's paying me a hundred euros a day "retainer" to take care of project-related stuff (mostly Boutelle). This is more than my typical take-home on days I work a full shift, so I don't really *need* to go back to the Green Empire so soon. But what else am I going to do? It also gives me some extra money to sock away or help Chloe with the bills.

So far, I haven't had to do much for my retainer, because Boutelle was still missing. The feelers I put out in Portsmouth haven't produced yet. Getz is seeing who's available. I've called Boutelle's U.S. phone two or three times a day since I got back and got *nada*.

Until this morning. His voicemail message is different, and his mailbox isn't full anymore. That makes me figure he's still alive. Like Ricky Ricardo said, he's got some 'splainin' to do. The Mainwaring exhibit closes in thirty-six days.

Boutelle's studio is in half a crappy brick warehouse on Jefferson across Ballona Creek from Culver City. It's not the kind of live-work space realtors try to sell to tech workers with lots of money and no time to spend it; it's more like the kind of live-work space meth cookers have. The big blocks of a dozen different shades of red paint outside (covering graffiti) have a kind of Abstract Expressionist vibe. That is, in the early afternoon, like now; at night, the area has a kind of zombie-apocalypse vibe.

Since nobody answered the first three times I knocked on the industrial metal swinging door next to the big roll-up, I channel my inner Carson and pound the shit out of the door. "Wake-up call, Sim. It's your paycheck."

Locks start clacking. The door finally squeaks open. A woman in a white wifebeater, with rat's-nest blond hair and Slavic cheekbones, stares out at me like I've disappointed her for the rest of the day. There's a cigarette (unlit, unfiltered) dangling from the right side of her mouth.

Damn it, Sim, already? "Looking for Simpson Boutelle. It's business."

She doesn't seem to understand, or care. She sparks up the cig and blows the first lungful up to the sky. In daylight, she doesn't look as old as she acts—maybe mid-to-late twenties.

I try again. "Boutelle? Here?"

She picks a flake of tobacco off her tongue and flicks her little finger to get rid of it. Then she nods behind her and lets me in.

The studio's roughly fifty feet square, cluttered, and dim from the trees blocking the clerestories along the back wall. It smells like turpentine and bad cooking. I thread my way through the obstacle course to where I remember Boutelle's lair being. In the far back corner, I find his bed—a mattress on the floor—with him sprawled face-down on it. I check his throat for a pulse and actually find one. That's a good start.

The noise of the fridge opening makes me look up. This is when I realize that the wifebeater's *all* the woman is wearing. She's too blond, too tattooed, and way too skinny to be worth checking out, though. The bottle of Stone Smoked Porter she's holding up over her shoulder is a lot more interesting, though—I guess Boutelle's spending his fee before he gets it. We bond over a bottle opener, then she strolls to the sagging blue-floral sofa and curls up with her beer and her smoke.

I pour a red Solo cup full of cold water on Boutelle's head. Ever see an elephant seal waking up? That's the kind of noise and thrashing I get from him.

After he's done flailing, Boutelle squints up at me. His hair's partly plastered to his scalp, which makes it neater but not any more attractive. He mumbles, "Matthew, m'lad. I… I was about to ring, but—"

"Get your clothes on and tell me where the *fuck* you've been for a week and a half." I'm still channeling Carson.

My beer's all gone by the time Boutelle shambles up to me in the working part of his studio. He's wet down the rest of his hair and managed to button his violet used-to-be-dress shirt correctly, so I guess he's sort-of awake. "Matthew, I can explain every—"

"You better."

He hems and haws and shuffles his feet some. "Yes. Well.

Y'see… I'd just settled in to watch *Eastenders*—I didn't want to break my parole, you know—when two villains appeared at my door. They were… rather *insistent* that I go with them, and of course I was in no position to refuse, so—"

Shit. Shit. Shit. "Who were they?"

He shuffles some more and surveys the stains on the concrete slab floor. "I never told you the story of how I came to be here, did I?"

"No, and I don't care. Who were they?" Tovorovsky's goons?

"Ehm, well… they belonged to a man of my acquaintance. McNichols, a true villain. We'd disagreed about certain transactions in the past—"

"How much do you owe him?" I don't know whether to be relieved it's not Tovorovsky, or pissed that Boutelle's sideways with some other gangster.

"Well… nothing any longer. Rather a bit before, or so he claims. I dashed off a few Goya brush-and-ink works while I was his guest—nothing so very difficult—and he declared my debt settled. I can't say we parted fast friends, but, well…"

Original Goya drawings can go for a million bucks or more at auction. He owed this McNichols *that* much? "How'd he find you?"

"Ah, that." He pokes a brownish stain on the concrete with his toe. "He, ehm… led me to believe he has a colleague in a credit card processing center. He must've learned of me when I checked into the hotel."

I almost throw my empty bottle at him. "*I* checked you into the hotel, with *my* agency card. Try again."

He clears his throat and tries to look bashful but doesn't quite pull it off. "Yes, of course, of course. My mistake. It may have been when I visited a local… ehm, *establishment* after we arrived. For some harmless entertainment, of course. I had to pay the young lady—"

"You went to a *whorehouse?*" Steam's starting to come out of my ears. If he'd gotten busted…

"No, no, no, no, no. A gentleman's club. The Playhouse, I believe it's called. Great fun." He spreads his hands and smiles. "Matthew, m'lad. It's all sorted now. No harm in it. Everyone's happy, and now I'm at your service."

If I didn't need him, I'd fire him. I need him. My brain's throbbing. I take half a dozen calming breaths before I can turn down my volume control. "You've burned. A week. Of your four."

If this bothers him, he doesn't show it, damn him. "Yes, yes. Not a problem. Just give me the snaps and I'll be on it double-quick. You may rely on me."

"Stop saying that."

Julie's sent me a few flirty texts, and I flirted back. It's not enough. We spent three weeks together almost nonstop and now I miss her. Especially at night. It didn't take long to get used to having someone in bed with me again.

A couple days after Boutelle resurfaces, I'm on a half-full Santa Monica Big Blue Bus after six hours at work. My burner phone pings with a text. Only one person in the world has this number.

Hi, handsome. Can you talk? She punctuates.

The nearest other rider is two seats away. Still, this isn't a conversation I want to have in public. Going home ill call u soon.

OK.

Twenty minutes later, I get off the bus and start my three-block walk to the pool house I share with Chloe. It was 51° and cloudy when we left Portsmouth, and some of the leaves were turning gold; here it's 73° and sunny and looks the same as it did in February.

She picks up on the second ring. "Matt?"

"The one and only. Can you talk now?"

"Uh-huh. I'm home. It's good to hear your voice." Her voice is all warm and purry. I'm glad my work pants hang loose on me. "Is it warm out there? It's freezing here. I need someone to keep me warm."

We chat for a few minutes along those lines. If I wasn't out in public, I'd ask her, "What are you wearing?" As it is, I walk past the house and have to double back.

"This isn't just so I can hear your voice," she finally says. "I want to send some translations to you. How should I do that?"

Damn. Work. "Go to Gmail. Log in as 'mattsimon09,' all one word. Once we hang up, the password will be 'devillardi,' all lower-case. Create the message, attach the files, but don't send it. Text 'done' when it's ready. I'll log in and get the files. Got all that?" Many thanks to Dave Petraeus for this security hint.

We tease each other for another couple minutes, then Julie says, "Sorry, darling, there's someone at the door. Talk to you soon. Miss you."

That feels good. When was the last time someone called me "darling"?

By the time I get home and change, Julie's left a draft message in the mattsimon09 email account. She's added a comment: "Stefan found something!"

Yes, he did.

Geisman found Wolf Kinigader's grave in Friedhof Aigen, a cemetery in southern Salzburg. An Erna Thalmann of Spumberg claimed his body in February 1946 and paid for his burial. She also paid the plot rent every ten years until 1997, when she was buried next to him.

Kinigader had *two* somebodies in Salzburg. Somebody else has paid the plot rent for both graves since Erna died.

Ute Kinigader.

I sent Geisman's discovery to Olivia three days ago. I didn't expect an answer so soon. But when I get home from work this afternoon, it's waiting for me.

The Salzburg *Grundbuch* lists a dairy farm in Spumberg (a village southeast of Salzburg) that's owned by a Thalmann family trust.

Gotcha. A quick check shows Ute Kinigader has no online presence. It's not a huge surprise; if she's Kinigader's daughter, she'd be in her seventies by now. But she's probably still alive. The Salzburg cemetery system lets you search the last few years' worth of burials online, and her name doesn't show up.

Maybe she knows where her dad stashed his paintings.

Monday. Twenty-seven days to closing.

Julie's sent me a few of the Kinigader records. Since Allyson let me bring my work laptop home, I can even read this stuff without going blind. It's all kinds of interesting in a really geeky way. Fake-provenance research can be like writing a historical novel, figuring out how to put real people in imaginary situations. This'll be the biggest bogus provenance I've ever built… if I can pull it off.

If fucking Boutelle actually gets some work done.

The same woman opens his studio door. Different shirt, same pants. I've never seen Boutelle with the same woman twice, so maybe it's love. Or her wardrobe.

He's dressed and on his hind legs this time. "Matt, m'lad! Welcome! Come here, come here, and see what I've wrought." If he's put out from last week's flaming, he's not showing it.

He whips the cover off the canvas. At least he's put in the ground—the major background color, a deep oxblood—and left an area for Dorotea. Not that she's anywhere to be seen. "Great work, Sim. You painted one color. That took a week?"

"No, no. Where's your faith, m'lad? Have I ever let you down?"

Recently?

He makes a big show out of turning around the canvas. There's a Winsor & Newton stamp burned into the stretcher's top crossbar. The canvas back is aged, and the tacking margin is like what I remember from the portrait. Boutelle clicks on the big flatscreen monitor hulking over the nearby workbench, attached to a laptop. A high-res photo of the portrait's back fades up. Once the picture stabilizes, I can tell the color on the copy is a dead match for the original. It looks great. Except… "Where's the labels?"

"Ah! Exactly the right cue." He bashes a key on the laptop a few times until the monitor fills with a huge close-up of one of the Russian labels. Then he hands me a manila folder with a crinkled, faded-yellow rectangle of paper perched on top. It's the same label. It's perfect.

"Are all of them done?"

"Of course, of course." He sweeps his hand toward five more manila folders lined up on the bench, each with a different size, shape, or color of label on top. He points to the one I'm holding. "Fair Inessa tells me this one belongs to the restorer."

"Inessa is…?"

"The young lady." For once, he lowers his voice. "You've met. Twice now."

It takes me a moment to process this. It sounds worse every time I rewind and replay. "You showed this to her?"

"Why, of course. I don't read Russian, don't you know."

"You showed this to your girlfriend." Because even he should know that's a bad move.

"Is that a problem?"

I step closer and drop my voice as far as I think I can get away with. "You understand this is illegal, right? This isn't one of your Studio Direct projects."

"Of course I know." He's using his outdoor voice again. Then the cartoon light bulb switches on over his head. "Oh, I see, I see. You worry that Inessa will grass us, aren't you? Well—"

"Keep your voice down, for chrissake."

"Put your mind at ease, m'lad." He claps my shoulder not quite hard enough to dislocate it. "She's no reason at all to go to the plods." At least he's not shouting anymore. "She's here on the QT, you see."

Oh, great. I squeeze my eyes shut until the psychic pain dies down. "ICE is looking for her? She busted her visa?"

"No, no." Now he's down to normal human speaking volume. "I'm not aware she bothered with a visa. No, there are some people she's keen to avoid. Rather a rum lot, I believe."

I'd really like to pound my forehead on the workbench, but the last thing I want is to leave DNA evidence. "She's running from the Mob?"

Boutelle turns up his meaty hands. "That *may* be so. She has such a charming way with English, but I do sometimes miss the nuances."

I count to ten, then twenty, then think about going to thirty until I see that Boutelle's losing focus. "Sim, promise me something. You won't show any more of this to your girlfriend. You won't tell her what it's for." A wad of bad vibes drops on my head. "You… *haven't* told her, have you?"

He frowns. "Of course not. I'm not mad."

It's easy to lose track of that fact. "Good. Promise me."

"Anything for you, m'lad." He wraps an arm around my shoulders and almost pulls me off my feet. "Besides, it's not illegal 'til I sign someone else's name to it."

A week comes and goes. Twenty days before the exhibit closes.

Len, my PO, does his quarterly home visit with me. He'd wanted to do it while I was still in Portsmouth, but I was able to put him off. Because he needs to talk to the people I live with, Chloe's taken off early from work to be here.

At only five-nine, Len's not all that much taller than Chloe in her heels. He's wiry, looks sort-of like a completely bald Sam Waterston, and has a voice like an engine running out of oil. He could also totally kick my ass—he's an advanced black belt in Brazilian *jiu-jitsu*. Still, he cuts me a lot of slack because I don't cause him problems (that he knows about).

So he goes down his checklist and pokes around. Chloe and I spent the past couple nights dusting and vacuuming. The pool house is cleaner than it's been… well, since Len's last visit.

"Got your pay slips for your freelance gig?" he asks. This is his first visit since I started working for Allyson. I hand him a folder of invoices I wrote for an A&E firm I've never seen but really exists. Allyson must have a load of dirt on the owner.

I'm in the black Brioni slacks and Z Zegna green-and-gray microprint shirt I bought for the Milan project. Chloe's still wearing her work clothes—a knee-length, cap-sleeve black sheath and three-inch heels—and her shoulder-length, white-blond hair's brushed out and shiny. She cleans up well. When she sits next to me on the sofa, she wraps her hands around my arm. Anyone peeking through the window would see an upscale Angeleno couple. If only they knew.

Out on the front step, Len hands me his checklist and report. "Sign here." I'm a *model probationer*. Who knew? "You should just marry that girl and get it over with."

"I've told you—she's into girls."

"So? There's no sex after the wedding anyway." He stows the paperwork in his black vinyl portfolio. "Keep your nose clean. Stay away from criminals. Say 'no' to drugs. You know the rap."

"Yes, sir."

Once he drives away, I change clothes and head off to see my pet art forger. Gotta make a living.

Boutelle's getting not much work done on the portrait. Maybe Inessa's distracting him too much, or they have to hide from the

Mob.

I send pictures of the Russian labels to Carson for translation. Her reply:

1 Moscow museum of modern art

2 Tovorovsky collection

3 V shishkin conservator

Just like her—not even a "hi." Oh, well.

MMOMA opened at the end of 1999. Why isn't there a label from the Hermitage or the state archives or the Soviet Army? Who kept it between 1945 and whenever Tovorovsky picked it up?

Then I think about something I saw in the lab. I bring up a high-res picture of the back of Dorotea's portrait and spend some time going over the rough spot. No signs of repair, no patching, no reweaving. It looks like somebody ripped something off the canvas. A label?

Federal court booted Bowen's claim against the Russians twice. Because there's no proof the Russian government ever had custody of the portrait, it doesn't fall under their cultural property law. So it was totally in Tovorovsky's best interests to make any government markings go away. I'm sure any paper records went in a shredder, too.

While I think about this, another realization head-butts me: if we're going to pass off the real portrait as a new find, the three surviving Russian labels need to disappear. I'm just thrilled I'll have to attack Dorotea's portrait again.

I'm getting daily emails from both Carson and Allyson. *Is it done yet?*

No, it isn't done yet. Thanks for reminding me. It's like the clock is on fast-forward everywhere except Boutelle's studio, where it's going backward. Now I'm going to his place every day straight from work to see what three or four random brushstrokes he's made since last visit. I'm practically best friends with Inessa now, even though she hasn't said a word to me.

I go there on the fifteenth when the copy's supposed to be done. Fourteen days before the exhibit closes.

Still not finished.

The rough-in's there. The column fragment looks fantastic, but Dorotea's face is still a blank and her dress has no beading. Things are not happy between Boutelle and me. But there's a limit to how much I can beat on him; the last thing we need at this point is to have him say *to hell with it* and leave us with an unfinished canvas.

Thirteen days.

I watch Boutelle take forty-five minutes to put three brushstrokes on the canvas. He needs two beers to do it. Inessa's gone someplace; is he pining for her? Did she ever put on pants?

Twelve days. No change from yesterday.

Eleven days. Boutelle doesn't answer the door.

I can't sleep. My eating habits suck, too. Stress is beating the hell out of me. Boutelle was my idea, and he's blowing it. If he doesn't deliver, the best thing that'll happen is, I'll never work for Allyson again. The worst? I still don't know if people survive getting fired by her.

Ten days. Still no answer. What's he doing? Is he alive?

Nine days until the exhibit closes.

"Jesus, Sim. It's beautiful."

Yes—the portrait's finally done. And it's gorgeous. I compare it to the photo on the big screen, and I can't find a single flaw. Even the signature is perfect.

"Have you baked it yet?" Forgers have been known to bake their work in industrial ovens to set the paint. Boutelle happens to have one of these. He also makes pizza in it.

He's standing behind me with his arms crossed, just radiating pride. He's also radiating chemical stimulants and no sleep for God knows how long. "Of course, of course. Yesterday." He claps my shoulder. "Is it everything you wished for?"

"It is." I scowl back at him. "It's also almost a week late."

Boutelle holds his arms out, his hands palms-up at shoulder height. "I could work only so fast as Sargent could guide me. Inspiration can't be rushed."

I shake my head. I've heard that before, just not from a forger. "Come on, let's get this thing in a box."

Chapter 43

Commercial Road's empty but not dark when Carson and I leave the Painter's Arms pub around 11:10. The streetlights flood the pavement with hard, contrasty white light, and several upper-story windows glow yellow with safety lights. All the stores are closed, of course. So is the Christmas Market, a string of temporary booths running down the center of the street, made up to look like log cabins with holly and pine boughs strapped to the eaves of their pitched roofs. The trees planted down the middle of the street—still stubbornly green when we left—now have their fall colors on, and drifts of leaves are settling around lampposts and trash cans. It was full dark by five. We have the place to ourselves except for a couple guys walking through fast.

Four days left before the exhibit closes.

The Jubilee Fountain is silent when we reach it. They apparently turn off the water at night so people don't dump laundry detergent in it. Carson drags me around the east end and under the overhang outside Debenham's—a local department store—blocking the sharp-edged wind. The display windows are full of Christmas stuff. From here we have a straight-line view into the Mainwaring's front lobby and the two guards gabbing at the reception desk.

Carson slaps my wrist when I pull my phone to get the time. "Put that away." She hikes her coat cuff and checks a man-sized, stainless-steel watch with a big bezel. "Eleven twenty-four."

"Since when do you wear a watch?"

"Since I do surveillance. Here." She spins me around so I'm facing away from the museum, then steps close and winds her arms around my neck. "Watch my six."

Ah. We're boyfriend and girlfriend again, snuggling for a few minutes out of the cold. I wrap my arms around her waist and pull her a bit closer. We're both so bundled up, all I can feel is padding. She makes a face at me but doesn't back away.

A few months ago, I hardly ever had any physical contact with a woman. Now with Julie, Carson, and Gianna, I'm making up for lost time. Of course, I keep hearing Julie's voice from before she went to her room: "Don't have too much fun out there. Save your strength."

"Guard just took off," Carson whispers. "Eleven thirty."

This is why we're here—to time the guard patrols. "How long are we staying?"

"Two full rounds." In other words, two hours if the patrols are on a half-hour schedule. It's mid-forties now and getting colder.

We adjust our hands and knees to get as comfortable as we can in this cold. Carson's just a couple inches shorter than me, so it's easy for her to look over my shoulder. My view is of an empty Arundel Street, a pedestrian mall that leads into the Jubilee Fountain's east end. Mist halos surround the streetlights. We manage some snippets of conversation. The minutes creep by.

Carson asks, "When's the picture get here?"

"Friday. It's going to Gillian's box." As long as Customs doesn't screw us over.

Footsteps echo off the walls. Quick, sharp; hard-soled shoes, in a hurry, getting closer. A cop? I check Arundel: nothing. Carson glances north on Commercial, then nods south. "That way." Then she's nuzzling me. Our noses are dancing; her mouth's about a whisper away from mine. Anyone going by will see us having a private moment.

The sound changes. It's clearer, less echoey. Carson edges her nose away from me and lets her eyes track someone going up Commercial. I steal a peek at the back of a big woman (I think) in white *faux* fur and high-heeled boots, charging away from us. When s/he disappears around the Burton menswear store on the opposite corner, we both sigh.

I ask, "Why don't we stand on the corner?"

"Camera."

"It can't see us here?"

"No. Inside the store, looking out."

We settle down again. It's still cold on all the parts Carson isn't touching. Time goes by. "Got a plan yet?"

"Yeah."

I wait for her to say more, which she doesn't. "Care to share?"

She tugs her black knit watch cap farther down her ears. "Princess has the party invites." There's a reception for the end for the exhibit right after closing on Sunday. "We go in with her, hide in the basement. Come out when the party's over and the cleaners are gone. Kill the power, swap the picture, walk out the back door."

"You make it sound so easy."

"My part is." If eyes can smirk, hers are.

All I have to do is dismount the portrait, remove the original from its frame, install the copy, and rehang it. In the dark. While I'm waiting for a guard to come bust us. No problem.

"Guard's back," Carson says after some while. "Midnight."

Only ninety more minutes in deep freeze. "He's jamming if he can cover the whole place in half an hour."

"Yeah. Maybe not paying attention." Bonus for us. "Other guard's moving." She breaks our clinch, presses her back against the display window, then peers at the museum.

I feel silly just standing there, so I slide behind her in time to see the guard disappear into an elevator. "Starting at the top?"

"Easier to walk down than up."

They're spending roughly eight minutes on each floor. We've got a schedule. If the guards leave the podium on the half-hour, their sweep of the third floor—where the exhibit is—will start eight minutes later and end at roughly quarter-past. If we time things just right, we'll have half an hour of working time between patrols. Enough time? It'll have to be.

We just get ourselves arranged again when we hear something that makes us both cock our heads. It's like a big alarm clock going off a long way away. We look around to try to figure out what direction it's coming from.

"Museum," Carson says.

I twist so I can see behind me and spot a blue light I hadn't noticed before, strobing at the south end of the Mainwaring's façade. "What the hell...?"

"Shhh." She fiddles with her watch. Maybe thirty seconds later, I hear the first of two police sirens cook off somewhere in the night. They get closer awfully fast.

I have a bad history with sirens. "We gotta get out of here."

"No. It's an opportunity."

For what?

Carson's solid and calm and totally focused on her watch, which is good, because if she wasn't, I'd be running down Arundel by now.

So I hold onto her and listen to the sirens get closer. Blue flashes start bouncing off the walls across the street. There's an engine, car doors, a radio scratching. Every single way this could go bad zooms through my head every few seconds.

"Five thirty-three." Carson stops messing with her watch. "Turn around."

I turn around. A cop's heading our way, not quite jogging, shining a flashlight in my eyes. A huge shot of shit hits my heart. This is exactly the worst thing I can think of, and it's happening. Right. *Now.*

Carson snuggles up against my back, wraps her arms under my armpits and grabs my shoulders. It probably looks cozy, but she's holding on tight. Did she feel me running away before I did?

"Sir? Mum? Please show me your hands." The cop drops the flashlight beam to my chest. He's young and round-faced. Some glow from the nearest streetlight shows that his nose and cheeks are pink from the cold. He stops just outside grabbing distance. "What are you about here now, this late?"

Carson whacks her knee into the back of mine. I guess I'm talking once I find where I put my voice. "Um… me and my girlfriend, we were up at the pub. We stopped here to get out of the wind for a few minutes. Then the alarm went off."

"Miss, please step out from behind him." Carson edges out to my right. The cop's eyes twitch back and forth between me and her. "Your identification, please."

Another rush of shit to my heart. Will these fake IDs stand up to a police check? They'd better. Between the coat, the gloves, and my hand shaking (not from the cold), it takes some doing to get my wallet out of my back pocket and my fake driver's license out of the wallet. Carson, of course, has hers out in seconds. The cop takes them, backs up a few steps, then starts talking into the radio mouthpiece clipped to his shoulder.

Carson slides her hand around mine. "Calm down," she whispers in my ear.

"Easy for you to say."

"IDs are solid."

"Even with all the databases and stuff?"

"Haven't busted one yet."

The cop shoots a glance our way. Carson kisses my cheek, I guess to firm up the "girlfriend" thing.

While we wait, I distract the moths in my stomach by watching the drama in the Mainwaring's lobby. Two cops are talking to the guard by the desk. There's a lot of pointing and talking on radios. One cop charges toward the elevators while the other keeps writing down what the guard's saying. The one thing that makes me feel better about all this is that so far, nobody has a gun.

I steal a peek at Carson. Her eyes are glued to the lobby window. It's like she's watching the Stanley Cup.

"Matthew Simon?" The cop's walking toward us.

Gulp. "Yes?"

He holds out my license. "Thank you." When I take it, he says, "Lisa Carson?"

Lisa?

Carson takes her ID. "Thank you, officer."

The cop steps back, then gives us one more going-over. "Best be on your way."

"Yes, sir." I drag Carson away as fast as I can get her feet moving. It's like trying to walk a cat on a leash. "Lisa? You've been hiding 'Lisa' from me?"

"Not my name. Just something on an ID." She finally stops pulling back when we can't see inside the museum's lobby anymore. "Wonder what tripped the alarm."

We hurry toward the end of Commercial and our parking lot. "Did you get anything out of all that?"

"PD responds in five and a half minutes. Two units at least. No armed response."

"Is that good or bad?"

"Just is."

We both look to our right as we cross Edinburgh Road, the end of the pedestrian mall. Flashing blue lights reflect off the kebab-shop windows at the mouth of Fountain Street, which leads to the courtyard behind the museum. Carson slows down for a few steps until a building cuts off our view.

I ask her, "You didn't plan that alarm thing, did you?"

"No. Someone else."

"Smoking Man?"

She shrugs. "If they're casing the lab, they're casing here, too."

Chapter 44

Friday. We steal Dorotea in two days.

Yesterday was about me buying tools and things in Bristol. I'm sure Portsmouth has fine hardware stores, but Carson told me, "Don't make it easy on the detectives," so I went out of town.

Since Wednesday night's alarm thing, Carson's been jumpier than a cat around a vacuum cleaner. She's constantly looking out windows to see if we're being watched. If we need to use the car, she scans it with a phone app and a plug-in wand before we go. She also checks the wheel wells and engine compartment—for what, she won't say. It's weirding me out to the point that I'm seeing shadows in the shadows.

Carson's also forbidden Julie from leaving her room unless she's Gillian from head to foot. "If they're watching," Carson tells her with a lot of finger-jabbing, "they need to see *her*, not you." Since that's a lot of work, Julie's been staying in her room unless she's in mine across the hall. Even though the clock's ticking down to the big show, she's bored.

I should've figured that wouldn't turn out well.

Carson and I pick up Boutelle's fake at the Royal Mail delivery office in Shirley, a district northwest of downtown Southampton, at around five-thirty Friday afternoon. She found a white Transit van somewhere (I didn't ask), which is useful, because I doubt we could stuff the 40" by 58" Airfloat Strongbox into the Jag's back end. One side of the box took a hit somewhere between Culver City and here, but not enough to hurt the painting. I peek inside once it's settled. The fake Dorotea still looks beautiful.

We finally have everything we need to pull off the swap. All's right with my part of the world.

Carson pushes past me to climb into the cargo bay. The Transit's about the size of a minivan, but she seems to fill up the back. "Get going. Follow the GPS."

"Are you gonna be all right back here?"

She gives me her *really?* look. "Got no problem with small places. Move it."

We crawl through in-town and highway rush-hour traffic for almost an hour before the GPS takes me off the M27 at Fareham west of Portsmouth, then into what looks like farm country. Boarhunt Road, a narrow, paved slot between walls of green, leads me to a dirt path that ends in a weathered wooden fence.

When I let Carson out of the back, she's the Polish flower girl again, this time in a beaten-up blue jumpsuit. She drives us the final four-ish miles to the hotel and lets me out at the driveway's mouth. "Fifteen," she says as she pulls away.

We're staying in the Portsmouth Marriott Hotel on the north edge of the city. It's another typical soulless business hotel, a seven-story International-style box with a busy lobby and a harried front-desk staff. They probably forgot us ten minutes after we checked in.

To burn time, I stop at the bar and grab an overpriced beer. I'm just about at the bottom of it when I get a text from Carson. `@freight elevator.`

`Meet u upstairs.`

We join up at the fourth-floor elevator lobby, almost halfway between the freight elevator and my room. While I drove us out of Southampton, she'd moved the canvas from the Strongbox to a form-fitting cardboard carton that's a lot less conspicuous. She also scraped all the labels off the Strongbox and chopped it into pieces small enough to stick in a dumpster. It's a waste of a $193 box, but one less connection the cops can find.

"Bring it in," I tell Carson while I dig out my keycard and open the door.

"Hi, lover." Julie's voice. "I was wondering when you'd get back."

Oh shit oh shit oh shit…

She's made a little nest for herself with my pillows so she can sit up against the headboard. Both bedside lamps are on and give her skin a warm glow.

And other than her readers and the book propped on her thigh, she's naked.

"I hope you've had dinner." Julie's using her purry, dusky voice.

"'Cause I'm ready for des—" Her mouth drops open.

I shouldn't look behind me, but I have to. Carson's there. Her lips have disappeared. She's turning bright red, but not from embarrassment. Her eyes should've set Julie's hair on fire by now. They might still.

Carson gives me the most poisonous look she's ever aimed at me. Then she turns on her heels and storms out.

Oh shit oh shit oh shit…

Julie's sitting up with an arm crossed over her nipples. "Who was that?"

That stumps me for a moment until I realize she's never seen Carson in disguise. "That was Carson, undercover."

Her eyes balloon to the size of fried eggs. "Oh God." Tiny voice. "Oh God." One hand wraps around her throat, the other covers her mouth. The book bounces off the carpet.

There's about three thousand things I want to ask her, but the first one that gets loose is, "How did you get in here?"

Now she gives me the whipped-puppy eyes. "I took one of your room keys. I… I wanted to surprise you."

"You sure did." Now what do I do?

"Is Ms. Carson… really mad?"

"She's…" There's no way to sugar-coat this. "Yeah."

"Oh, God." She buries her face in her hands. "I'm sorry. I've ruined everything."

The break in her voice makes me think that crying's coming next. I perch on the bed next to her, wrap an arm around her shoulders and pull her against me. "She'd've figured it out eventually. Carson's smart. We'd have said something or done something…" Except we'd been really careful until now, and Carson doesn't always notice what she's not looking for—case in point: Aurora. Still, I have to try. I give Julie a squeeze. "It was a nice thought."

She sputters. "Just really awful, horrible timing."

"Well…"

She straightens up and wipes her eyes. "I should go. I—"

"Why? She won't come back." I kiss her temple, then get up and prop the box against the wall next to the desk.

"That's the copy?" Julie's got her knees pressed to her chest and her arms around her shins. Her voice is still a little rough.

"Yeah. It's gorgeous. Don't take it out of the box yet." I wait for her to look up at me. Still the whipped-puppy eyes. "I gotta go try to fix this with Carson. You might as well stay here. I'll be back when I'm done."

If Carson doesn't break my neck first.

Carson doesn't pick up when I call and ignores my texts. I know she has to dump the van, but I have no clue where she'd go after that. Instead of flailing around like I did after Boutelle ghosted, I go straight to my higher power—Olivia.

Carson went to the last place I'd expect: the Florence Arms.

I take a cab to Ladbrokes, an OTB place a couple blocks east of the pub, then walk around in circles for a good twenty minutes until I work up something to say that might not set off Carson again.

She's in the far corner of the half-full back room, hunched over her empty glass like Snoopy the vulture at the same table where we met Miranda a century ago. Good thing I got another scotch along with my double vodka.

I gently set her scotch down and carefully slide it next to her empty. She glares at me. I can feel the notches she's carving in my ears. I pull out the nearest chair and perch on the edge, like I could actually get away if she comes over the table at me. Her eye-mounted laser cannons are burning through the back of my skull. "Look, I'm sorry about—"

"You're fucking the client." I've heard friendlier growls out of pit bulls.

"Well, she's not technically the client. She's—"

"You're fucking. The client."

What can I say? "Um… yeah."

"Thought you were smarter than that."

"You told me to keep her happy."

"Not what—" Her throat makes a long, guttural sound. "How long?"

"Vienna."

"Fuck." Carson drops her stare, then shakes her head like it hurts a lot. "What're you telling her in bed?"

"What?" I get another blast from the laser cannons. "We're not talking about work, that's for sure."

She sags back into her chair and stares across the room at nothing in particular. Long, deep breath. Head shake. "Okay. You needed to get laid. I get that." She sounds… explosive. "Just hook up with someone. That's what I do."

Whoa. I wasn't expecting that kind of insight into Carson's mating habits. I'd love to pursue that, but now's about as not the right time as possible.

"Why not that redhead from the front desk at the Hilton?" She finishes off the drink I brought her, then hunches over the empties. "She was young, cute. Way she looked at you, her panties'd be on the floor before you're done asking. Fuck her brains out. Who cares?" She stabs a finger in the hotel's general direction. "But the Princess? Really? Why?"

She's hated Julie from the moment they met. Yeah, she's pissed about the whole client-babysitter thing, but it's deeper than that. Territory? Pack dominance? "Because I like her. She likes me. She's nice. She's normal. We get along."

"Wonderful. You into old women? That it?"

"There's some damn sexy older women out there." Like Allyson. I won't mention her, though. "I've come to appreciate that mature women seem to know who they are and what they want. That's very attractive."

Carson snorts again. "Right. What's your mom look like?"

Now *that's* a low blow. "She's 61, blond, and turning into a bird." I hope there's enough edge in my voice to back her off. "I'm *not* sleeping with my mother, thank you very much."

We end up in a frowning match. "You're stuck with her now, you know."

"What does that mean?"

"What do you think? You get tired of her, she beats you up, whatever—can't dump her." Finger-jabbing goes with this. "That'll piss her off. Last thing we need, especially now. She asks you to marry her, better fucking say 'I do.' Until the job's done, she owns you."

I slump against the back of my chair and let my head fall back. Yeah, Carson's right, but she's rubbing my nose in it. Maybe I deserve it; maybe she's out of line. It's funny—I came in here ready to kiss up to her to get back on her good side. Now she's just pissing me off. "I'm a big boy. I can handle this."

"You better." Carson reaches across the table, grabs the front of my sweater and drags me close. "Listen. You do this shit again—"

"Define 'this shit.'"

"Fuck the client. Fuck another op. Fuck Allyson—"

Where'd that come from? She can't know… can she?

"—Do that again on a project I'm on? You'll never work another one. I'll make sure of it."

We're close enough for me to get a full dose of the scotch on Carson's breath. It's strange, but I'm not afraid of her right now. Just pissed. I manage to pry her hand off my sweater. "Carson… the only way you get a veto on who I sleep with is if I'm sleeping with *you*."

It takes twenty minutes of walking around to cool off enough to be able to sit in the cab back to the hotel. On the way, I wonder why I said what I did to Carson—about how she gets a say in my mating habits only if she's part of them. Where did that come from?

At the hotel, I get a glass of white wine and a double vodka from the bar and carry them up to my room, where Julie's curled up in bed. We talk for a long time, avoiding the big subjects—who we are, where we're going, what we want from each other—that we probably should discuss. At the end, we're sitting very close.

I kiss her behind her ear. "I like you."

Julie slides her hand over my thigh. "I like you, too."

"Yeah?" She nods. "How much?"

"Get a little closer and you'll find out."

"Darling?"

Julie and I are spooned together, warm and comfortable. She's hugging my arm against her chest. Her hair smells like fresh rain on grass. The bedside lamp throws soft shadows over our bodies. Until now, every woman I've been with has been slender and sleek. Julie's body is lush, curvy. Voluptuous. Now I know what I've been missing.

I climb back out of the twilight I've been floating through. "Mmm?"

"Can I tell you a secret?"

"Sure." *Just don't move.*

She rolls over to face me. Oh, well. "Promise not to tell anyone?"

Her waist is like a valley between her ribs and her hips. It's perfectly sized for my hand. "Okay."

She slides her fingertips down my flank, over my hip, then back up. Up and down. It's sending me back into that twilight, which is fine with me. "I know… I know you're not happy about giving Oma's portrait to Ron." Her voice is as soft as the rest of her.

Wait, what? "Why are we talking about this now?"

"Shhhh." She kisses me to shut me up. It works. "Just listen. I know you don't like it. I don't either. Well… you don't have to do it."

I'm still muddled enough to not be tracking this. "What do you mean?"

"It's simple, darling. He doesn't own her."

I trap her hand so my big brain can get out of park. "He doesn't?"

"No." She gives me a big smile. "She's mine."

Chapter 45

Talk about breaking the mood...

I prop myself up on an elbow. "You'd better explain that."

Julie arranges her pillow so she can sit up against the headboard. "I'm sorry to pop this on you like this. I've wanted to tell you, but..." She bites her top lip and looks off into space. "I needed to know I can trust you—"

"We've been sleeping together for how long? And you just *now* figure that out?"

She sighs. "I know. It sounds silly to me now, too. I *do* trust you. I mean, well, look at us. And we'll have Oma's portrait in a couple days. I have to tell you now. I'm sorry."

I kiss the point of her shoulder. Forgiven. "So how do *you* own Dorotea?"

Julie does some more of that staring-into-space thing while she strokes my forearm. "It's about Oma's and Opa's wills." She looks at me, a little sheepish. "You want to hear this?"

Part of me wants to go back to cuddling. The rest is awake and trying to work all this out. That part wins. "Yeah. Tell me."

She settles in and folds her hands on her stomach. "Okay. Oma and Opa got their wills redone a week before *Anschluss*. I guess they saw what was coming and wanted to be ready. They sent copies to Viktor's Swiss lawyer—that's how I got them."

I pull the white duvet from around our knees up to Julie's armpits, which is all kinds of wrong. "If I'm going to have to hear about wills and codicils and all that, I need to concentrate."

She lifts an eyebrow my way. "Am I that distracting?"

"You bet."

"Good answer." She kisses the tip of my nose, then folds her hands on top of the duvet. "So. Opa's will left everything to Oma in case he died first. If she died first, then he split their belongings between the kids. Uncle Leo would get the real property, any cash—"

"Did they have any real property?"

"Not yet. I guess he was thinking ahead. Anyway, Uncle Leo would get any cash or investments, and the art. Mom would get the china, the silver, the linens, and the furniture."

"She got screwed."

"Well…" She bobs her head side-to-side a couple times. "Kind of. I've thought about it. First, they had *really* nice china and *really* nice silver. They were wedding presents. Also, I think he thought that by the time any of this would happen, she'd be married off and living in her husband's house and she'd already have her own china and silver. She could sell Oma's and Opa's and get a mint for it. But it would've been nice to give her some cash, too."

"No joke." This is now officially the weirdest conversation I've ever had in bed. That's saying something, considering the off-the-wall shit Janine came up with. "What was Dorotea's will like?"

She holds out her right hand to me and wiggles her fingers. When I take it, she pulls my hand down on her stomach and covers it with both of hers. Too bad the duvet's in the way. "Um… well, it starts out like Opa's. If she died first, he'd get it all, and if he died first, she split their stuff between the kids. But she was a little more even-handed. Uncle Leo still got the real property, but he only got half the cash and investments. He got the furniture to make up for it, which kind of makes sense, because then he'd have a fully-furnished house for his wife when he got married. Mom got the rest of the money, the china, the silver, the linens… and the *art.*"

Aha. "So Herschel died first?"

"Yes."

"Can you prove it in court?"

"I think so." She turns my hand loose and twists so she can face me. "How far have you gotten in my book?"

"Herschel and his brothers just got thrown in Dachau."

She nods. "June 1938. The Nazis sent them to Mauthausen in August. They were some of the first prisoners to get there, so they'd have been helping build the camp. Enough records survived that I found out Opa worked in the accounting office. That may be why he lived so long." She shakes her head. Her eyes are getting squinty. "The Nazis were idiots. They wrote everything down. *Everything.* Opa died on September 19th, 1939. I know the name of the guard who shot him. He was Gerhard Wandler, from Styria in Austria. It's crazy that I know that." She swallows and looks away.

"I'm sorry." Because what else can you say? I wrap an arm around her waist and pull her against me. She touches her forehead against mine and sighs. "Did you look him up? Wandler?"

"No." Julie sniffs and sits up. "I don't want to find out he went home and had a family and died in bed with his grandkids holding his hands. I couldn't take that."

Can't blame her. I give her a few moments to get herself together again. I hate to have to ask this next question. "What about Dorotea?"

Julie sighs again, wraps her arms around her shins, then rests her chin on her knees. "She went to Lichtenberg first, then they transferred her to Ravensbrück when it opened. It was all women and some kids then. Not much documentation survived the war— the SS burned most of it. The Polish Underground saved some, and some of the earliest stuff ended up in the Reich archives. That's where Stefan found some infirmary records for the camp's first year." She stares at the desk. "Do you still have that postcard of Oma?"

"Yeah. You want it?"

"Yes, please."

I slide out of bed and fish the postcard out of my laptop case.

She holds it in both hands, gazing at it like she can see through it to wherever her grandmother is now. Then she brushes a fingertip over the portrait's hair. "They'd have cut her hair off by then. Or she would've, because of the lice. It was a labor camp. Siemens, AEG, Daimler. A lot of that was later, though. They'd send the young, strong women out to build roads and things. I don't know what Oma did there. But I know she checked into the camp infirmary on September 18th, 1939 and was there until the 23rd. That's when her number shows up on the clinic's daily report under 'died.' Having prisoners die was strange enough back then that they still kept track."

There's an ache in Julie's voice that makes me want to bundle her up in my arms and rock her and tell her it's going to be okay. When I try, though, she grabs my hand and holds on tight while she keeps staring at the postcard. If that's all the comfort she wants, that's what I'll give her, though I wish I could do something more.

You are. You're stealing back her painting.

Yeah. It's pretty clear that's where this is headed. Like it isn't complicated enough.

I finally ask, "Does Cousin Ron know?"

She hands me the postcard, then flops back against the headboard. "Sort of. I gave him the wills. I showed him the thing from Mauthausen. I showed him the Ravensbrück clinic log from the eighteenth." She puts on a grim half-smile. "I maybe didn't show him the log from the twenty-third."

I sag against the headboard and massage the throb building behind my ear. "Why not?"

She gives me the kind of look I usually get from Carson. "Think about it. How hard would he try to get Oma back if he knew I own her? None. He wouldn't get anything from it. I need him to think he's going to get her right up until I tell him, 'Oh, by the way.'"

"He can sue you for fraud."

"How will he know? Stefan won't testify against me. He's my lawyer."

"Who pays him?"

"Ron, but Stefan's *my* lawyer. *I* signed the retainer with him. It doesn't matter where the money comes from." She slides against me. "And you won't, will you? After... everything? Us? You don't want Ron to get her anyway. And, well, you're the one who'll have stolen her."

I open my mouth a couple times, but nothing comes out. I never figured she could be so calculating. I don't want to follow this down to its logical end, but... "Is that what... what *this* was all about?" I wave my hand over the bed. "Did you do this to—"

Julie's eyes get huge. Her mouth falls open. "No! No! How can you think that?" She backs away. "I never expected this. I'm glad it happened, but I never planned you and me..." Her face starts to melt. "Is that what you think of me? That I'd... I'd..."

"No." I reach out to touch her face, but she pushes my hand away. "I don't want to think that way about you. I don't want to wreck this... whatever this is we've got. But..."

Then it dawns on me why I'm getting more confused with every word I say. I can't tell if she's acting. I thought I could read her, but I can't, not right now. Why isn't her face red? Why isn't she tearing up? I've been around people who've been faking it for so long that I can't tell the difference between real outrage and the fake kind anymore.

I put up my hands. "Look, I'm sorry, I—"

She backs out of bed. "I can't stay here. I need to go. I need to think."

What am I seeing here? The hurt in her eyes, the trembling chin—she'd have to be a hell of a good actress to pull that off if it's not real. Then again, she *is* a good actress. She totally nailed Gillian. But what happened between us felt real up until a couple minutes ago.

A spike of panic blows through me. "No, please, stay, let's talk—"

"No." She bats my hand away again. "I'm upset, you're upset. No." She rushes to the desk chair and starts throwing on her clothes. "I thought I could trust you to—"

"You *can.*" I scramble out of bed and catch her arms before she can pull on her sweater. This time, she doesn't fight me off, which gives me a little hope. "I'm surprised and confused and... please don't go, not like this. I want—"

"No." I can barely hear her. She slowly twists away from me, then struggles into the sweater. "I need to spend a night away from you so I can think. Find me after breakfast. I'll be ready then." She reaches out to brush my jaw with her fingertips. Then she's gone.

I stand there watching the door close. I have to try hard to breathe right. I blew it. I totally fucked up. I feel like twenty kinds of shit.

The worst part: the little voice inside me that's usually right? It's asking, *Did you fuck up? Or is that what she wants you to think?*

Chapter 46

I pass Carson in the hall on the way to breakfast this morning—Saturday—and she walks by like I'm not there. When I find Julie in the restaurant, she frowns and looks away. I hate this shit. On top of it all, if this doesn't get worked out by tomorrow night, swiping Dorotea's portrait is going to be about a hundred times harder.

I haven't been able to find out which brand of hardware the Mainwaring's using to hang its art, so I have to look at all the major players. There are only so many variations on cables and hooks out there, and I think I'm seeing them all.

Julie taps at my door a bit after eleven. She gives me a look that's half-hurt and half-pissed off. "I thought you should see this." Frosty. She holds out a printout of an email.

"Look, Julie, I'm sorry—"

"You should be." She turns and stalks back to her room. Her door closes louder than it needs to.

I watch her door for a minute to see if she'll come back out and help negotiate my surrender terms. She doesn't. I sigh and take her gift back to the desk.

During the break—when we were still talking—Julie told me Geisman had been trying to contact Ute Kinigader. Geisman sent Julie this translation of Ute's reply a couple hours ago:

```
Fraulein Kinigader was not born
when her father died. She remembers
nothing of him. If you must ask
questions, you may come, but it may
be a waste of your time.

With respect, B. Leininger for U.
Kinigader.
```

At the bottom, Geisman says he doesn't know who B. Leininger is, but he'll keep digging.

I go to the window to watch the wind beat on the trees and drive the gathering clouds across the washed-out sky. Ute said she didn't *remember* anything about Kinigader, not that she didn't *know* anything about him. That sounds fishy. If I was a little kid and I found out parents are supposed to come in pairs, what's the first thing I'd ask my mom? *Mommy, where's my daddy?*

Erna—the mom—must've told her *something*. Maybe there's papers in a drawer somewhere. Maybe there's a salt mine behind the house. Maybe pigs fly out there. It's gotta be worth checking out... I hope.

Carson abuses my door a bit after two. When I open up, she grumbles, "She in there?"

I haven't quite gotten around to telling her that I pissed off Julie. I've already heard the *I told you so* in my head. "No. It's safe."

She pushes past me, glances at the bed, then drags me into the bathroom and turns on the bathtub faucet.

I know what that means. "Seriously? You think I'm bugged?"

"What do you think?" She bites off the words. "Allyson called."

I stand there blinking for a few moments. "All by herself?" Carson nods. "I thought she doesn't do that."

"She doesn't." Carson crowds me and drops her voice so I can barely hear it over the running water. "She asked when we'll be done tomorrow."

"Why does she care?"

"Good fucking question. Told her I don't know. She says, 'Pick a time and stick to it.' Told her, two a.m. She says, 'Be out by two.'"

"Can we do it by two?"

"Doesn't matter. Gotta be out by then."

None of this makes any sense. I guess that shouldn't surprise me. I try to avoid Carson's eyes drilling through me so I can think. "Something must be happening there, or around there."

"No shit."

My brain takes a lot of time to make a very short leap. "Smoking Man?"

Carson shrugs. "Thought about that too. Surveillance at the lab, the alarm the other night… but nobody's on our tail? Like they already know where we are, what we're doing."

"Who'd you tell about Wednesday night?"

"Olivia, in case we got jacked up. You?"

"Nobody." Olivia tells Allyson, Allyson tells…?

"Not even your girlfriend?"

"*Especially* not her." This makes no sense. "Allyson's working with somebody *else* who's making a run against the museum? That's the stupidest thing ever."

Carson rolls her eyes. "You haven't worked for her long enough to see the stupidest thing ever." She hooks her thumbs in her jeans' front pockets. "Cleaners get done on time, we can make it."

"Yeah, about that…" I'd spent the past couple days both with the hardware catalogs and reviewing everything I know about how turn-of-the-century European paintings are put together. "I know you want us in and out fast, but I can't rush through it—I have to leave both pieces absolutely unmarked. I need an hour."

"Won't get it. Power comes back in fifteen, maybe twenty minutes tops. Sooner if they got bolt cutters."

Bolt cutters? She hasn't told me many details of her plan yet; another thing that's got me spooked. "Look, we've talked about this." I'm trying to keep my voice calm—we're still working out the last fight, we don't need a new one. "Taking apart a painting takes time. I can do it only so fast. You can say 'do it faster,' but that's like telling a chicken to fly higher. It just isn't gonna happen."

Carson's face gets all dark. "Power comes on, cameras come on. Figure it out." She plods to the door.

"Carson?"

She stops to look over her shoulder.

"Are we speaking again?" Say yes…

"No." She twitches her head toward Julie's room. "Keep track of your girlfriend." She bangs the door shut on her way out.

Chapter 47

Sunday. Twelve hours to showtime.

Not only does Carson not run with me, I don't even see her. I kind of miss watching her run away from me. I pretend I'm chasing her through the sleepy streets so I can keep up a decent pace. While I run, I think about what I'll do after my shower.

I need to practice taking apart a painting. Hey, it's been four years.

I clean off my desktop, cover it with a towel, then haul out a landscape I'd picked up in an antique store outside Bristol while I was shopping for tools. It's the kind of thing you'll get if you describe Impressionism to an artist who's never seen it, then tell him to paint one. Luckily, it was cheap. It's about thirty by forty—smaller than Dorotea—and the artist (who I've never heard of and hope to keep it that way) helpfully brushed "1919" next to his scrawled signature. But it's put together in roughly the same way Dorotea is: the stretched canvas is set into the frame, then nails go straight through the stretcher into the sides of the frame's rabbet. There are fourteen little rusted nail heads down there, four on each long side, three on each short.

No problem... right?

I haul my tools out from under my bed, start the timer on my phone, then get to work. I have to winkle out each nail without damaging the stretcher or the frame. It's nothing new for me—I used to do this at the gallery—but I'm as rusty as the first nail I finally lever out with my cat's paw and a thin-bladed chisel. This may be the original hardware.

Each nail fights me all along its inch-and-a-half length. As metal rusts, it becomes rough and starts to bond with the wood. This shouldn't be a problem with Dorotea; she's been out of her frame at least a couple times, including once only a month and some ago. But she's bigger and probably has more nails. I kick myself again for not counting holes when we were in the lab.

The last nail squeaks out of the stretcher. I hit the "stop" button on my phone's timer. Forty-two minutes.

Shit.

Two nails came out seriously bent. I straighten them out, but I know they won't be happy being pounded back into the frame, even using the same holes. More time lost.

The hour I wanted seems like way too little. And Carson says I have to do this in twenty minutes? Sure.

I reassemble the painting—total time, an hour eighteen—and think about what I can do differently. There's not a lot. I reset the timer and try slipping the chisel's edge under each nail's head and twisting slightly to get it started. It works only because the nails are already loose (as they should be for Dorotea). This knocks off a few minutes, but leaves scores on the stretcher.

Rinse, repeat.

And again.

And again.

By almost lunchtime, I'm down to under an hour, but not by a lot. And this is on a piece that's smaller than the one I'll be taking off the wall tonight. I still have yet to figure out how to pound nails through the new stretcher without it sounding like a construction site.

This isn't going to work.

I spend lunch in the hotel's Cast Iron Grill thinking about this problem without coming up with any bright—or even dim—ideas.

Carson blocks the restaurant entry just as I'm about to finish my beer. She points at me (it's like those cartoons of Death pointing at his next victim), then over her shoulder. You bet I follow her.

We end up in her room. She closes the door. "They're watching."

Shit! I'd been wondering how long we'd go before this happened. I plop down in one of her armchairs. "Did you see Smoking Man?"

"No. Two guys in cars, one in the parking lot, one across the street." Her arms are crossed tight enough to crack ribs on a normal human. "Showed up last night."

It had to happen, I guess. We needed more ass pain. "What do we do about it?"

"*We?* You don't do shit." She lets her shoulders fall back against the door. Because she wants to lean, or because she wants to keep me here? "Asked for another car last night. It'll be here by four. I'll drive the Jag north someplace at six. You take the Princess to the party when the shadows follow me."

"How do you get to the party?"

"Not your problem."

I guess we're not over the Julie issue yet. "Actually, it is. If you're not there, I can't do anything."

"I'll be there."

"When? What if these guys try to stop us? What if they don't follow you?"

Carson purses her lips. Did I finally manage to ask her something she hasn't thought of? "Call a cab. Leave from the Premier Inn over there." She pushes away from the door, then yanks it open. I guess I'm dismissed. "They get in the way, I'll deal with it. You stay on goal. Got it?"

Now's not the time to tell her I still need an hour or more with the portrait. "Yeah. Got it."

The next three hours take about ten minutes. No matter how much I molest the crappy landscape, I don't get any faster. The look Dorotea gives me from her postcard is absolutely lethal. The sky gets nastier every hour. *Go ahead and rain,* I tell the weather gods. *Everything else is turning to shit.*

It starts to rain.

I watch the gutters fill up and the leaves get plastered to the asphalt while I try to dredge up some better ideas. The one that keeps coming up seems like the worst I've had for months, but it's the only one that helps solve my problem.

Carson jerks her door open a few seconds after I pound on it. "What?"

"Ever unframed a painting?"

"What do you think?"

"I think it's time you learned."

She grumbles all the way into my room. Then she sees the

landscape turned face-down on my desk and the grumbling stops like she's turned off a faucet. "What's that?"

"Get over here. It won't bite much." She edges closer. "This is what the back of a painting looks like. It's set up roughly the way Dorotea's portrait should be. I've been practicing on it." Here we go… "I have good news and bad news. The bad news is, it's taking me over half an hour to get the canvas out of the frame."

"That's too long."

"No shit. The good news is, I know how to cut that time in half." I hand her a slim chisel, a cat's paw, and a putty knife. "You're gonna help."

We get to work once Carson stops squawking and sputtering. She's over-cautious at first, but after a few tries she gets the hang of it. She's pulling nails like a pro after an hour. We're able to get the canvas loose in around twenty minutes by the time it's completely dark outside.

"Still too long," Carson says, this time without the hard edges.

"Now you know why." I drop into the desk chair. "I've done everything I can. I pre-drilled the copy's stretcher. We're moving as fast as we can without breaking anything. It takes as long as it takes."

She nods. "I'll buy us some more time."

Chapter 48

The rain turns into a steady light drizzle that reflects light from the windows on both sides of the street. I've changed into my blue Canali suit and wish I had a raincoat. (It never rains in Southern California.) In a few minutes, I have to get Julie-as-Gillian to the party at the Mainwaring.

But while I watch the rain, I'm seeing something else. The end of Heibrück Pacific fiveish years ago. The end of my old world.

We didn't watch the Steel Sparrow's press conference through the gallery's windows. There were too many cameras looking in. No, I watched it with Gar in his office, livestreaming on his computer. Actually, I did most of the watching; he spent most of the time pacing and muttering, "This is bad. This is bad."

Ida Rothenberg stood in front of our window under our name and logo, just so nobody'd miss where she was. She wore a white suit that was a touch large for her. It almost matched her hair. She had to stand on a stepstool so the reporters could see her head over the podium.

"Many years ago, the world saw a great evil." She sounded like Dr. Ruth, with a gravelly voice and a thick accent. "We defeated that evil, but we did not eliminate it. It still lives."

She talked about the Nazi looting of Europe's art treasures and what her family lost to it. She talked about the camps, and how she survived when most of her family didn't. How the laws came either too late or too flawed to help the people of her generation get their property back. How her painting flew along just out of reach, falling into one set of hands after another. How it was stolen from a museum it never should've been in. How it came to this gallery. How we sold it. (She didn't know about Feng, or she'd have talked about him, too.)

"I will never get back my art," she said. "My grandchildren will never again see it. For me, this story is done. But there are thousands of people like me who face the daily disappointment and loss.

Children who want their parents' most loved possessions. Grandchildren and great-grandchildren who want their birthrights.

"So I must do what I can to help them push through the complicated laws and stubborn officials and expensive lawyers and the people such as these in this gallery that continue the Nazis' work." That hurt. "I will not let the Nazis win. I can do one thing only to help these people who are like me: I can give them the attention of the public, and the politicians, and the courts. The people who *can* help them. I can make certain that my words will live on after me, because they will be my last words."

Then she took a pistol out of her purse, stuck the muzzle under her chin, and pulled the trigger.

The gunshot breaks me out of the flashback, like it usually does. That saves me from seeing the blood again, hearing the screams from the reporters, and feeling my heart drop like a rock into my shoes.

You should have tried.

Chapter 49

The reception in the "Stealing Beauty" gallery would be okay if I wasn't wound up tighter than a tick on crack. There's lots of free Champagne, for one thing. I get one last shot at my favorite pieces in the exhibit as I trail along behind Julie, who's in full Gillian-schmoozing mode. She's still giving me the cold shoulder. She's really good at it.

But Carson's way late. She hasn't answered my texts. Did the shadows get her? If they did, what would they do with her? Should I be out looking for her, or call Olivia to find her?

She's smart, I tell myself. *She's tough. She can take care of herself. Right?*

Or is she still pissed enough at me to hang me out to dry? Would she do that? I hope not. Hope's not really a plan, though.

If she doesn't show up soon, this project is over.

A photographer's drifting through the crowd, snapping the happy party animals. Security cameras are one thing—I've never seen a still from one that wasn't a piece of shit—but a focused, well-lit, full-face color portrait is a whole other animal. Julie may survive ending up on the museum's website, but I totally can't afford the publicity. It turns into a dance, with me pivoting away from the front of his lens and Julie mastering the just-in-time head-turn.

Tovorovsky's here, too, hovering around Dorotea in the back half of the exhibit. He's had enough time to research Gillian by now. Maybe he already knows who she really is. I can't risk letting them meet again. I see him just in time to steer Julie the other way and I spend the next hour keeping her in the exhibit's front half, waiting for an explosion.

Time goes geologic on us. I swear the clock runs backwards a couple times. Every security camera I walk under looks like it's glowing... and watching me.

When I'm right on the edge of grabbing a full bottle of booze and chugging it, Carson shows up. Her fitted black cocktail dress isn't nearly as extreme as the clingy blue jersey one in Milan, but it's eye-catching anyway: knee-length, sleeveless (her arms are as chiseled as her calves), slit neckline. She's a very healthy woman.

And she's so calm and normal (that is, Carson-normal) that my insides unkink enough to let me breathe a little. I never figured Carson would have a calming effect on me, but right here, right now, she does.

Four hours 'til showtime.

We send Julie back to the hotel at nine and slip down the midpoint stairwell. Carson's heels sound like little gunshots as we charge through the basement. It's all pipes and conduit, bare fluorescent strip lights, work benches, machinery, concrete everywhere. We end up at a locked metal door painted a medium gray. She growls "Get in" once she picks the lock.

It's a closet. Am I going to end up in a closet on every assignment?

The back and right walls are lined with metal utility shelves piled with cans of paint and assorted junk. Six feet wide at most and shrinking every second I look at it. I force down an extra-deep breath and edge in. Before I can even get oriented, the door clunks shut. It's like the inside of a mineshaft.

Carson's phone flashlight app pops on. Now the place looks like the inside of a horror movie, all contrasty bluish-white glare and weird pitch-black shadows. All the color's blown out of the room. She shoulders past me and drags a dark backpack off the bottom back shelf. "Sit."

I take off my suit coat and settle on the concrete floor. I can't relax, though; from the inside, the closet looks about half as big as it did from the outside, and it's still shrinking. I try to watch Carson instead of the walls closing in. She squats, zips open the backpack, then drags out rolled-up dark clothes and a pair of dark gym shoes.

Then everything turns black again.

For a few moments, all I can hear is my own breathing and a vague rustling where Carson should be. "What are you doing?"

"Changing. Not doing this in a dress."

I hear a zipper, then more rustling. The thought of Carson

stripping down to her underwear right next to me distracts me for about two seconds. Then I'm back to obsessing about being buried alive. Phobias suck.

Carson's in her ninja costume when she turns on the light again. I pull off my tie, fold it in half and roll it into a coil while she puts away her dress and heels. I'd like to change, too, but my backpack's in the Volvo station wagon Carson got for us. "How'd you get that in here? The Polish flower girl again?"

"Uh-huh. Came in with the caterers." She sits with her back against the blank wall, then shuts off her phone.

Dark. Again. I fumble my tie into my coat's breast pocket, lean back against the wall, and try to think about things that make me happy. Julie? That ends up being all about her being mad at me now. Gianna? Well, I've mentioned what that's like. Beer and puppies get me only so far. I swear I can hear the walls grinding closer. I could turn on my phone, but that'll just show me how small this place really is. When it's dark, I only imagine how small it is.

I whisper, "Carson?"

"What?" She sounds irritated.

"You should know... Julie told me something Friday night." I repeat what Julie said about the wills and her owning Dorotea. Maybe I drag it out because I don't think about the damn closet while I'm talking.

Carson's quiet for too long, the kind of quiet that I think happens in the eye of a hurricane. Finally, she grumbles, "Fuck."

"Is this bad?"

"What do you think?" She makes a noise like breaking a rock in her throat. "Should've seen it. Nobody works that hard for something they're not gonna get."

"What do we do?"

"What we *don't* do is fuck the client." I can hear her stew for a while. "Bowen gets his picture. Princess can sort it out—"

"But it's *hers*—"

"Not our monkey, not our circus." That crackles as it flies past me.

Of course, Ida picks this moment to barge in and say, *you should have tried.* "If Bowen finds out it's Julie's, she'll never get near it again. That's not fair. Her grandmother left it to her mother, who left it to her. If we take it away from her, we're..." ...*screwing her like*

I did Ida is what I don't say, but what's in my head.

Carson sighs. "Look. I get it. She should have it. It sucks." Her voice is quieter, with fewer sharp edges. "We don't do 'fair.' We get the client what he wants. We get a paycheck big enough to drink our conscience away. That's why I hate knowing who the client is." Pause. "Took me time to get used to it, too. If that helps."

It doesn't. Talking about it probably isn't going to change Carson's mind, though, so I let it drop… for now. So now it's both dark and silent. When we're talking, I can ignore what the walls are doing, but when it's quiet, it feels like I'm alone, which freaks me out more.

Suck it in. It's fine, you're fine. Carson's here. The walls aren't moving. You're fine.

*Bull*shit, *I'm fine. The closet's the size of a shoebox.*

Suck it in… suck it in…

"What's wrong?" Carson's voice startles me, not because it's loud—it's only a couple notches above a whisper—but because it's so sudden.

"Nothing. I'm fine."

"Bullshit. Sounds like you're running a marathon."

If I tell her, I'll never hear the end of it. "It's nothing."

She makes an exasperated noise. "You sick? Look, you barf, you're licking it up."

Before I can scratch up an answer, I hear footsteps outside. Rubber soles, heavy steps. They turn a corner—I can hear the pivot—get closer, stop right outside. I hear the *snick* of Carson's metal baton telescoping. My heartbeat fills my ears.

The doorknob rattles. I levitate. Then I remember: it's locked.

The feet walk away.

It takes a while to scrape myself off the ceiling. Even Carson needs to take a few deep breaths. I don't relax until I hear her baton click back into its shell, and then I don't really relax, I just go back to listening to my heart try to claw its way out of my chest.

There's rustling, then something touches my forehead. I barely stifle a scream while I bounce off the floor.

"Ease off!" Carson sputters. "For chrissake. What's wrong?"

That was her. Her hand on my forehead. "I don't do so well in small places."

She sighs. "Claustrophobia?"

"Um… yeah."

"Since you were inside?"

"Yeah. I mean, I was always a little claustrophobic, but it's a lot worse now."

"I'll bet." Her voice is softening. That helps all by itself. "Want the light on?"

"No. That makes it worse. Sorry."

Carson sighs again. "Everyone's scared of something. C'mon, sit."

I ease back down on the floor and try to find a position that doesn't shut off too much circulation. There's scratching, then I feel a hard bicep press against my softer one. Her hip bumps mine. "This better?"

She's warm and solid and safe. My stress level starts nosediving in seconds. "Yeah. Lots. Thanks. So, what are you scared of?"

No answer, of course. She settles in. "What helps?"

"For this? Talk. It distracts me. Look, I'm sorry, I—"

"No worries. You talked to me, out at the lab. My turn now."

I remember that—her out in the bushes after midnight, watching the Mainwaring's lab, me in the car a block away. What goes around…

"What you wanna talk about?" Carson asks.

This whispering in the dark takes me way back to when I was little and I shared a bedroom with Dianne, my big sister. I could talk to her about anything and she'd never make fun of me or use it against me or tell on me. We moved to a bigger house when I was eight and I got my own room, but we'd still sit in the dark and talk. Dianne's still the only person I trust completely. There: something that makes me happy.

"Anything. Whatever." That doesn't get her going. "Are your folks still around?"

Pause. "Yeah. In Edmonton. Yours?"

"Yeah. They're divorced now. I never thought they'd do that."

"Wish mine would."

"Why?" No answer. "What happened with Aurora?" Still no answer. "You know, if we're going to talk, you have to say something."

"Yeah. Nothing personal, okay?"

We sit there for I don't know how long. I can hear her breathe and feel every time she moves. When I turn my head, I can pick up what's left of her soap or shampoo, something that smells like sage. This is way more intimate than I ever imagined getting with Carson. Not that it's bad or anything, just… unexpected.

"What's the plan? You never told me."

She shifts and rotates her shoulders. "Get to the power panels at one. Throw all the breakers. Put blown fuses in the main shutoff. Lock the panels with new padlocks. They gotta cut the locks and fix the disconnect before they can power up again. Call the Princess, get the fake and your tools out of the car. Go up the stairwell to the third floor. You swap the picture. Go out the back. Princess picks us up and we're gone."

I roll that over in my head. "It sounds so simple the way you tell it."

"One problem."

"Only one?"

"One big one. They'll know we're here."

She's right—that's a big one.

"I'll block out the cameras on the way. We get forty, maybe fifty minutes of dark and no alarms. An hour if we're damn lucky." If I listen hard, I can hear *I hope*. "Power comes on, they see what I did to the cameras, they call PD. Then we got guards *and* cops inside looking for us."

There's nothing about anything she said that makes me feel good. It's hours away and my stomach's already knotting up. "Why wait until one? We have to be out by two."

"*Because* we have to be out by two. Other guys should be here by then. Maybe PD catches them, not us. Thinks they did all this."

Figuring the odds gives me a headache. "If this works, we're buying lotto tickets."

"Princess better come through, or we're fucked." She had to say that, didn't she? "Get some Zs. We got three hours."

Sleep? Is she kidding? "You have an alarm?"

"Set my phone. Go to sleep."

Maybe ten minutes later, Carson's deep, even breathing tells me she's out. I'm still wired like I've had ten Red Bulls. My brain's full of all the ways this can go sideways. When that doesn't keep me busy enough, all my spidey senses are out waiting for the walls to start closing in again, or the guards to bust in here with dogs the size of rhinos.

I need to go to sleep so I don't drive myself nuts. I doubt it'll work, but I close my eyes, lean my head back against the wall, and try to match my breathing to Carson's. In. Out. Innn. Ouuut. Innnnn…

Next thing I know, Carson's shaking me. Her phone light's on; she's wearing her black hood. "It's time."

Chapter 50

"Ready?" Carson's fingertips are resting on the big red handle on the main electrical service disconnect, a gray metal cabinet mounted to the basement wall.

She'd told me that once the lights go out, we're going to be real busy. I totally believe her. "Ready." I think.

"On three."

I'm in front of one of the two main service panels next to the meter stack, which is next to Carson. I rest my fingertips on the breakers controlling the feeders to the subpanels on each floor. My hands are sweating in my blue nitrile gloves. My job starts when the main service is down: I have to set all the breakers to their halfway, tripped position, so they look like they overloaded.

When she hits "three," Carson yanks the disconnect lever down, cutting the grid power. The lights die. I expect everything to go silent, but it doesn't. The HVAC and pumps and other mechanicals keep grinding away, probably on a separate feed.

Carson snaps on her new fashion accessory: a headset with a small LED spotlight on the center of her browband. She rips out the disconnect's fuses with her heavy elbow-length black-rubber gloves, then slots in new, blown ones.

The clock's running.

I sidestep from the domestic panel to the security system's panel and flip all its breakers, too. I can imagine little red LEDs going dark all over the museum.

Voices. We both freeze.

Carson switches off her headlight. I twist off my red Mini Maglite. The world disappears except for the battery-operated exit signs and fire lights.

The voices are off to our left somewhere. The way sound bounces down here, it's hard to tell where. But they're getting louder. And my insides are getting colder.

A splash of red light zips up in front of me. I trace it back to

Carson's little black flashlight, which must have a red gel on it. She whispers, "Lock 'em up."

I take the padlocks she's holding out, close the panel doors as quietly as I can—which sounds like a three-car accident—then click the padlocks closed in the hasps.

The voices are definitely louder. My insides are definitely collapsing into a softball.

"Stairs're over there." Carson runs the red circle along the floor off to my left—the same direction the voices are coming from. "Go to the ground floor, turn left. Princess should be out back in a couple minutes. If she shows up."

"What about—"

"Go."

I go on the balls of my feet. I'm still wearing dress shoes, and even with the surgical booties Carson made me wear, hard soles make a big noise in a concrete cave. Just as I turn a corner to the stairwell door, I look back and see a slight red glow at the disconnect. Carson has to swing the handle back to "on" without making any noise. We want the museum guys to think it's a power surge or circuit fault until they figure out it isn't.

There's footsteps to go with the voices, now: two guys, rubber soles (they squeak now and then—they're that close). I glance back in Carson's direction in time to see the red glow disappear. *Get out of there!*

There's no way I can help her now. I don't even have a coin to throw to make a distracting noise. The voices and footsteps get louder and more distinct. When I see a light pool from a flashlight slide by, I slip through the door and creep up the stairs.

Except for the exit signs, the back hallway is darkish and quiet. I tiptoe-run down the hall to what must be the back door, actually a set of big double doors with panic bars (appropriate name for those). I stand there for a moment, trying to ignore the question my rational brain keeps asking: what's out there? Guards? Cops? Tovorovsky's thugs?

Fuck it. At least I can watch the BBC in a British prison. I shove the door open.

It's dark out there. A Transit van is sleeping in the parking lot's far corner, next to the building being renoed. Other than that, *nada.*

Julie's at the wrong courtyard. She blew us off. She's been arrested.

Tovorovsky's goons dragged her away. All this takes only an instant to rocket through my mind. Then it repeats, and repeats, and repeats.

I step through the door. No spotlights hit me, no blue flashing lights turn on. Another step and I'm even with the back wall. No snipers have shot me yet.

Off to my right, I see a white car nose and a grille with a single chrome slash across it. I've never been this glad to see a Volvo before.

Julie's rolled down her window by the time I get to the driver's door. She's wearing a dark sweater and her car coat. She asks "Are you okay?" like she actually cares.

"Yeah. We took down the lights. Unlock the doors?"

I dump my coat and change into gym shoes and a black sweater. Now I feel more like a burglar. I then grab both backpacks and hurry to the back hatch, which is open by the time I reach it. Boutelle's copy of Dorotea is in a canvas envelope, a rectangular black cloth sack with a Velcro closure.

On my way past the driver's door, Julie says, "Be careful." Again, like she means it. I'll have to figure that out sometime when my brain isn't full.

Carson closes the door behind me as I stagger inside, loaded down with all this stuff.

I drop her backpack at her feet and wrestle the canvas into a more secure carrying position. The last thing we need is for me to fumble this thing and have it go bouncing down the stairs. A pool of red light from Carson's flashlight fills this section of the hallway. I look back at her, do a double-take. "What's that?"

She's extended an aluminum tube with a three-pronged claw on one end. The claw's holding what looks like half a black egg. Instead of answering me, she props open the door again, leans out, and shoves the egg over the camera bubble above the doorway. Aha.

She whispers, "Let's go."

I follow her up two flights of concrete stairs. The only light is the red wash from her flashlight, which she's using for her footing, not mine. I stumble a couple times, but I don't go down (thank God). She stops at the second-floor landing and does the egg-sticking thing again.

I ask, "We're not going in there, are we?"

"No. They don't know that."

On the third floor, we push through into the short hallway that leads to the exhibit. The red light reminds me of submarine movies. Carson covers the camera bubbles all along our route to Dorotea.

"How many of those things do you have?"

"Three dozen. Cheaper that way."

Paintings blur by in the shadows. Every time we turn a corner, I expect to see a wall of guards waiting for us. When I was a kid, I always wanted to hide out in a museum and see everything at night. I don't think this is what I had in mind. Be careful what you wish for.

Carson screeches to a halt. Dorotea's there, hanging against the opposite wall, staring at us. She's all, *you took long enough, didn't you?*

I lean the copy against the next wall. My heart's banging away—not just because I half-ran here while hauling Dorotea's double, but because I'm here, almost alone, with a multi-million-dollar piece of history that I'm about to steal. I run my flashlight beam over her, trying to work myself up for what comes next.

"Twelve minutes," Carson hisses. Already? "Where's your mask?"

"Aren't the cameras off?"

"They'll come back on."

Good point. I break away from lusting after Dorotea and start to get myself together. I pull on my hood, lay out my tools, and cover the floor in front of Dorotea with a cheap dark-blue quilted mover's blanket. Then I do something I've wanted to do since the first time I walked in here: I look behind the portrait. I stare at the picture hooks for a few seconds. If it's not one thing, it's another. "Carson? This' gonna take two people."

"Why?"

"You want the full rundown?"

"Shit, no."

The full rundown is, the Mainwaring uses Picture Display Systems security hooks: machined aluminum blocks about an inch tall with a wire latch over the hook's open end. I'll need both hands to open the latches and guide the hanging wire free while she keeps the canvas from falling.

Carson grabs the top and bottom of the frame. I make myself as flat as I can against the wall. "Up a smidge." She raises the frame just enough to take the weight off the hook, which is perfect. I reach in, flip down the latches, then worry the hanging wire out of the hooks.

"Okay, on the blanket, face-down. Slow."

The painting doesn't look like much when it's flat on its face. In a way, that makes the next part easier; I can pretend this is that nasty landscape I was taking apart in my hotel room.

Carson holds out her headband with the LED. "Here."

"Don't you need that?"

"Not now."

I fiddle the thing over my hood, look down, then switch on the LED. Compared to Carson's red flashlight beam or even my little Maglite, it's so bright that I wince. "Time?"

"Twenty-one."

We've hardly even touched Dorotea yet. "Let's get to work. Do those two sides." I point to the portrait's top and left edges.

Carson nods and grabs tools.

Luckily, the nails are new and come out without too much of a fight. Except for one—there's always one—down in the lower right corner that's acting like it's bent or stuck. I skip over it to get the rest out. Carson's doing okay; she mutters only three or four F-bombs along the way. Nail squeaks sound like dying hyenas. I keep waiting for the goon squad to come charging through the gallery. While I'm busy, though, I can ignore that mental picture… mostly.

The last stubborn nail comes out looking like a banana. I tap it flat while Carson pulls her last two nails. When she finishes, she sits back on her heels and pumps her fists in the air like she just won a race. Then she shines her red light on her watch. "Forty-three."

Seventeen minutes before the other guys show up. "Where are you going?"

She's on her feet with her grabber stick in her hands. "Gonna cover more cameras."

"Why? You got these, right?"

Even hooded and in the dark, I can see her you-dumbshit look. "Want 'em to know exactly where we were?" Then she's gone, nothing but an occasional red spot on the ceiling.

I ease Dorotea out of her frame and carefully slide her out from under the hanging wire. Looking at her will just distract me, so I don't. I prop her against the wall, face-in, then skin the envelope off the copy. Make sure she's heads-up. Fit the top of the canvas into the frame's rabbets just below the hanging wire. Gently slide it up. Sliding, sliding.

Not sliding.

The canvas stops about a half-inch from the top rail. I scramble to the top, lift the canvas free, and feel along the rabbets on both sides. Fairly smooth; no nail heads or knots or anything. I move halfway down the long side, settle the painting's foot in the frame's bottom, and lower the top in place. It won't go in.

The top is too wide. Not by much—a sixteenth, maybe—but enough.

After swearing some under my breath, I think back to the lab and me with a measuring tape. Did I measure all four corners? No: I took one width and one height. There wasn't enough time for anything else.

I swear some more.

Okay, a sixteenth isn't much. I can shave that out of the rabbet with my chisel. They won't notice until they pull the copy out of the frame. I hope.

The elevator clunks into action. Someone's coming up.

If I had any brains left, I'd panic. *Get to work.*

The frame looks like it's walnut, a good hardwood that's had a century to dry and harden. Hard enough, in fact, that I can't get a shaving started by hand. I don't want to use a hammer (too much noise), but I can't keep skating the chisel's edge along the wood, coming up with nothing. Not with the elevator on its way up.

"What's wrong?"

It's Carson. I don't even glance up. "Canvas doesn't fit."

"Fucking kidding?"

Now I look up. "Hold the frame."

She pins the frame against the mover's blanket while I brace the top left corner against my knees. The elevator stops grinding, but I don't hear the *ding* as the doors open—it must've gone upstairs to the admin offices. No time to think about that. I use a white Thor soft-faced hammer to tap the chisel's base. *Thuk thuk thuk.* I get a smooth shaving off the top half-inch of the side rabbet, clip it off at the head rail, finish the edges a little. Good thing Dad taught me how to use tools on his job sites when I was a kid.

Carson whispers, "Five minutes."

"Five minutes what?" I line up the canvas' top and lower it into the rabbet. It's tight, but it fits. I drag in that breath I haven't taken for the past few minutes and wipe the sweat off my forehead with my sleeve.

"Before the guard gets here. If that was a guard in the elevator."

Doesn't it ever stop? I stare at her. "Seriously? They're not downstairs?"

"Only need one at the door."

Five minutes might as well be five seconds. "You cover up all the cameras you need to?"

"Down there." She thumbs west, past me, toward the exit. "Not up there." East, toward the exhibit's start.

I start slotting the nails into the pre-drilled holes in the copy's stretcher. "Get the original in the bag."

There's only twelve nails; I drilled fourteen holes. Oh, well. I spread a hand towel under the first nail to protect the canvas and knock the nail into the frame with the soft-faced hammer. *Thuk thuk thuk*. Now it sounds like I'm using a sledgehammer. Then I move to the opposite side and do the same.

"Two minutes."

I hammer in the next two nails. Just as I line up to do the next one, I hear a door slam at the exhibit's far end. I freeze.

Carson makes a "T" out of her hands. *Time*. No shit.

Footsteps. Rubber soles. Coming closer.

Chapter 51

I wave my hand to catch Carson's attention, point to the portrait, then to the wall. She nods. It's easier to get the hanging wire into the hooks than out of them. I straighten the *faux*-Dorotea while Carson folds up the mover's blanket with the tools inside it. I just hope the canvas doesn't fall out of the frame while we're gone.

The footsteps are getting closer. One guy; probably the regular patrol. A white glow reflects off the ceiling about halfway between us and the exit. It's moving toward us.

Carson yanks my arm and tosses her head back the way we came.

We scurry through the serpentine toward the exhibit's halfway point, where the stairwell is. We can't run—too much noise—and the only light we can risk is Carson's red-gelled flashlight. I have Dorotea in the cloth envelope. Every time I bump the canvas with my knee, I think, *sorry, sorry.*

The light blob's maybe two turns behind us when we break out into the midpoint lobby. Carson quick-steps toward the corridor with the restrooms, freight elevator, and stairwell. I can just barely catch up. I whisper "Wait!" as she starts to open the stairwell door.

"What?"

"We can't leave. I only got half the nails in."

"So what?"

"So the minute they take it down, they'll know what we did."

Even in the red lightwash, I can see Carson grimace. She pivots, whips her lockpick set out of her back pocket, then fiddles with the women's-room lock. The guard's footsteps are getting louder.

She pushes open the door, shoves me inside, then eases the door closed behind us. She hustles me past the double sinks to the two stalls. "Get in. Feet off the floor."

I've been in a women's restroom before (long story), but not to hide in. I close the door but don't latch it, climb up on the toilet seat, squat, and settle Dorotea on the toilet-paper roll next to me. The blanket muffles the tools clanking next door as Carson does the same thing. Then we wait in the dark for the guard to catch us.

As we wait, I have time to obsess over Dorotea's gallery. Did we leave anything behind? Did we mark a wall? It would've been easy to do, working fast in the semi-dark. Did the guard find a tool we forgot? Did any loose nails fall out of the frame? What if one of Carson's black eggs pops off a camera?

A hinge squeaks. A flashlight beam dances around the floor, across the stall doors. I made the mistake of holding my breath once I got on the toilet, and now I really need air. Now's not the right time. Which is louder, gasping, or passing out and falling off?

More footsteps. The light sweeps under my stall door.

Thomas Crown never had to hide in the women's toilet. *Please* please *don't open it…*

The guard's not that thorough. The light streaks under Carson's stall door. The footsteps walk out. The door closes. A key turns in the lock.

At least I can breathe again.

I don't move until Carson snaps on her red light. If my knees had their way, I wouldn't move then, but they don't get a vote. I get to the door in time to see Carson flip a thumbturn, one of those little levers that throw a deadbolt. She flicks the red spot to Dorotea. "Leave that here."

Every synapse in my brain screams *no!* It's an act of will to lean the painting against the wall. Carson pushes me out, locks the door behind us, then grabs my sleeve and drags me back to Dorotea's gallery. Spread out the blanket, move the tools, take down the painting.

The lights blink on. Already?

"Fuck." Carson's head snaps up like a bird dog hearing a pheasant take off.

"That was fast."

"We got our hour." She growls. "They'll know we're here in a minute."

"Why then?" I'm busy looking for an MIA nail. Did the guard find it?

"They'll check a camera they think's down, find my cover." She cranes over her shoulder. "What?"

"Found it." I hold up the nail. It was below the empty spot where Dorotea was.

"Move your ass. If the PD isn't here, it's coming."

I seat the stray nail and start knocking it in. "Is it two yet?"

She checks her watch. "Yeah. Hurry up."

I can hear the OT clock ticking as I finish off each nail. When the last one's done, Carson grabs the hammer out of my hand and buries it in my backpack with the rest of the tools. It doesn't take long to get the portrait back on the wall—we've got lots of practice now—but every minute goes by in a second and I'm seeing reruns of my visions of guards swarming us.

Carson folds the blanket, mashes it into her backpack, then zips it closed. "Time to go."

We rescue Dorotea from the bathroom. Carson cracks the stairwell door and presses her ear to the opening. After a moment, she eases the door closed, then shoves me back the way we came. "Move!"

"Why? What—"

"They're coming!"

"They" slam through the stairwell door when we're three turns away. Bootsteps, clinking metal, the *swoosh* of rubbing nylon. They're *way* too close.

We slalom through the second half of the exhibit, running as fast as we can without making noise. It sounds like an anchor falling when the tools in my backpack clank. As the guys behind us get closer, the noise they're making covers up our noise. Do they know we're just ahead of them?

We hit the end of the building and the stairwell door. The cops or guards or whatever are maybe thirty feet back and gaining on us. The red sticker above the panic bar says "Alarmed Exit." Carson pushes through anyway.

No alarm.

I hustle up the stairs behind her—how does up get us out of here?—and hit the fourth-floor landing just as our cop friends crash through the door below us. We freeze.

Heavy breathing. Two pairs of boots thunder down the stairs. The door slams.

Carson picks the lock on the door in front of us. I whisper, "Any cameras up here?"

"No. Come on."

We're in the admin offices, back by the restrooms. I have to trust that Carson knows how to get us out of this. It doesn't make me feel any better, but at least I don't have to come up with any bright ideas of my own. Not that I have any.

We hustle south down an aisle flanked by cubicles, with Carson's red light leading the way. At the end of the aisle, we reach a white-painted metal fire door. At eye level there's a yellow triangle sticker with a lightning bolt—either Harry Potter's in there, or high voltage is—with an "Authorised Persons Only" sticker next to it. Carson picks the lock.

It's pretty crowded in there: three big A/C units, vented through the west wall by big aluminum ducts, and all the usual fire-suppression gear and water piping. I don't pay a lot of attention, though, because I've locked on something I didn't expect: a bookmatched set of fire doors in the east wall. The only thing that way is... the roof?

Carson says, "Come on," the first time either of us have talked out loud since we walked out of that closet about a year ago. She charges the doors, drops her pack, pulls out a long wire with a flat copper tongue at each end, then starts fiddling with the alarm contacts at the top of the left door, the one with the lever set and deadbolt. After a few moments, she carefully opens the door. No alarms, no flashing lights.

She tosses her backpack through the maybe two-foot gap, then slides out sideways. "Give me the picture." I pass Dorotea to her. "Backpack." I give her that, too. "Careful."

Broken wire = alarm = cops. I'm very careful.

It's drizzling out here on the roof. It won't hurt Dorotea much unless we let her soak in it, which I have no intention of doing. The skyline's pretty dead—marker lights and the orange glow from the mercury-vapor streetlights, but not much from windows.

I follow Carson south to a ten-foot dropoff onto another roof level. Carson shrugs off her backpack, sits on the ledge, then slides off and lands in a crouch. I drop her pack to her when she holds up her arms, then mine, then Dorotea, fighting a breeze that wants to turn her into a UFO. I jump and end up on my ass in a puddle, with my knees ringing like bells.

It looks like someone's having a party to the west. Flashing lights. Echoes of shouting.

We creep to the west edge and peek over the pipe railing into the courtyard behind the Mainwaring. There's five cop cars down there, each with its strobing blue light bar going full blast. Two guys are face-down on the asphalt with their hands behind their backs. As we watch, a cop in a rain slicker hauls up one and hustles him into the back of a patrol car.

"Smoking Man's people?" I say, not really a question.

"Not us. All that counts."

Off on the east side of whatever building we're on, four more cop cars are giving Commercial Street a disco vibe. The whole Portsmouth PD must be here. Clearly, we're not going out that way. "Now what?"

Carson backs away from the edge. "Downstairs."

Huh? I follow her to what looks like a two-hole outhouse with a fire door on the south side. She picks the lock and throws the door open.

I ask, "No alarm? No cameras?"

"Nope. Get in."

"How do you know?"

She waits until she's inside before she gives me The Look.

The stairway is low-ceilinged, steep, and narrow, with two sharp bends. I have to hold Dorotea upright and edge her around to get through. We come out in what looks like storage for a clothing store: rolling pipe racks with hanging bundles of clothes in white plastic dust covers, stacked cartons from China, Bangladesh, and Turkey, a couple dismembered male mannequins, a beat-up filing cabinet, some "autumn sale" posters piled on a work table. Enough street light's coming through the front windows that we can move around without hurting ourselves. Through the back windows we get the cop lightshow from the courtyard.

"Now what?" It seems like I've asked that a lot tonight.

Carson eases her backpack onto the table, sighs, and rolls out her shoulders. "Wait."

"For?"

She boosts herself up onto the table's edge. "PD got two suspects, maybe more. They'll search the whole place. Find what I did to the cameras."

"Those eggs—they're opaque?"

"Uh-huh. Fits over the standard camera dome. Museum staff will look around, see nothing's missing. Most of the PD'll be gone before dawn. Just criminalists and detectives left."

"And then?"

"Out the front door, maybe the back, whichever's quieter. Store opens at 9:30."

She sounds pretty sure about all this. I hope it works the way she says. "What about Julie? Isn't she waiting?"

"Told her to go back to the hotel. Gave her a burner, said I'd text her."

Huh. I find an office chair with a busted arm, slip off my backpack and sit. Sheer luxury. "What about the dudes the cops caught?"

"They'll say they never got into the museum. Maybe they didn't. Detectives'll think there was someone else, maybe an insider, setting up the place for them. Spend a lot of time looking for a ghost." She shrugs. "Glad it's not my case."

I pull my phone for the first time since Julie left the party. It takes a while to get a connection after I take it off airplane mode. "Ever miss it? Being a cop?"

A pause. "All the time." She says this softly, almost to herself.

I have six text messages. Six? They're all from a local number. I figure spam until I see the first one. "Carson? You told Julie to go to the hotel?"

"Yeah. Why?"

Shit. Shit shit shit. "She texted. It says, 'Police talked to me. They have Gillian's name.'"

Chapter 52

"God, I'm sorry, I'm so sorry." Even over a bad connection and a cheap phone, Julie sounds like she's flying apart. "I thought I'd stay close in case you needed something, or you had to get away fast. I was just trying to help—"

Carson asks, "Where'd you go?" We have my phone on speaker and we're huddled over it at the table.

"To the mall parking lot. It was close. I thought it was safe, there was no one there, I thought I'd just wait, but, well, I'm so sorry, and I'm scared—"

"Julie, breathe. Please." I try to keep my voice calm and soothing, even though my brain's busy figuring out how screwed we all are. "Just tell us what happened."

A big sniff bursts out of the phone. "I was across the street from the back entrance. Just sitting. I had the radio on, some classical music, trying to calm down. It was… I guess, five 'til two, maybe? A police car drove by. I thought they'd just keep going, but the next thing I knew, they were behind me and shining their high beams at me."

This is around the time when the museum guards would've called the cops. The only reason I'm not freaking out yet is that I'm talking to her on her burner phone. She wouldn't have it if she was in a cell.

"It was a policewoman. She looked so young. Anyway, she asked me what I was doing there. I didn't know what to tell her, so… I said I'd been at a party at that pub, the Painter's Arms? And I had a little too much to drink and I was waiting to… dry out a little so I could drive home. She asked me for my ID and I gave her Gillian's. It was the only ID I had; I didn't have any choice. Then she asked me for the registration—"

Carson whispers, "Fuck."

"—so I gave her that, and she asked if it's my car, and I said mine was in the shop and this was a loaner. She went back to her car."

Another sniff. "I was so scared. I thought I'd ruined everything." Her voice is so small, so unsteady. I want to reach through the connection and wrap my arms around her. If she'd let me. "She came back and asked if I'd take a breath test. I blew in the thing and she said I scored a fourteen, which I guess is way under the limit, so she said I could go but I should be careful."

We'd spent almost two hours at the party and Julie always had a Champagne flute in her hand. I'd worried about it then. I guess it paid off.

Carson's digging her fingertips into the tabletop. Her arms are rigid, and she's glaring at the phone. "Where are you now?" That comes out sharp and hard.

"At the hotel. I drove around a little to see if she'd follow me, but she didn't, so I came back here. I've been here since."

I ask, "Are you okay?" Carson shoots me a glance that ought to kill me.

"Yes. No. I don't know. My hands are still shaking." Forty minutes after. "Is this… bad?"

Carson clamps her eyes shut. "Yeah. Tell the cop about the hotel?"

"No. No. She didn't ask."

Something broke our way, at least. "Good. That's good. Julie, hold on for a second, okay? I'll be right back." I hit the mute button. "How bad is bad?"

Carson's knuckles are glowing white in the semi-dark. "They got her fake name and fake address. Got the car's registration plates, so they got our supplier. She was near the scene of a reported burglary with a bogus alibi." She pins my ears back. "How bad's it sound?"

Pretty bad. "I guess we've gotta dump the car."

"No shit?" She whips out her phone and stalks away.

I take a minute to think before I turn off mute. "Julie? Still there?"

"Uh-huh. I'm so sorry, really—"

"I know, I know. Look. Carson's going to clean this up. But Gillian has to disappear. Tear up all her ID and flush it. The contacts, too. Get—"

"I don't have to throw the clothes away, do I?"

"You should. You don't—"

"But they're *beautiful*." It's like she's pleading with me to not kill a kid. "I love them. And they're *so* expensive. Can't I keep them?"

She's got a point—it's like eight grand worth of clothes and they look great on her. "Bury 'em in your suitcase. You'll need to do something with your hair and makeup so you don't look like her."

"Um… I can wash my hair and not blow-dry it. It'll go flat."

"Great. Do it. Stay in your room. We won't be back for a few hours." Anything else? Think. "Whatever you do, don't call anybody or talk to anybody. Okay?"

"Okay." Long pause. "Did… did you get her?"

"Yeah."

Julie sighs into the phone. "At least that went right. I'm so sorry—"

"It'll be okay. I'll see you in a few hours. Try to get some sleep."

"How?"

No idea. "Bye."

Carson's glooming at me from one of the rolling racks. "She gonna behave?"

"Yeah." Probably. I grind the heels of my hands into my eye sockets. Most of my adrenaline is gone and I'm. *So.* Whipped. "What about the car?"

"We're dumping both cars. They'll do the swap at six. They don't want to wait 'til daylight."

The light show out back hasn't stopped yet. "How do we do that? We're stuck in here until the cops leave. *If* they leave."

Carson pads to the far-right front window and peeks around the jamb. She stands there for a good two minutes, watching. I know better than to interrupt her. She finally says, "Nobody's outside with the patrol units. Must be in the museum. That's an opportunity."

To get arrested? "What are we doing?"

"We? *I'm* getting out. *You're* staying here."

Chapter 53

I'm glad she has a plan, because I sure don't. Of course, if I had one, it wouldn't include me sitting here waiting to get collared with the take.

Carson's plan involves her changing back into her party clothes. She makes me look out a back window while she puts her dress on. It also involves her swiping my black sweater, which is part of her cover story. It's her boyfriend's, or now her ex-boyfriend's, since they fought going home from a party and he chucked her out of the car. (Don't ask me where she gets this stuff.) She takes a couple swallows from a half-empty bottle of rotgut we find in the filing cabinet so she'll have some alcohol on her breath, just in case.

Why her and not me? She uses a totally plausible but ultra-sexist argument I'd never say out loud: "I'm a woman. They'll buy it from me. You'd be face-down on the street."

There's no alarm on the store's front door—even though a sticker says there is—and a thumbturn opens the deadbolt. We lurk in a shadow waiting for the cops to disappear inside the museum again. I tell her, "You should be crying. For your character."

"I'm mad at the son of a bitch, not sad." Her imaginary boyfriend's in deep shit.

"Doesn't matter. It'll make the cops feel sorry for you."

She sighs, then licks the heels of her thumbs and drags them across her eyelids. Her mascara smears enough to sell the story.

When it's clear, she slips out of the store and starts wandering south toward the train station's taxi stand. She's wrapped her arms around herself for show and hunched her shoulders against the cold. I watch through the shop window as she makes it to the south edge of Debenhams on the other side of Commercial.

A foot cop flags her down.

I can't move and can hardly blink while they talk. She points up Commercial, shrinks some more, wipes her eyes with my sweater sleeve. I'll bet she's even pretending to shiver.

The cop scopes out her legs, then lets her go. He doesn't even ID her.

If the thug thing doesn't work out, Carson should try acting.

Two hours ooze by. I'm upstairs, sitting in the busted office chair. I've already toured the store (men's casual, streetwear, and fitness, nothing that does anything for me), sent Chloe a chatty email about Brooklyn (where I'm supposedly staying), played some solitaire on my phone, and paced about five miles. So far, I've resisted pulling Dorotea out of her bag; it's too dark to see her properly, and I can't risk turning on my flashlight. There's one cop car left in the courtyard, along with half a dozen normal cars. There's also blue-and-white police tape around the Mainwaring's back door.

I'm exhausted, wide awake, scared, and bored. It's like my first night at PEN.

Carson's plan was to catch a cab to the hotel, then drive the Volvo back here by five and pick me up on the corner of Edinburgh Road. I think I'm supposed to just walk out of here with Dorotea under my arm. That sounds pretty sketchy to me, especially with roaming foot patrols out stopping walkers. Or are they? I haven't seen a cop on the street or in the courtyard for over an hour.

The thing is, I haven't heard from Carson since she walked out the front door. Not a call, not a text. Did she make it? Is she in a cell? Is she dumping Julie's body in the harbor?

My work phone rings. Buzzes, actually.

"Matt? Did I wake you?" Julie's voice, low.

"No." I check the time. "Why are you up so early?"

"I can't sleep. I've tried, but I can't." Silence, except her breathing. "Matt? I'm sorry."

"I know. We'll make it work, don't—"

"Not that. I mean, yes, that too, but… I haven't been fair to you, and I feel bad about it."

"How so?"

She sighs. "I've been thinking about Friday night? What I said, and what you said? And… well, I… um… if you'd said what I said, I'd probably have said what you…" She makes an exasperated sound. "I'm making such a mess of this."

"No, keep going." She's trying to apologize for going off on me. I'd been wondering how long we'd be on the outs. But why now, in the middle of all this?

"I didn't… oh, God… I didn't sleep with you to keep you from testifying against me. I… that was never what I wanted. I never *planned* to sleep with you at all. It's just… well, I haven't had a real boyfriend for almost two years."

That's just wrong. I don't want to say it, though, and risk derailing her.

"Then suddenly I'm spending a *lot* of time with this really nice, smart, good-looking guy. We have a lovely dinner in a beautiful city and we walk and talk and we really open up to each other, and…" She sighs again. "Well, what's a girl supposed to do? Anyway, the only 'plan' was to get you from where we were standing, into bed. That's it."

Wow. That's the nicest thing anybody's said to me in years. Now I really feel like a shit about the other night. "There were probably nine million ways I could've said what I did without hurting you. I'm sorry."

"I know. I am, too. I forgive you. I wish you were here. When are you coming back?"

There's a definite subtext to what she's saying that I'm way too strung out to parse right now. Is she being flirty or needy? "Soon. Carson's taking care of it. In fact, I should probably get off the phone in case she tries to call me. I'll come by as soon as I get back. Okay?"

"Okay. Be safe."

"I will. Get some sleep, okay? I think it's gonna be a long day." I click off.

So we're on again. My rational, usually right side wonders if the timing is too convenient. Is she making up now because she's maybe in trouble? I hate thinking like that, but in my world, hardly anybody actually means what they say.

I spend the next half-hour trying to sort this out. The problem is, I got so used to trying to decode Janine—kind of like breaking those Enigma machines the Germans had in World War Two— trying to figure out all the sketchy people at the gallery, and working the angles in prison, that I have a hard time dealing with normal people. Julie's normal… I think. Hope. What she said on the phone just now sounded, well, reasonable. Or did it?

My work phone buzzes. It's Carson. "At the corner."

I scurry to the left front window to spot her. There's a tree in the way. Figures. "Is your cop still out there?"

"No cops out. No nobody out. Get down here."

"What about cameras?"

"Camera's aimed south on Commercial. I'm at the bus stop by Barclay's. Move it."

I'm about to ask another stupid question—*are you sure?*—when the line goes dead.

There was plenty of time for me to figure out how to haul three backpacks when I finally got to leave here. The pack Carson hid in the closet held her burglar costume, the headlight, and our electric screwdrivers. I've put her tools in with mine and stuffed her clothes in with her leftover black eggs. I pull on my pack (it weighs a ton), pick up Carson's two by their top handles, sling Dorotea under my free arm, and ride the pint-sized elevator to the ground floor.

It's still darkish outside except for the streetlights between the shop door and Debenhams. Luckily, three mostly naked trees filter a lot of that light into weird, dark crosshatching on the sidewalk. I remember three ATMs attached to the Barclay's between me and the corner. ATMs have cameras.

It's not gonna get better later.

Fine. I swing open the door and step through before it closes on me.

It's cold, but my heart's pumping so fast that I feel sweat chilling on my forehead. Anybody looking will see a dude in a dress shirt and dark slacks freezing his ass off, carrying too many backpacks and some big, black rectangular thing. I hope nobody's looking.

I walk quickly enough to look like I'm going somewhere but slow enough so my backpack doesn't clank. It's maybe fifty yards from the store to where Carson's waiting, but with every step I take, the corner retreats two. I'm hyperaware of the tree branches rattling in the breeze, the buses wheezing away from the stops farther down Commercial, and every light on every pole, window, doorway, building, and airplane between here and the harbor.

If I get stopped—if anybody looks in these backpacks—I'm done. It's over.

The bright red-and-yellow TheWorks storefront crawls by on my right. The ATMs are next. I stop, set Dorotea down, and get a grip on the stretcher through the cloth envelope. If I let her side skim the paving blocks, she should be just below the cameras' fields of view. Maybe.

First ATM. I look away.

Second ATM.

I snag a corner of the canvas on an uneven paver. The impact almost knocks Dorotea out of my hand. I stop, adjust my grip, wipe my forehead on my sleeve, and move on.

Third ATM.

I'm at the corner. I suck in a lungful of cold, damp air. There's no white station wagon. But there *is* a burgundy Jaguar sedan parked between the crosswalk and the bus shelter.

Carson helps me get Dorotea into the trunk. I say, "Seriously? Isn't Smoking Man watching this thing?"

"No. Drove around forty minutes to make sure. Get in before we get busted. We gotta dump this thing."

Chapter 54

The car swap involves me driving the Volvo behind Carson into the middle of nowhere. Then I get to hide in the bushes with Dorotea and the backpacks while Carson argues in Russian with the couple of skeevy dudes with the replacement car. I'm not worried for her at all; I *am* worried she'll make me help bury their bodies. But everybody goes away alive.

We head back to town in a black Citroen C5 Tourer station wagon with left-hand drive and a Belgian license plate. I surf the news sites with my work phone on our way to the hotel. It doesn't take long to find what I hoped I wouldn't. "It's on the Portsmouth *News* website."

Carson's jaw sets.

I read out loud:

> What may have been an elaborate attempt to rob the Mainwaring Gallery in Portsmouth city centre was foiled early this morning by museum guards and the police.
>
> Hampshire Constabulary took two unidentified men into custody on suspicion of attempted burglary at the Gallery premises on 115 Commercial Road.
>
> Museum officials have not yet determined whether any items were taken from the Gallery.
>
> In an official statement, DI Stella Newling said that the suspects were found to be carrying tools and masks. The police are seeking one or two possible accomplices who may have fled the

scene.

DI Newling encouraged members of the public to step forward with information that may be of assistance to police enquiries.

Carson says, "Fuck."

My stomach starts doing weird twisting things. "Are those accomplices their guys... or us?"

It's almost eight a.m. by the time we work our way back to the hotel. Camera avoidance, of course. I'm in my room just long enough to take off what's left of the wrinkled, sweaty mess of my dress shirt when Julie taps on my door. Big dark circles around her bloodshot eyes, no makeup, flat and scrubby hair, everything drooping.

She says, "Gillian's on TV."

A glossy blonde pops up with the 8:30 BBC South news bulletin on the *Breakfast* morning show. "Hampshire Constabulary are seeking a person of interest in their expanding enquiry into this morning's attempted burglary at the Mainwaring Gallery in Portsmouth." A not-great Identikit sketch of Julie-as-Gillian appears. Julie sounds like she's choking. "The woman, using the alias Gillian Hardwick, may be associated with two suspects already in custody and possibly two to three more suspects at large. A Hampshire Constabulary spokesperson described the plot as 'elaborate' and 'sophisticated' and encouraged witnesses to contact South Eastern CID with any information."

Julie slumps on the end of my bed with her head in her hands. I know how she feels.

Carson sees the same bulletin fifteen minutes later. She stands in front of my TV, arms crossed, and frowns at the screen all the way through. When the Identikit sketch appears, she closes her eyes and shakes her head. What I can see but Julie can't is the red slowly clawing its way up Carson's throat. If she was a volcano, geologists would be plastering her with sensors.

At the end, she stands still for what seems like a long time, staring at the carpet. She throws a nasty look over her shoulder at

Julie, who hasn't said a word since Carson walked in. Then she turns so she can look at us both. "We're done here. Pack."

"Where are we going?" Julie's scraped up some strength for her voice from somewhere.

"Not your problem. Pack."

Julie sits up straight and squares her shoulders. "I should dye my hair. It's still Gillian's color."

I nod. "She's right, you know. It's the single biggest change she can make."

Carson rolls her eyes. "Why don't you have that already?"

"Because I thought I could keep my new hair. We weren't supposed to get caught."

Carson stabs her finger toward Julie. "That happened 'cause you didn't do what you were told."

Julie ought to shrivel up into a little pile of ash, the way Carson's fuming at her. She doesn't. She stares back very calmly. "I know, and I've already said I'm sorry. But someone needs to get some hair dye for me so I don't look like Gillian anymore."

After a few seconds, both women are looking at me. "Whoa, hold on. You know how weird it'll look for a dude to go shopping for women's haircolor? They'll remember."

In another few seconds, Julie and I are looking at Carson. She tries to hold out but eventually rolls her eyes. "Whatever. What do you want?"

"John Frieda Precision Foam Color, Medium Chestnut Brown. It'll cover Gillian's highlights, and it's almost my real color. Boots has it." Julie hikes her eyebrows. "Do you want me to write it down?"

"No. Pack."

Julie doesn't move.

"*Now.*"

Once the door closes behind Julie, Carson sighs and massages her neck. I didn't realize until now how tired she looks. "We're splitting up. Can't have her and the picture in the same place."

My first thought is, *are you nuts?* But once my rational brain kicks in, I see her point. We make a big target all in one place. "How does that work?"

"You two take a train to France. I'll—"

"Wait. Shouldn't we split up three ways?"

Carson snorts. "Think Princess'll make it past the city line on her own? Besides, you gotta keep her from turning herself in and ratting us out."

"She wouldn't do that." I don't think...

That gets me a rude noise. "Fuck yeah, she would, to stay out of jail. She's your problem—deal with it. I'll drive the picture to Dover, catch a ferry. You get stopped, I give the picture to Allyson. That a problem?"

I'm not liking the part about *you get stopped*. Somebody's got to plan for that, though, and better her than me. "You think the cops are going to find us?"

"I'm betting on it."

Chapter 55

Back a hundred years ago when Allyson briefed us on this project, she said the M25 is "infested" with cameras. It's not just that road, though. It's the whole country.

You never realize how many cameras are watching you until you don't want any of them to see you.

Carson and I keep the front desk clerk busy while Julie does the express-checkout thing. She's wearing Carson's gray hoodie, which is tight on her but covers her still-damp hair. We can't dodge the cameras on the light standards in the parking lot; we can only hope that nobody really cares yet.

It takes over three hours to get to Ashford—a city southeast of London that I've never heard of until now—after skirting practically every city on the southern English coast for the hundred miles east of Portsmouth. It's slower than the motorways, but most of it is two- or four-lane roads out in the countryside, so there aren't as many cameras. Every fourth car seems to be a cop, though, and every little town feels like a speed trap or checkpoint. A heart attack every few miles.

Carson's totally fixated on the road, following every speed-limit change and warning sign to the letter. Julie says maybe ten words the whole way, and she can't look at Carson straight-on. None of that helps ease the tension.

Carson dumps us off at Ashford International Station, the last (or first, depending on which way you're going) Eurostar railroad station before you hit the Chunnel. Cameras in the concourse, on the escalators, in the corridors. TVs showing Gillian's Identikit sketch on Sky News. Airport-style security at international check-in. Guards carrying machine guns. The French immigration dude at passport control spends too much time looking at Julie before letting her pass.

Then we sit for an hour and a half in international departures. More guards, more cameras. Only the fear keeps me awake. Julie's wired and nervous. I'm pretty sure she's going to draw cops because they'll think she's on meth.

Luckily, the only video monitors I can see have train schedules on them. Just as I think we've caught a break, though, I check the news on my work phone and choke.

The BBC has a photo of Gillian.

It's not a great picture—it's grainy, like they blew it up too much—but it's a three-quarters front view of her in her emerald-and-white Carolina Herrera cocktail dress, talking to a man and woman whose faces are blurred out. The hair's different, but if you look at bone structure and not makeup, the face is the same.

Just when you think it can't get worse...

Then the train, the conductor—did he spend too much time looking at Julie?—the rocket-sled ride to France. Other passengers walking by. The gal with the snack cart, parked next to us for what seems like an hour. Julie passes out before we even hit the tunnel. I've been running on fumes for hours, too, and everything takes me three times longer to do. I don't dare give in to the nap that's calling my name, though. I don't want to wake up in a cell. I've done that before.

Somewhere under the Channel, I nod off.

Paris is the last place in the world we should go. The army's in the streets because of that terrorist attack less than twenty days ago. The Gare du Nord, where our train pulls in, looks like what happens after a military coup.

But the news from Portsmouth hasn't made it to France yet. Everybody on the platform and the arrival hall looks like us—jumpy and paranoid—so we blend right in. And if you want to get from anywhere to anywhere in France by train, you have to go through Paris. So here we are.

I have texts waiting on my work phone. "Carson made it onto a ferry okay. She landed at Calais around 4:30. She'll meet us in Reims."

Julie's still scrubbing sleep out of her eyes. "Where's that?"

Good question. I look it up on Google Maps. "About eighty miles northeast of here. It's on the main highway from Calais."

The good news: there's a train to Reims in half an hour. The bad news: it's at another station, half a mile away. We won't make it if we take a taxi—the traffic's worse than West L.A. at five p.m. So we walk through the creeping dusk. We pass soldiers or cops about every thirty seconds. There's CCTV cameras everywhere. Partway there, a two-tone police siren keys off behind us; we both nearly jump across the street. Why are so many women giving Julie the side-eye as they go by? Do they disapprove of a grown woman wearing such a déclassé outfit? Does the hoodie make her look like a terrorist?

We reach the Gare de l'Est with minutes to spare. More cameras, more cops. Another conductor on the train, taking a little too long to punch our tickets. A guy across the aisle, scoping out Julie. Leching on her? Wondering where he's seen her before?

I keep myself awake (barely) by obsessively cycling through the news websites. We're just out of Paris' suburbs when I get another shock. Britain's Channel 4 has a grainy still frame from a Mainwaring security video; it shows a person dressed all in black slipping past a gap in a wall. I recognize Carson's shape.

When's my photo going to come up? Will it be like Carson's (totally useless) or Gillian's (the next best thing to a portrait)? Will it get all the way to America? Will my PO see it?

It's dark out when I meet Carson in the lobby of the Novotel Reims Tinqueux, what passes for a business hotel in a light-industrial suburb of Reims. I can't tell you how relieved I am to see her. All the time I didn't spend imagining myself or Julie in a French prison, I spent chewing my nails over the thought of Carson ending up in a cell or being gunned down by rogue *flics*.

She's sprawled on one of the low-slung, dark-leather easy chairs next to a wall punctured by square storage niches. If anything, she looks worse than Julie, who looks basically dead. I've been avoiding mirrors for several hours now. "Any problems on the way?"

Carson yawns and stretches. "Road work. Traffic. Where's your girlfriend?"

"Eating dinner in the restaurant over by the Ibis." That's the hotel next door. "I figure it's better if she doesn't check in. I'll sneak her in through the side door so they don't get a copy of her passport.

I'm bringing Dorotea in, too. No *way* I'm leaving her in a car outside."

Carson tosses the car key at me. "Don't get too comfortable." She groans out of the chair, wavers a bit, then rolls out her shoulders. "We left a trail a six-year-old could follow. We got a long way to go."

Chapter 56

It's early Tuesday afternoon before we haul our sorry butts out of bed. Lack of sleep and adrenaline overdose does that to you.

In the meantime, the Mainwaring story's blown up.

A failed museum robbery is one thing; a fake rich divorcée who drops money on that museum before disappearing is too good to ignore. The Gillian party picture is everywhere.

But now there's Identikits of me and Carson, too—at least, faces with our cover names under them. I'd freak out if they weren't so bad. They made me look like Ryan Gosling (as if), and Carson looks like a runway model. Still, our names are out there now.

But nobody seems too interested in us; it's all about the glamorous *femme fatale*. There's interviews with the people who really live in Gillian's supposed house ("No, we had no notion"), with Fallbrook ("We value Ms. Hardwick's contribution to this museum and hope we can get this misunderstanding sorted very soon"), even with someone who claims to be her friend ("It's not the first time she's been squiffed and had to sleep it off in a car") (wait, a fake friend? Olivia, is that you?). Charley Hill, who's billed as "the world's greatest art detective," did the expert-opinion thing on ITV ("There's much more to this than we're seeing"). At least three different clips from Pierce Brosnan's *The Thomas Crown Affair* are showing up in the various TV news reports. And that's just Britain; my Google search found headlines (and Gillian's picture) in France, Spain, and the Netherlands.

The Mainwaring's still saying that nothing's missing. It's true in a macro kind of way.

We sit in the Citroen in the parking lot's far northwest corner. We have a view of the hotel's peach-and-white stucco walls and the entry canopy shaped like a ski jump. Why the car? It's the only place we can think of that's definitely not bugged and lets us see eavesdroppers as soon as they see us.

Things are pretty frosty when we get together. Carson gives Julie an if-looks-could-kill look, which doesn't kill Julie (yet) but keeps her quiet. Then Carson grumbles a bit.

I'm up in front with Carson. I ask, "How does this work?"

"Olivia's shipping our backup IDs to Stuttgart." Carson throws me a significant look. "Yours and mine. She's on her own."

I glance at Julie in the back seat. All I can see is the top of her head. She sniffs.

"Good thing those sketches are such pieces of shit," I say. "Though you came out looking pretty hot."

Carson snorts. "Eyewitnesses are fucking useless."

We bitch about being on TV for a few minutes, but our hearts aren't in it. Eventually we turn to a new topic: now what?

I say, "Let's take Dorotea to Geneva. Olivia says Allyson has a space in the Free Port. We put the portrait in there and nobody'll find it, ever."

"What's that buy us?" Carson's strangling the steering wheel's rim with both hands. It's a thing with her.

"Well, first, we won't get caught packing it around. Second, we'll buy some time to figure out how to launder it." It's the first reason that interests me the most. I'm not looking to sit on a hot painting very long, not with my fake name in the news.

"I thought we were going to use Ute Kinigader for that." Julie's finally found her voice again. Her eyes are still red from crying after she saw the news.

"If Geisman comes through, then yeah. But that could take weeks, maybe months."

She's nursing a big go-cup of coffee and an oversleep hangover. We were so exhausted last night that we spent fourteen hours in bed and didn't fool around once. "Even so, shouldn't we take Oma to Austria? That's where we'll need her to be."

"It is. But where do we put her until we work out how to pass her through Kinigader?"

Carson says, "Go to Vienna. Have Rodievsky store it 'til we need it again."

"Who's Rodievsky?" Julie asks. Carson ignores her.

I ask, "Will we get it back?" Because the man has uses for stolen canvases.

Carson snarls at me.

We wrangle over this for a while. Carson starts the car every ten minutes or so to run the heater. It's 42 degrees outside and windy, and even with three of us in here, the cabin cools off fast.

A white Renault with a blue light bar swings into the parking lot. Police, not guards. Julie ducks behind Carson's seat. The cops turn right and prowl past us. There's no reason to worry, right? The Citroen was in Portsmouth for only a couple hours, and it's got Belgian tags. But Julie's in the car with us, and so are our IDs, and so is Dorotea.

The cops hang a uey at the end of the lot, crawl past us again, then work their way around the front of the hotel.

I say, "It's clear, Julie." She peeks around Carson's headrest before she sits up.

"Callin' it." Carson yanks the key out of the ignition. "Two votes for Austria. That's where we're going."

"But—" When did this become a democracy?

"Pack your shit. I'm checking out." Carson flings open the driver's door and lunges out. "You check out when I get back. If we gotta be a target, we're gonna be a moving target."

"I know these things take time, Stefan." Julie's voice is back to sounding like Gillian's: firm, in charge. It's good that phones are sturdy, because as tight as she's holding hers, it ought to bend in half. "I'm just saying that now we have this lead, we should follow it up as soon as we can. Ute's how old? Seventy? What if she dies next week?"

It's about seven hundred miles from Reims to Vienna. We're on the A33 skirting Nancy, the last sizable French city we get near before we hit the German border. We've seen a lot of rolling hills and green fields over the past couple hours. Pretty, but not all that interesting.

"Yes. I understand." This sounds like, *what kind of shit are you saying?*

I twist to look at Julie over my seat back. I give her the pushing-down, dial-it-back hand signal.

Julie sighs. "Sorry to be so pushy. The exhibit's over. Oma's portrait is going back to Russia. If Ute's got something we can use to prove the Soviets took it from her father, we can go back to court, right?" She listens, not happily. "I *know* it's a long shot. But what else do we have? I can't get this close and then lose her. I won't."

Even though we're getting only half the conversation, it's better than dead silence, which is what we had until now.

"She said to come talk to her, right? At least, that's what that Leininger person said. So make an appointment." More listening. "Because I want to go with you to see… Stefan, hear me out." Julie holds up a hand like the lawyer can see her. "She's a link to Oma's portrait and the other three paintings. Even if all I do is sit in the corner and listen, I still want to be there. But think about this—she might tell me something she won't tell a lawyer, or a man. Maybe I can make a woman-to-woman connection. Isn't that worth a try?" It's good that Geisman can't see the expression on her face. "Stefan, I have to insist. Please make an appointment to interview Ute as soon as possible. I'll meet you in Salzburg. Yes, I'm on my way now. Please call me when you have a date and time. Thank you." She thumps the disconnect button a lot harder than she needs to, then growls, "Lawyers."

Carson glances in the rear-view mirror. Her lips push up in that "huh" look, like when you see something that surprises you pleasantly.

I didn't expect this, either. Is this take-charge attitude another gift from Gillian… or was it always there, and I didn't see it until now?

Ninety minutes later—as we're passing the Roppenheim Style Outlets on our way to cross the Rhine—Geisman calls.

He has an appointment to interview Ute Kinigader on Wednesday, December 9, at ten in the morning. Eight days from now.

Julie grins as she hangs up. "We're going to Salzburg."

Chapter 57

When you think "Salzburg," you probably think of the place in *The Sound of Music*. Baroque palaces and churches, overwrought fountains and statues, formal geometric gardens, castles on hillsides, cobblestones, pastel yellows and pinks and blues on the walls. That place really exists. It lines the River Salzach for maybe a mile in the city center, and it's really pretty.

That's not where we're staying. We're staying in the airport-warehouse-light industrial-shopping mall part of town three miles or so southwest of the river.

The Austria Trend Hotel Salzburg West is attached to the city's big McArthur Glen Designer Outlets mall, which is so close to the airport that it's easy to count the windows on the departing airliners. The hotel may be next to an outlet mall, but I didn't choose it—that was Carson's call. It's big and impersonal and the front-desk staff is pretty busy, which means they don't notice when I bring in an extra person (Julie) and a big rectangular thing in a black bag. It's also near a major highway in case we need to make a run for it.

Geisman's coming next Monday. That leaves us four and a half days to catch up on our sleep, wash clothes, and sightsee. At least, that's what Julie and I do; God knows what Carson's up to.

I also do homework. Even though I don't expect to find Kinigader's lost paintings stacked up in Ute's living room, I figure I should know what the pieces look like just in case. So I start going through the couple hundred items in Kinigader's February 1945 inventory to try to find photos.

This is harder than it sounds. Unlike books, paintings don't always get titles; the artist may not assign one, or a painting comes to be known by its subject. If the artist gives a work a name other than "Untitled," it's usually in the artist's native or adopted language, which isn't always the version other people use (*The Scream* is really *Der Schrei der Natur*). The *Mona Lisa* is a good example. We don't really know what Leonardo called the portrait, but his assistant, who inherited it, listed it as *La Gioconda* in his papers. "Mona Lisa" didn't come around until Vasari made it up maybe fifty years later. Bonus degree of difficulty: in some Italian dialects, it's "Monna Lisa."

And in this case, we also have the Nazis and their minions dicking with the titles to make them more acceptable to the good Aryans buying them. That's how Klimt's *Portrait of Adele Bloch-Bauer I* became *Woman in Gold*, and Julie's *Dorotea DeVillardi* became *Italian Girl* (or, to make things even more complex, *Italienischen Mädchen*).

Sound fun? That's what I deal with for four days.

It isn't all about staring at screens. On Thursday, Julie and I go to the Altstadt, the pretty part of Salzburg. The Mainwaring story hasn't made it here yet, and we use cash or my new cover's credit card (I'm now Michael Harmon), so it feels pretty safe. It's the first time I've seen Julie smile since we left England. We end up singing "Do Re Mi" in the Mirabell Gardens, which I'm sure nobody's ever done before. Surprise—Julie can sing. She's no Julie Andrews, but she has a clear mezzo voice and can carry a tune.

On Friday, we visit Wolf Kinigader and Erna Thalmann.

Friedhof Aigen is in a southern suburb of Salzburg, in a neighborhood of mostly postwar apartments and attached homes. The cemetery's a series of tree-lined meadows bordered on two sides by pastureland and on a third by railroad tracks. The burials are Germanically restrained—there's none of the over-the-top craziness of Milan's main cemetery, which I visited for that project.

Julie navigates us along the asphalt walkways under mostly naked trees, using a paper map she got from the front office. We're the only ones here, except for the occasional squirrel taking advantage of the tropical day. (Fifty degrees in the Alps!) We reach our destination after half an hour of poking around: two plain rectangular granite markers standing side-by-side in a far corner of one of the smaller parterres. Just names and years, no decoration, no "beloved" or "devoted," no glass devotional candles or flower vases. Forgotten except by Ute, who doesn't have much time left.

Is this how I end up? Planted in an obscure hole under a chunk of rock so generic it should have a barcode? I can think of a lot of people who'll be happy to drink to my final exit, but hardly anybody who'll care what happens to whatever's left of me afterwards.

At least it's kinda pretty here. I wonder if I'll even get that.

Julie threads her fingers through mine. "I can't imagine what Erna was going through back then. Nineteen, pregnant. Having to bury a man she hardly knew." She shakes her head. "I couldn't have done it. I was nowhere near grown-up enough at nineteen. I could barely cope with Anthony when I was twenty-five."

"Were they even married?"

She shrugs. "Since the gravestone says 'Thalmann,' I guess not. I tried looking for them at the city registrar's office but didn't have any luck. We really don't know anything about her except that she paid for his grave until she died and she's buried next to him. That says a lot right there."

Talk about devotion. What's it like to have someone like that?

Since Erna's here with Wolf, it's reasonable to assume she never found anybody else. I can't decide if that's incredibly romantic or just plain sad. Sometimes there's not a lot of difference.

Friday night, after dinner. I'm at the blond-wood table in our room, slaving over the free WiFi to find lost paintings. Julie's curled up on the bed with her laptop on her lap, working on her book. It's warm and quiet except for keyboard tapping and mouse clicks.

Then Carson pounds on our door. When I open up, she frowns at me, then tosses her head back toward the hallway. I follow her a few steps down from my room.

"She in there?" Carson grumbles.

"Yeah."

"Got clothes on?"

I sweep my hand toward the door. "Want to check?"

She scowls. "Seen enough of her. Come on."

"Where?"

"To see Allyson."

"To... *what?*"

Allyson? Here?

This happened in Milan. We both got chewed out. It wasn't fun.

Chapter 58

Carson lets me knock on the door. Allyson answers, stares at us both for a very long few seconds, then opens the door wide. No hello; no "thanks for coming."

This time isn't going to be fun, either.

It's a suite, as usual, with a closed pocket door separating us from the bedroom. It has the same cream walls and Scandinavian wood furniture as my room. Allyson points toward the blocky moss-green sofa. Carson and I sit like good little girls and boys. Then Allyson stands on the other side of the coffee table, her arms folded, glaring at us.

She's wearing an Alexander Wang above-the-knee pencil dress with thick, wavy vertical black and white stripes. She does body-con *so* well. When I look closer, I see that the stripes on her full-length sleeves and at her hem are slit, with whispers of skin showing in between. It'd be totally hot if she wasn't about to take my head off.

"I have two very unhappy clients." Her voice is as stiff as I've ever heard it. "Mr. Bowen's representative is now wanted in Britain. I told you *explicitly* to protect her from any compromise, and you failed. You can imagine that he's livid. I would be too. You can also imagine what effect this will have on any future projects with him or his company. Do you have an explanation?"

I swap a glance with Carson. She says, "Got the picture. It's under his bed."

The points of Allyson's jaw bulge for a moment.

I should be more scared than I am. But I've thought about nothing other than this for the past five days, trying to put pieces together. If I'm going down, I'll go down fighting. "Have you heard from Bowen since Wednesday afternoon?"

"No. I expect he'd said everything he needed to."

"Maybe. Or maybe because Julie called him when we got here Wednesday afternoon. That was the first time he heard we actually got the portrait."

"Short conversation, too." Julie had made the call in the car, so Carson got to hear it. "Seemed happy. He didn't bitch her out."

One thing about Allyson: she's adaptable. (I was going to say "flexible," which she is, but in a completely different context.) Feed her some information and she crunches it instantly. If it changes the state of her world, she switches up without slowing down. What this means is that her angry-boss glare from a few seconds ago is turning into something more speculative. "You're implying Mr. Bowen will be willing to sacrifice his cousin if he can get the painting."

I nod. "If he runs the rest of his life the way he runs Alivian, he's probably willing to sacrifice anybody once he gets what he wants."

Carson leans back in the sofa. "Gonna be interesting when she tells him the picture's hers."

Both of Allyson's eyebrows jump up. She watches Carson for a few moments. When the follow-up doesn't come, she switches targets to me.

I give her the capsule summary of how Julie inherited Dorotea. "I've looked at the wills and the camp papers. It seems to check out."

Allyson closes her eyes, props her right elbow on her left wrist, and slowly rubs the space between her eyebrows. "Thank you for providing another way to make the client angry." She refolds her arms and gives us both an annoyed look. "You've yet to tell me what you intend to do about Ms. Arnlund."

I've been thinking about this, too. "Nothing."

Allyson has the most expressive eyebrows. "Explain."

"First of all, Gillian's the 'person of interest,' and she's gone. Julie's traveling on her own ID. But what do the cops really have on Gillian? Carson, you're the cop. What can they do?"

"Fuck all. Maybe false representation, if that's even a crime. Museum says nothing's missing. No crime there. No connection between the Princess and the two hosers they busted. All they got is proximity, and that ain't a crime either." She elbows me. "He's right. Nothing to do."

We didn't rehearse this. I just tossed the ball to her, and she ran with it. Almost like a team. I need to buy her a nice dinner or a good bottle of scotch to say "thanks."

I pick up the thought. "Another thing. This is news only if somebody dies or something disappears. Any day now, there'll be a scandal or a terrorist attack, and the media'll forget all about it. Tell *that* to Bowen. Ask him how long it took the media to stop beating him up for Ceraphan." The cancer drug Julie told me about on the train from London.

Allyson's lips are pursed, but she's nodding now and then. Like I said, she's adaptable. "Assuming he accepts that, I'm still left with another very angry client—"

Carson says, "Tovorovsky?"

Allyson pauses, then swivels her eye-mounted laser cannon toward Carson. "Why do you say that?"

"He was a client. Stiffed you on his last project. What's he owe you?"

"More than I'm willing to write off." The heat's out of Allyson's voice; it's wary, now. "I'm pursuing… other options against him."

I say, "Why don't you have a seat? We can talk like people."

She flicks a look at me that I'd rather not get again, then eases into an armchair next to the couch. "Go on, Ms. Carson."

"Guess you're not the only one suing him." She thumbs toward me. "He says Tovorovsky's broke or something."

I say, "Not broke. Cash crunch. Asset sales, restructuring, debt extensions. And that's just what's happening in public." That old saying, *if you owe the bank a grand, it's your problem, but if you owe it a million, it's the bank's problem?* It's totally true.

Carson takes the handoff. "They always seemed to know where we were gonna be." The thumb again. "He didn't tell the Princess. I only told Olivia. When you made me pick an exit time, it's clear, eh? You're working with them. What other client wants to take off the place at the same time?"

Allyson leans on a chair arm and crosses her legs. Her skirt rides up her thigh. Bonus. "Let's assume for a moment that you're correct. Why would I work with Mr. Tovorovsky again, and why would he want to steal something from the museum?"

Carson leans her elbows on her knees. "You want your money. No lawyers. Nothing public."

"Go on."

Carson looks at me. I guess it's my turn. "Tovorovsky got Dorotea in '99, but he lent her out for the first time last year. It's a twofer for him—he gets the piece out of Russia around the asset controls, and the exhibit credit gives him maybe a ten-percent bump to the piece's auction price. So now what? Maybe he needs to sell it to clear some debts.

"The thing is, Sargent's prices have been all over the place. He was hot before the crash, but not so much now. Dorotea's his last oil, and it was lost for fifty years, so that'll raise some interest. But even if Tovorovsky could get someone like me to shill the piece at auction, say he pulls down five million. That's five times what Sargent's portraits usually go for now, but it's hardly worth getting out of bed for. Follow me so far?"

Carson's eyes are glazing. Allyson's focusing on me so hard that I'm starting to feel burn marks on my forehead. She nods. "Go on."

Like I said, I've been thinking about this for a while. The more I explain it, the more right it feels. "Now, the Mainwaring had to insure the piece. It's a standard thing for traveling exhibits. Who knows what valuation they used? I'll bet Tovorovsky bought himself some really high estimates. Eight mil, ten mil, whatever. So what happens if somebody steals Dorotea from the Mainwaring?" I pause so they can think that over. "He'll probably put her in a free port somewhere. He gets his insurance payout after a few months. Maybe he sues the museum for negligence and gets some more bucks out of them. But he still has Dorotea. What's next?"

Carson chuckles. "Sells her to some other crook."

"Uh-huh. One of his buddies in Russia, or some dude in the desert. Even if he only gets low seven figures for her, it's free and clear to him and it all adds up to more than one of the big auction houses would ever sell her for." I point at Allyson. "He pays you off, maybe at a discount? No legal fees?"

I get nothing from her.

"Did I get any of that wrong?"

Well, not quite nothing: the corner of her mouth curls up a notch.

"He got caught," Carson says. "Fucks things up."

I nod. "Yeah, some. *He* didn't get caught; his minions did. He's probably paying them good money to shut up. Or they'll get shanked in prison. But let's say the very worst happens. Someone talks, and the cops manage to follow it back to him. Think they'll ever hang it on him?"

Carson snorts. "Be serious. He'll pay off someone."

Allyson sits up and wraps her hands around a knee. "I see your point. The burglary would have been a very low-risk operation for him. Assuming any of this is correct, of course."

I say, "Of course. If he did it the same night we're there, he might be able to throw the dirt on us. Maybe shop us to the cops."

"This is all very interesting." Allyson pushes out of her chair and paces to her minibar. "Assuming any of it is true. The fact remains: my other client is very upset that you interfered with his operation. Ms. Carson, I believe you committed to leaving the museum by two a.m.?"

Carson shrugs. "Took longer than we thought." Which is true.

That gets her a nasty look from Allyson. "What exactly should I say to the client?"

I elbow Carson. She says, "We thought of taking it in transit. He could do that."

Allyson finishes pouring a miniature of white wine into a glass and starts pacing around the room. "Mr. Friedrich?"

"Sure, why not. He's got the people to do it."

Carson adds, "Just so they don't fuck it up again." She points to the minibar. Allyson nods. On her way over, Carson says, "Client know what we were doing?"

"No, only that you had an objective in the museum. Given what that was, it wouldn't have been wise for me to tell him, would it?" That's pretty much her confession that "the other client" is Tovorovsky.

I ask, "Now what happens?"

Allyson considers me over the rim of her wine glass. "Assume I'll be monitoring your progress very closely until this project ends successfully." Her tone's eased up, so I guess we're only sort-of in the doghouse.

"Meaning, both clients pay you?"

"Of course."

Carson fishes a scotch miniature out of the minibar, then flips me a Stoli while Allyson's back is turned.

Allyson turns to me, notices the baby vodka I'm twisting open, then shoots Carson a *really?* look. Carson shrugs. "You have the painting now. Explain your endgame. How does Mr. Bowen take possession?"

"Assuming Julie doesn't get it first?"

Allyson scowls at me. "I'm still trying to imagine how I'll explain *that* to him."

"Family politics." Carson takes a slug from her mini-scotch. "Not our problem."

"I'm *sure* he'll see it that way."

I tell Allyson my proto-plan while she nurses her wine. Unlike the Tovorovsky stuff, my "plan" for Ute Kinigader sounds flimsier the longer I talk about it. But it's all we've got so far.

When I finish, she gives me a long stare. There's some eyebrow action, too. "Ms. Carson, what's your opinion of this… scheme?"

Carson leans her butt against the counter over the minibar. "Dunno. He knows how this shit works. I don't."

I guess that's better than her saying *he's fucking nuts*. Still. "Look at it this way—it's so far-fetched, nobody'll believe it's a setup." That sounds lame even to me.

Allyson sighs. "When does the lawyer arrive?"

"Monday. The interview with Kinigader is Wednesday morning. We scope out the place, then come back a night or two later and plant the canvas."

"*If* conditions are right."

"Yeah. If it looks doable."

Allyson carefully sets her glass on the coffee table. "I expect you to have a backup plan before your meeting with the lawyer. Something that will work without needing a long chain of events to go exactly right." Her boss tone is back. "Until then, don't make my life or this project any more difficult. Do you understand?"

"Yes, ma'am."

"Ms. Carson?"

"Clear."

"Consider yourself warned. You may go."

Chapter 59

Remember the Mainwaring story? Winter Storm Desmond drove it off the front pages in England. Every day that nothing new happened, it fell farther back in the European press.

Until Sunday.

According to this morning's news, the police finally cleared the scene at the museum Friday night. The canvases loaned to "Stealing Beauty" started going home midday Saturday.

Early Saturday evening, an "art transport vehicle"—the pictures show a plain-wrap white van that looks a lot like the one we watched take Dorotea from the museum to the lab—headed northbound out of Portsmouth on the M275 freeway on its way to London. Two black Range Rovers forced it into a guardrail. One SUV trapped the driver and guard in the cab, while ninjas from the other one blew the rear doors and grabbed the three paintings inside. Nobody was hurt (except their pride and, probably, their careers in security) and the Range Rovers rode off into the sunset.

Of course, Boutelle's copy of Dorotea's portrait is the main kidnappee.

Suddenly, even flooding in western England is less interesting than this "Hollywood-style" (they all say it) heist by the "M275 Raiders" (the *Daily Mail's* name for them). The British news is full of this on Sunday morning, and by Sunday evening it's spread to the Continent. Because it's connected to art and the Mainwaring, the press immediately links it to last Sunday's hijinks at the museum.

Which means Gillian's picture is on TV again.

Julie groans, "Doesn't it ever stop?" She won't quit watching the news, though, no matter how hard I try to pry her away.

I swap a glance with Carson. It looks like Tovorovsky took our advice.

Chapter 60

Geisman arrives at the central train station a bit past noon on Monday. Instead of work clothes like last time, he's wearing pressed blue jeans, heather-green nubuck day-hiking boots, a wine-red, crew-neck sweater, and an aqua wind shell. I guess if he gets bored, he can go hiking in the mountains I can see from the plaza outside the station.

I take Julie to greet him. The German and Austrian news have run small stories about the M275 art heist but don't mention Gillian; it seems safe enough for now.

When they get done cheek-kissing, Geisman shakes my hand. "Herr Simon, I am very pleased to see you again." We have to risk using our old covers so we don't have to explain why we have new names. "I have the photographs you asked for, although I cannot say I fully understand why you want them."

"I don't fully understand it, either." We go outside and angle across the plaza toward the blue-gray glass box of Forum1, the shopping mall next to the station. It also has the closest parking. "I guess I'm trying to put images to the names on the list. How many did you find?"

"Forty-three. I expect that some of them are on the internet already."

"I'll take 'em anyway. Thanks."

We claim the Citroen from the parking garage and start on our way back to the hotel. The roads here aren't as narrow or as tangled as the ones in Portsmouth. I guess this is the one upside to having your city bombed to pieces.

Julie asks, "Did you find out anything more about Ute?" She's in the back seat with Geisman. It feels like I'm practicing for my new career with Uber.

"Very little, I fear. Beata Leininger is her carer. I spoke with her briefly when I arranged for our interview. Frau Kinigader is blind and is becoming frail. She also does not understand or speak English.

Frau Leininger attends to her every second day. She will be present during our meeting. She would not share any further information." I catch his nervous smile in the rear-view mirror. "I doubt that we will be welcomed with kind thoughts and open arms."

I ask, "Does Kinigader have any other relatives we can talk to?"

"He must have, of course." Geisman tries to make eye contact in the mirror, but we're moving around too much. "If we knew his family heritage, we could trace his relatives. Unfortunately, we do not yet. There are several people in Austria with the 'Kinigader' name, but how do we know they are part of the correct family? Perhaps Frau Kinigader can assist us."

Yeah, good luck with that.

After Geisman checks into our hotel, we meet in the restaurant to go over the questions he'll ask Ute at Wednesday's interview. The list takes up three pages, with diagrammed branches depending on her answers. Until he told us Ute's blind, I'd been considering showing her pictures of some pieces in her dad's inventory to see if she'd react. Oh, well.

Tuesday night. We see Ute Kinigader tomorrow.

Geisman's been hiding out at the city registrar's office all day. I've been working Kinigader's inventory. Julie pretends to write her book while she worries.

My brain hurts after another long brainstorming session with Carson, trying to come up with backup plans. The only progress we made was racking up a bigger bar bill. Everything we come up with has at least one of two problems: either it doesn't pass the smell test, or it's more of a long shot than the Ute plan.

When I get back to the room, Dorotea's out of her bag, propped against a wall. Julie's sitting on the floor next to the bed with her arms wrapped around her knees, facing the portrait. "You gotta be careful about having Dorotea out in the open," I tell her. "What if I was housekeeping?"

Julie looks toward me, but not at me. After a few beats, she turns back to staring at her grandmother.

I put the "do not disturb" sign on the front door, then sit next to Julie, my shoulder against hers. I wrap my hand around the inside of her thigh and give it a little squeeze. "You okay?"

"I can't believe she's really here," she finally murmurs.

"You don't sound too happy about it. What's wrong?"

She shakes her head. "I've been at this for almost eight years. Now what do I do?"

This sounds like project post-partum depression. One of Gar's clients wrote novels, and she got the same way when she finished one. "Start an interesting hobby?"

She sniffs, a more polite version of one of Carson's snorts. "Maybe. The rest of Oma's paintings are still out there someplace. I told Stefan I want to find them, but..." She sighs. "Those are just things she owned. This"—she waves toward the portrait—"this is *her*. What's left of her."

"If you're right about the wills, those others belong to you, too. There's three on Kinigader's list."

"I know. I might need them to buy off Ron so he doesn't sue me once I tell him they're mine." She shakes her head like it weighs a lot. "Not that I'll have a way to do it once he cuts me off. Stefan doesn't work for free." She gives me a long look. "Neither do you."

I can't tell if she's fishing for a volunteer or just saying the way things are. "You only get to steal one."

That gets an almost-smile out of her. She turns back to the portrait and admires it for a long while. "You know, this is all incredibly unfair."

"You're getting Dorotea back." I don't say, *what else do you want?*

"I don't mean for me. I mean for everyone else. They say there's what, a hundred thousand? Two hundred thousand artworks still missing from the war? I don't think anyone really knows; I think they're just guessing. And they're not just from Jewish families. The Nazis stole from everyone—churches, museums, cities. Private collections owned by gentiles. And that's just the Nazis—the Russians stole something like a million and a half pieces at the end of the war. A lot of it's still in storage at the Hermitage and the Pushkin. No one really knows what they've got." She lets go of her legs and wraps her arms around herself. "All those innocent people who'll never get their stuff back. I did; they won't. That's what's unfair."

Now I get it. I thread my arm around her shoulders and give her a one-armed hug. "So go to work for them. Once you get Dorotea back, you and Geisman have a pretty powerful story. Randy Schoenberg's career took off after he got Maria Altmann's Klimt away from the Austrians. There's an interesting hobby for you."

Julie smiles a little, maybe wistfully. "I'll say." She loses a staring contest with her grandmother. "All we need is a happy ending, right? You'll get that for me?"

Can I? "Sure. One Hollywood ending, coming right up."

Chapter 61

The Thalmann farm is outside a sprinkle of houses called Spumberg, roughly twenty miles and several decades south of Salzburg. The house is at the end of a gravel road at the top of a broad meadow. A few brown-and-white cows watch us grind up to the house and get out on the gravel forecourt.

Julie wraps her hand around my elbow. She whispers, "My God, it's beautiful."

A rich, green carpet stretches from the gravel's edge to the base of the snow-covered Alps across the broad Salzach River valley. Sturdy, white-walled houses with red or brown roofs are drizzled over the slopes below us. It's so quiet, I can hear the branches clicking in the light, cold breeze jostling the trees fifty yards behind us.

Geisman points across the valley. "Those mountains you see are in Germany."

Berchtesgaden is just southwest of us. Eagle's Nest—Hitler's mountain getaway—wasn't much more than a mile from the frontier. I wonder if Wolf Kinigader knew that.

The house is four window bays and a door wide, mottled white plaster on the ground floor, weathered brown-stained wood plank on the upper floor and gable. The pitched wood-shake roof projects several feet beyond the building envelope, creating deep eaves to keep the snow and ice off the walls. A balcony runs across the entire front exposure, supported by heavy, carved-wood brackets. I can't see much of the two-story timber barn on the far side of the house, but I'm sure Carson will check it out while the rest of us are inside.

Geisman marches up to the peeling four-panel front door, squares his shoulders, and knocks three times. He's wearing a shark-gray loden jacket and vest with green trim over a white dress shirt and black slacks—a little bit country and a little bit rock-'n'-roll. Somehow, he pulls off the look.

A stocky, late-thirties honey-blonde in a forest-green tracksuit opens the door. She throws some German at him; he hands it back.

This goes on for a while until the blonde—who must be Beata Leininger, since she isn't seventy or blind—makes an unhappy noise and lets us in.

Geisman thinks we're all here to grill Ute. He and Julie may be, but I'm not. I need to get the house's floorplan and document any art I see. It's the only way we'll know whether it makes any sense to plant Dorotea here. That's Plan A. There's no Plan B worth a damn.

Inside is dark woodwork, dark hardwood plank floor, and white hand-troweled plaster walls. We're in a dim hallway that seems to stretch all the way to the back door, with doorways on both sides. But what draws my attention are the paintings on the walls: landscapes and still lifes, mostly Romantics and early Impressionists as far as I can see (which isn't very). In a farmhouse in the middle of nowhere.

Imagine that.

I don't get a chance to look closer. Leininger herds us to the left into what looks like a living room. A wood fire's crackling in a stone hearth on the other side of a rag area rug. The four sash windows let in sunlight softening in the gathering clouds. A few pieces of country-plain furniture—yellow pine turned gold under old shellac—take up regular positions around the room, nothing more than a couple paces from anything else.

Leininger holds up her hand to stop us, then hurries to the old woman sitting on a rocking chair in the room's far corner. She straightens the woman's heather-blue cardigan as she murmurs something German to her. Then she waves Geisman to come closer. "She is Ute Kinigader."

Geisman launches into what's probably a self-introduction in German. Ute puts down her knitting—how do you knit when you're blind?—and turns her face toward him. She has sharp features, a high forehead, and steel-gray hair pulled back in a bun behind her head. Outdoor life left her with deep wrinkles and sunspots. Even from the center of the room where I'm standing with Julie, I can see that Ute's milky eyes aren't really aimed at Geisman.

She says, "*Grüss Gott, Herr Rechtsanwalt*" and carefully nods her head. Her voice is soft but clear.

Geisman introduces Julie and me. Leininger brings a straight-backed wooden chair for Geisman, then tells Julie and me to sit on the settle in the room's center. Then Geisman turns on his pocket recorder and starts with his questions. In German.

Julie leans across me toward Leininger, who's perched on the armchair next to the settle. "Excuse me, Ms. Leininger? Could you please translate for us?"

After giving us a grumpy are-you-serious? look, Leininger crowds onto the settle next to Julie. "Frau Kinigader says she is born in this house in 1946…"

So starts the guided tour of Ute's life. Measles at twelve (which blinded her), leaving school at fourteen, milking cows, being overlooked by the local boys, learning from her mother how to run the farm, yadda yadda. The cardigan and the shapeless navy-blue housedress hide her body but can't disguise the wide shoulders and thick arms she probably got from pushing cows around and hauling pails of milk. "Frail" isn't the first word I'd think of to describe her.

I glance around the room while Geisman and Ute are doing biography. There are two paintings here: a genre scene on the front wall near Ute's rocking chair, and a landscape on the wall next to the door we came through.

I spend a moment on the second one. If J.M.W. Turner did Dutch landscapes, they'd look like this—a mottled Impressionist sunset, faceless figures walking on ice, a ghostly windmill almost lost in the misty distance. Nice. I'm willing to bet my pay for this project that no dairy farmer ever bought this at the local gallery.

"Herr Geisman asks if Frau Kinigader's mother tells about her father." Leininger has more of an accent than Geisman, but not enough to sound like a 1940s movie Nazi.

I start paying attention.

As relayed by Leininger, Ute says Erna told her Wolf was an important man in the Ostmark (Austria's name after Germany took over) and was doing "the people's work" in Salzburg. He did business with influential men in the Reich government. And Jews killed him because he was successful.

This last one has me doing a mental *wait, what?* I turn to Julie, whose jaw has dropped. I guess I don't need to ask if Ute actually said that. Instead, I ask Leininger, "Is that exactly what she said?"

"Yes." She shrugs. "You are not in Wien, Herr Simon."

I guess not. Being Hitler's neighbor must've rubbed off.

Leininger keeps reporting. Ute says Erna told her Kinigader was handsome and sophisticated. They met in a shop in central Salzburg as the war was ending, before the Americans came. He had to hide because he'd been important in the Party and the Jews and Communists were hunting him. Erna's family took him in. She and Kinigader fell in love. For Erna, there was no other man.

Okay, somebody here is delusional or gullible. Kinigader was at best a fence with a permit, a small gear in the huge Nazi machine. There's no way we'll ever find out if he fed this story to Erna and she bought it, or Erna cooked it up and her daughter didn't know any better. Maybe a little of both.

"Herr Geisman asks if Frau Kinigader has a photo of her father and mother."

Ute looks toward the settle and aims some German our way. Leininger answers, then bustles into the hallway. The moment she disappears, I pop out of my seat and zoom in on the sunset painting. I shoot a picture, then plug the signature into the StolenArt app that's my community service project. Yes, I get bars up here, and a surprising result.

I check for Leininger. She's still gone. I rush to Geisman, grab his notepad, and scrawl, *Ask about paintings in hall + this room.*

He frowns, then writes, *Why? Special?*

I point toward the sunset. *By Johann Jungblut. Quasi-Impressionist, Dusseldorf, 1880s. How did it get here?* I underline the last sentence twice.

Geisman peers at the painting, purses his lips, then makes a note on his list of questions.

I shift to the painting near Ute's chair. It's not a genre scene; it's a Nordic Christ visiting a farm family in their home. StolenArt tells me the signature belongs to Fritz von Uhde, a.k.a. "Germany's outstanding Impressionist." There's nothing Impressionistic about this canvas, though. The religious theme probably made it unpopular with the urban Nazis, though apparently not the rural ones.

Ute startles me by saying something. She's picked up her knitting again, but her face is aimed at me.

Geisman clears his throat. "She asks why you stand there but say nothing."

Her spidey-sense must be really good. "Tell her I'm looking at the painting. The one with Christ in the farmhouse."

Ute nods when Geisman translates, then asks a question.

"She asks if you are interested in art, Herr Simon."

Geisman was careful to not mention art upfront. We both figured that Ute might not want to talk if she knew that's what we're after. So how do I answer and not blow the deal? "Tell her... tell her that her mother had interesting tastes. Or was it her father?"

"Herr Simon!" Leininger's voice, cold and hard. She's in the center of the room frowning at me, cradling a leather-bound album that's seen better days. When I look her way, she stabs her outstretched arm toward my empty spot on the settle.

Leininger's the guard dog. Good to know.

I slow-walk to the settle while Leininger marches the album over to Geisman. Too bad I didn't get to see Ute's reaction. It could've been interesting.

I'll find out later if anything useful comes out of the interview. It's time to do what I came here for—especially documenting the art that doesn't belong here—before Geisman runs out of questions or Ute runs out of patience.

I flag down Leininger as she approaches the settle. "Excuse me, where's the toilet?"

She's busy watching Geisman, who's studying a picture in the album. She waves toward the back of the house. "Go to the kitchen. The door is at your left."

I hope she stays distracted.

When I hit the hallway, I pull my phone and shoot pictures of the art, including close-ups of the signatures. I'll look them up later. There's a closed door halfway down the hall, opposite a narrow staircase. When I peek inside, I find a small room—maybe a study—furnished as a bedroom. Ute's? I'd bet money on it.

There's no art in the kitchen. The small bathroom's attached to the house next to the back door. I flush just for form, then hurry back to the hall in case Leininger comes looking for me.

I text Carson. Anything?

No.

Whats in the barn?

Old cow shit. This is how I know I'm texting Carson and not some neo-Nazi holding her hostage.

I'm standing at the foot of the stairs. Should I go up? Of course I should... *not*. Or should I? It looks like Ute lives on the ground floor, but what's up there?

Let's find out. Going upstairs.

I step as carefully and lightly as I can on the left edge of each tread to cut the chances I'll bend a tread and cause some huge squeak. The staircase is clean, but narrow and steep; I'll bet it's not to code. I edge around the landing and up the next flight to the second floor.

Like downstairs, the hall runs the depth of the house. The only light is from the double-hung windows at either end, and they could use a wash. My eyes adjust to the murk after a few moments. There are five doors: three open on the other side, two closed on my side. I risk turning on my phone's flashlight app. Across the hall, an open door shows me vague furniture shapes under sheets that probably started out white.

Voices murmur up the stairs behind me. I have time, but how much? Getting caught by Leininger could blow any hope we have of planting Dorotea here. Still, I need to check out the closed rooms.

I creep out of the stairwell and hug the hallway walls, heading toward the house's front and the first closed door. I turn the old-school brass knob, but the door won't open. The tarnished brass trim plate has a traditional keyhole for a skeleton key. Nobody's watching—not even ghosts as far as I can tell—so I bend to peek through the keyhole.

There's light, but it's so dim it makes the hall look like bright sunshine. I kneel and hold my phone so the screen can shine through the gap between the door and the floor. Not much light gets in, but what does picks out more white sheets. The shapes under them are too long and continuous to be furniture, but I can't see enough to tell what they are. I push the phone's camera lens in the gap and shoot a couple pictures blind, hoping the flash will light up something.

A locked room full of stuff that doesn't look like furniture. Maybe it's nothing—boxes, books, luggage. Or maybe it's something. I text Geisman: `Ask if erna kept her out of any rooms or places.`

I've been gone over ten minutes. I should see what's in the other closed room, but I've gotta be moving the needle on Leininger's suspicion meter. They're still talking… for now. I brush the dust off my knees, slink back down the stairs, and walk into the living room.

Geisman glances up at me, then back to Ute. Leininger glares at me as I walk back to the settle. When I'm a couple paces away, Julie pops up and trots to me. "Are you okay?" Her stage-whisper is just loud enough for Leininger to hear. "Is your stomach still upset?"

She's covering for me. Good job.

I rub my belly. "Yeah. Last night's dinner is kicking my butt."

I try not to startle when she gives me a you-poor-thing hug. She whispers in my ear, "Where did you go?"

"Later."

She leads me back to the settle. Leininger's still scowling at me. I give her what I hope is an uncomfortable smile. "Sorry. Stomach bug."

I can't tell if she buys it, but at least she stops looking at me like I'm a cockroach.

Geisman riffles through his notes. Ute rocks her chair. We have one of those awkward pauses. Then Ute breaks the silence.

"Frau Kinigader asks why Herr Geisman has such interest in her father."

I cross the fingers on the hand Julie's holding. Geisman has an answer; none of us know how Ute will react to it.

"Herr Geisman says his associates find recently some of Herr Kinigader's papers." This makes Ute frown and rock toward him. "He says he is unable to find more information about Herr Kinigader. He has hopes that Frau Kinigader can help with his research."

He checks his phone, nods, then starts another question.

Leininger says, "Herr Geisman asks if Frau Kinigader's mother forbids her to enter any room or place in the house or on the ground."

Ute stands. She does it a lot faster than someone who's supposed to be frail ought to. She looks to somewhere vaguely in the middle of the room. "Beata?"

Leininger's on her feet in an instant. "*Jawohl*, Ute?"

Ute says something short and stern, then cuts through the room, touching every piece of furniture along her way. She makes hardly any noise except for the occasional scratch of her shoe on wood. It's like she's gliding, not walking.

"Frau Kinigader says…" Leininger frowns as she thinks. "Frau Kinigader is tired and must rest." She holds her hand toward the doorway. "She tells me to see you to outside. Please."

Ute doesn't *look* tired.

Chapter 62

Julie asks, "Stefan? Did we learn anything from all that?"

Geisman twists in his seat to look back at Julie and me. "We have now a photograph of Wolf Kinigader. That is most useful. We can look for him in other photographs and perhaps learn who he knew and who he worked with." He gives us both an uncomfortable smile. "Ute Kinigader is either, how do you say… simple and knows only what she was told, or she is quite intelligent and gives away very little. I must review my notes before I can make a decision about which is more likely."

I say, "Carson? What did you see?"

She's busy edging us around a tractor on the lane-and-a-half-wide road, so she doesn't answer for a few seconds. "No salt mine. Nothing in the barn. Junk and spiders in the basement."

Geisman looks like he just swallowed one of those spiders. "Fraulein Carson. I will ignore that you entered her house without permission."

Carson shrugs. "Door was unlocked. That's an invite." Not that she lets locks stop her.

I scroll through the pictures I took in the house until I find the ones I shot under the door upstairs. They're a little blurred and not all that bright, but I can probably clean them up on the computer. I zoom in and out, trying to figure out what I'm seeing. It's too hard to tell on the small screen. Later. "There's the art. How else would those pieces make it onto a dairy farm in the mountains?"

Geisman settles into his seat and watches the pastures roll by. He nods. "That is potentially interesting. Does it appear on Herr Kinigader's inventory?"

"I'll look when we get back to the city."

"Thank you. Please tell me what you find." He sighs. "Julie? I do not think we have learned as much as you may have hoped for. I am sorry."

I'm not so convinced he's right.

◼

I hit the computer as soon as we get back to the hotel. While I download photos from my phone, Julie wraps her arms around my neck from behind and rests her chin on the top of my head. It's distracting, but in a good way.

"When you left the room back there, where did you go?"

"To the back, and upstairs."

"You went *upstairs?* What's up there?"

"Old bedrooms. It doesn't look like anybody uses them now— Ute sleeps downstairs. There were two closed doors. The one I tried was locked." Would Carson teach me how to pick locks if I asked? Something to think about later. "Here's what's in it."

The best under-door picture is blurrier than I thought once it's blown up to laptop-screen size. The bottom half is overexposed hardwood floor and World's Dustiest Rug. The top third is a dim monochrome strip, light gray fading to dark. In between, there's diagonals of random dark tones.

Julie asks, "What's that?"

"I have no idea. I'll have to mess with it." I start organizing photos by location and order.

Julie settles on the end of the bed, kicks off her shoes, then starts to wander. Her face is all closed and semi-unhappy. She paces to the window to watch the sky turn lead gray, then turns on and mutes the TV, then tries to build a nest on the bed with the ridiculously flat pillows (I've eaten fluffier pancakes), then picks up and sets down her laptop. "Darling?"

"Hmm?" I'm trying to concentrate on the signatures I shot so I can figure out whose paintings I'm looking at.

"Is this how it worked on your other jobs?" She sounds annoyed. "You think you're going to get some answers or learn something important, and… you don't?"

I've only got two other agency projects under my belt before this one, but… "Yeah, that's about right. This time, though, we learned Ute's got art she probably shouldn't have."

"What do we do about it?" She's using that eager, let-me-at-'em tone she had at the start of all this.

I watch her watch me for a few moments. "We keep trying. I need to look at these canvases, see if they're on a registry or on

Kinigader's inventory."

"How can I help?"

"You can't yet. I need to put a list together first."

She watches me some more. "Okay." But I can tell it's not.

Eight canvases. Six different artists. No big names that would shoot up a flare. No Rembrandts or Van Goghs or Vermeers. None would clear low six figures in an auction. These are the kinds of paintings that get stolen every day but rarely make the news.

I hope someone wants them back.

The Austrian Code of Criminal Procedure says that police can search a place with a warrant if there are "objects or traces which must be ascertained or evaluated" (the Google Translate version) connected with a crime. If we can link one—*just one*—canvas back to Kinigader, it should be enough for Geisman to push the local cops into raiding Ute's house.

I give Julie photos of two canvases and tell her how to get to the desktop version of StolenArt (still in beta, but it works okay). "Here's how this goes. Punch in the first artist's name. Johann Jungblut. He did that sunset painting in the living room. Now hit 'search.' Okay, this list is all the hits for Jungblut in all the databases StolenArt searches."

"That many?" She scrolls through the list. There must be a dozen and a half hits.

"Just for laughs, try 'Rembrandt' and see how many come up." I guide her through how to process the search results, comparing my photos with whatever's in the database entries. "Got all that?"

She nods. "If I start dancing, you'll know I found one."

I kiss her forehead. "If you find one, I'll dance with you."

The problem she's going to have—which is going to drive her nuts—is that some artists do multiple versions of the same scene. It's hard to tell the difference sometimes, especially using the crappy pictures that come up in the databases. I expect a lot of false alarms.

I start going through Kinigader's February 1945 inventory. Between Geisman's photos and my own, I have pictures for 53 of the 219 works on the list. Unfortunately, none of those are hanging on Ute's walls.

Luckily, Kinigader sorted the entries by artist name. I look for an artist on the inventory. If he's there, I check the titles for any plausible candidates. It's slow going. Not only was the original list in bad shape, but the scan I'm working from washed out some of the text.

Of the six artists hanging out at Ute's, five are on the inventory. There's plausible titles for seven of their paintings. That's the good news.

The bad news? There's no way to tell if the works we saw are the same as the ones on the list. That Jungblut with the sunset is a good example. "J. Jungblut, Sonnenuntergang" is entry number 96 in the inventory. But Jungblut painted dozens of sunsets. Which is the right one?

Julie finishes with the first two paintings I gave her—no joy—so I pass her another two and go back to staring at the inventory.

Then I have a thought: I already know what the paintings look like. Why not search for the artist and see if any turn up? So I try that. I look at hundreds of pictures. Nada.

Actually, that's good news. The search engines don't get into the databases Julie's using. Bad news would've been finding a brand-new image of one of Ute's paintings on Pinterest. That would mean a copy's floating around somewhere, or the one in Ute's house is a fake.

Julie drags me to dinner at the tapas place in the mall so we don't have to go outside in the snow much. We're both tired and our eyes are bloodshot from all the screen work. "We'll find something," I tell her, even though I don't believe it myself.

Back to the room, back to the computers. Julie takes the next two paintings. I start checking the links she's already found. The ones with pictures aren't the right ones, though a few are close. The ones without pictures... well, who knows?

By eleven, Julie's on the last two paintings. I've gone back to that photo I took under the locked door. I don't have Photoshop, but I have ACDSee, which is picture-organizing software that happens to have a basic editor in it. I bring up the photo, draw a marquee around the mottled dark stuff between the dusty rug and the gray sheet, then spend some time messing with the contrast, sharpness, luminance and chrominance levels to drag out whatever detail's in the picture. It's fighting me, or maybe I'm not doing it right.

I'm leaning my head back with my eyes closed when Julie says, very softly, "Darling?"

"Yeah?"

"I think I've got one."

I look up. Julie seems more awake than she has in hours. "For real?"

"Yes, for real. I've been staring at it for ten minutes, trying to figure out what's different, and I can't."

I stumble over to perch on the edge of the bed. She hands me her laptop. I'm foggy enough to have to puzzle out what I'm looking at. It's a slightly blurred black-and-white photo of a still life: a dozen big, pale roses arranged in a metallic pot, resting on an off-white cloth printed with large paisley designs. There's a couple fallen petals and a bunch of dark grapes.

Even without color, I recognize the work in an instant. It's hanging in Ute's hallway across from the stairs. I sort through the thicket of windows Julie has open until I find one with the photo I took. The roses are blush pink, the pot is copper, the paisleys are red and green, and the textured background is a moss-green wash. But as I compare the two side-by-side, I can't see any difference.

Now I'm starting to get excited. The black-and-white image is from lostart.de, the official German registry for Nazi-era looted art. I switch to the database entry. Clara von Sivers, 1897, 55 cm by 70 cm (about right). Circumstances of loss: Munich, 1937.

Julie asks, "Is it the right one?"

Munich. A short train ride to Salzburg or Vienna. A quick search shows me that Von Sivers cranked out about a bazillion floral still lifes in the late nineteenth century, some with roses, some with copper pots, some with paisleys. But Ute's is the only one I find with *these* roses in *this* pot on *those* paisleys. I've spent enough time going over the inventory that I know it by heart. Entry number 187: "C. von Sivers, Stilleben mit Rosen."

"Yeah. Yeah, I think it is."

Gotcha, Wolf.

It's around 2:50 when I finally give up on sleeping and slip out of bed. Julie's so zonked, she barely makes a sound. I don't know why I can't sleep. Maybe it's because I keep ending up in the crack between the twin beds the hotel shoved together to make a king. Or maybe it's because there's a loose end.

We'd run to Geisman's room after Julie found the von Sivers canvas. He was still awake and still working, even though it was almost midnight by then. He looked at the pictures and the lostart.de entry, massaged his chin, then smiled. "This is exactly what I needed. Most excellent." It was the most excited I'd seen him get so far.

It may have solved his problem, but it didn't solve mine.

I pad to my computer, wake it up—the screen glare's almost painful—and bring up the good under-the-door photo. The dark area I'm trying to decipher is still resisting. It's brighter now, a bit sharper, a collection of mottled rectilinear shapes separated by thin, dark lines.

Wait a minute.

Just for kicks, I turn up the contrast again. The dark lines get darker, and the mottled shapes become more obviously rectangular. I turn up the saturation on the red channel and get a bunch of red splotches on the rectangles, but not on the lines. The same when I up the saturation on green. Some blobs look like long fingers running from left to right, tapering as they go.

Of course.

I know what this is.

Chapter 63

I catch Geisman that morning as he leaves his room to check out. It's early, and Julie's still asleep. "I've got something to show you."

He squints at me for a few seconds. He may not be completely awake. Then he gestures for me to follow him to the elevator. "Did you find more paintings in Frau Kinigader's house?"

"I found several."

His forehead crinkles. "Really? You have been very busy. Are they listed on Herr Kinigader's inventory?"

"I don't know. I can't see them."

That gets his complete attention, which is what I wanted. He stops to frown at me. "I do not understand. What exactly do you find?"

I show him the under-the-door photo on my laptop. He stares at it for a while, purses his lips, tilts his head to one side, then the other. "Please, will you explain to me what is this?"

"It's unframed paintings, face to back, with a sheet thrown over the top. Those are the edges of stretched canvases." I give him the thumbnail sketch of what I saw upstairs in Ute's house.

His face clouds over as he listens. It doesn't look like he's mad, exactly, but he's not a happy camper. "Doing this is an offense in Austria. It may be also in your country. I cannot use this photo." He leans closer. "The colors are paint, yes?"

"Yeah. See these two? The paint ran—that's the stripe."

"I see." Geisman stands straight and examines me. He's wide awake now. "Herr Simon. I appreciate the effort you have made to help. Finding the von Sivers painting was most useful. But I cannot be associated with your illegal actions, even indirectly. Goodbye, sir." He heads down the hall toward the elevators.

Seriously?

I start after him. "Maybe I wasn't clear. We've got a house where a Nazi art dealer left at least one painting. There's at least one locked room full of paintings upstairs. Are you saying we have to ignore that?"

Geisman stops, bows his head slightly, then faces me. "I am saying, Herr Simon, that you offer me no proof that I can present to a judge. I can request a warrant to seize the von Sivers because we have actual proof that it is the object of a criminal act. When the police deliver that warrant to Frau Kinigader, she may simply surrender to them the painting and the need for a search disappears. This is how the law is enforced in my country. Yours may be different." He turns and drags his roller bag the last few feet to the elevator lobby.

This, I didn't expect. "Seven of the eight pieces downstairs may be on the inventory." I realize how loud I'm getting and dial it back. "Shouldn't you at least get those? Get some real experts after them?"

His mouth is tight, and he's fidgeting with his roller bag's handle. He leans forward to push the "down" button. "Perhaps. The proof for the others is inconclusive. I must consider whether including them will put at risk my request for the warrant."

"But… isn't your whole gig about finding stuff the Nazis stole?"

"It is not. My work involves estates. I find heirs and lost property. I find assets that husbands and wives hide from each other. If I may say, I am very good at this work. It is why Julie engaged me to work on her behalf. I am not an activist. I am an officer of the court. I must follow the law."

This is when Ida drops in to tell me *you should have tried.*

I am trying. *I can't piss him off.*

Try harder.

I give myself a three-count to make sure I don't say the wrong thing. Then I slide between Geisman and the elevator. "You know, everything the Nazis did followed the law."

Geisman's head draws back a couple degrees. His eyes narrow.

"They went out of their way to make sure everything they did was legal. They changed the laws to cover themselves. They had lawyers and judges who—"

"What point do you make?" It's the first time I've heard Geisman raise his voice. I hit a button. I can't tell if it's the right one.

"My point is—"

The elevator door dings open behind me. A bellhop and a sixtyish woman look at us like it's too early in the morning to deal with our kind.

"Sorry," I tell them. "We're going up." I turn back to Geisman when the door rumbles closed. His mouth is mashed shut. "My point is there's legal, and there's right, and sometimes the two overlap. This time, they don't."

He shakes his head. "I have heard this argument in the past. Unfortunately, it is not—"

"What you can take to a judge? Look, Geisman, I've spent a lot of time with lawyers. I've learned that you guys can make white black and up down when you need to. I've—"

"You do not understand." His half-karate chop startles me. "When the police take the von Sievers painting from Frau Kinigader, it will be news throughout this country. There are people, political parties, that still take the National Socialist line. Solicitors will represent her for no cost because it follows their ideology. They can appeal the warrant all the way to the European Court of Human Rights. They have so much money. I, however, do not. They do not hesitate to attack, personally, people who oppose them. I cannot afford to lose all of my clients save for Julie—"

"So you're scared?" Ida's screaming in my ear, *try, try, try*. "There's also people who're *against* the nut jobs. They'll support you. Think about what this is *about*."

"I do nothing else, sir."

"Do you?" When did I get so close to Geisman? We're breathing the same air. But I have to make him see so Ida will leave me alone. "There's a room in that house that has a hundred, maybe two hundred canvases in it that've been missing for Seventy. Years. The Nazis—remember them? The worst—"

"Yes. I am aware of the Nazis. I grew up being aware of the Nazis. I—"

"Good. They took those paintings right before they murdered the owners. There's another room that may have more. Julie's paintings may be in there. Kinigader might be the new Gurlitt. Are you gonna let that go?"

Geisman looks away. His face is flushed and he's breathing hard. "What do you expect of me, Herr Simon?"

"You're a lawyer. You know how the system works. That means you know how to game it to get what you want. That's what I expect. That's what Julie expects."

"Are you mad? Frau Kinigader is an aged… blind… *milkmaid*." He shakes a finger at me with each word. "These people, they will make her the martyr if we pillage her entire—"

"Fuck her."

Geisman's eyes get real big.

"She's a Nazi and a bigot. Stick her in front of a camera and let her run her mouth. Nobody except the whack jobs will speak up for her."

He shakes his head. "If you believe that, you know nothing of my country."

I'm running out of arguments. Ida's still yelling at me. *You want this so bad?* I ask her. *You're gonna help.* "Ever hear of Ida Rothenberg?"

"No. Who is this?" The changeup seems to confuse him. He cocks his head like he's not sure he heard me right.

Now all I have to do is get through the story without reliving it. "Holocaust survivor. She spent half her life chasing her family's paintings around the world. She was closing in on one in Los Angeles when some little scumbag gallery sold it out from under her. It was her last straw. She killed herself on TV to make people pay attention to what happened."

His eyes do all his talking for him: big, round, horrified.

I take a step back physically as well as metaphorically. "I won't give you the photo, but you can't unsee it. We both know what's in that room. We both know you can give maybe dozens of families closure. You can decide to do the right thing. Or you can decide to walk away, and maybe you get to live with your own version of Ida because *you* became her last straw. Your choice."

We stare at each other for what seems like a long time. He finally reaches around me to push the "down" button again. "I must take the early train to Wien. I will consider what you say during the trip. In any event, I will work with the Häschke family, the owners of the von Sivers, to recover their painting." His voice isn't exactly normal, but he's got it under control again.

That's the best I'm going to get from him right now. "How long will it take? With the von Sivers, I mean."

"The request may be several months waiting, but it will be heard. Our court system is not swift, but it is fair for the most part. I will inform Julie as matters progress."

"Thanks." I stick out my hand. He looks at it, then at me, then he shakes it.

The elevator opens behind me. I step out of the way.

He pulls his roller bag in after him, then stops the door from closing. "You may not credit this, but I do believe in doing the right thing, as you put it. I am also a realist. Those two things do not always work well together." He nods at me. "Please give my regards to Julie. Goodbye, Herr Simon."

Chapter 64

Carson says, "Months?"

"It's the courts. You know how that goes."

We're strolling aimlessly through the outlet mall the hotel's attached to. With its skylights, cream walls, forest-green railings, apple-green columns, and the colorful geometric patterns on its ceramic-tile floors, it could be anywhere in America, except there aren't enough fat people. It's early yet and only moderately busy, meaning we can have a conversation without worrying about being interrupted or overheard or drawing any attention.

"Tell the Princess yet?"

"Not yet." And I'm feeling guilty about that. She's probably still sure that Geisman's going to come through for us. I'm on the fence, wondering if the what-would-Jesus-do line was over the top. But Carson and I need to get our waterfowl aligned so I'm ready when Julie starts asking her first thousand questions.

"Gonna?"

"Well, yeah, I have to. I thought we should talk first."

She nods. I can't say why exactly, but I get that she's a little pleased by that. "Getting in the house'll be easy. Old woman may not even lock the door. Old people don't sleep hard, though. She may hear us coming in or going up the stairs."

"I got up and down without anybody noticing."

"Geisman and the old woman were talking. So was the nurse. It's different."

As usual, she's right. "So what's the plan?"

Carson glances at me, then cracks a tiny smile. "You said it already. Go in the front, up the stairs, drop the picture, leave. Not hard. Maybe wait for a windy night so there's noise outside." She messes with her phone for a short while. "Supposed to be a storm coming in late Friday, early Saturday. Snow, wind gusts. That should make some noise, cover our tracks. No moon on Friday."

In other words, get ready to go tomorrow night. I wasn't

expecting to move quite this fast. But then again, why wait?

Well, maybe because we did the breaking-and-entering thing less than two weeks ago and my heart rate is just now getting back to normal.

Carson stows her phone in her back pocket and shoves her hands in her front pockets. "One thing. Princess goes home now."

"*Now?* Why?"

I get a glance that's colder than the air outside. "She almost fucked up everything in Portsmouth. Not giving her a chance to do it again. We're done with her. Time for her to go."

"That's… abrupt."

"Too bad."

"But, well, she'll want to stick around for when we plant Dorotea in the house."

"Too bad. She's got no part in it. Won't risk her fucking up again."

I'd always thought we'd have more time to… to what? Wind things down? Run off to Vegas together? Get into a huge fight so we won't mind going our very separate ways?

Carson watches me for a while with her head cocked. "What'd you think was gonna happen when we're done?" It almost sounds like she's interested.

I've been so into the moment that I haven't thought about the end game. Has Julie? "You know that scene at the end of *Casablanca?* Rick and Ilsa at the airport?"

"You're Ilsa?"

Nice. "Just saying—it's the best breakup scene ever." We walk a ways. "I'll miss her."

She sighs. "You in love with her?"

More walking. More thinking. I hadn't planned to have this talk with Carson. "Right now, it's enough to be around someone I like who can hold me at night. That's the best. You can't buy that."

Carson slowly shakes her head. "Gotta learn to keep it light. A weekend. Fun and done. Women like that too, you know. You'll tear yourself up, getting attached like this."

That sounds like the voice of experience. "I'm not built that way."

We walk for a while. Carson finally says, "I'll tell her. I'll be the bad guy."

I didn't expect that. I thought she'd rub my face in it, like she did before. "No. I need to. I owe it to her to tell her face-to-face. We're grown-ups. We'll… deal."

Yeah. Keep telling yourself that.

Chapter 65

It takes me an hour to get back to the hotel room. I have to stop at the hotel bar along the way for a couple overpriced drinks that don't make me any braver. Opening a bar at 6:30 in the morning is genius. As I leave, I'm shocked to see it's not even lunchtime yet—it feels like it should be the middle of the night.

There's a "*Bitte nicht stören*" sign on the door when I finally get back to the room. Inside I find the curtains closed and Julie curled up in an armchair with her chin on her knees. Dorotea's propped against the foot of the bed with the bag like a puddle around her.

Julie looks serious and a little sad, the same way I feel. We watch each other for a few moments. "I was worried when I woke up and you were gone." She sounds disappointed and a little wary, the same way I feel.

"Sorry. Geisman caught an early train. He should be back in Vienna by now."

Her mouth knots up. "You should've told me. I wanted to say goodbye."

"He said he'll be in touch. He's going to work with the other family to get a warrant to get their painting back." I can't tell her that Geisman might stiff her if he decides to be a lawyer instead of a human. She'll find out soon enough, one way or another.

She sits up. The lights turn on in her eyes. "He is? That's wonderful! Did he say how long that'll take?"

"Maybe a few months."

"That's great! I'm glad for them." She switches focus to Dorotea. "What about Oma?"

I perch next to Dorotea. "I've been talking to Carson about that. We'll figure something out."

"What do you want me to do?"

I'm not ready to answer that. "Like I said, we'll come up with something."

The sun leaves Julie's face. She leans forward, clasps her hands between her knees, and peers at me. "What's wrong?"

Tell her.

Tell her.

"I didn't get much sleep last night." Coward.

I don't want to hurt her. Even though I'm not 100% certain whose side she's on, and even though there's no non-sci-fi future that contains an "us," I still like her and I don't want to hurt her. She doesn't deserve that.

I glance away from Julie toward Dorotea. She's giving me the stink-eye. She knows what I'm not saying.

Julie slowly sits up straight. Her eyes blink too fast. "No. You can't. Not now, not when—"

"It's time." Even after thinking about nothing else for an hour, I still don't have a better comeback.

Her jaw sags. "But... we're not done yet. We still have to—"

"Your part's done." That came out too fast and too hard. I dial it back a lot. "You're wanted. Gillian's wanted, whatever. We can't protect you. Whatever comes next, you can't be part of it. If your picture shows up in the wrong place..."

That hangs in the air between us for longer than I expect. "What are you going to do with Oma? Put her in Ute's house?"

"We have options." Like that list of dumb ideas we built to make Allyson happy. "Whatever we do isn't the end. Like Geisman said, this'll take months to play out all the way. There's no reason to stick around and lots of reasons to go."

"But we need to finish this part, right?" There's an edge to her voice that wasn't there a few seconds ago.

I take a deep breath. She's not going to like this answer. "Me and Carson need to finish it. Gillian has to vanish. That means you have to vanish, too."

Julie's face is starting to set in stone. She bolts from her chair, yanks open the curtains. Her eyes are aimed out the window, but I can tell they're not seeing the gloomy clouds sliding across the pale gray sky. "You're trying to get rid of me."

She's hearing what she's afraid of hearing. "I want you to be safe at home." I want to hug her but stop just shy of her back. "The longer you stay here, the better the chances the British cops will get serious about finding Gillian. We can't risk involving you in anything else."

She wheels around and aims a trembling finger at my nose. "I've spent almost eight years working on this. *Eight years*. And now we're *this far* from the end"—she holds up her thumb and index finger about a quarter-inch apart—"you're throwing me out? *You*, of all people?"

Ouch. I expected tears, not this. "The ending happens when Dorotea comes out of hiding. You can't stay here until then. Hell, *we're* not staying here that long."

"'We' being you and Ms. Carson."

"Yeah. We do what we do, and we're gone. Then it's all up to the lawyer. Besides, what're you going to do here? Sit and worry? Bug Geisman?"

Julie brushes past me, stalks to the other side of the room, stops, then spins to face me. Her face is pink. "After everything that's happened… everything we've done… I'd expect that… that you'd be on my side. That you'd let me see this through."

I feel like a complete tool until I realize something: I'm not hearing the word *us*. As in, *what about us?* Or, *how can you do this to us?* Maybe she's too upset to think about the *us* part of this. Maybe she's being more grown-up about our relationship than I am.

Or maybe (my usually-right inside voice says) *us* happened so Julie could keep me committed to the cause. *Her* cause.

I push off the bed and take a couple steps toward her to see if she'll throw something at me. She doesn't… yet. "You want to get your grandma's portrait back, right?"

After a long staring match, she drops her focus to the carpet and nods.

"I want that, too. More than you know. A few months from now, she'll resurface. All you have to do is be ready to pull the trigger on your claim the moment she does. Let me do that for you."

Julie looks up at me through her lashes. Her temperature's dropping, but busy things are happening behind her eyes. She gazes at Dorotea. "You will? You promise?"

"I promise."

She drifts to the portrait, presses her fingertips on the edge of the canvas. Her eyes and mouth and jaw soften like ice cream in a warm room. "When do I leave?" The heat's gone.

The voice I shouldn't listen to, but usually do, says *not yet*. "The agency's booked you a Lufthansa flight out of Munich tomorrow, early afternoon. It's direct to JFK, so you'll only have to go through

one set of European security. All they had left was business class—
hope you don't mind."

Julie's fingertips tap the canvas like she's typing. After a few
seconds, she smiles a little. "I think I can survive that." She steps up
to me and eases a hand onto my chest. It's warm even through my
sweater. "Tomorrow afternoon, huh?" Her index finger trails down
my chest and hooks into my waistband. "Is that 'do not disturb' sign
still on the door?"

"Yeah."

The finger yanks me against her. "Good."

We don't say anything after "good." We start soft and relaxed,
as usual, but Julie slowly becomes more intense, almost rough. This
is a whole different side of her, one she kept to herself until now. Is
the slow-and-easy Julie the real one, or this take-charge, demanding
version? I'm too busy keeping up to think about it.

Now she's on her side, her head propped up on her right hand,
the fingers on her left scuffing through my chest hair. Her body's
next to me, but I can tell her brain is somewhere in low Earth orbit.

She re-enters the atmosphere. "May I ask you a personal
question?"

I glance to see if she's being funny, but her face says *I'm serious.*
"What did we just do?"

That gets me a scolding look. "There's intimate and there's
intimate. I don't want to make assumptions." She peers into my eyes
like she's looking for the bottom. "How old are you?"

"That's a hell of a question to ask now. Why?"

"I've been trying to put together the things you've told me about
yourself and it's not adding up. That bothers me. I'm wondering
what you left out."

"Does it matter?"

"Yes. Besides, you know how old I am. Fair's fair."

It'd be easy to lie. She'd never know. The problem is, do I lie
high or low? Eventually, I go for the truth. "Thirty-seven."

Julie'e eyes go round. "*How* old? I thought you were in your
forties!"

Not the first time someone's made that mistake. I tap the gray on my temple. "It's this, isn't it? It runs in the family."

"Well… maybe. Yes. I mean…" She makes a face. "Now I feel like a cougar."

"I'd have to be half your age for that. I'm pretty sure it involves leopard prints, too."

"I look terrible in animal prints."

"Everybody does."

Julie shakes her head. She gives my chest a pat and my forehead a peck, then slides off the bed. She spends longer than she strictly needs to picking up her clothes and draping them over her side of the bed—not that I'm complaining.

Then the suitcase comes out.

I ask, "What are you doing? You don't have to go 'til tomorrow morning."

"Why wait?"

"Seriously?"

She takes her time putting on her lingerie. Then she walks on her knees across the bed and kneels next to me. "Sit up." I do. She caresses my cheek. "You're sweet. You know you're part of my adventure, right?"

I'm not sure what to say.

"I know, it must be hard for you to think like that. 'The fling.' But that's what this is, isn't it?" She pats my cheek. "I mean, I had lots of fun. You were so good to me. I'm not used to that. But it's over now, right? That's what you told me. It's time to go home to my real life." Her hand slips to my chest, right over my heart. It's hard to ignore, but I'm waiting to see some kind of emotion come into her eyes. "We're not going to move to, oh, St. Louis to meet in the middle. We don't belong in each other's real life." Her eyes narrow a bit. "Please tell me you didn't think this was forever."

I swallow. It's one thing to have my brain say all this; it's a whole other thing to hear Julie say it out loud, so matter-of-factly. "No."

She kisses my forehead, then slips off the bed and pulls on the rest of her clothes.

I watch her pack for a while, listening to my inner voices cuss at each other. Then I slide off the bed and start gathering my clothes.

"Oh, don't get dressed." There's an almost flirty something in Julie's voice. "I like seeing you that way."

"You're dressed. Besides, I have to have clothes on to take you to the station."

"Don't worry. I'll take a taxi."

"You don't have to do that."

Julie stops in mid-move with a folded powder-blue polo in her hands. She looks at me for a long time, like she's untangling me. "Darling… we've already said goodbye, right?" She nods toward the bed. "In the very nicest way. Do you really want to shake my hand in the train station? Tell me, 'Have a nice trip'?" She arches her eyebrows.

Well… yeah. No. How can I argue when she's right?

When I can trust my voice, I say, "Well, if it's not going to be me, then find yourself a guy who'll treat you right. You deserve it."

"Thanks. Same for you. Go find a girl your own age to play with." Julie takes a handful of ziplock bags into the bathroom. When she comes out, they're full of her makeup and shampoo and other colorful little bottles. "Here's an idea—how about Ms. Carson? She's been jealous since the day we met."

It takes a moment to process that totally left-field idea. "Carson? Jealous?"

"Uh-huh. Women can tell, you know. I was on her territory. Just a thought."

Before I know it, Julie zips closed her suitcase, slides her laptop case over the pull handle, and drapes her black car coat over the whole thing. She stands in front of Dorotea and takes one long, last look, then puts her fingertips to her lips and gently touches them to the canvas' edge. She whispers, "See you soon."

Julie steps to the window, where I've been standing since I got my clothes on. There's about two inches of air between us. She looks into my eyes for a long time. Then she smiles a bit and brushes the backs of a couple fingers under my chin. "We'll always have Vienna."

She struts to the door. It's Gillian's walk.

She doesn't look back.

Chapter 66

I spend the rest of Thursday wandering around the Altstadt, soaking up the architecture. I just don't want to stay in the hotel room now that it's empty. Ever notice how when you're newly alone, everybody else around you seems to be paired up?

At dusk, I discover the sprawling Christmas market in the plaza next to the cathedral. I think, *what the hell*, and call Carson. She likes these kinds of things. Not only does she answer her phone, but she meets me there.

She asks, "You tell her?" when we meet up.

"Yeah. She's gone."

Carson nods. We don't talk about it anymore. We don't talk much at all. But as we wade through the art glass, knitwear, baked goods, *glühwein*, and the knots of Salzburgers getting their yuletide on, I find I'm more glad for her company than I ever imagined.

Friday morning. After breakfast and my run, I spend some quality time with Dorotea. I'll never have another Sargent in my hands ever again, so I need to take advantage. Also, I need to think about something besides Julie.

I pull on a nitrile glove, kneel in front of the portrait, and touch the canvas. I can feel the texture around Dorotea's head and hands where Sargent reworked their original positions. He did that a lot. He'd rough in some basic forms on the canvas in pencil, then do all his drafting with his brush. But sometimes he'd decide he wanted his subject to look somewhere else or have her hands somewhere else and he'd have to redo some of his work. Other things, like the beading on Dorotea's dress, are perfectly flat—he did that in one shot. Which is amazing.

I check the back again. I soaked off the three Russian labels over the past week. There's lighter spots where they used to be, but no way to prove what was there. I hope that's good enough.

"You're going home," I tell Dorotea. "Just one more stop, then you're back with your family."

For the first time since I started talking to her, Dorotea looks pleased.

I meet Carson in the garage at eleven that night. She went to some effort to find a parking space that's not close to a security camera. We stash Dorotea in the back of the Citroen and our luggage behind the front seats. We're not coming back.

The sky's clouded over and the wind's kicking the trees and stoplights around. There's not much action on the streets even though it's Friday night. People with any sense are snug at home.

We don't talk until we're outside the city on the open road. We're each in our own little bubbles inside the car's bigger bubble.

Carson flicks a look at me. "You're quiet."

She noticed.

"Thinking about the Princess?"

"She has a name, you know." I don't bother sanding down the edges on that.

"Yeah. Julie. You make her cry? That what's bothering you?"

I remember Julie saying that Carson's jealous and have to swallow the first couple things that jump into my mouth. "No. It turned out, she dumped me." It's not the first time. It's just... well, I didn't expect it from her. How she changed in an hour. Or was she changing all along, and I didn't notice? "I was her 'adventure.'"

She nods. Some road unspools under our headlights. "It's hard. We're mutts. Don't fit in the real world. Make a connection, then you gotta break it. Do that a few times…"

Funny—that's sort of what Julie said. Now that Carson's on the subject… "That weekend when Julie and I were in Vienna? When we got back, and you were all happy?"

"Was not."

"Bullshit. You got some. That's what it was. Who was he?"

"None of your fucking business."

Even though it'll probably make her want to hurt me, I can't stop pushing. "Come on, share. You know who I was sleeping with. You even saw her naked. Cough it up. Who was he?"

Carson doesn't take her eyes off the road. That's normal for her. What isn't is that if her eyebrows crunch down any farther, she won't be able to see. But she knows I've caught her. She burns holes through the night for a good, long time. "Kiwi."

"A New Zealander? Cool. What, some student?"

Her snort sounds like a horse. "Give me some credit. Special forces. Their SAS. Some exchange program thing."

You know what? This is great. Carson's human. "Good job." I put up my fist for her to bump. She ignores it. "Did you get together again—"

"Stop." Her ears are turning red. "Wasn't looking for a boyfriend, all right? Leave it." She lets the silence hang a long time. "Like I said. Keep it light."

"Teach me how to do that."

"Can't teach it." She glances at me. "Just gotta learn."

By the time we reach Spumberg, the wind is howling through the river valley and the trees are thrashing like weeds. It's seriously dark up on the mountain—no streetlights, no moonlight, no window lights on the few houses. Even the cows are safe inside.

Carson rolls past Ute's driveway and keeps going another couple hundred yards until she reaches a pullout next to the forest. We park facing downhill.

I ask, "Where are we?"

She shuts down the car, then peels off her gray hoodie. She's wearing her ninja costume under it. "About a hundred meters from Kinigader's house, through there."

"Can you find it in the dark?" I swap my burgundy sweater for my black one. Now I'm ready to skulk.

"GPS can."

The trees shimmy like club dancers in a blender. Tiny white BBs of snow are falling sideways. I'm *so* looking forward to taking a three-by-four-foot, million-dollar kite outside in this mess.

Carson hands me a pair of hospital booties and two pairs of nitrile gloves. She slips her own booties over her black gym shoes, then snaps on both pairs of gloves.

"You're putting those on now?"

"Won't leave traceable footprints, won't get local dirt in our shoes. Do it."

It's not only blowing hard outside, it's crazy cold. The wind wants to rip Dorotea out of my hands. I manage to hold on, though, and once we get into the forest, the wind's not as bad. That doesn't mean I'm not still afraid of breaking the portrait's stretcher. The booties are slippery. I stagger through the trees while I try to keep Carson in sight and try to not drop Dorotea or let tree limbs skewer her. The only upside is that with all the noise, a whole army of our clones could march by without Ute hearing us.

After what seems like a couple hours, we reach the edge of the trees behind the house. It's a dark shape against a darker background. It makes a fine windbreak. There are no lights, not that I expected any. Ute doesn't need them, after all.

Carson pauses on the back step, takes off her booties, turns them inside-out into a ball, then puts on new ones. She holds Dorotea while I do the same. I'm not quite sure why we're doing this, but if she tells me to, I'll do it.

The back door isn't even locked. Carson eases it open just enough to slide through the gap, then takes Dorotea from me. Once I'm in, I gentle the door closed and slowly untwist the knob. It's even darker in here than it was out there.

Carson clicks on her red flashlight beam. There's nobody in the kitchen or the hallway. That's when I start breathing again; I was half-expecting to see some Japanese-horror-movie ghoul standing there, ready to send us to hell. The noise is about a third of what it was outside, but the house's creaking and popping against the wind. That's good—it'll cover any noise we make. But it's bad—we'll never hear Ute coming.

We wait for what seems like an unreasonably long time, though it's probably less than a minute. Carson ghosts to the hallway's mouth, waves her flashlight around a bit, then motions for me to follow her. I've never concentrated so hard on walking in my life. Reaching the stairs seems like a major hike. Luckily, Ute's bedroom door is closed and the hall floor doesn't squeak. Yet.

By now, my heart's doing what it does when I run with Carson: pounding so hard it feels like it'll explode. It's cold in here, but I'm sweating.

Climbing the stairs was hard enough when I had light and both hands. Now I have to go up in the dark (Carson's lighting the steps with her flashlight, but that's not much help), while holding Dorotea at an angle so she doesn't hit a tread nosing, *and* trying not to move too far from the left-hand wall. The last thing we need is for some loose nail to squeak.

I move in slow motion, one step at a time. Dorotea's not all that heavy but holding her like this for so long is hitting me right in the shoulders, especially after the weird way I had to carry her through the forest to keep her safe. But I do okay…

…until the second step from the landing. My foot slips, and I lurch my other foot wide to keep from crashing down the stairs.

Creeeeeak.

The noise sounds like it's going out over a stadium loudspeaker. Of course, it happens between gusts, so there's almost no other sound to cover it up. I stand there tied in a pretzel, terrified to move, waiting to hear Ute's door open or to find out she has a guard dog we didn't see before.

Fifteen seconds. Thirty seconds. No door.

Carson takes Dorotea from me. Now that I have a free hand, I can grab the railing and haul myself back against the wall. I shake out my arms and shoulders once I'm on the landing, then take the portrait back. Carson flashes the "OK?" sign; I nod. I don't need to breathe yet.

We make it to the second floor without falling down or making more noise. I lead Carson to the door I looked at on Wednesday. She examines the lock, then hands me her flashlight and starts poking tools from her backpack into the keyhole. It seems like her hands barely move, but her forearms are working really hard. After a while, I hear a tiny *click*. She slowly twists the knob, then eases open the door inch by inch. I expect a haunted-house sound, but get only a low-level whine from the hinges. When it's open, I pull my Mini Maglite from my pocket and light up the room.

It's a smallish bedroom, no more than ten by ten. No furniture, and the window's covered by a thick curtain. Three rows of covered canvases, sorted by size, run left-to-right across the room with narrow aisles between them. There's gotta be almost two hundred paintings in this room alone.

Good god. What's in the other room?

Carson whispers, "Well?"

I lean Dorotea against the wall outside the door, then press the toe of my shoe against the dusty carpet. The light-blue bootie doesn't pick up much dust. I tiptoe along the baseboard to the far left-hand wall. Kinigader left a foot-wide clear area down there; it's like he wanted to be able to get to individual pieces, not just pile up a mess. Which means all this is probably in some kind of order. If I'm going to file Dorotea correctly, I need to figure out that order.

I carefully lift the edge of the sheet covering the front of the first canvas at the end of this row. It's a typically over-busy Rococo scene of putti screwing around, signed "Vander Aa/1776". Next is an Andreas Achenbach seascape with sailboats. I don't have to go too far to see that these are all within a few inches of the same dimensions, arranged by artist name. The next row over has noticeably larger canvases, and the third one is larger still.

None of them are as big as Dorotea.

I wave my flashlight at Carson to get her attention, then point toward the other closed room. She disappears. I sweep the flashlight beam around the ceiling. No water damage that I can see, no fallen plaster, no mold. This is one well-built house.

Carson's got the other room open by the time I get there. This one has fewer paintings—maybe seventy or so—but they're larger than the others, arranged in two short rows with more variation in the sizes. I wave in Carson to help with the coverings.

We head for the row where Dorotea should belong. The first painting is an Impressionist view of sailboats in a harbor, signed "Adrion." Another Impressionist, this time of what looks like a courtyard at a country estate, signed "Agafonov" in Cyrillic. (That's what Carson says, at least.) On it goes. De Clerck. Kaiser. Oenicke. Rabe. Finally, the "s" paintings, starting with a sticky-sweet Romantic portrait of a girl in peasant dress holding a tambourine, signed by Jules Salles.

I spend a long time staring at the next painting.

Carson grabs my hand and aims my flashlight at the face in the portrait.

She whispers, "Fuck. Me."

Chapter 67

The piece needs a cleaning. You'd expect that after seventy years in a farmhouse. I can't see any damage to the canvas itself or to the paint surface, though the harsh light makes it hard to tell. But there's no doubt about the subject, no possibility that this is a study or some similar woman in one of Sargent's recycled poses.

Dorotea stares back at me. She's saying, *took you long enough.*

Carson stabs a finger over her shoulder, toward Tovorovsky's Dorotea. "What. The *fuck*. Is that?"

I pull the portrait's top toward me so I can look at the back. There are three labels, all in German: one from a framer in Vienna, another from Otto Scheunebrunner, and a sticker with "WK Jan '45". Nothing in Russian. A handwritten dedication, in Italian, signed by John Sargent.

I gently set Dorotea back against the next painting. "That back there is a copy."

"How do you know? Maybe this' the copy."

"No. The forger had access to the original, but he didn't copy the back. He missed Sargent's dedication to the DeVillardis, or ignored it. This one's the original."

A copy. We stole a *copy*. All that effort and stress and expense and risk, and we stole a copy. Miranda getting racked up in the car crash. Julie almost being caught by the British cops. Me and Carson almost getting caught… how many times? For a copy.

Tovorovsky bought or took a copy from the Hermitage or wherever.

Did he know?

Carson whispers, "Now what?"

Good question. "We put everything back and go."

She points at the Dorotea we brought with us. The copy. "What about that?"

I shrug. "Take it with us."

My brain's racing around in circles, trying to catch the random thoughts pinging through my head. If Tovorovsky knew, was this all a setup to dump the fake and get real money for it? When did he figure it out? If he didn't know, was it because nobody bothered to authenticate it, or because nobody could tell the difference?

The upside: we don't have to plant Dorotea's portrait here because she's been here all along.

Carson flashes her red light in my face. "Wake up. We're outta here."

We put back the tarps (I guess these canvases were too big for sheets) the way we found them. Carson rearranges the dust to cover up what we disturbed. We tiptoe out, lock the door. Carson goes to lock the other door while I start downstairs. It's only marginally easier than going up. When I reach the landing, I set down fake Dorotea to give my shoulders a break. There's another pause in the wind outside. It's quiet for a few moments.

I hear a muted *scratch* downstairs. Then another.

I risk a peek around the wall to the ground floor.

Ute's door is open.

A soft bump behind me makes me swivel. Carson just stepped onto the first stair. I grab my flashlight and shine it at her, then hold up my hand to signal "stop."

I try to stop breathing, which isn't hard. My heart's trying to bust out of my rib cage. Okay, she can't see us, but don't blind people get superhero hearing to make up for not seeing? Did we make something squeak upstairs? Did we whisper too loud?

Another peek. I see a vague human shadow in the dark, just outside Ute's door. It's moving, but I can't tell what it's doing.

"*Hallo? Wer ist da?*" It's Ute.

The wind picks up again. The house groans and creaks.

Ute approaches the stairs. She stands at the foot, not moving. Is she listening? Is she chasing a random noise, or does she know she's not alone?

She turns. "*Sie sind hier nicht willkommen.*"

I glance back at Carson. She's creeping down the stairs using the wind for cover.

Ute shuffles toward the front of the house. I can't hear her footsteps anymore, and she disappears once she passes the staircase.

"*Mutti?*"

Wait. *Mommy?* Does she think this place is haunted?

Is it?

"*Mutti? Bist du das?*"

This is creepy. It's also a little sad. She lost her mom almost twenty years ago. She never married, maybe never had a boyfriend, doesn't know any relatives. She pays people (or, the Austrian government does) to take care of her. And she's alone in dark that lasts forever.

I never want to be like that. Never.

Her shadow drifts back to her bedroom door. Ute stands there for what seems like a long time, listening to the wind or her mother's ghost or my heart banging away. "*Hallo? Hallo?*"

She fades into her room and shuts the door behind her.

I can feel Carson behind me—a big, warm presence a couple inches away. As usual in these kinds of situations, having her there brings down my heart rate a couple notches.

There's music. Something classical and complicated-sounding with a choir and orchestra. For a moment I wonder if this is like the ballroom in the Haunted Mansion, but it's coming from behind Ute's door. The radio, or a CD. I doubt it's Pandora.

Carson whispers, "Go."

We make it down the stairs without raising an alarm.

The last thing I hear from Ute's radio before we go out into the falling snow is the choir singing "Hallelujah."

Chapter 68

Olivia sounds perfectly awake when she answers my call. "How may I help you?"

"We need to talk to Allyson."

There's a pause. "I see. Give me your message and I'll pass it to her."

"No. We need to talk to *her*. Face-to-face."

A longer pause. "I... see. Please send to me the location and time. I'll notify her. This is... *important*, I trust?"

"Very."

Grünecker Strasse passes through a belt of trees flanking the Isar River a mile shy of Munich's airport. A track runs south into the trees. It's too scrubby to be a forest, but there's enough cover to screen us from the road.

It took four straight hours of driving to get here, including the hour backup at the German border from the temporary immigration controls trying to screen out Syrian refugees. It feels good to step into the cold night air, stretch out my back, and blast the cobwebs out of my skull.

The sky north of us glows from the airport lights, but where we are is middle-of-the-night black. My phone says we're an hour early for our meet with Allyson. I guess Germany's in a different time zone from Austria.

Carson crunches through the frost toward me, a dark shape in a dark place. She's rolling out her neck and shoulders. "Know what you're gonna say?"

More or less. "Want to hear it?"

"Nope. This is your show."

"Wrong. It's *our* show. You're in this too. Ben Franklin said something about hanging together or hanging separately."

She sighs. "Wonderful. Talk."

I do. After a few minutes, we move back into the car. Carson makes some changes. When I'm done, she sits quietly, strangling the steering wheel.

She says, "This was a good job. I'm gonna miss it."

Allyson arrives right on time. I don't know how she always does that. When she rolls up behind us, her car's ultra-bright bluish headlights make the Citroen's insides look like a supernova just went off behind the back seats. Carson grumbles; it takes me a minute to get my night vision back.

It's an Audi, of course, and Allyson's driving. She marches to meet me at the Citroen's back hatch, which Carson popped for me. I'd been wondering what Allyson would wear in the middle of winter, in the middle of a forest, in the middle of the night. The dome light in the Citroen's cargo area shows me a dark hip-length Moncler Anastasia down parka, cut close to her body with a bright silver zipper slashing diagonally across her chest. Her black slacks and turtleneck fade into the night.

"I trust there's a very good reason for us to be out here at this hour, Mr. Friedrich." Her voice is colder than the air.

"There is. Remember why you briefed us personally at the start of the project? Same reason I'm briefing you personally at the end."

Her lips purse. Even in the semi-dark, they look good that way. Her eyes flick to my right. "Ms. Carson."

"Allyson." Carson stands about two feet away from me at the edge of the light pool. I guess she wants to be a bad target.

I pull the fake Dorotea out of the Citroen and hold it out to Allyson. "This is Tovorovsky's copy of the Sargent. You can give it to Bowen. Tell him to keep it under wraps until you say it's clear."

She scans the black rectangle for a few moments before she lifts it out of my hands. "This is the original?"

"It's Tovorovsky's copy. Tovorovsky's minions swiped the copy Boutelle made for me."

Allyson's watching me very closely. "Is there a reason you keep using the word 'copy'?"

I let the question hang. Timing is everything. "I want to confirm something. The contract you signed with Bowen—does it specify you have to deliver the actual, original *Dorotea DeVillardi*, or the one Tovorovsky owns?"

"Actually, neither. It's our standard services contract. He gave me his instructions verbally so there'd be no paper trail. He mentioned Mr. Tovorovsky rather often."

"Seriously? You work that way?"

"It's not uncommon. Also, 'no paper' doesn't mean no video or audio." She rests the *faux*-Dorotea on the toes of her boots. "Where exactly is the actual, original *Dorotea DeVillardi*?"

I glance toward Carson. She says, "Farmhouse. Thirty clicks south of Salzburg. With a bunch of other pictures."

I give Allyson a short recap of our night, what we found in Ute's house, and Geisler. She listens hard and nods now and then but doesn't interrupt.

At the end, she pats the top edge of the canvas she's holding. "So this one—Mr. Tovorovsky's painting—is also a forgery?"

"Yeah."

"And you propose that I give a known forgery to the client?" Her voice isn't happy.

"I propose you give him what he asked for."

Allyson's eyebrows say impolite things to me. "Ms. Carson, do you agree with this?"

"Couldn't happen to a nicer guy."

"I see." Allyson turns back to me. "I'll assume I shouldn't tell the client where the original portrait is."

"No. When the lawyer springs it from the farmhouse, Julie'll put in a claim for it. Her grandmother and mother gave it to her, and she's got the paperwork to prove it. She won't have to get it away from Bowen because it was never his."

"He won't be happy with us."

"He's not happy with anybody. You already said he's not going to hire us again."

"Besides," Carson says, "how'd we know there's another one?"

Allyson smooths an eyebrow with the tip of her right middle finger. I think it's her version of a cry of pain. "What do you propose I do with my other client?"

My turn. "Tovorovsky? Tell him he has sixty days to cough up your money."

"Or?"

"Or you'll give the insurance company documented proof that the stolen piece is a contemporary fake. The value of his claim goes to zero."

"Do you have this proof?"

"I do. I took pictures every time I went to Boutelle's studio."

Allyson nods. "And the lawyer?"

I'd distracted myself from thinking about Julie leaving by trying to figure out how to put some steel in Geisman's spine. "There's this group called the Austrian Committee for Social Justice. They put up money to defend lawyers and journalists who get in sideways with the far right. Once you give that thing"—I wave at the *faux*-Dorotea—"to Bowen, you should talk him into donating six figures or so to the group to give Geisman some top cover. That is, if he ever wants to get the portrait out of his basement." Personally, I love the idea of muscling Bowen into giving a chunk of change to a bunch of civil-society warriors. It smells like karma.

Allyson stares into the middle distance with her lips pursed. She strokes the part of her throat that the turtleneck doesn't cover. Finally, she comes back to Earth. "Just so I understand, Mr. Friedrich: you propose to defraud our clients and lie to them. Is that correct?"

Well, when you put it that way... "Yeah. For the greater good."

She bores holes into my forehead for a few seconds. I'll start smelling burnt flesh soon.

Then a flicker of a smile breaks out. "You may have more aptitude for this business than I credit you with. Ms. Carson? Anything to add?"

"Nope. Just wanna go home."

"Olivia can see to that." Allyson hefts the *faux*-Dorotea. "As usual, this has been informative and educational. Of course, this conversation never occurred."

I ask, "Not even on audio or video?"

Allyson smiles—*oh, the shark has/pretty teeth, dear*—then turns and leaves.

Chapter 69

FOUR MONTHS LATER

When the Germans found Cornelius Gurlitt's stockpile of paintings in February 2012, they kept it quiet until a magazine broke the story a year and a half later. The government got kicked in the teeth—repeatedly—for it. I guess Austria learned a lesson from that. The Häschke family filed a motion in a Salzburg court just before Christmas to seize their von Sivers still life from Ute. The court issued the warrant just two months later—a nice, broad warrant. Geisman did the right thing. The February 23rd *Art Newspaper* headline said, "Another Nazi-Era Art Hoard Found in Salzburg."

I was here—literally, at this same table outside the store in downtown Santa Monica—when I read the article. It was 81 degrees and blue skies here, but the Austrian cops in the pictures were wearing parkas and knit hoods. The cops confiscated 268 paintings from Ute's house including the von Sivers, which ended up in most of the news photos. The story didn't play over here because the Super Tuesday freak show coming up a few days later sucked all the air out of the country.

I noticed, though. And I knew that the moment I read that headline, the clock had started ticking on the Austrians finding Dorotea.

A month and a half later, I'm back at this table on my morning break with a cup of milk and a marked-out raspberry muffin. I open the browser on my phone and see that the Google news alert I set up in February has hits. The *Art Newspaper* headline I pick first says, "Kinigader Hoard Yields 126 Nazi-Loot Artworks."

Dorotea gazes out at me from the picture in the article. She looks very pleased with herself.

The article talks about the Austrian provenance task force reviewing the hoard, using documents discovered during the raid and also provided by "victims' advocate Stefan Geisman of Vienna."

(Heh.) Unlike the German experts, who took basically forever to ID Gurlitt's looted art, the Austrians are moving at warp speed. They've identified eighteen pieces that the Nazis definitely stole (including Dorotea), another sixty-three probables, and forty-five possibles out of 160-ish paintings examined so far. They got up a website with pictures (kinigadervorrat.as) within three weeks of the raid.

I lean back and let myself think about Julie again.

I haven't heard from her since she said goodbye in Salzburg. The few times I started writing an email to her, I deleted it before I hit "send." Still, I wonder what she's feeling right now. It's gotta be exciting for her. She probably thinks she's getting the canvas she bonded with after we knocked over the Mainwaring. Will she be able to tell the difference?

Julie's back at school now; her entry in the staff directory doesn't say "sabbatical" anymore. I'm waiting for her book to come out. I can't wait to see what she says about Vienna and Portsmouth. I hope she's happy with how it turned out—I am, and I would be even if we hadn't been together. I still miss her sometimes. And I hope that every once in a while she thinks about me, and she smiles.

Another article in the *Art Newspaper* asks how having Dorotea show up in the Kinigader Hoard will affect the case of Tovorovsky's "stolen" Sargent. He apparently doesn't have anything to say about it to the press. The Hampshire Constabulary detective in charge says the PD will probably re-evaluate the case very soon. By the way, they're still looking for Gillian Hardwick or for anybody who knows who she really is.

Tovorovsky's screwed. If he files an insurance claim, they'll laugh in his face. Not even the people who buy on the black market will give him much for his now very famous fake. He'll be pissed. I wonder who he'll take it out on.

Cousin Ron's asshattery finally got him into more trouble than he could skate over. He was part of the congressional inquisition last month that also roasted Martin Shkreli and Valeant's Howard Schiller over Big Pharma raping consumers and health insurance companies. His testimony disgusted so many people that the news media now refers to him as "embattled CEO" or "discredited CEO." (Business Insider calls him "soon-to-be-ex-CEO Bowen.") I doubt he'll have much bandwidth to fight Julie when she tells him she's getting the real Dorotea.

I cleared almost $49,000 on this project. It dropped in my Singaporean account in late January. I've been parceling it out since then to everybody I owe money to. I have to lay down a credible string of invoices for freelance work to account for this lump of money; it'll take until summer to use it up. I padded my expenses (Bowen can afford it) and used some of the money to get Chloe a gift certificate to the spa at the Peninsula Beverly Hills for Christmas. She deserves more for putting up with me.

And the Steel Sparrow? I haven't had an Ida dream for a few weeks, now. I know I haven't fully atoned for what I helped Gar do to her—that'll take going to Shanghai and dragging her painting off Feng's wall, something I'll probably never manage to do. But maybe, just maybe, she's cutting me a little slack for having done something good for another somebody like her. Maybe Dorotea (the ghost, not the painting) had a word with her.

However it worked, I'll take the little bit of peace it's brought me.

The Adventure Continues...

CHASING CLAY: The Next Matt Friedrich Art Caper

It's pure white, deep blue... and dirty all over.

Disgraced gallerist and ex-con Matt Friedrich has sixty days to find the source of 800-year-old smuggled Southeast Asian antiquities. If he fails, he may be buried next to them.

Buy CHASING CLAY today at your favorite online bookselling site!

Like What You Read?

Share your experience with friends! **Leave a review** on your favorite online bookselling site, on a readers' social network (such as Goodreads) or promotion site (such as Bookbub), or just on your blog or Facebook wall. Someone told you about this book; please pass on the favor.

About the Author

Lance Charnes has been an Air Force intelligence officer, information technology manager, computer-game artist, set designer, *Jeopardy!* contestant, and is now an emergency management specialist. He's had training in architectural rendering, terrorist incident response, and maritime archaeology, but not all at the same time. Lance's Facebook author page features spies, archaeology, and art crime.

Official Website
https://www.wombatgroup.com
Sign up for Lance's newsletter! Be the first to find out about new books, special deals, and the occasional giveaway.

Facebook Author Page
https://www.facebook.com/Lance.Charnes.Author

Goodreads
https://www.goodreads.com/lcharnes

The DeWitt Agency Files

Matt Friedrich has a very particular set of skills that he learned while working in a crooked L.A. art gallery, and other knowledge that he gained while hanging out in federal prison with Wall Street types who had bad lawyers. He's out on supervised release and working for $10 an hour at Starbucks to pay off over half a million in debts and restitution.

Matt's the DeWitt Agency's newest employee. The Agency "fills needs" for not-always-honest people and organizations. When a client has a need to fill that involves art in whatever form, Matt gets the project.

Follow Matt around the world, where he sees new places, meets new friends, avoids new enemies, and discovers (or pulls off) new scams. If he plays his cards right, he can make a lot of money, pay off his debts, and build a new life. All he has to do is not screw up...which is much harder than it sounds.

Praise for the DeWitt Agency Files

"*The Collection* is a breezy read in the way the very early Leslie Charteris' Saint novels were breezy: entertaining with an underlining of grit below the surface..." – *Criminal Element*

"Interlacing storylines give this series its charm... It's nice to have some modern *It Takes a Thief* escapism to slip away to in this world gone awry. Suffice it to say, I can't wait for The DeWitt Agency Files #3." – *Criminal Element*

"A brilliant heist story filled with fascinating art history reminiscent of Dan Brown or Steve Berry. Only better." – *Seeley James, author of the Sabel Security thriller series*

To learn more, go to your favorite online bookselling site, or to https://www.wombatgroup.com/dewitt-agency-files/.

The DeWitt Agency Adventures

Carson used to have a life. Then a crooked superior in the Toronto Police Services framed her for corruption, her husband turned out to be a serial cheat, and her father didn't pay back the millions he borrowed from Gennady Rodievsky, a Russian *mafiya* godfather.

Now Carson (that's only one of her names) answers to two masters: the DeWitt Agency, which "fills needs" for not-always-honest people and organizations; and Rodievsky, the criminal she tried to take down as a detective.

Follow Carson as she shuttles around the world, dealing with friends and enemies, victims and tormentors, fighting to do the right thing in places where even the right thing may be wrong. Someday she may pay off her debts, work out her demons, and be free of a life that can kill her in an instant... but will there be anything left of her when she does?

Praise for The DeWitt Agency Adventures

"A breakneck tale where enemies and friends are often indistinguishable and the heroine's life is literally minute-to-minute. Highly recommended." – *DP Lyle, award-winning author of the Jake Longly and Cain/Harper thriller series*

"Charnes, a capable writer, crafts an exciting and alluring storyline...The author provides enough breakneck action and unexpected circumstances to keep readers entertained, while the Ukrainian backdrop is well conceived." – *The Booklife Prize*

To learn more, go to your favorite online bookselling site, or to https://www.wombatgroup.com/dewitt-adventures/.

Thrillers by Lance Charnes

DOHA 12: An International Thriller

Jake Eldar's and Miriam Schaffer's names may kill them.

An assassination in Qatar thrusts twelve innocents into the crosshairs of a hit team bent on revenge. But two of them refuse to die quietly.

> "*Doha 12* is an exciting and hard-to-put-down read of fiction, not to be overlooked." – *Midwest Book Review*

Buy DOHA 12 today at your favorite online bookselling site!

SOUTH: A Near-Future Thriller

Luis Ojeda owes his life to the Pacifico Norte cartel. Literally. Now it's time to pay.

In 2032 America, ex-coyote Luis Ojeda must get FBI agent Nora Khaled into war-torn Mexico with her family – and a secret that will rock the U.S. government.

> "*South* is a riveting work of action/adventure suspense that is a real page-turner… Lance Charnes demonstrates a truly impressive knack for deftly creating a complex and thoroughly engaging story…" – *Midwest Book Review*

Buy SOUTH today at your favorite online bookselling site!

www.ingramcontent.com/pod-product-compliance
Lightning Source LLC
Chambersburg PA
CBHW071531110726
47908CB00007B/1846